To:—
Rick & Sonya
dear friends,
with thanks for
many kindnesses
from *[signature]*
& Dorothy

Paris, Sept. 16, 1975

The Dice of God

The Dice of God

JOACHIM G. JOACHIM

STEIN AND DAY / Publishers / New York

First published in 1975
Copyright © 1975 by Joachim G. Joachim
All rights reserved
Designed by Ed Kaplin
Printed in the United States of America
Stein and Day/*Publishers*/Scarborough House,
Briarcliff Manor, N.Y. 10510

Library of Congress Cataloging in Publication Data

Joachim, Joachim G.
    The Dice of God.

    I. Title.
PZ4.J618Di   [PS3560.016]   813'.5'4   74-78523
ISBN 0-8128-1721-4

For Dorothy

Acknowledgments are due to the Penguin Books Ltd. and Mr. E. F. Watling for the lines quoted in Chapter Six from his translation of *Antigone* by Sophocles. The play was performed at the Herod of Atticus Theater in the summer of 1969 as part of the Athens Festival, but poetic license has been used with regard to the actual performance in the novel.

Part One

1

Hilary eased the small green car down the Sounion road, shifted into third gear, released it into fourth.

"That's the way, baby, that's the way, my Josephine.'"

He spoke often to his car, coaxing it, praising it, sharing a joke with it. "Come on, girl, come on."

When the engine of the battered old machine overheated, Hilary would pull up by the road and wait for it to cool down, personally hurt and anxious for its health. But when he was happy, Josephine seemed to share his good spirits, responding with sudden leaps to his lavish endearments. And Dr. Hilary Grey, Doctor of Philosophy and wandering professor of the world, was especially happy that evening. It was Sunday, the Greys' first Sunday in Greece that summer.

"That's the way, baby. Ah, she's a darling, my Josephine."

His wife was not amused.

"I wish I hadn't agreed to come," she said.

"But I want you to come, Isabel. We're invited, both of us."

"It would be nicer for you to be alone. It's you she wants to see—naturally."

"Now, Isabel, that's nonsense. After all, it's been many years; she's buried one husband, got rid of the second, she's a baroness. She wasn't the Baroness when I knew her."

Then she was only Angela. Hilary remembered the luscious body sprawling naked on the sand, still shaking, moments after they moved apart.

"I don't know, I'm really not feeling well. I doubt that she'll be pleased to see me, and I don't think I want to see her. I wish you could take me back to the hotel."

"Don't be silly, Isa, love. Of course she wants to see you."

"I thought you said it was her secretary who invited us."

"Yes—Inge. I've told you, Angela wasn't there."

"You know I don't like mixing with people I don't know, going places where I don't know what to expect."

"The Old Lion has got his daughter engaged. It won't hurt us to have a leg of chicken and a glass or two of wine, would it? An extra bottle won't put Leonides in the red, I can tell you."

"It's Angela I'm afraid of."

"The Baroness. Remember to call her that."

He, of course, would call her Angela. Suddenly he was young again and he pressed his foot down and the small car leaped forward obediently. Angela. He mustn't be too effusive tonight, he mustn't be . . . Let her make the gesture. He drove past the Voula Church, past the Queen Anne Nightclub and Hotel. As the road sloped gently uphill, Josephine's pace slackened and other cars began to overtake them. My heart's still young, he said to himself. I still have a claim on life. It was a mistake to wish to relive the past, perhaps it was a mistake to expect so much of the evening—those had been happier times and Hilary had been thirteen long, hard years younger. *I should have kept a journal, an erotic journal.*

Josephine reached the top of the incline and started the descent, quickly now, even eagerly. Christ, nobody would dim their lights; from the opposite lane came a continuous stream—cars, trucks, scooters, motorcycles—all driving back to Athens in the cool of the evening after a day spent on the beaches of Saronikos. Below the steep cliffs of Vouliagmeni, yachts rode at anchor in the bay.

The launch from the *Hesperides* was waiting, and some of the guests were being helped into it. Hilary smoothed back the strands of his hair with one hand as he looked out for a place to park.

"I suppose the Baroness needs her old lovers around her," said Isabel. "She must be getting on now."

"You're a cat, but you look lovely, so I'll forgive you. It's not every day we're invited on board a yacht." He looked out over the bay and pointed to the gleaming white lines of the ship three hundred yards away. "There she is. Come on."

Isabel stood motionless.

Hilary went around the car and took her arm. "Come on," he said and waited for her fear to subside. "You look lovely. There's nobody like you, Isa, when you try. Let's enjoy tonight, shall we?"

They were already in the launch and it was beginning to move when a silver sports car braked on the quay and a young man got out and jumped into the boat. His black shirt was unbuttoned halfway down his chest, his hair fell over his forehead; a girl took him by the arm and kissed him on the cheek and Isabel heard some of the guests calling him Mark. When the launch drew alongside the yacht, he got out first and helped the others up to the gangplank.

Isabel thought she could manage by herself, but when the boat rocked with the swell, she nearly lost her footing. As Mark seized her elbow, he put an arm around her and held her, just a moment longer than necessary. Isabel felt wrapped up, enclosed by this handsome stranger. When she tried to thank him, she couldn't pronounce the words properly, and she hurried up the gangway without waiting for Hilary, who was busy talking to someone in Greek.

The Old Lion, stripped to the waist, was talking into the telephone, scratching his brown stocky chest as he shouted into the receiver.

"You stay near her. Give her the pills every half-hour, and no drink, do you hear me? . . . Yes, idiot, no drink, no matter what she says."

Leonides waved to Mark to wait. "The eunuch is grilling my liver on burning coals, the motherfucker." He shook his heavy head and spoke again into the mouthpiece. "Keep her quiet, whatever happens. Tell her I'm on my way, I'll be there as soon as I can."

He banged down the telephone.

"I admire the man, whoever it was, who cut off his balls," he said. "One day I'll take a knife and cut what's left of him right down to the root." He scratched his chest again and beckoned to Mark. "Come here, what are you afraid of? What are you hiding from me?"

"As I said in my cable, sir, the deal is set. Our terms."

Leonides stared at him with dark, opaque eyes.

"Spill it out, then, gypsy. Give me the news, I want to hear the whole story."

"I even managed to get the final clause included, sir."

Mark started buttoning up his black shirt. It was always a strain to talk to the Old Lion, but Mark had a secret respect for his brains and guts. Certainly he would rather work for him than for a smooth, soft-spoken nonentity, however much he got paid.

The party celebrating his daughter's engagement begun, Leon Leonides was still wearing shabby white trousers rolled up at his bare ankles. Behind him, on the wall, dozens of tiny lights showed on a world map the positions of his fleet; half of them were oil tankers and most of the rest were tramps. On his desk, three feet high, stood a model in gold and crystal of the *World Seafarer*; portraits of the ancestral Lions hung on the wall of the cabin. Leonides himself looked very much like a pirate. The only difference, thought Mark, noting the Old Man's espadrilles, was that some of his ancestors had found it more comfortable to go about barefoot.

"Talk to me, gypsy!"

As Mark began his account of the trip to the Japanese shipyards, the people he had met, the negotiations, Leonides leaned back in his leather armchair, eyes half closed, concentrating. Once, the telephone rang, but he insisted he was not to be disturbed—unless the Baroness called him. When Mark finished, the Old Lion's face remained expressionless.

"I suppose now you will ask for a raise. Well, you won't get it." As though he

11

had been contradicted, his voice grew louder. "What do you need more money for? In Beirut it's the Phoenicia, in Cairo the Hilton, in Kuwait the Sheraton, in London the Savoy, in New York I give you my apartment, bastard, with a beautiful black woman thrown in to suck you to sleep. Yours is the highest expense account on our books."

"It includes entertaining the clients for the firm."

"Ah! I said buy *them* a girl for the night to keep them happy, did I say the firm would pay for *your* whoring around?"

He was shouting, but from long experience Mark knew he was pleased.

"How is Midori, gypsy? A good tail, a great asset to the Tokyo office. You saw something of her, Markos, eh, Markos?"

"Not in the way you think, sir."

Leonides got up and came round the desk.

"You young people get sentimental, you don't know what a piece like Midori wants. Next time we're there together I'll demonstrate—I'll fuck her across her office desk just for your benefit."

He walked across to a cabinet and poured himself a whiskey. He did not drink during the day, and he had been waiting for the good news from Japan. Now he could relax, he could drink as much as he liked. But he wouldn't offer the gypsy a drink; he could drink outside, but not in his office when there was business to be discussed.

He moved close to Mark and put an arm around his shoulders.

"We've done it," he said, hugging him. "Cheer up, boy, we've done it, you and I!"

He raised his glass and drank. There was a knock and Leandros Leonides, the Old Lion's son, came in. He was dressed in immaculate white. The father, suddenly constrained, released Mark.

"What is it?"

"The guests have arrived. They're asking for you."

"What do they want of me? You're there, you look after them. I've already explained to Van that I've got to go ashore tonight."

"Aunt Zoe wants to speak to you."

"Well, tell her I'm busy. Whatever your aunt's cackling about, it'll keep."

"Father, I've some friends on board, they want me to show them the casino after the reception. Is that all right with you?"

Leonides smiled. "No sooner does poor old papa make some dough than you plan to throw it away. Go ahead, Leandros, Markos will be here tonight. He'll be in charge."

Leandros turned to Mark. "Hello," he said, not offering his hand. "I've heard everything went well."

"It was a good trip," said Mark, who disliked discussing business with the Young Lion.

12

When Leandros had left, his father poured himself more whiskey.

"If I didn't know that his mother was as virtuous as the Statue of Liberty —God rest her soul," he muttered and crossed himself, "I'd suspect he was born the wrong side of the blanket. Where the hell did he get those blue eyes from? And the fair hair, it's a mystery to me. The Lions always had dark eyes and hair—black, like you. . . . Come, I'll show you something."

He went to the opposite wall and drew back a curtain.

"What do you think of this?"

At first Mark didn't recognize the lightly draped figure with one breast exposed as the Old Lion's younger sister, Angela. The eyes were smoldering, the red mouth was a little open . . . Mark turned away. He had only seen the Baroness once, after her husband had left Greece for the schloss in Bavaria. The Old Man seemed to keep her confined, which only fed the many rumors about her.

Leonides stared at the painting.

"It's good, isn't it?" he said finally. "The Baroness is a real Lioness. Clive Bellingham did it, and the pose was his idea—or more likely hers. I wanted her in national dress, like Bouboulina or Queen Amalia, something suitable to hang up there with her forefathers. Well, now it's done, I can't be angry, it's so like her. I'll make out a check and you can give it to him, he'll be here tonight. He pretended he didn't want payment, the high-hat Britisher. Shall I write five thousand dollars or is four thousand enough? The value of a picture is something I'll never understand—I know some of our friends pay millions for them."

"Five thousand, I should think."

"Four thousand five hundred, and don't listen to any crap from him about not accepting it. I shouldn't think his pension's as much as that."

He handed Mark the check.

"I want you to stay here this evening. The Baroness isn't well, and I'm flying to Zurich tomorrow. Go mix with the people on deck and keep an eye on things. Thalia's engagement is good for us. For the firm. The Sullivans own half of Pittsburgh. Don't run off with a skirt and leave your post—if you have to fuck do it here, near the telephone. And don't overdo the drinking. Remember, you're in charge. Still, the firm has always believed in combining business with pleasure . . ." The opaque eyes were suddenly bright. "Katia is probably up there, waiting for you. But remember, she's only fifteen. A virgin. Don't rape her, gypsy, because if you do I'll castrate you and make you eat your balls!" Leonides grinned. "Bastard," he squeezed Mark's shoulder. "I wish I were your age. That little niece of mine looks such tender meat."

The telephone rang and he took it up, ready to shout at the caller. Then his features softened, his voice changed.

"Angel, don't be frightened. I'm coming now, I'll be with you in a few minutes . . ."

13

As he spoke, he waved Mark out of the cabin.

Hilary looked again at Inge's long bare legs showing under the short skirt, hitched up as she perched on the bar stool. He drained his glass.

"I'll just get myself another."

He was talking with Isabel and Sir Clive Bellingham, a tall man with a trim, grizzled beard. Having already had plenty of champagne, Hilary felt genial and expansive. On the way to the bar he met a waiter carrying a large tray of hors d'oeuvres and reached out for a lobster patty, his eye still on Inge.

She was talking to Leandros.

"Are you sure your father won't mind?" Her flaxen hair streamed over her shoulders. As she talked she kicked her legs high, spun around on the stool, and helped herself from the tray. "Hi, Prof!" she called to Hilary. "An old friend of your father's," she said, introducing him to Leandros.

Hilary shook hands with the Young Lion and congratulated him on his sister's engagement.

Leandros nodded politely.

"I'm afraid my father's not here tonight, Dr. Grey. He was called away suddenly."

"Oh, that's all right," said Hilary, who felt relieved not to be meeting the old ruffian yet. Even now he could not quite understand how his teaching contract had been so suddenly terminated and his residence permit rescinded. He had been warned, Angela had warned him well in advance and had even given him the gun. "When he keeps quiet, that's a dangerous sign." Hilary had turned over the automatic. "Do you know how to use it?" "Of course. But what can he do to me?" "You'd be surprised."

He picked up a glass of champagne and looked around again for Angela.

"Are you coming with us after this?" Inge asked Hilary. "We're going to the casino."

"I've no money," he said.

"I'm broke, too. But I'm going with young Leo."

As the guests moved about under the shaded, colored lights of the main deck, Hilary peered through the crowd, still hoping. The small orchestra played popular tunes, and some couples were dancing. Hilary began regretting it all, his confidence began to ebb; Angela didn't want him and she had only had them invited to give herself time, to get rid of him tactfully.

"The Baroness is very late," he remarked tentatively.

"The Baroness is not coming," said Inge, still swinging her long, slim legs.

"I hope she's not feeling indisposed."

"I'm afraid she is. She asked me to pass on her excuses."

"Did she? Well, I suppose I'll see her some other time."

"The Baroness will have to go abroad. She's not well."

14

"Can't I see her before she leaves?"

"She'll go early tomorrow morning. To Switzerland."

"I suppose Mr. Leonides will travel with her?"

"I suppose so."

"Will she take her child with her?"

"What child? The Baroness hasn't any children."

Hilary's mouth felt dry.

"I thought she had one. A boy. From her first marriage."

"Well, I certainly haven't seen any child. Or heard of one."

Hilary started to drain his glass, then set it down. The champagne was going to his head.

The band stopped; a slim young man whose naked chest gleamed with oil began to play the electric guitar, and a girl wearing a red sequined dress came up to the microphone.

"That's Eva," said Inge. "Jewish, of course. Isn't she gorgeous?"

Hilary spotted an unoccupied canvas chair and set off. He stopped, waiting for Inge to follow him, then went on and flopped down into the chair. There had been a time when they would sit at Zonar's, he sipping ouzo, Angela whiskey. She did come then, she had plenty of time for him then. Hilary would make love to her later—they would drive down to the coast and he would have her on the sand or on the back seat of the car.

Eva's voice was husky, very professional. As she finished her song, she turned and looked at Hilary. The rhythm seemed to vibrate right through her supple body.

Inge sank into the chair nearest his. "Do you like her?"

Hilary didn't answer. As Eva's voice curled around him, he remembered cupping Angela's breasts in his hands and how they spilled over, luxuriant; he remembered the husky voice saying, "Bite me, Hilary, bite me . . ."

"Do you like her?" Inge asked him again.

"She's very good."

Hilary took her hand and watched Eva. Angela had been spoiled, of course; she had only to stretch out her hand and take what she wanted. Hilary could close his eyes at any moment and see her lazy, sensuous walk, hips swinging, head thrown back, the round breasts moving under her dress as if they had a separate life of their own. "Do you want me to kill him?" Hilary had asked, not meaning his words. "No, I don't want that." She put one foot up on the edge of the car seat, her skirt drawn high to show her full, smooth legs. "What's it to do with him, anyway?" he asked her. "Why not let your husband do the worrying?" "He's my brother, Hilary. I married Kriton, but Leon is still my brother." "I don't understand." "It's not necessary to understand." "He's your brother, you don't sleep with him, do you?" "That's my business, Hil." "What's my business, then? What do I *do* with this?" "Keep it with you. Just in case." It was exasperating, but he turned and saw her marvelous legs and took his right hand from the wheel and patted the inside of the thigh nearest him. He was confident then, his hand stirring her to warm, moist softness as the convertible sped through the countryside in the setting sun, the breeze cool and Angela so warm.

Perhaps she needed me, thought Hilary, and in all these years I have written only once.

The young guitarist put down his instrument and came forward and danced alone to the music of the band. His long hair swung back and forth as he jerked his head; the heavy medallion hanging down his chest caught the light and glittered.

"He's available, Prof," said Inge. "If you fancy him."

Hilary wasn't really listening to her. "What's that?"

"You can always find him at the Bacchanalia. I'll take you there if you like."

Then a belly dancer sidled onto the floor and Inge leaned forward in order to see better. "I took lessons in the States in oriental dance. I was pretty good."

"You don't say." However keen the enthusiasm, Nordic Inge didn't have the Arab shape.

The dancer swayed and stamped, her broad haunches shaking under the filmy green gauze, the strong bare feet thumping. The drummer played furiously, and she threw off her veils and her brassiere, her brown melon breasts jumping under the streaming raven hair. The men practiced tolerant smiles, but their eyes were intent.

"*Yiaish el-Arab!*" Hilary called out, clapping his hands to the rhythm, his eyes on the deep navel in that fluid, twisting belly.

Mark bowed to Isabel, and when Sir Clive Bellingham introduced him he kissed her hand. She recognized him at once from the launch.

"I'm sorry to interrupt, sir."

He handed over the envelope.

"Are you sure this is for me?"

"From Mr. Leonides. He hopes you'll be good enough to accept it."

Sir Clive guessed what was in the envelope and put it away without opening it. When Angela had asked him to paint her portrait there had been no mention of money; he had accepted only because he found the request flattering. Clive had worked for several days at her house when, suddenly, she presented herself without clothes and demanded that he paint her in the nude. He finally persuaded her to drape her lower half in a swath of velvet; the idea of one exposed breast appealed to his poetic nature. He had succeeded in painting an idealized woman whose face and figure flowed from the canvas. It was the Baroness, it was Angela, it was all mysterious, unattainable women. The colors captured the desirability of that supple body, yet the flesh was so luminous as to seem ethereal, the eyes were inviting yet aloof. When Angela pulled him down

16

to the couch, Clive, shocked and bewildered, suddenly realized the mistake he had made. . . .

"I'll be back," he said. "Excuse me, I'll bring Hilary over to meet Mark."

As Eva's voice floated among the guests, Mark remembered that he had meant to buy her something in Tokyo—some jewelry, a brooch or a bracelet.

Isabel waited for him to speak, a little nervous at being alone with him, apprehensive of his presence and his silence.

A waiter came by, and Mark took two glasses of champagne and handed her one. When he searched his pockets for his cigarettes, his fingers touched the letter from his lawyer. He lit a cigarette absently; then, remembering Isabel, offered her one.

"I don't smoke."

There was a scar on the back of his right hand, running all the way from the root of the middle finger to the wrist.

"You must have hurt yourself," she said.

"When I was a child. I don't recall exactly how it happened."

He usually told people he had caught the hand on a barbed-wire fence, but he was too preoccupied now to go through the story again. He hadn't seen his wife for years; he hadn't even tried to find out about her. The letter from his lawyer explained that Jennie was at last asking for a divorce—was she planning to marry again?

He turned to Isabel. Now he noticed how perfect she was. Her skin was flawless; the body under the close-fitting dress was beautiful. Her thick honey-blonde hair fell heavily on her shoulders.

"Are you one of the Leonides?" she asked him.

"No. I work for them."

"We're here for the summer," she ventured. "You haven't met my husband, have you?"

When Mark was introduced to Dr. Hilary Grey, the professor could only nod. His mouth was full of a creamed crab canapé; he held his glass in one hand and a lobster patty in the other. Soon, however, he was talking easily, telling Mark about his former residence in Athens, his scholarly projects, his hope of finding a cottage in a village or on an island somewhere and spending the next two or three months writing. In the middle of a long and rather entertaining story concerning one of his adventures in the Middle East, Hilary suddenly stopped and looked down at his empty glass with amazement.

"One moment. I'll be back." He inspected their glasses, nodded sagely— "Refills for all, I'll pass the word along"—and moved toward the bar.

"Shall we dance?" Mark asked.

She looked at him, at the black eyes so close to hers. The black shirt set off his dark good looks; he was very attractive, she thought, but vain and too sure of himself. She liked the way his hair fell over his forehead in front and curled at the nape of his neck in back. The idea of going into his arms intimidated her—it would be like giving up something.

"No, thank you," she said. "I'd rather stay here and watch the others."

But she agreed to go with him to look around the yacht and see the lights from the small town of Vouliagmeni shining on the hills beyond.

Mark took her hand as they walked along the deck. His walk, his movements were lithe and graceful. He helped her climb to the bridge and pointed out the yachts anchored in the wide bay.

"Are you rich, too?" she asked, teasing him. "Do you have a yacht?"

It would have been nice, really nice, to have been able to tell her yes and invite her on board.

"No, I don't have a yacht."

"Not yet?"

"Well, I'm always hoping. I travel hopefully, as they say."

"But you haven't arrived, have you?"

Her light words had struck a nerve, and he looked across the bay with somber eyes. He hadn't arrived, it was true, and time was running out. He wasn't even good enough for a raise—hell, how could anybody "arrive" who wasn't his own man? This lot tonight could buy and sell Greece. Money, just money—what couldn't one do with money? The rich lost no love on each other, still less on him, and no embraces from the Old Lion could deceive him. He was useful to them and they knew it, but he was an outsider, a parasite, a beggar eating only what was put into his bowl. Money—how it all came back to that, what it must be like to have enough, to be truly free. He thought of Jennie's asking him for the divorce and closed his eyes. *I could always marry Katia*, he thought. *That's one way of arriving, isn't it?* Then he opened his eyes and saw Isabel's pale hands clasping the rail, saw the long delicate fingers.

He looked up, and their eyes met.

"Cigarette?" he asked her.

"Don't you remember? I don't smoke."

"I'm sorry."

He wanted to touch those slender hands, to take them in his and caress them. Then Katia called his name, and he turned toward her. Isabel moved a few steps further on and waited.

"Her brother was arrested this evening," Mark explained when they were left alone.

"How terrible!"

"Oh, he was asking for it. He flourishes the flag of revolution a bit. He's a student at the university."

"What will they do to him?"

18

"Give him a good beating, shave his head, and by then the Lions will see to it that he's released."

"What do you think of all this? What is your opinion?"

"I'm practical. I have no opinion."

"But aren't you interested, Mark? Surely you don't support this regime."

"I support any regime that lets me get on with my affairs in peace."

She looked at him, shocked. But Mark took her hand and smiled, and the thought suddenly came to her that he was not expressing his true feelings, that it might be dangerous for him to do so.

"You don't trust me, do you, Mark."

He wasn't sure what he was supposed to trust her about, but at once he put his arm around her shoulders and led her away from the lights, into the shadows.

"Of course I trust you," he murmured.

On their way, they nearly stumbled over two bodies lying intertwined between high-piled coils of rope in the darkness. Isabel stopped, but Mark led her on, talking to her to dispel her misgivings.

"What's the name of this student?" she was asking.

"Jason."

"Jason . . . He must be brave."

She sounded very innocent.

"I suppose you could call him brave."

They stood near the prow of the ship. The sea below was dark and patterned with paths of light beaconing out from neighboring ships and from their own decks. The sounds of dance music drifted toward them through the warm summer air.

Isabel was intensely aware of Mark, his closeness, the lemon scent of his cologne. She stepped aside, but Mark came even nearer.

As he leaned over the rail, the breeze lifted her hair and a long, perfumed lock fell across his cheek. She was delicate, like a leaf before the wind; she looked as though a gust would blow her away.

Mark bent and kissed her hair.

Isabel stepped back, but he went to her and put his arm round her waist. Sensing her nervousness, he gestured toward the entrance of the bay, where a line of small bright lights were moving slowly out toward the open sea.

"It's the *gri-gri*," he said. "A schooner tows the fishing boats out to sea, and they put down their trawls."

As she felt his arm tightening around her waist, she told herself that it would soon be over, that it wouldn't be necessary to make things strained and awkward by protesting. Then she felt his lips behind her ear, on her cheek, and the old fear suddenly surged up, choking her. He was just lifting her chin to kiss her when she struck him hard across the face with her open hand.

19

She backed away from him, biting her guilty hand in distress, then turned and fled, without once looking back.

"Gently, baby, gently, my Josephine."

Hilary drove the small green car delicately, as if afraid that the old engine might at any moment break into a gallop. The cool pine-scented breeze blew down from the wooded slopes of Vouliagmeni; then, at Kavouri, the wind coming down Hymmetos through the gap between the hills of Voula and Varkiza whipped Isabel's long hair against her face and into her eyes.

"The whole trouble started just over there," said Hilary. "Your Churchill and Eden came over to help the royalists cheat the partisans."

Isabel was confused; her body was still trembling, her head was hot, she could hardly hear what he was saying.

"The Russians had betrayed them first, when they gave the British a free hand in Greece in exchange for the Slavic countries. The partisans had most of the land in their grip, then Stalin stabbed them from the rear. That's how the powerful arrange the destinies of the small nations, that's how it's done."

The champagne had done its work. Hilary talked wisely and grandly, reviewing the world, criticizing the affairs of all humanity. "We Americans understand what money can do. The Reds wanted to play it with theories and rhetoric, then, when the rubles failed to roll in, the dreamy-eyed patriots didn't see much reason to carry on. . . ."

On the top of the hill he almost ran over some soldiers who were checking all cars driving into Athens at that late hour. The soldiers peered under hoods while the passengers were moved out and searched. An officer came over to the green car, but when he realized that Hilary was not a Greek he waved him on.

"That's the world, that's the colonels' world," Hilary said and pressed down on the accelerator.

Josephine made a leap and he calmed her down skillfully, keeping her near the curb, holding the wheel steady.

"I shouldn't think they'll last very long," he continued, quite as if Isabel were paying attention to him. "They'll make a thorough mess of the country first, then we'll have democracy again—with a king or without, not that it really matters. The colonels and their friends will still rule the country, albeit from the back room, with a little advice from our CIA, I admit. That's how it was before and that's how it's going to be. Greece, the cradle of democracy! Still, it's better than Bulgaria, I'll grant you that. You can still get a glass of decent champagne here."

Hilary stole a guilty glance at Isabel.

She was staring in front of her, the wind still blowing her hair across her face. Hilary leaned over and wound up her window.

"Better now?"

20

"Yes, thank you."

"You were very beautiful tonight," he said, pleased that she had spoken. "I searched for ages, but I couldn't find you. At first I thought you were with Mark Stephanou, but then I saw him in the saloon, playing cards, and there was no sign of you. I hope you didn't spend the rest of the evening alone, did you?"

"I was all right."

"I think that man made a packet tonight. They were playing for high stakes, and I saw him collecting a pile. Ah, well, lucky at cards, unlucky in love. I wonder. Quite an eye for women, I'll bet. I liked him."

He had hoped to spark her interest, but she seemed too preoccupied to play up to him. It was quite possible that Mark had entertained some secret hope of making a conquest with Isabel. If so, he must have been disappointed, Hilary thought, smiling.

"He didn't try to make a pass at you, did he?"

Isabel was gazing out the window, one hand clenched against her breast. As he turned and looked at her profile in the lights from the street, waiting patiently for her to speak, he thought that the head poised on that slender neck resembled a flower on a fragile stem, the white stole providing the calyx.

Hilary stretched out a hand and patted her knee.

"Tender paw," he whispered. "Tender paw."

It was an old joke of his which Isabel had learned to accept and even welcome; it was his way of comforting her. While driving on the long desert roads of the East he would look out for the moments of her distress and, almost automatically by now, stretch out his hand and pat her knee: "Tender paw, tender paw."

She smiled at him.

"It does my heart good to see you looking so beautiful," he said.

"Thank you, Hilary. You looked very nice, too."

He stroked her knee again. It was one of those exceptional moments when he felt that they were drawing close to each other, that they might still have something to give each other. One inch more, one step nearer, a little more warmth . . . but little things were so often the most difficult to achieve.

"You're very good to me, Hilary," she said quietly.

She rearranged her stole and removed Hilary's hand from her knee, very gently. Hilary glanced at his rejected hand, then put it hurriedly back on the wheel.

It isn't fair to her, he said to himself. I deserve what I got, Isabel was not for me, I should never have got involved with her at all.

When he first met her, she had worn the pained, bewildered expression of a child lost in a nightmare, unable either to retrace her steps or to decide in which direction she wanted to go. But there was her beauty, her low-pitched gentle voice, and something else, something fine about her that appealed to Hilary

—rather to his surprise, for she wasn't his usual type. Again Hilary blamed himself for not giving her the sort of life she was meant to lead. Many times he had toyed with the idea of Isabel's falling in love with a man who could understand her better than he could, a man whom she could understand better than she did him. It had been wrong to marry her, she must only have accepted him out of her sickness and loneliness—but why go over the old mistakes again? If someone were to take her away from him, if there were a chance of happiness for her, he would accept the situation and be glad for her. And he would be free. I'd invite them both for a drink, he reflected, and toast their health and wave a farewell hand.

Again he felt a sense of companionship and tenderness. He leaned toward her.

"Really, you were very beautiful tonight, Isa, love."

Isabel smiled her sad, patient smile.

"I wish you wouldn't keep repeating the same compliment," she said.

2

"No, I don't want the bungalow," Hilary said. "And I doubt that I'll go to the island this summer. You can tell the Baroness that, if you like."

"Why get worked up about it?" Inge asked. "Nobody's making you go."

She drove very fast, having informed him gleefully that one of the traffic cops was sure to run her in for dangerous driving.

Hilary took strands of her flaxen hair and rubbed them between his fingers. He liked her perfume; her warm, young female presence and all its promise seemed very near. Her black dress was short and skimpy, and as she sat at the wheel she showed, unconcerned, long, slim thighs.

"What sort of a place is this club we're going to, anyway?"

"The right sort. There are pretty hostesses to help get you in the mood, to titillate you—if you need titillating. I like that word: *ti-til-lat-ing.*" She rolled the syllables on her tongue, glancing at him slyly.

Two girls were walking across the road, holding hands. Inge nearly ran them down as they jumped, squealing, onto the pavement.

"That'll shake them up!"

"Be careful, Inge."

"I've been driving since I was fourteen."

"You must have had an indulgent father."

22

"My father was what all girls' fathers ought to be. He was strong and reckless and didn't care a damn."

Hilary was intrigued.

"What did he do?"

"He was a racing driver. One of the greatest. He broke all the records, the papers were full of him. We traveled everywhere together. It was fantastic!"

"What about your mother?"

"She was a coward. She left us for a bank director in Copenhagen and we went to the States right away."

"You never saw your mother again?" he asked, still looking at her legs.

"My father was better off without her. He had me. When he crashed, I didn't even see why I should wire and tell her."

"I'm sorry about your father."

For an instant she looked even younger, less confident.

"It's all right. I'm over it now, and anyway I'd been expecting it. I had this sick feeling in my stomach every time he climbed behind the wheel. . . . Two months before he was killed, the Lions invited us on a cruise—Angela was crazy about my father. They would've got married, I'm sure, if he hadn't been killed. Anyway, when Angela gave me this job, I stayed in the bungalow at first, the *kalivi*, whatever that means."

"It means 'hut.' "

"Well, it's quite luxurious for a hut and very useful to Angela. When she's on the island, the overflow of her guests stay at the *kalivi*. But she's not there now, and I don't think she'll be back for a while. So the bungalow's vacant, free. She wanted me to tell you that."

He understood. He would "overflow" to the hut, part of the crowd, excess luggage to be stowed away.

Hilary shook his head.

"Okay, Prof. Never mind. It was only an idea."

"It was very generous of Angela, very thoughtful."

She must still feel guilty about his dismissal from his job so long ago; she could even have been an accomplice in his deportation.

"You were her lover, weren't you?" Inge asked him.

"One of them."

"I'll bet you were a good one."

She reached over and gave his arm a light pinch.

"What was your way-out specialty that made her take you up?"

"What was my—you could do with a good spanking, you know."

"I'm not a little girl," she said, but she put out her tongue at him. "Maybe you like spanking *big* girls—right, Prof?"

He felt his heart racing—soon he must make his first move. Then they turned the corner, and he saw the neon sign of the Bacchanalia blinking and

23

flashing out into the street. Inge maneuvered the big car into a dark alley nearby and switched off the lights.

Before Hilary could reach over and kiss her, she was out of the car and waiting for him to follow.

At the end of a corridor they went through a doorway, screened by a beaded curtain, which opened directly into a bar. Its stools were covered in red vinyl; the footrail and the ashtrays were of brass. The bar area was bright, but the rest of the room was softly lit, and, beyond a small dance floor and the tables, Hilary got a confused impression of alcoves and bays secluded in the shadows behind columns and velvet-curtained arches.

It was difficult to see just how far the room extended. Here and there a white sofa caught the mellow light from the red-shaded lamps. Hostesses in short tunics and high heels were circulating, talking and drinking with the customers. Three of them were lounging against the bar, not far from where Inge had perched herself on the high stool next to Hilary's.

"Hilary gazed approvingly at Inge's exposed thighs.

"How did you find this place?" he asked her.

"I came here with Mark."

"Have you been seeing much of him, then?"

"Why? Do you mind?"

She smiled and touched his hand.

A man in a white dinner jacket was playing a jazzed-up version of a popular tune on the piano. The subdued murmur of voices was punctuated now and then by the shrill laugh of a woman or the voice of a waiter repeating an order; nobody seemed to be listening to the music.

The bartender placed their drinks in front of them. Inge was studying the mural on the wall opposite them.

"Look at it, Prof. It's like a Pompeian brothel, isn't it?"

Hilary slid his hand beneath her skirt; stroked and kneaded the inside of her thigh as he looked up. The mural portrayed nude women in every imaginable erotic posture, their flesh rosy and impossibly opulent. Some of their amorous adventures were grotesquely indecent, some merely amusing. In one of the central panels a bull with lowered horns was eternally charging a plump beauty who was encouraging him, her teeth, breasts, and buttocks gleaming. In the next panel she was triumphantly dragging the bull, now limp, by the tail.

"It's quite charming, don't you think?" said Inge. "And look at *that.*"

She pointed to a less innocuous section of the mural.

"Isn't he big! I wouldn't like that to go inside me." But her eyes were shining.

Beyond the mural, pianist, sofas, girls, were all enveloped in a rich ruby glow, and Hilary was gathering courage to lead Inge away into the shadows lurking beyond the arches and curtains. Inge's knee kept nudging his and

24

Hilary's always volatile spirits soared toward euphoria.

He raised his glass and clinked it against hers.

"*Yia sou*, Inge!"

"Down the hatch, Prof!"

He put his hand high up on her thigh and patted it.

Mash'allah, Inge! You're a good girl."

"Would you repeat that first bit, please? I didn't get it."

"Ah, that's my fluent Arabic breaking out. One day I'll give you my entire repertoire, all ten phrases. Five religious, five obscene."

At that moment Eva joined the pianist on the small stage and began singing in her husky, insinuating style. Her purple sequined dress clung to her supple figure, leaving her shoulders bare, exposing most of her breasts. When she had finished the song she came down from the stage to the center of the dance floor and looked around, smiling, as the audience offered its applause. Then the sharp notes of an electric guitar sounded and Toni, the young man who had played at the party on the yacht, plucked out a melody. Eva raised her arms and began moving her body, very slowly, every movement deliberately languid.

"I like this," Hilary said.

"What did I tell you? *She's* titillating, isn't she?"

Hilary put his arm around Inge's waist and squeezed the firm flesh under her dress.

"Let's go somewhere else, somewhere intimate."

"Why?"

"Somewhere I can show you how an old teddy bear can hug and kiss." He was doing his act. "Let the grizzly bear embrace the innocent maiden and smother her to death."

"You're funny."

She turned away to watch Eva, and Hilary felt deflated, suddenly embarrassed. He was too old for these bright, silly girls, he shouldn't have tried.

Inge slipped her hand in his, her eyes still on Eva.

The band took over and people came onto the floor to dance. Some of the customers danced with the hostesses; some of the hostesses danced with each other until a man came to claim them.

"It's interesting," Hilary said.

"It's human. Do you like it?"

Inge squeezed his hand and gestured vaguely behind her.

"They show 'adult' films in the room down there."

"Did Mark take you to one of them?" He would have liked to see a blue film with Inge.

A girl came up to Inge and embraced her.

Inge gave her a playful push.

"This is Chloe," she explained, and the two girls went away to dance.

A man wearing dark glasses slid onto her stool next to Hilary's and ordered a whiskey.

"I think I saw you on the *Hesperides*," he said.

His mustache and long side whiskers were charcoal black. "You're a friend of Mr. Stephanou?"

"Yes, well, we met at the reception."

"Markos is my friend, too."

As he stretched out his left hand to take the whiskey, Hilary noticed that his right sleeve hung loose and empty.

"We do business together, Dr. Grey."

Hilary wondered how he knew his name.

"Oh, really? What kind of business?"

"Quite legitimate, of course, what did you think? I have a travel agency in Athens, I organize a stream of tourists all the year round for the hotels of Markos' firm. We're the main customers of the Kalamos Village. We've got hundreds of people there now—the real rich, the money people."

"Where is this tourist village?" Hilary asked.

"My God, how long have you been here, man?"

He finished his drink and insisted upon paying for Hilary's.

"The Kalamos Village was my idea, my suggestion to Mr. Leonides. Half the island belonged to them, but the Lions are seamen, they don't understand that you needn't run after money, that money can come and knock at your door."

He got to his feet.

"Markos is here somewhere tonight. Suppose we go and find him, what do you say?"

"I don't mind."

Hilary put down his glass and followed him down the corridor until they reached a closed door.

"By the way, my name is Nubar Ohanessian," he said. "I'm an Armenian," he added unnecessarily and, with his one hand, pushed open the door.

There were perhaps twenty-five or thirty people in the room, some gathered around a roulette table, some playing dice, others cards. The air was thick with smoke. No music could be heard here—only the click of the wheel, the voice of the croupier, and the occasional tense murmur from one of the tables.

Mark was playing cards at the far end of the room with a number of people standing around his table. He seemed tired and dissipated, with shadows beneath his eyes, a cigarette drooping from the corner of his mouth, his tie loose, and his shirt open at the neck.

The waiter came and put a drink in front of Mark. He took one sip and set it down, his eyes never wavering from the cards. Nubar left Hilary and went to his friend. Hilary thought Mark raised his eyes, but he gave no sign of recognizing the Armenian.

26

Gambling had no fascination for Hilary. The air was too close, the smoke hurt his eyes, and after a while he began wondering what was happening to Inge. I'd better go and find out, he said to himself, and went back to the bar in the other room. The young guitar player was performing what Hilary could only have described as a pelvic dance; Inge was nowhere to be seen. . . .

Hilary found an unoccupied sofa and sank down into it, almost spilling his glass of beer. Toni had finished his dance and Eva was back at the microphone. First she sang a haunting Greek song, her voice plaintive; then she sang in French and in English, closing her eyes and swaying a little in time with the music.

Mark came over, carrying a brandy, and sat on the sofa with Hilary. Eva saw him, and the husky voice became even more suggestive.

"She sings wonderfully," said Hilary. "Where does she come from?"

Before Mark could answer, Toni leaned over the sofa and embraced Mark. As he put his arms around him, his hand pressed against something in the inside pocket of Mark's jacket.

He kissed Mark lightly on the cheek.

"You don't take any chances, you don't."

Mark ignored the remark and stubbed out his cigarette. A tall man with finely drawn features was looking down at them.

Toni released Mark.

"Don't be discouraged, sweetie. Life is hell sometimes," he said and sauntered away.

The newcomer sat down with a great show of weariness and glanced around with shrewd gray eyes; then he smiled, and Hilary decided he was not much older than himself, only graying at the temples and smelling of lavender.

"I had a chance to speak to the captain," he said. "After you'd left, Markos. Jason Kommenos is at the camp at Dionysos."

"When will he be released?" Mark's feet were propped up on the low table in front of him.

"What's the hurry? The boy, I understand, is mixed up with the student organizations—one of the leaders, as far as we can make out at this stage. There is evidence that he authored a certain leaflet distributed around the university, calling on the students for disobedience and revolution."

"He's just a boy. The Lions will send Jason abroad to study—there's no reason to keep him in."

"Now, my dear Markos, you're a clever man, you must understand we've *had* our revolution, the country is well on its way to normalization. We don't want this sort of . . ."

"He's just a student," Mark said. "And the Lions certainly are staunch supporters of the colonels."

"We know that."

Mark took his feet from the coffee table.

"And what am I to tell Mr. Leonides when he returns?"

"To keep an eye on the younger Lions. Come on, Markos, give me a cigarette. I've been running about all day and I haven't any on me."

Mark offered his case; the other man took it up and examined it carefully. He had rather small, delicate hands, the nails carefully manicured; his hair, streaked with silver at the temples, was beautifully groomed in smooth wings over his ears.

"Thank you, my dear boy." He put a cigarette into an amber holder. "What a pretty case you have, Markos. I was going to ask you if it was gift, but, I've just remembered, I shouldn't pry into your private life, should I?"

He snapped the case shut, eyeing it with subtly exaggerated admiration. "Platinum, I see. Give me a light, will you?"

As Mark flicked his lighter, Hilary noticed that it too was platinum and, like the case, monogrammed in gold.

The man inhaled deeply.

"I can see that whoever tries to win your affections will have to bid against very high stakes."

His pedantic Greek seemed to fit the mannered voice. He turned to Hilary now and gave him an appraising stare.

"Please introduce me to your friend," he said to Mark in English.

"This is Dr. Hilary Grey. He speaks Greek." Then, to Hilary, "Superintendent Mikhail Lazaros. He's a cop."

"It's nice to meet a friend of Markos," Lazaros said. "What are you doing in Athens, Dr. Grey? If I may ask?"

"I'm on holiday." Hilary sounded to his own ears oddly defiant.

"Ah, the joys of a tourist! On holiday. No cares, no distractions, no running about on matters of business. We working men envy you, don't we, Markos?"

Mark took a long pull on his drink. Lazaros, not at all disconcerted at the lack of response from Mark and Hilary, saw that their glasses were empty and clicked his fingers for the waiter.

"Markos, what are you drinking—brandy? This is my round. And you, Dr. Grey? Ah, I see you're a beer drinker." He ordered a brandy, a bottle of beer, and a small whiskey for himself—"with water and lots of ice." He turned to observe Eva, who was doing a little dance as an introduction to her next song. "A rather . . . spirited young woman," he said. Then his eyes came back to Mark.

"It was a shame they wouldn't let you see the captain. All of the big catch ended up in the captain's in-box so to speak. It's nothing to do with my department—still, when a thing like this happens, there is work to go round for all of us. And it was interesting to go through the list. Apparently some of our friends will never understand that the game is up, that it's better to leave well enough alone. Papademas was your friend, wasn't he?"

28

Mark did not answer, and Lazaros turned his attention to Hilary.

"Once Papademas was campaigning and went to a village to speak. But first, Dr. Grey, he called the grocer and, in the square, he paid all the outstanding bills of the inhabitants. The villagers voted to the last man for this fine philanthropist."

The superintendent smiled, drank a little more of his whiskey, drew lightly on his amber cigarette holder.

"Papademas spent thousands to win in one of our democratic elections, he became a minister with hardly anything left in his pocket. And so, within a year, he was a millionaire. A profitable business, our democracy—thank God we haven't democracy any more."

Lazaros then noticed Nubar Ohanessian lurking in the shadows.

"No, I don't think Papademas really was your friend, Markos. He didn't claim to be so, and you weren't interested in politics. He's a friend of your Armenian friend over there, shall we say?"

When Mark again did not reply, the superintendent finished his whiskey and stood up.

"I'm very happy to have met you, Dr. Grey. Good-bye, Markos, I hope I shall see you soon. I didn't say anything to offend you, did I?"

Mark stood up too and offered his hand.

"Good-bye," he said. "Please don't misunderstand me, I'm not very good company tonight. My luck was out at cards. Cards, as you once told me, will be my ruin. And women, didn't you say that?"

"I think, Markos, you're still bitter with us for the time you spent in our care. But you must realize that we have a job to do."

Lazaros seemed to be eyeing Mark, waiting, this time, for a response.

Finally, Mark smiled—a smile, Hilary suspected, that had cost him a great deal of effort.

"I had nothing to do with it," he said. "But I don't hold it against your people. They were deceived."

"How charitable of you."

Lazaros turned and left them, as if on cue, conscious of his exit.

Mark called the waiter.

"Let's have another drink, Hilary, let's wash away his taste from our mouths."

"A fine idea." Hilary was glad for the chance to talk to his new friend.

"How's Mrs. Grey?" Mark asked. "I'm sorry, I meant to ask you before."

"Isabel's fine, thanks. She wouldn't come out with me tonight. Sir Clive brought her his book on the island and she stayed home to read it."

Hilary noticed the Armenian signaling to Mark with his good arm from the other side of the room.

"It's good you reminded me of Isabel, Mark. It's so late, I should be going really."

29

But he finished his drink before saying good night.

The street was dark and nearly deserted, and Hilary stumbled against the closed shutters of a kiosk on the corner. That reminded him—Inge had barely avoided knocking into this kiosk as she was looking for a place to park.

Inge . . . where was the little so-and-so? When they had arrived, all the surrounding streets were full of cars; now only a few were left.

Hilary thought of going back to the nightclub and searching for her, but he decided instead to set off on foot toward Omonoia and pick up a taxi there. Then, as he began to cross the road, he saw in the dim glow of a street light that the big car was still parked where Inge had left it. She might be waiting for him, he thought.

He walked over to the car.

The street light shone on the empty front seats, and he was about to head off when he heard a noise. He stepped up to the car and looked through the side windows; yes, there was somebody on the back seat, a woman, her dress pulled up. One of the street girls, perhaps—no, wasn't it Chloe, that hostess from the Bacchanalia? Then Hilary made out another female figure, crouched on the floor at the darker end of the back seat—her head between the thighs of the reclining hostess, who moaned and pulled at the other girl's hair. The crouching figure gasped, her face upturned now, her mouth open, her tongue still lolling out. It was Inge.

Hilary stood mesmerized, watching their bodies as though he could see nothing else. Inge's head went back between Chloe's legs, and the moaning and gasping started again. Hilary was turning to go, when Inge lifted her head and saw him.

"Fuck off, Prof. You're not wanted here," she said, and went back to her task.

3

Hilary's green eyes looked back at him from the mirror; they were pensive, cryptic, questioning. Behind the eyes there were only hollow spaces. He stooped and inspected himself more closely—as if, by attentive examination, he might establish himself as someone who had the right to occupy a certain amount of room in the world.

His fair skin was burned from the Mediterranean sun, and his chestnut hair, the seawater and sand washed out of it, was wildly unruly. He brushed it back over his ears and smoothed it at the sides with his fingers. There was still, even after shaving, a faint shadow along his jaw. Carefully, as if handling something explosive, he picked up Isabel's box of "Invisible Veil" face powder and started patting it on with a piece of cotton.

Isabel came out of the bathroom wrapped in a pink towel, her hair bundled up on top of her head, her legs glistening with water.

"Sport Light is just your shade," she said.

She was obviously in a good mood.

"It's all very well for you," he said. "You forget that I'm older and my need is greater."

Not very old, really. Hilary took a deep breath, expanding his chest, watching the result in the mirror. He could work on stomach exercises or, better still, he could do a lot of swimming this summer. He buttoned up his shirt and tucked it inside his trousers.

Isabel came to the dressing table to collect a jar.

He lifted his face for her to see.

"I think my complexion is really improved, toned down for the evening, don't you?"

But Isabel, busy with her own preparations, went back to the bathroom. He heard the shower raining down again and felt the old exasperation; he started putting on his tie, determined to ignore it, even as he tried to ignore her obsession for washing and cleanliness. She'll stop in a moment, he told himself, she can't go on forever; she's been in and out of that blasted shower for the last two hours. She'd have to stop soon if they were ever going to be ready for their guest. And Hilary wanted them to be ready; they would have dinner on the terrace and he would even offer Clive a drink afterward; surely an ambassador, even a retired one, would know enough not to stay beyond eleven o'clock, not after seeing Hilary apparently falling asleep in his chair. The strait and narrow gate of the Bacchanalia would be open, and the place really began livening up close to midnight. After sending Isabel to bed with a nightcap, Hilary enjoyed driving up to Athens and having a beer or two with the girls there.

Again he called to Isabel; there was no answer and he stood at the glass door of the shower stall and called her once more. The water was streaming down her shoulders over her small, soft flowerlike breasts and down the silky blonde pubic hair. The face, totally absorbed, was raised toward the deluge; the hair was now covered in a yellow plastic shower cap.

There was a knock at the door and Hilary, stifling once again his desire, pulled the bathroom door shut. The maid came in, carrying a large basket of white and red carnations.

"This has just arrived, m'sieur. It's for the madame. Please look, there is also a box."

31

The box was wrapped in gold paper and tied with red satin ribbon. When the girl had gone, Hilary, without waiting for Isabel, tore the paper off a green leather case, noting that its contents came from Zolotas Jewelers in Athens. He opened the case and took out a long necklace of turquoise and gold.

Isabel came out of the bathroom, naked, and took the necklace in her hands, not quite knowing what was happening. Then she saw the white card from Mark Stephanou among the carnations. On the back of the card was a short note asking Hilary to persuade her to accept his little present.

"I can't," she said. "It's impossible."

But she lifted the necklace in front of the mirror and Hilary, in admiration, took it from her and put it round her neck. It was a blue and gold river in the valley of her breasts.

"Your eyes look just the same color as these things," said Hilary. "Apparently you made a conquest."

This must be Mark's peace offering, she thought, and as she lifted the gold and turquoise, her hand seemed to burn as if she had struck him across the face only that moment. She moved closer to the glass and let her hair fall, timidly arranging it around her shoulders in front. Then, as if she had only now realized she was undressed, her cheeks flushed.

She pushed her hair back and unclasped the necklace.

"I can't accept it, of course. He should have known better than to think I would."

"Keep it, old girl, keep it! It looks perfect on you."

"I'll keep the flowers. Please send this back for me."

Hilary put it back in its case.

"All right," he said softly. "I'll probably see him tonight. After we've finished with the ambassador."

The hostess, eyes narrowed against the smoke of her cigarette, turned to Hilary.

"Foreigner?" she asked lazily.

"That's right, but I can speak Greek, if it helps."

"You never know what may help."

Toni came to the bar and asked for a Brandy Alexander.

The hostess nudged Hilary. "He's a nice boy, isn't he?" She turned to Toni. "How's business for the loveliest boy in Athens?"

Toni smirked, and Hilary decided he had too much makeup on, even for cabaret.

"Do you think so, my love? You haven't tried me yet. Or have you, and I've forgotten?"

"I'd love to try you, *agori mou*. But I thought you preferred men."

"It's a lie, dear. Shall I prove to you that I like girls?"

32

"But come, confess, you do go with men, don't you?"

"I'm in the trade, I'll slip it to a man if the price is right."

"And what's the price to slip it to a girl?"

"There's no charge for that, dear. I *adore* girls—they always give me presents afterward."

In the shadows Hilary noticed Chloe carrying a long-stemmed glass. He turned away, embarrassed. An American airman was ordering old-fashioneds for himself and his companion, who now climbed onto the bar stool next to Hilary and placed her plump hand squarely on his shoulder to steady herself. Her face was on its way to being the battered wreck of a pretty woman, but the brown eyes under the penciled brows were unexpectedly soft. When she was finally seated, showing an expanse of plump legs and breasts, she made a *moue* at Hilary.

"Thanks," she said.

"Any time."

She indicated Hilary to her companion with a nod.

"Just like Benny Webster, isn't he, Sam?" She spoke English with a strong Greek accent. "My poor Benny! Do you remember how he'd cry like a child when he'd had a few drinks and we had to put him to bed? *Panayia mou*, he was heavy!"

She beamed at Hilary, as if expecting him to collapse at any moment.

"British?" she asked.

"American."

"So was Benny Webster. He lived with—he rented a room in my house for eighteen months, all the time he was stationed here. He used to say sometimes, when he got *nervous*, that he was only a bum, but he was really a clever man. Very clever, very intelligent, *believe me*."

"I'm sure he was," Hilary said.

"He was a photographer, he took pictures of film stars and other famous people."

She leaned over to whisper to Hilary, her smell was a blend of face powder, perfume, and sweat, not unpleasant. "He took many pictures of women—in the nude, you understand?" Then she resumed in normal tones: "He was a famous photographer. Remember, Sam?"

"I certainly do remember Benny Webster."

"I am an *artiste*," she informed Hilary. "I have an academy of ballet in Athens. Are you interested in the dance?"

"Sometimes."

"You must come and see my academy."

She searched in her bag for her card; Hilary assured her that it wasn't necessary, that he was bound to come across her again, but she was unconvinced. She borrowed a ball-point from Sam, fished out a squashed cigarette

33

pack and wrote her address on it in bold, childish letters. Then she removed the last two cigarettes from the pack and handed it to Hilary.

"I am called Daphne," she announced. "I live off Omonoia."

"Daphne what?"

"Madame Daphne." She wrinkled her nose at him.

"All right. Next time I come downtown . . ."

She turned back to her companion. Hilary took the empty Papastratos pack with the address on it and put it in his pocket, rather hurriedly, so that Mark, who was coming at that moment toward the bar, would not see it.

Mark was glad to see Hilary and anxious to find out how his present to Isabel had been received.

"Where have you been?" Hilary asked. "I come in here almost every night, and I never see you."

"I've been traveling abroad, and then I had to go to Alea for a few days."

"At least it's cooler on the islands—it's been hell in Athens. We climbed up to the Acropolis this morning. My feet still hurt and I may never feel cool again."

"Now why did you do that?" asked Mark, smiling. "I haven't been up there for years."

"Isabel read somewhere that the best time to see the Parthenon is under the midday sun of a hot summer day. Thank God for the marble steps. I sat there in the shade and leaned against a column while she roamed about. She had her *Guide Michelin* with her and checked on every single stone to make certain that nothing was missing."

"How does Isabel take the hot weather?"

"Oh fine, just fine. Mad dogs and Englishmen, you know. Now I remember, I promised to thank you for the flowers and the necklace. It was very kind of you. Why did you send such an expensive gift? Isabel feels she shouldn't accept it."

"It's a beautiful necklace, and she's very beautiful. I want her to have it. Souvenir from Greece."

"When can you come and have dinner with us at the Venus?"

For days Mark had been thinking how he might get to see Isabel, but now he hesitated.

"Thanks, but I'm busy these days. Later I'll tell you."

"What keeps you so occupied?"

"Work. All kinds of problems and headaches. Mr. Leonides is returning soon, and then I'll have a little more time to myself."

"He was in Zurich with his sister, the Baroness, wasn't he? I understand she was sick."

"So I've heard."

"She offered us a small house she has in Alea, but I don't think we'll go."

"I suppose you want to drive around and see the country?"

34

"We've seen enough of the country. I want to rest, I want to think, I have a project I want to give a try to."

"What kind of a project?"

"I have some ideas I want to put together. Perhaps write a book . . ."

"What's the subject?"

"Greek demotic poetry."

"I like poetry."

Hilary turned to him, his eyes alight.

"Do you really?"

"I used to know many of the klephtic ballads by heart. Tell me about your project."

"I've borrowed the major collections from the libraries here and I'm trying to trace and classify the unifying characteristics of this rich tradition that flourished during the long Ottoman rule, during the War of Independence. I want to pick out the themes, illustrate them with clear English prose translations, compare them with the themes from the Odyssey and the Iliad."

"That's exciting, Hilary. How did you hit on the idea?"

"I wrote a book on the Homeric poems once, when I was at Columbia. It's turning yellow in the university libraries. Then I came to Greece to see the land and sea of those marvelous heroes and began learning the modern idiom and reading the demotic poetry. . . . Well, the heart was the same, the ancient spirit was still alive here."

As Hilary unfolded his ideas, Mark warmed to his enthusiasm. Hilary was a rare man, a scholar, totally removed from the concerns of business. Mark hoped he hadn't hurt him by sending the necklace to Isabel. He got the bartender to refill their glasses, and Hilary insisted that Mark recite aloud for him some lines from the ballad of the mother with the seven sons and the one daughter, "the only one, the dearest, the most beloved." Matchmakers came from Arabia to ask for her hand for their prince; all the brothers refused except the youngest, Constantine. When the plague killed all the boys, the distraught mother wept and blessed the graves of the six, but cursed the place where the youngest son was buried and reminded him of his oath to bring back her daughter if she were ever left alone. The grave opened and Constantine rose up and rode to the East to fulfill his promise. . . .

"Mark, you're crying," Hilary said.

"Yes, isn't it silly?"

Mark rubbed his eyes with the back of his hand; for some odd reason he had been reminded of his baby son Emil who died, neglected, while his father was locked away in jail.

As the Greys were getting up to leave after a coffee at the Byzantion one evening, Isabel saw Mark buying cigarettes from the kiosk at the corner.

She touched Hilary's arm.

35

"It's Mark."

"You're right. Wait here, I'll get him."

Mark immediately invited them to his apartment close by to have a drink.

"Are you sure we should come now?" Isabel asked. "Isn't it too late?"

"All time we spend asleep is time wasted," pronounced Hilary.

Isabel wondered if Hilary had really tried to return the necklace. Having something so valuable from Mark upset her. He doesn't want me to forget, she thought, *he* hasn't forgotten. She always carried the necklace in her purse, sometimes angry, sometimes grateful to him, but she had never put it on again. She now decided to leave it behind in the apartment secretly. She felt relieved at the idea—now she could sit back and look at him without any feelings of obligation.

As Mark led them through the entrance hall she noticed his eyes, alert and watchful. In the elevator she imagined herself running her fingers through his curling hair, but when she caught his eye, she looked up to watch the floor numbers flashing above them. Isabel felt excited, yet uneasy; it was like crossing a frontier. Then, when they entered his apartment on the fourth floor, she·was disappointed. It was small and impersonal, more like a hotel suite, totally lacking the kind of clutter that might yield a clue as to what its occupant was like.

"What about some sherry?" Mark asked her.

"Thank you."

She watched him pouring the drink—calmly, easily, quite as if nothing had ever happened between them. Perhaps he has forgotten, she told herself. But her guilty hand trembled as she took the glass.

Hilary discovered the ouzo on the bar and, bottle in hand, went to the kitchen to find the ice.

"I've no cellar to show you, not even a fireplace," Mark said. "I do have a balcony—or would you rather sit inside?"

He waited for her to decide; their eyes met and she found she could not answer. Finally, a noise came from the kitchen and she was released.

"Let's go outside," she said, taking a sip of her sherry.

Mark opened the door to the balcony and stood back for her to step out.

"How do you like the Parthenon from my balcony?"

He rested his hand on the parapet, and Isabel looked down at the scar.

"How lucky you are to see it always like this," she said.

"Lucky? Yes, I suppose I am. Next weekend is the full moon, and the ruins will be open to the public."

"How lovely! Would you like to take me to see the ruins by moonlight?"

"What do you think?"

"I'm frightened of open spaces at night," she said, almost to herself. She moved a little away as Hilary rejoined them.

Hilary came out and handed Mark a glass of ouzo.

"Any news of Jason?"

"He's still in detention camp. But Mr. Leonides will get him out when he returns."

"Poor kid! What bastards they must be."

Isabel's eyes dared Mark over her glass.

"He isn't interested, Hilary. He's a practical man."

"Don't be so impertinent, my love. Perhaps Mark has his reasons not to parade his feelings."

Mark sipped his ouzo and said nothing. Isabel found herself hating this male conspiracy of silence.

The doorbell rang abruptly. Isabel watched Mark pause with his glass near his lips. Then, very carefully, he put his glass on the parapet and went to answer the door.

"Markos Stephanou?"

"Yes?"

"You're wanted at headquarters."

Hilary and Isabel had come in from the balcony and were standing just inside the room.

"What's it about?" Mark asked.

"They'll tell you at headquarters."

One of the officers, a heavily built man with bushy eyebrows, looked steadily at Hilary; but Hilary was not to be intimidated.

"What on earth's going on here?" he demanded. "Mark is our f iend."

"We know that, Dr. Grey," said the swarthy policeman, spacing out the words as he opened the door for Hilary and Isabel.

"It'll be all right," Mark told them. "I'll come see you tomorrow."

They walked down the corridor in silence. Isabel, not quite certain what had really happened, had forgotten to leave the necklace behind. At the elevator she turned back. Through the open door of the apartment, she saw Mark putting on his jacket as the officers waited to take him away. Mark's eyes met hers for an instant and Isabel thought that he smiled at her, but she was too far away to be sure.

They drove home, Hilary talking all the way, Isabel only half listening. It was a hot night, no leaves stirred, and a sticky salt-sea humidity hung in the air.

Isabel showered, cleaned her face with tonic lotion, brushed her hair, and lay naked in bed, pulling the sheet halfway up. What will they do to Mark? Where will he spend the night? If they torture him . . . She turned uneasily onto her side. Perhaps he did stare at me. But when I dared him to take me to see the Acropolis by moonlight he didn't suggest a time, he didn't take me seriously. Perhaps he'll call later, he said he would come and see us tomorrow.

Tomorrow. It was already tomorrow.

Isabel turned over again, her back to Hilary, trying to drift off to sleep. She still had the necklace and now she decided to keep it to remember him by if anything went wrong, if he never called, if he never returned from the hands of those men. The necklace was in her purse and she fought the desire to put it on and sleep with it. Hilary was still awake, he would see it if she did. . . .

Hilary got up and opened the venetian blinds to let in as much air as possible. From the terrace downstairs a dim light shone in and as he went back to bed he saw Isabel's buttocks outlined under the thin white sheet, arched up as she lay on her side facing away from him. I'll call and find out about Mark tomorrow, he was thinking. Perhaps they only wanted him in connection with that student. Policemen can look brutal even when they're on routine business. Mark didn't seem particularly worried, it may not have been anything important. He said he would come round to see us. We could have dinner together.

Again Hilary noticed Isabel's curved body in the dim light.

"I met someone the other night," he announced. "Not a silly girl, a mature woman."

There was no response from Isabel.

"She gave me her address, she wants me to call on her. Oh hell, you wouldn't understand."

Looking at Isabel's body, he quietly slid his hand down and started touching himself.

"She's a ballet teacher. She wants me to screw her, do you hear?"

Isabel turned on her stomach and buried her face in her pillow.

Hilary had an erection, but the lonely passion had deserted him with the years and however much he tried he couldn't come to a climax.

"Christ, it's hot tonight."

He fell into an uneasy sleep, only to wake up much later drenched with sweat, feeling out of his dream, out of the past, Isabel's pounding fists upon his head and shoulders. It was five nights after their wedding, it was past midnight. . . . He had come home half drunk to find her showering in the bathroom of their hotel room; he had tried before the gentle way, the sweet endearments, the tender kisses. He had caressed her between the legs with his fingers, he had gone down and licked her with his tongue and succeeded in arousing her; but every time he tried to penetrate her, always at the crucial moment, she would cry out and turn away, imploring him to give her time, to have patience with her.

That night he hadn't called for her to come, he'd kicked open the bathroom door to see her under the shower, the water running down her body in glistening streams. She had begged him to wait for her to finish, but he had dragged her to the bed and wrestled with her. Her thighs were locked together

38

and nothing could make her knees relax. She shivered and cried and her eyes accused him, horrified, the eyes of a trapped animal. Hilary felt again the pounding of her fists. . . . He had slapped that perfect face and Isabel cowered and left the bed, went to the bathroom to cry alone. I was drunk, I was drunk, he said to himself now as he had so often, knowing deep inside that he had drunk too much on purpose, in desperate need of an excuse that would enable him to do just what he had done.

Isabel never once referred to that dreadful night, but how could he ever forget the way he had found her the next morning, huddled on the bathroom floor, her eyes blank, the tears dried on her cheeks, her hair disheveled about her white face? He had taken a step toward her and stretched out his hand, only to help her to rise, but she fled from the bathroom and stood at bay near the window, as far away from him as she could get.

"Isabel," he said, "I'm sorry. I'm terribly, terribly sorry."

"Don't touch me," she whispered.

Hilary had sworn that he would never again try to force her, that he would never so much as ask her unless she wanted him.

Not once had she showed that she wanted him, ever.

4

Mark tried to find out what it was all about, but neither of them would tell him. The jeep went down Solonos Street, past the School of Law, then turned sharply left down Massalias and came to an abrupt halt before a place Mark knew well. The yellowish stucco walls of the ugly old building bore posters advertising the National Lottery; a man, fatuously beaming, was breaking through a screen of thousand-drachma notes above the slogan *You win, you win, you're a double winner.* It was a bad omen; the grinning man, the money, the slogan. Feeling depressed, Mark looked away for a moment, across the road to the tall marble statue of Athena high above the roof of the Academy. Her spear was pointed toward the Parthenon.

Around the corner from them, Mark knew, was the entrance to the Offices and Museum of Criminology and the National University Laboratory of Forensic Medicine and Toxicology.

"Who is dead?" he asked them.

"You'll see soon enough. Don't ask questions."

They went through the swinging doors, up the steps, down a long corridor.

A policeman saluted and opened the door; the body was on a trolley in the middle of the empty room. Mark stood by the door and stared at the outline of the still form beneath its white sheet.

"Come here and take a look," ordered the inspector.

He approached, his eyes still fixed on the sheet; it was impossible to tell whether the body was that of a man or a woman. The smell of disinfectant was strong, and the chill of death crept over him.

"I want you to be careful what you tell us. This wasn't a natural death."

The inspector took one end of the sheet and lifted it off the head and shoulders, exposing the white breasts, still firm and full on the thin dead body.

When Mark's eyes focused, he saw her face: the glazed eyes, the open mouth, the cheekbones more sharply defined than ever, the long hair spread out, a violent shade of red. Oh, God. No, no . . .

They waited for him to say something, but he could not. Inspector Notaras finally spoke.

"Well, is this Jennie Stephanou, born Jennie Mastroyiani, or is it not?"

He hadn't seen her for three years, but he was still her husband. The police always picked on the husband.

The inspector turned to his sergeant.

"How old would you say she was?"

"Thirty-three? Thirty-five?"

"How old was your wife?" asked Notaras.

"Twenty-four, I think."

"You see, sergeant? She was only twenty-four, but she had a habit and that makes a difference."

He moved to the side of the trolley and raised the right arm of the corpse; it was scarred with needle punctures, some of which had suppurated and were evil-looking even now. He let the arm drop, then leaned over and lifted the left one.

"There are fewer punctures, sir."

"Correct, sergeant."

Of course, Mark thought, Jennie is left-handed. Then he realized—Christ, what was he thinking?

The inspector went to the basin and washed his hands with carbolic soap.

"Bring in a dope merchant," he told the sergeant, "and I'll get you promoted before you can say 'needle'!"

Mark ventured nearer and with a trembling hand tried to close her eyes, but the lids wouldn't move, and as he lifted his hand, they stared up at the ceiling like a doll's.

The sergeant covered the corpse carefully, the legs, the body, the face, the shapely breasts, the too bright hair. Then he jerked his head toward the door and Mark followed along the corridor to the pavement outside. He was feeling sick; pain drummed at his temples and stomach. He leaned his head against the wall beneath the lottery man still beaming, still telling him that he was a double winner.

He woke up when somebody turned off the light that had burned above him, unshaded, all night. He shook out his jacket—he had used it as a pillow on the wooden bench—and reached for his cigarettes. Then he remembered that he had smoked the last one the night before.

The door to the white-washed room was unlocked, a constable came in, followed by a boy carrying a Turkish coffee and a glass of water.

"How are you off for cigarettes?" he asked.

Mark gave money to the boy and he was sent to fetch two packs of Players. The constable gave Mark one of his while they waited. He smoked it and drank some coffee which made him feel better, but he worried about the confrontation ahead, not knowing what direction the questioning would take.

"I'm sorry about your wife." The constable shook his head. "But this is life. We shall all die."

He closed his eyes; behind them he could see the violent red of Jennie's hair. There was a time when her hair had been a natural auburn; he had loved to run his fingers through it, to help her fasten it up. She had changed the color while he was in jail—when he saw her after his release, at the inquiry into the death of Psaros, she was well dressed and *soignée*, snug in a fur coat, avoiding his gaze, flaunting the cascade of dyed hair, her friends waiting outside to take her away . . .

The constable led him to a large lavatory.

"I'll be outside," he said, but when Mark walked from an open urinal to the washbasins, the constable reappeared and stayed with him, leaning against the wall.

Mark hung his shirt on a nearby hook and splashed his face, neck, and shoulders with cold water. He passed his fingers over his jaw; he could do with a shave. In the mirror over the basins, his skin looked firm and suntanned and this comforted him obscurely. He combed his hair carefully, then reached for his shirt. It irritated him that he had to put the same one on again; however much he smoothed the fabric, it was still creased. He put on his tie, used some toilet paper to wipe off the dust from his shoes, and washed his hands again.

"I'm afraid it's not permitted for you to make any phone calls. But if you have any messages for your family, I'll see they're safely delivered."

For his family?

"No, no messages. Thanks all the same."

He put on his jacket. His handkerchief was no longer fresh, so he put it into

41

a side pocket. Again he studied his reflection: he looked presentable, but he wished he had his razor with him. In the mirror he saw the constable waiting and turned to follow him down the endless corridors.

Again the fear came back to him and he stopped, involuntarily.

"They'll only ask you some questions," said the constable. "Then they'll get you to sign a statement."

Mark went with him up the stairs and into a large room where he was given a seat. Two police officers were busy with papers; a middle-aged army major and two captains were leaning back in their chairs, their desks empty. As Mark had expected, the central desk was occupied by Inspector Notaras of the Athens Bureau of Narcotics.

Notaras asked him to give an account of his movements the previous day, so Mark went over it all—the work with the Piraeus office, with the architect designing the new buildings going up on the island of Alea, with his secretary; the drive to his apartment in Kolonaki, then to the sea, for a swim . . .

"Where was that?" asked Notaras.

"A small beach about half a kilometer beyond Vouliagmeni."

"Alone? Don't you like the company of other people?"

Mark did not answer.

"Tell us, Stephanou, were there *any* other people on the beach?"

"No."

"Who saw you, then?"

"Anyone who happened to be passing on the road above, I imagine. I wasn't hiding."

"What happened when you got back to Athens?"

"I stayed home, I had some work to do. Then I went out."

"What time was that?"

"Eleven, I think. I walked down to Kolonaki Square, and I met some friends."

"Had you arranged to meet them there?"

"No."

"Then what was the purpose of your going out?"

Mark had been planning to go to see Eva at the Bacchanalia, then go home with her. He'd wanted to talk to her about Jennie.

"I went out to buy some cigarettes," he said. "Players, to be precise."

The inspector was not amused.

"Then?"

"Get something to eat, I suppose."

"But you met, by chance, Dr. and Mrs. Grey waiting for you?"

"They weren't waiting for me. We met, as you say, by chance."

"Foreigners?" the middle-aged army major called out.

"Yes. He's an American professor. His wife is English."

42

"Why are they here?"

"They're on holiday."

"What kind of doctor is the husband?"

"He's not a doctor of medicine. He's a professor."

"Communist?"

"No."

"He's not against us?"

"I'm certain he supports the government," Mark told the major. "He's a philhellene, an admirer of Greece."

"What about you?"

"I support the government."

"What is your opinion of the Revolution?"

"It saved the country from anarchy."

"Did you vote in the referendum?"

"Yes, of course."

"For which party did you vote before the Revolution?"

"I had never voted before."

"You are not interested in the destiny of your country? In the time of Pericles any citizen not taking part in public affairs was called an *idiotes*—an idiot, in fact. Did you know that?"

"Yes. But I never trusted any of the politicians."

The major smiled at his colleagues. He was done.

Inspector Notaras tapped with his pencil on the desk. He had been in the service for eighteen years, he had never liked army officers, and he resented the major's interruption.

"Now listen to me," he told Mark. "We've spoken to Dr. Grey, who seems to like you. How long have you known him?"

"I met him this summer."

"Did you? Do you know that this Hilary Grey was here before, teaching at the American College? That his residence permit was suddenly revoked, and he had to leave the country?"

"No."

"And do you know the reason? Communism. Fraternizing with the *koukouedes*. His best friend here was a prominent member of the KKE. Why he was allowed in again is a mystery to me."

The major broke in again.

"Are you a Communist?"

"I'm against communism, I always have been."

"What did you do about it?" asked the major. "How did you help to keep your country free from the infection?"

Mark had nothing to say to that and after a short pause Notaras tapped his pencil on the desk.

"Your wife had intercourse not more than one hour before her death. You screwed her yesterday, didn't you?"

"No. I hadn't seen her for three years."

"Well, somebody screwed her, and instead of the fee, he gave her a little too much heroin. Unless she made a mistake and gave herself an overdose. Do you think that's likely?"

"I don't know."

"Suicide? Did your wife have any reason to want to kill herself?"

"I don't know."

"Is it true she was a prostitute?"

"I don't know."

"What *do* you know?"

"I haven't seen her for the last three years."

"Now, there's no hurry. Just sit there and think it over and tell us when you've decided to speak the truth."

He got up and went out of the office. It was a quarter to ten, and Mark wondered what was going to happen next. He found himself thinking about Jennie's funeral rites. There were no relatives to be informed. Her friends would not want her now; as the next of kin, he would have to make the arrangements.

Notaras came back, carrying a file. He went to the desk and began looking through the papers.

"When did you say you got married?"

"In 1963."

"I see here that you were imprisoned in 1963."

"That happened afterward."

"Were there any children?"

Mark didn't answer.

"Any children?"

"No."

"What was the crime for which you were sent to jail?"

"There was no crime. I was framed."

"I repeat my question—what was the charge?"

"Transporting drugs."

"And your wife was a heroin addict, wasn't she?"

"Not when I was with her. I didn't know she'd become one, until last night. Until I saw her at the mortuary."

"You were sent to jail," he consulted his folder, "for three years—framed, as you put it—on a charge of transporting dope and now your wife is found dead, murdered probably, and certainly a drug addict. Curious, isn't it? Do you yourself suspect anyone as the murderer?"

"No."

"Do you know of anybody who would have had any conceivable motive for killing her?"

"No."

"Do you still say it wasn't you who screwed her last night? It was you, wasn't it?"

"I haven't seen my wife for the last three years."

"When you came out of prison, you didn't go back to her?"

"No."

"Why not?"

"I didn't want to. We didn't like each other."

"Was it, in fact, because she had left you and gone to live with her lover?"

"Something like that."

"It's true, isn't it, that your wife's lover was killed in a car accident some time after your release? Did you try to make it up with her after that?"

"No."

"Why not?"

"It was too late. I've told you—we didn't like each other."

"You liked her well enough to make her pregnant before you married her! Perhaps you only married her because you made her pregnant?"

Mark did not reply.

"Did you marry her because you made her pregnant, or didn't you?"

"I don't remember."

"You don't remember! You didn't remember that there'd ever been a baby, did you? You lied about that! The poor girl is dead— *dead*, do you hear? She didn't die full of years, and I don't think she killed herself. Somebody killed her. Did *you*?"

"No."

"Did you have any reason to kill her?"

"No."

"Did you have any reason to get somebody else to kill her?"

"I've told you—no."

"Look here, Stephanou, you were in the clink and your wife was being fucked around Omonoia and you found her living with one of the fuckers and apparently plying her trade successfully during the past few years and you say there was no reason for you to want her out of the way—*kerata!*"

"She was nothing to me anymore. She was not my responsibility."

The inspector stood up, looked around the room, and pointed to Mark.

"You hear that? His wife was a common *porne* and it was nothing to him!" His voice rose higher. "He wasn't responsible! She was free to do what she liked!" Then he turned on Mark. "Why, then, didn't you get a divorce? You had evidence, there was plenty of evidence!"

There was no answer to that, Mark didn't clearly know the answer himself.

45

The disillusionment had been too much, the bitterness too great, the prospect of the humiliation of the procedure unbearable. As long as Jennie hadn't asked for a divorce, he could avoid facing the truth: he was not ready to come to terms with reality. It was only recently that he had heard from his lawyer, but poor Jennie hadn't given him time to think, time to decide.

"I guess it might seem like that," he said.

"You guess, motherfucker! *Skata!*"

The army officers looked uncomfortable—these police methods with a bereaved husband seemed to them in poor taste and not likely to lead anywhere.

Inspector Notaras got up.

"I haven't finished with you yet, but next time you'd better have something to say which sounds like the truth. That is, if you want to walk out of here alive."

"I would like to speak to my lawyer."

"You don't speak to any smart-aleck bugger of a lawyer until I've finished my end of the business," he said and walked out.

Mark spent the rest of the day locked up in the room where he had spent the night. An officer brought him his typed statement and he signed it. The friendly constable sent for coffee and sandwiches and stayed with him while he ate them, talking in a relaxed way about Crete and Herakleion, his home town; his young son who was first in his class at the gymnasium, and his oldest daughter for whom he would soon start building a house to marry her off—"the sooner the better, Mr. Stephanou. At twenty they tell you the girls are too old, at twenty-five nobody wants to marry them." As he left to go and report to his chief, he said, "They may want to ask you some more questions and they may not, but I shouldn't let the inspector worry you." Then he added, "I'm sorry about your wife, I really am."

At four o'clock he returned and took Mark back to the office where he had been questioned that morning. Superintendent Mikhail Lazaros was behind the desk where Notaras had sat.

Mark tried to shake off his apprehensions; Jennie had died of an overdose, it was only natural that Lazaros be involved sooner or later.

"I'm sorry we've had to keep you like this, Mr. Stephanou."

Superintendent Lazaros's voice was gentle.

"But you see, this woman was your wife and such a death is bound to result in disagreeable consequences for those connected with her. Theodore Papademas knew her, by the way, as indeed he knew various other people who were either addicts or distributors."

Lazaros questioned Mark about his job and his movements; he was particularly interested in his various journeys abroad, but he affected not to know that Mark had spent a lot of time on the island of Alea during the past three months, looking after the Kalamos Village.

"What exactly do you do there?"

"We're building a tourist village. A complex of hotels, bungalows, shops, swimming pools, tennis courts . . ."

"I thought the Leonides Maritime Enterprises was a shipping firm."

"The family came originally from Alea. They're developing a stretch of land they already owned there. This, of course, with the full agreement and approval of the government." Mark turned to the officers. "My firm is doing its best to promote the economy of the country."

"Are you the manager of this complex?"

"No, I'm the connecting link between the various directors of departments and the firm."

"And your friend, Nubar Ohanessian, what is he doing there?"

"He has a travel agency, he does a lot of our publicity."

"I have here your file from my department's records." Lazaros said softly. He leafed through the pages and shook his head.

"I can't understand why we don't have a complete record on you after your release from jail. I see here that you claimed you were wrongly accused, but that's hardly a reason for not keeping the records up to date. It seems you were interviewed routinely by an officer of the Asphalia in April 1967, just after the Revolution, but after that—nothing."

He looked at Mark with a plaintive expression, as if it were Mark who was to blame for some inexcusable negligence.

"You were also questioned in connection with the running down of Psaros the previous year, but that was before the Revolution. Anyway, there were all too many persons who would have been happy to see Psaros out of the way—the police were faced with *un embarras de richesses*, as it were. And you had an excellent alibi, I must confess."

He glanced around, but the officers in the room were unresponsive.

"You were sent up in 1963," he said, suddenly businesslike again. "Do you still say that you were unjustly accused?"

"I was framed. I didn't have anything to do with it."

"Who was it who framed you, then?"

He paused. Then, "I don't know."

Lazaros raised his eyebrows. "Did you never try to find out, didn't it interest you sufficiently?"

"It interested me. I never found out who it was."

"Had you found out, would you have taken matters into your own hands?"

"That's hypothetical, isn't it?"

"Is it really?"

The superintendent leafed backward through the pages.

"Why did you leave the navy? Didn't you like it?"

There was a definite stir of interest in the ranks of the military. The officers looked at each other and then the major leaned forward across his desk and addressed the suspect.

"Were you a naval officer, Stephanou?"

"Yes."

"When did you enter the academy?"

"In 1957."

"What was your first ship after you were commissioned?"

Lazaros interposed.

"Markos Stephanou was acting lieutenant, he had a promising career ahead of him, which, alas, did not materialize. Our friend left the navy—not voluntarily, I am sorry to say—he was court-martialed and cashiered."

"Court-martialed! Why?"

"Why not ask Superintendent Lazaros?" said Mark. "He knows all the answers.'"

It was his first show of temper that day. He had promised himself that he would stay cool, but the repetitive, plodding questions were beginning to fray his nerves.

"He was court-martialed for misappropriation of funds." the superintendent said smoothly. "That's the answer gentlemen."

He looked at the officers, then back at Mark. The eyes were suddenly pitiless; he seemed secretly excited by the abrupt crack in Mark's composure.

The major faced the suspect with a new distaste.

"Misappropriation of funds? You mean embezzlement? You mean you robbed the service—you, an officer?"

"It was a sports club fund," said Mark.

Lazaros had finished fitting his menthol cigarette into his amber holder.

"How were you connected with it?"

"I was the acting treasurer. The treasurer was on sick leave."

"Quite a heavy responsibility for you to undertake. How much money was entrusted to you?"

"About fifteen thousand drachmas."

"What was the charge against you in connection with this fund?"

"That I borrowed ten thousand drachmas from it."

"Was 'borrowed' the word used when you were charged?"

"No, but it would have been the correct word."

"In that case, did you plead 'not guilty' to the charge against you?"

"No. Technically it was true."

Superintendent Lazaros puffed delicately at his cigarette.

"Let's not indulge ourselves just now in dialectics."

"All right," said Mark. "I took the damned money, yes, but I intended to pay it back—I borrowed it."

"Did you really expect the naval court to see it that way?"

"No, I didn't."

"Then why did you take the money in the first place? Didn't you expect it to be discovered?"

"No, I thought I had time to replace the money. Then an unexpected audit was ordered, there was nothing I could do about it."

"Why did you take just ten thousand?"

"That was what I needed, what I had to have to pay some urgent debts."

"What kind of debts?"

"Gambling debts."

"Where did you incur these debts?"

"On shore. A club in Piraeus."

"The name?"

"The Red Leopard."

"Red is a dangerous color at the best of times," observed Lazaros. "But why didn't you try to raise the money in a more honest way?"

"I did try, but I couldn't raise it."

"Why didn't you ask your father?"

"My father was dead. There wasn't anyone I could go to for that amount of money."

Lazaros fitted a new cigarette into his amber holder, and the major took up the interrogation.

"You don't seem to have done very much for your country, do you, what with one thing and another? Disgracing the service, going to jail on some sordid charge, drifting around ever since, from what I can make out."

Lazaros watched Mark closely; he saw the tightening of the sensitive mouth and he guessed the effort to appear unruffled. The major seemed to be well into his stride; Lazaros leaned back in his chair with eyes half closed, smoking, listening to the proceedings as if they were being provided for his entertainment.

At that moment the door opened and two soldiers brought in a gangling, bespectacled boy of about nineteen, his hair cropped almost to the roots, a raw cut on his upper lip. The soldiers saluted the major who looked at the frightened young man between them.

"Ah, you look better now, Kommenos. It was all that hair that was weighing you down—we'll make a man of you yet! Now, this is what we're going to do. We're going to give you a chance to continue at the university in the autumn, but now you'll be sent back to your island and you are not to leave it until the first of October. Then we'll see. You will report to the police every day. We thought at first to send you to the army straightaway, to whip you into shape, but never mind—you can graduate first if you behave yourself. I can tell you, you won't get another chance and you should feel damned grateful for this one."

Then he smiled, quite a warm smile, like a father who must admonish his son but remembers always that it is he who will one day have to continue the family tradition.

"You've been a very stupid boy, Kommenos, but you're young and there's hope for you yet. Be careful whom you make friends with. We have the assurance of your uncle that there'll be no more trouble, so don't let him down. Your uncle is a serious man, see how far he's gone! Listen to what he tells you, take his advice. Do you understand what I'm saying?"

"Yes," said Jason, biting his lip. He looked around and saw Mark for the first time.

"You know each other?" asked the major.

"Yes, sir," said Jason.

They've obviously scared the shit out of him, thought Mark. And from the look of him, they beat him up before the Old Lion had time to intervene.

"Where did you meet?"

"On Alea, sir."

The major looked at Mark as though he were about to say something to him, then decided against it.

"Straighten up, young man!" he said. "You may go now, but remember what I've told you. You'll be put on the *Gorgona* tomorrow morning at nine. Now get out!"

When Jason and his escort had left, there was a brief hiatus. The major sighed deeply, found a penknife in his drawer, and whittled away vigorously at an already sharpened pencil.

"About this foreign couple you've been around with," he said finally. "What sort of a professor is he? Has he asked you for any information about our country?"

"No, of course not. Nothing like that. As I've said, Dr. Grey is a great admirer of our country. He speaks the language, he's a Greek scholar."

"It doesn't follow," said the major.

One of the captains suddenly addressed Mark.

"Where do you live in Athens?"

"I've an apartment in Kolonaki."

"What is the name of your parish church in Kolonaki?"

Mark hesitated.

"You don't go to mass very often, do you? Many people have become very clever nowadays, they've given up the ancient traditions and put nothing in their place."

Mark inclined his head politely, but made no comment. His detached composure infuriated the major.

"You have had many advantages," he said. "You should have become a credit to your country, you had every opportunity for worthwhile service, but you threw it away."

50

He leaned forward, aiming his words.

"We have places for the cynical, the flippant, the idle, the selfish, the amoral, the parasites, the *antichristoi* and the *antihellines*. There are camps, there are prisons, there are islands . . ."

Lazaros cut him off.

"Oh, but Stephanou is no political agitator."

"Are you sure of that, Superintendent?"

"Quite sure. He's not the type. I assure you, he won't worry your people. He's my department's headache, if anyone's."

He rang the bell for the guard, who took Mark back to the whitewashed room. Then he picked up the intercom.

"Look here, Notaras, nothing is coming out of this. We'll have to do some field work. . . . Yes, of course, we shall get him in the end, but we need a charge that sticks first and we want to find out who his associates are. . . . No, you have more important duties. I'll put two of our men on him myself. . . . We'd better wait till we've got something more concrete before we send his dossier to Interpol. Now tell me, who is our man on Alea? . . . Demetris who? What's his job? . . . I see. Antiquities and detective work go well together, don't they? . . . Never mind that, can we trust him? I'd like to see that report. And get this Demetris over to me tomorrow. . . . By the way, why is he doing this? What does he want from us? . . . Good, good. I'll see him first thing tomorrow morning."

"These soldiers live in a world of their own," said Lazaros. "One has to play up to them, humor them sometimes."

He was driving Mark through Athens in the evening traffic. It was ten o'clock, and the crowds were coming out of the early shows at the cinemas.

Mark did not know where they were going; he felt tired and frayed and in no mood for conversation. If he could he would have declined the superintendent's company and gone directly to his apartment. But he had reached the stage of lightheaded tiredness that day when a few more hours, a few more vexations, did not seem to make much difference.

"Very intense, that young student. He's lucky to have Leonides behind him."

Lazaros did not turn toward Mark but spoke as if to himself.

"By the way, I'm deeply sorry about your wife. I didn't have a chance to express my condolences before. Shocking. But you hadn't seen her for a long time—to all intents and purposes she was no longer your wife, I understand."

Mark turned and looked at him. Lazaros glanced back, smiled nervously, then concentrated on the road ahead. His shrewd eyes were veiled as he maneuvered his Morris Minor through the traffic.

51

"It's very tiring, all this questioning," he said, his voice melancholy. "I've been on duty since early morning."

He drove the car into the garage of a block of apartments somewhere on the southern slopes of Lykavitos.

"Come along."

They went up in the elevator in silence. At the third floor they got out, and at the end of the corridor Lazaros halted and took out his key ring.

"I live here," he said. "Come in."

It was a corner apartment, the bedroom windows opening to the east, toward Pendeli; the living room's balcony doors overlooking the American Embassy, the Hilton, the sweep of the town down to Phaleron. On the piano in the living room there was a photograph of a handsome young man in officer's uniform; beside it was a bowl of pink and white roses.

"You must be exhausted," said Lazaros. "Do sit down somewhere and I'll give us a drink."

He went over to a tape recorder first and switched it on.

"Delius. I hope you like it—he's one of my favorites."

He gave Mark and himself a whiskey with a little water and plenty of ice, collapsed gracefully into an armchair opposite Mark with a great show of exhaustion.

"A little whiskey is just what I need after the day's work. Is yours all right? By the way, I thought you came out of it very well today."

The whiskey burned Mark's throat, but its warmth gradually dissolved some of his tension and he felt himself beginning to relax.

Lazaros' voice was soft, companionable.

"You live in Kolonaki, don't you? I used to live there, years ago, before I posted up north. I wanted to get a place in Kolonaki again, but prices have risen so much. Kolonaki is not anymore for such as us poor cops. But this is all right, don't you think?"

"It's very nice."

"Not bad, not bad. I've got quite an efficient woman who comes and cleans for me. I always do the flowers myself, though. A little beauty in this prosaic world is not amiss, do you think?"

"They're very nice."

"In fact, I should have bought some new ones today, but I've been too busy and unless one goes on foot it's impossible. I buy my flowers from the flowershops around the corner from the Vouli."

He noticed Mark's empty glass, picked up the decanter, and poured him another.

"Plenty of ice again?"

"Yes."

"Take off your jacket, if you like. It's still so hot, isn't it? When I'm out I switch off the air conditioning, it's so expensive—do you want it on now? No? I'll open the balcony doors, but take off your jacket if you think it's still warm."

He went to the next room and returned wearing slippers and a handsome housecoat of white silk. He made a fresh drink for himself, brought the decanter, and offered to pour a little more for Mark.

"You have noticed the glass?"

He brought the Waterford decanter nearer for inspection.

"It's a little hobby of mine—that's what I wanted to show you. But let's finish our drink first, there's no hurry."

Mark took off his jacket, they finished their drinks, then Lazaros got up and beckoned Mark to come see his collection. There was glass—Venetian, Bohemian, Waterford, Arabic, Turkish. First Lazaros pointed to the pieces from outside the cabinet, explaining how he had gained possession of each. Then he opened the cabinet and took out a deep blue glass, thick and slightly asymmetrical.

"Marvelous piece of work, don't you think? There's only one place in the world where they make these. A town in Persia, a beautiful place. They call it Hamadan, but of course to us it's Ekbatana—where Alexander the Great defeated the Persians."

He handed the heavy glass to Mark.

"Isn't it lovely?"

Then he showed him other things—an alabaster lion, a jade bowl, some blood-red Venetian goblets, a delicate glass narghile on a jeweled stand from Constantinople. "A sultan could have been proud of this, probably was," he commented, handling it affectionately.

The colors fused and danced like a kaleidoscope before Mark's heavy eyes. He was steady on his feet, but he felt dizzy, and knew that he was getting a little drunk. He had eaten only a sandwich that day and he was very tired—but now he felt he wanted another drink, perhaps that would help keep him going a bit longer.

Lazaros, as if reading his thoughts, refilled his glass from the decanter. Then the superintendent moved toward the piano and looked critically at the roses in their crystal bowl.

"They're fading—I'll tell my woman to throw them out tomorrow."

He turned to make certain that Mark was watching, then nodded toward the large photograph in the golden frame. For a moment he stood gazing at the young man in the picture.

"Vasilis. He was my best friend," he said finally. "We used to share a flat together. He was killed, betrayed and killed, during the Civil War. He fought for his country, but the Communists got him in the end."

53

Lazaros turned to Mark.

"Vasilis was a remarkable man; had he lived he would have made an ideal premier for this long-suffering country."

Mark was still silent, and Lazaros was disconcerted at the lack of any response. Vasilis had been like that sometimes, moody and withdrawn, suffering in silence, unwilling to confide. Mark had the same slim, graceful strength, the subtle strength of an ancient Greek athlete, only darker and more handsome, the features almost austere in repose. With Mark it wouldn't be a betrayal, it wouldn't be a degradation. Vasilis would have understood.

He walked to the tape recorder and raised the volume slightly.

"Marvelous music, isn't it? Thank God, there's always music."

They had often listened to music together, and Lazaros remembered the sharing with Vasilis, the warmth, the security, the quiet understanding, his generosity of mind and body; with him Lazaros had learned to find strength in self-sacrifice, dignity in humility. Mark was not Vasilis, he could never be, but he was there, flesh and blood, he was there.

"You must realize, Markos, I was only doing my job today. I have to go through the routine every time we have trouble on our hands."

Mark glanced at him and said, "Have you decided, then? Was it suicide, accident, or murder?"

"No, we haven't decided. But I have decided that whatever it was, it had nothing to do with you. It may be difficult to convince Inspector Notaras, but I'll try. I outrank him, of course, and I want to help you."

"I'm just as innocent now of any part in any crime as I was seven years ago—so you're getting a second chance to play fair with me, aren't you?"

"Why do you put it like that, Markos? I myself wasn't here to listen to your version, and we haven't charged you with anything, have we? Why do you want to remind me all the time that I'm a cop?"

He came and stood closer to Mark.

"I'm a lonely person, Markos, I don't make friends easily. I don't really enjoy being a policeman, you know. I was meant for the bar, but fate decreed otherwise and this was the nearest thing." As he spoke his voice was softer and gentler than ever. "I'm very sorry if this business distresses you so much. But, after all, you hadn't seen her for a long time, had you? It was all over, wasn't it? She was an unstable character, she wasn't worthy of you. But I understand. Death is not nice, really not nice at all. She wasn't always discriminating about her friends, though, poor creature, and I feel this may have hastened her end."

Mark loosened his tie, opened his shirt, lay back in the armchair, and stretched his legs. He had torn up all her photographs, he had burned all the letters a long time ago—there was nothing left to remind him of Jennie. He hoped the superintendent would let him go soon, otherwise he would fall asleep right there, in his chair. One arm drooped over the side and he closed his eyes and took a deep breath that was almost a sigh.

Lazaros took the limp hand and squeezed it.

"Are you all right?"

Yes, he was all right. For a moment he imagined that Lazaros was still holding his hand, then, realizing that he was, he made no attempt to withdraw it.

"I'm so tired," he said after a few moments of Lazaros' tender pressure. He stood up, and Lazaros put his arm round his shoulders.

"My dear boy, you *do* look tired. Would you like to rest for a while? Let me show you the bathroom, if you want to wash."

He opened the bathroom door, talking rapidly.

"I'll get you some fresh towels. You can shave, too—there's my razor, and some cologne."

The bathroom was spacious, green-tiled and well equipped and gleaming. Bottles and jars were arranged on shelves in perfect order, and one wall was almost entirely filled by an enormous mirror set into the green tiles. Mikhail Lazaros was rather proud of his bathroom.

"I've got a spare room—you can even spend the night here, if you like."

"No, I'll go to my place," Mark said wearily. "But thanks all the same."

"I wish you weren't so intent on going. Are you certain you want to go out like this—is it wise, when you're so tired? How will you get home?"

"I'll get a taxi."

"I can see the death of that unfortunate girl has upset you terribly. But you must have asked yourself before now—are women worth being upset about? If I may say so, you did very well to sever relations with her. I know it's sad, but she was a *foolish* girl and she was bound to come to a bad end in one way or another. Have they released the body from the mortuary yet? If so, I suppose you'll have the funeral tomorrow. Would you like me to come along—unofficially, of course, as a friend?"

"No, thanks. I need not trouble you."

"No trouble, Markos! Really, I'd like to if it would help."

He put his hand on Mark's shoulder.

"You don't mind my calling you Markos, do you? Somehow, it seems to come naturally. Why don't you call me Mikhail?"

Mark could not imagine it ever coming naturally to address Mikhail Lazaros by his first name.

"Thank you," he said, "but I'd rather be alone tomorrow."

His head was spinning; his and Lazaros' voices seemed to be coming from a long distance away.

"I'd like us to be friends, Markos. Drop in here sometimes for a friendly chat—off the record. If you ever feel like a drink and a chat, just ring the bell. Should you ever decide to talk to me about anything that might be worrying you, I might be able to help you more than you think."

He pressed and kneaded his fingers into Mark's shoulder and smiled at him.

"How strong you are, Markos! Are you certain you'll be all right?"

"I'm all right, I'm all right."

He turned to go.

"Good-bye," said Lazaros. "And try not to worry too much about tomorrow." He stood at the open door, watching him go down the corridor toward the elevator, but Mark did not turn back.

5

Isabel turned over Sir Clive's letter.

"He sounds so enthusiastic for us to go," she said. "The bungalow is right on the cliffs, not far from the villa Artemis."

She and Hilary were having after-dinner coffee on the terrace of the Venus Beach. A musician was playing the mandolin and singing softly at the other end. A young couple opposite them were holding hands and whispering to each other.

"The Baroness is in Switzerland," she added.

"I have work to do in Athens," said Hilary. "At the Gennadius Library."

I'm not a beggar, he thought. She's avoided me, ignored me, and now she offers her bungalow. No, thank you.

He finished his coffee quickly.

"I'll go and get a drink somewhere. Would you care to join me?"

"I'd rather stay here and look at the books Sir Clive sent us."

Hilary got up and left without saying good-bye.

He drove up to Athens, parked Josephine in a back street near Omonoia, and set off, not knowing which way to go. Ever since the police had questioned him about Mark, he had believed he was being followed. As if they had clairvoyant powers, he avoided planning his movements in advance—he would change his course halfway, frustrating them in their pursuit, as he liked to imagine.

He had plenty of time on his hands and he walked through the busy streets of night Athens, surveying the scene, savoring the festive mood of the crowds.

He could stroll to the lovely park, the one that Henry Miller liked so much; he could sit at Constitution Square and have an ice, or, better still, an ouzo; he could see a film or one of the open-air plays; he could even try his luck with a nice girl from a coffee bar—he could see them across the street, vivacious, well groomed, self-assured: They looked too young and challenging. Then he remembered Daphne. Madame Daphne. Hilary had kept her address, copying it carefully from the back of one Papastratos pack to the next; every time he threw an empty one away, he felt that he was giving her a little free advertisement.

He read the address again, checked the direction at a kiosk, and set off.

He was a little surprised at himself for not having looked her up before. After all, she was a female who had made it very clear that she was available, who knew about these things, who liked it and wanted it. Yes, this was what he should have gone after, the kind of woman he needed. It's a matter of cock and cunt, he thought, now lighthearted. That one wants me, we could do some beautiful ballet together.

Hilary stopped a passer-by and checked again on the address. A Mercedes taxi drew up beside him, its sharp-featured driver alert.

"I know this city very well. You want something, don't you?" He waited a moment, then added: "I know good places for you."

Hilary shook his head.

"I know some clean girls."

"No, thank you."

"I know some nice boys, if you like boys."

Hilary walked down several streets and then passed through a narrow passage between two blocks of office buildings which led to a small courtyard with a crumbling fountain in the middle. The house was dilapidated and in the Turkish style, the porch was lighted and at once he saw the large sign suspended on rusty chains above the porch: ACADEMIA CHOROU KAI MOUSIKES KYRIAS DAPHNES.

Hilary found a string of goat bells hanging from the main arch and pulled at it vigorously. The sound was fullbodied and curiously metallic. He waited for some moments, tugged again, and looked around him. Ranged on both sides of the door were earthenware pots of basil and mint, and, near the archway, an ancient and prolific laurel bush. Hilary wondered whether to wait another minute or simply leave. He walked to the laurel bush, crushed a leaf between his fingers and sniffed up the strong green country smell. He heard the bolt being drawn and he turned back; the door opened slightly and Daphne appeared. Her face was flushed, her hair was disheveled.

"Hello, Daphne."

The faded pansy-brown eyes in the battered face grew bright with pleasure.

"It was in the Bacchanalia, wasn't it?"

"Right."

"British?"

"Still American."

She was wearing baby-doll pajamas slotted with cherry-red satin ribbons; her bare legs were round and strong, if flabby at the thighs. As she leaned against the door, swinging one foot, Hilary could see the red varnished toenails of her small grubby feet through the open-work sandals with their exaggerated high heels. There was a stale, perfumed bedroom smell about her, not unpleasant.

"Hilary is the name. Don't you remember?"

She beamed at him.

"Of course I remember, *spourgitaki mou!* You remind me so much of my old friend, Benny Webster."

"This is where I came in."

Obviously gratified that he had remembered and sought her out, she stuck her tousled head through the door and kissed him on the lips, briskly but thoroughly.

"Not now," she said softly. "I've got a pupil here for a private lesson. Come back, *poulaki mou*. In about an hour."

Three fingers fluttered in roguish farewell as she closed the door.

Hilary loafed around the Omonoia district for an hour, then bought a box of chocolates from a kiosk and set off. When he got there the Turkish house was dark, but the door was open and the radio was on. Hilary lit his last cigarette and threw the pack with the address into the ancient fountain. He rang the goat bells, but there was no answer. Seeing a light coming from a door in the passage, Hilary walked in and put the box of chocolates on Daphne's crowded dressing table. He waited, then took off his shoes and his clothes; but as he lowered himself onto the old-fashioned double bed there was an angry yap and three white poodles, red collars around their necks, leaped out from under the coverlet. . . .

Hilary left Daphne shortly before midnight, pleased with himself but suddenly worried about Isabel. She had been acting strangely the last few days, withdrawn and silent, slipping away to wander along the seashore by herself, hardly eating anything. Sir Clive's letter had pleased her, but Hilary had been clumsy once again and killed her enthusiasm. He felt vaguely guilty. Perhaps he should take her to the island after all.

A stranger standing at the corner of the street seemed to be watching him. Hilary turned back and hurried away through another street. In a land where spying had become a national pastime and an excellent source of income—no doubt much of it coming from his own country—someone was bound to be shadowing him, writing ingenious reports in beautiful Greek to justify his paycheck if nothing else. By the time Hilary reached Tritis Septembriou he was almost running, but the crowds made him slow down. He crossed over to Leoforos Patission. Again he sensed the presence behind him—what was it? A scent? A familiar step?

He turned south toward the Pedion Areos, the Field of Mars. A patriotic drama was being performed at the open-air theater and Hilary heard the thunderous applause of the audience at what must have been the final curtain. He hurried through the park, choosing the darkest places; when he reached the other side, he walked into the open gates of an outdoor café, sat down at a table and ordered an ice, gazing intently at the platform where a graceful young man was balancing swords in his mouth, climbing ladders, leaning backward until his whole body was curved into an arc, the shining deadly blades poised directly above his throat.

Again Hilary thought of Isabel. He left his ice unfinished, got up, and —very cleverly, as he thought—made his exit through the other end of the enclosure.

As he stepped outside he heard behind him a languid voice which he recognized at once.

"Good evening, good evening to you, Dr. Grey."

Mikhail Lazaros pointed to the young man who was still balancing his swords inside the enclosure.

"How careless and confident he is! Yet he's really living on a razor's edge—*epi xyrou akmes*, as our ancestors would say. One slip and he'll be destroyed."

He fell into step beside Hilary as they came out of the park.

"Which way are you going, if I may ask?"

"Toward Omonoia," said Hilary. "I left my car there."

"But, dear Dr. Grey, this is not the way to Omonoia."

"I thought I'd stroll a little. It's too fine a night to spend indoors."

"Still, the pleasures of the boudoir are agreeable, indeed, if one has a relish for such entertainment. I'm going toward Omonoia myself, eventually. You don't mind, do you, if we walk together?"

Hilary stole a glance at Lazaros' pale, aloof profile. The son of a bitch knew all about him; he was the one who was having him followed.

"I'm meeting a friend there later, Dr. Grey. May I invite you for a little refreshment?"

"No thanks," said Hilary. "I should be getting home soon."

"Well, then, do let me ask, Dr. Grey, how are you enjoying your holiday? Have you made many new friends, have you come across some of your old friends?"

Hilary made no reply.

"I've heard in the office that from your previous residence here you knew a certain Takis Apostolides. Have you tried to contact him?"

"You mean the dentist? No, I haven't."

When Hilary had gone to look up his old friend, he'd found the dental clinic occupied by a urologist. Nobody seemed to know the whereabouts of Apostolides; his name was not in the telephone book.

"Your friend is not living in Athens any more, Dr. Grey. No, you have no reason to worry, Mr. Apostolides has at last realized his errors. His permit to practice was therefore returned to him."

"Where is he?"

Takis was one of the best friends Hilary had had in Athens, full of fire and determination, involved with the trade unions, preaching his own peculiar brand of Marxism to faithful and skeptic alike.

"I don't know the name of the village, Dr. Grey, but I have it from reliable sources that the dentist is doing a useful job now. The peasants need dental care, too, and the air must be so much healthier for him, up there on the mountains. Of course, as there is no electricity, he had to trade in his modern drill for a manual one—I'm sure the villagers don't mind, they're a hardy lot."

"What were his errors—that he had to be exiled to this God-forsaken place?"

"I think you know the answer to that, Dr. Grey. Your friend never tried to disguise his beliefs."

"But surely every man is entitled to his own . . ."

"Naturally. If he doesn't become a threat to the community. The Communists are just over the border, you must remember, looking through their binoculars down on the Aegean. We can't afford to take any chances here, Dr. Grey."

"If you're suggesting that the colonels took over to avert a Communist coup, you might as well know I don't buy it."

"Our country's place is with the West. But this is no America, this is no Britain. I understand the fellow travelers are making a lot of noise in the States these days—in Great Britain, of course, the Communist party is licensed by the government."

Lazaros looked at Hilary as if he held him personally responsible for the legality of the British Communist party.

"I take it you're not a Communist, Dr. Grey?"

There was some quality about Lazaros which made Hilary feel ridiculously like a child being questioned by an adult—who, while seemingly patient, genial on the surface, might at any moment take a very different tack.

"Now look, Superintendent, I'm not one of your nationals. I'm not obliged to tell you what I am or am not."

In his time Hilary had faced the extraordinarily humorless FBI inquisitors; he was not about to submit now to the questioning of a long-nosed Greek fascist policeman.

"There aren't many Communists left around here, I'm glad to say. They've been ferreted out, and those who haven't confessed and changed their minds are well looked after, thank God. Now it is corruption we must fight, that is our next enemy."

"What's that?"

"I'm sure you understand, Dr. Grey. The corruption that comes from social injustice, from cynicism, apathy, and lack of patriotic feeling. . . . Dishonest trafficking of various sorts, illegal organizations which exploit the follies and miseries of mankind."

"Drugs. That's your department, isn't it?"

"Yes, it is."

"Well, I don't take any myself. If that's what you're hinting at." In fact, Hilary had smoked a little hashish that very night with Madame Daphne—"Hashish turns me on, hard drugs turn me off," as she had told him.

"Have one of these, then." Lazaros offered his pack of menthol cigarettes.

"No, thanks. I'm trying to cut down."

"I should, too," said Lazaros. He clutched the pack to his chest, dropped his cigarette, and, with great effort, took from his pocket an enamel snuffbox and put a tablet into his mouth.

"Confound this pain!"

Hilary turned and waited for him.

"My heart is hurting me tonight. I think I must have some refreshment. Please join me, Dr. Grey."

Hilary, watching the spasm, wondered whether it was genuine or a piece of good acting.

"I have to be leaving soon," he said, but he gave Lazaros the benefit of the doubt and followed him to a café table on the pavement nearby. Down the street, opposite, was the Omonoia *plateia*.

"I like Omonoia at night, Dr. Grey. The lights, the fountains—so attractive! I left it a dark miserable square when I went to Salonika and I came back after my promotion to find it so very bright, so beautiful. Besides, a lot of our customers and a lot of our *potential* customers may be seen here—it's one of their habitats. I, too, like to wander about the streets at night. I cannot sleep sometimes for thinking of the evil at large among us, Dr. Grey."

They had hardly given their order—a hot chocolate with milk for Lazaros, coffee for Hilary—when the waiter returned to tell the superintendent that there was a telephone call for him.

"It's one of the disadvantages of my kind of work, I can never enjoy a quiet moment with a friend. Excuse me."

The police must have extrasensory perception, thought Hilary as he watched him threading his way gracefully through the tables. Unless, of course, they used this café for their contacts.

"That was Inspector Notaras," said Lazaros when he came back. "He asked me to say hello and many thanks."

"For what?"

"For your cooperation."

"I don't understand."

"The statement you gave to Inspector Notaras was of great value to our investigation. You may be pleased to know that it helped Markos in a way—Mr. Stephanou, that is. Your friend."

Cooperation? Hilary had only told Notaras when questioned that he and Isabel had first met Mark on the *Hesperides*, that they had only joined him by chance at the Byzantion.

"You haven't seen Markos recently. Have you, Dr. Grey?"

"No."

"He's on his travels again. Quite cosmopolitan and so charming—although a bit flashy in his tastes, shall we say?"

"After all, he has a very well-paid job, hasn't he?"

"True, true. A fine job, a very convenient job, and all his success achieved only four years after he came out of jail—a spectacular example of rehabilitation, alas, all too rare. How much do you suppose his salary is nowadays?"

"I've no idea," said Hilary. "And I wouldn't dream of asking him."

"The Asphalia is less inhibited, Dr. Grey, and it isn't always necessary even to ask. Markos gets three hundred thousand drachmas a year, something like ten thousand American dollars. Not exorbitant, but quite substantial for Greece. Plus an expense account, of course. I hasten to add that everything seems to be in order and that he always pays his taxes. But there are ways, Dr. Grey, of keeping the record seemingly straight—there are ways, you know. And Markos does have lavish tastes, even for a bright young executive with a good salary. An apartment in Kolonaki, an expensive sports car, all that jewelry, and, apparently, frequent trips to the casinos, from Beirut to Las Vegas, from Monte Carlo to Reno. It's all very intriguing, isn't it?"

He waited, unperturbed by Hilary's lack of response.

"I like him so much, it's really most distressing. But one does have to perform one's duty to society, if you follow me. We have to check on him from time to time. Still, *ouden kakon amiges kalou*—there is no evil without some good attached to it. It was, after all, through Markos that I met you. I do hope you and your delightful wife are enjoying your stay in Greece." Having stressed the word "delightful"—rather noticeably, even for him—he added: "It must be a pleasant change for Markos to have a respectable woman as a friend. I really must congratulate you, Dr. Grey, on being so broad-minded."

"What the hell are you talking about?"

It was Hilary's turn to wait for a response.

"See here, Superintendent—I demand an apology. And an explanation."

"Dr. Grey, I am sorry. Certainly I did not mean to offend you. You're a visitor here, a welcome guest, as the tourist people say. I thought you should know."

"Know *what?*"

"I'm a policeman, Dr. Grey. A cop, as Markos introduced me to you when we first met at the Bacchanalia. It's part of our job to observe the facts, to compile the records. Now Markos' record . . ."

Lazaros shrugged expressively. At that moment a girl arrived, embraced the man who was waiting for her, sat on his knee.

"I don't mean his record with women. That's his private concern, isn't it, Dr. Grey?"

Hilary banged the table and got up.

"Go to hell, will you?"

As he turned to go, he collided with Toni, who had just arrived to meet Lazaros.

6

Isabel spent the morning packing. The boat was leaving early the next day, and Hilary had agreed that it would be wiser to have most of their things ready before going into Athens for their last evening It took Hilary only a short time to dump his few belongings into a case. For Isabel, packing was a slow and highly organized operation. Every cosmetic bottle and jar had to be rinsed thoroughly, dried and wrapped in Kleenex tissues before going into her suitcase; her clothes were brushed and folded and tucked with tissue paper; her shoes went into individual plastic bags.

Hilary lay on the bed, trying to read between the lines of the government propaganda of *Eleftheros Kosmos,* watching Isabel out of the corner of his eye as she moved busily between bedroom and bathroom. He had settled his bill, ordering a packed lunch for them to take on the boat on Saturday morning. His dismay at the amount that he had had to pay still rankled. Why on earth hadn't he moved to the island earlier, why had he waited until his money was beginning to run out? Why hadn't he married a jolly, easygoing, Bohemian little thing who wouldn't have minded a room in a cheap pension with the bathroom two flights down?

By now Hilary had collected quite a pile of books, and his desire to begin his writing was stronger than ever. He couldn't write in Athens, with all that heat, with Daphne waiting for him every evening.

"I want to get busy this summer," he announced. "I've got the translations to finish and the commentary. Think of all the time I'll have on my hands on Alea to set to work with my mind at peace!"

Hilary's self-confidence was in the ascendant; there were no lectures to prepare, no tests to correct, no questions to set. Time—what he had always needed was *time*. Each summer vacation had slipped away, but this one, this Greek summer, would be different.

"I could do the typing," said Isabel. "I'm not an expert, as you know, but I'll improve."

"That's the spirit—that's a good girl! And I'll want your opinion about the translations, too."

"I'd like to help, Hilary. But I'm not a poet and I don't read Greek."

"You know what I mean, though. My translations will be in prose, more or less literal, and I'd like you to read through them and say what you think—do they make sense? Is the result satisfying on its own merits? Of course, I've got the commentary to prepare, the annotations, the introduction as well."

Hilary suddenly thought that on the island they could get their retsina directly from the tavernas, at a fraction of the price they had been paying for it in Athens.

"You never know, we might see Mark on the island," Hilary said happily. "He's connected with some project there, we're bound to run into him."

They hadn't seen Mark since that evening in his apartment at Kolonaki. When they heard, from Lazaros, the news of Jennie's death, Hilary called twice and telephoned several times, but without any success.

"I wish you could have persuaded him to take back the necklace."

"I couldn't very well *make* him take it back. Don't forget he's a Greek, Isa, they can be touchy about things like that."

"Perhaps I'll ring him again," he added. "It's not too late to ask him to come to the theater with us tonight, is it?"

To Hilary's surprise, Mark answered the telephone.

"I'm afraid I can't make the theater, I've a meeting to attend."

Could Mark manage a farewell drink after his meeting?

There was a pause at the other end of the line. Then, "All right, Hilary, I'll try."

Mark tried to eat, just to please Eva, to show that he appreciated her kindness, her hospitality.

"Try a little more," she urged him, standing by his side, rubbing herself against him, ruffling his hair. She was wearing a transparent negligee, her breasts and pubic hair showing through.

"Finish it up, Markos. It will do you good."

"You spoil me," he said, sorry that he had not remembered to buy her a bottle of perfume on the plane.

"I've missed you, Markos. And I didn't know where you were, to write to you."

"I missed you, too," he said, looking at his glass, turning it round and round. He hadn't promised to go and see the Greys, had he? He had only said he would try.

Eva's fingers moved under his shirt and down, squeezed under his belt, found him inert, stroked and held him in her hand.

"It feels so good inside me," she murmured.

"I'm sorry, Eva. I'm tired."

"Is it those Latin-American girls that drained you?"

She released him, kissed him tenderly behind the ear, laid her head on his shoulder.

"Next time I'll come with you. I won't let you out of my sight."

He caressed her hair.

"It's the long hours, Eva. The traveling."

"There's no hurry. I'm not going out tonight, I won't go to the club—I'll call them later and tell them I'm sick."

He could stay with Eva, she was devoted to him, he knew she had stopped sleeping with anyone else a long time ago. Her beautiful body was there, he could tell her he loved her and hold her close, as in the old days.

"Come now, Markos, let me help you undress."

She took him by the hand, but Mark wanted to finish his wine first. After all, Isabel was a married woman, married to a man he liked and admired. Isabel . . . She had said that he was indifferent to what was happening in the country and she was right; I've my own troubles, he thought, trying to remember what chores were piled up for him the next day at the office. But as he looked down into the empty glass, he saw Isabel's face, the lights shining in her clear blue eyes, a sea breeze blowing back that cloud of soft blonde hair, her long white slender fingers clasping a rail . . . Then his cheek stung.

"You think too much, you worry too much. Let me help you to relax."

"Some other time."

"Come and lie on the bed, anyway. I'll sit beside you."

Mark poured more wine into his glass, hoping to banish that patrician presence; but he couldn't drink and he wouldn't move from the table.

Eva sank down by his side and put her head on his knee.

Mark stroked her hair absently.

"We could be happy, we could always be together and I promise to be yours, only yours."

"I'm sorry, Eva. I've an important decision to make this evening."

"Come," she pleaded, with her eyes looking up at him.

"Some other time. I really am sorry. Jennie's part of it."

He tried to touch her face, but she sprang up and rushed to the bedroom.

He went after her, stood in the doorway. Eva was crying into the smooth sheet. He looked at her weeping and wished he could care.

"Come on, Eva, cheer up, don't cry like that."

"It's for Jennie I'm crying. She was an orphan, she was my friend. She's got nobody to cry for her."

Eva gave a sudden heartrending sob and stretched herself face downward on the bed, gathering up the sheets with both hands to cover her head.

Mark couldn't bear it any longer. He went out onto the balcony; the romantic strains of a popular song were coming up from the radio of the café below. Further down the street there was an open-air restaurant in a courtyard. He could see the waiters arranging the chairs and tables, spreading the cloth for a family group out for dinner. The two children were running about, their mother was calling to them, the father was drinking a beer. The boy must be about seven, he thought—had Emilios lived, he would have been about that big. By now he might even have had a younger sister the age of the little girl chasing a kitten under one of the tables. . . . Mark saw the mother picking up the girl, slapping her hand lightly, making her sit up properly at the table. The father smiled at the child and fed her tidbits from his plate of *meze*. Go on, tell him he's spoiling her—suddenly he imagined himself in bed with Jennie, planning the future of Emilios and his little unborn sister. . . . Gradually the dead face of Jennie crowded his daydream: the staring eyes, the lovely breasts, the bright red hair, the pallid skin, the prick marks of the hypodermic . . . Mark shook his head in distress, left the balcony, went inside.

Eva was sitting naked on the pink quilted stool in front of her dressing table, painting her eyes with intense concentration. Mark stood in the doorway and saw it all reflected in the mirror, the heavy breasts, the long dimpled back, the narrow waist, the flowing line of the hips, the cleft between the plump, curving buttocks. She had a marvelous ass and he was almost tempted.

"Why are you staring at me?"

The husky voice was indifferent, the bare torso straightened, challenging, as she went on making up. From where he was standing, he could see the small bottle of Seconals by her glass of gin. Eva took a sip. The professional mask was well in place, the golden eyes were tearless.

The telephone rang. She picked up the receiver and held it out without turning toward him.

Mark, who was expecting Leonides to call from London, had given Eva's number to his concierge. He had tried to reach the Old Man earlier that day, but could not get through to him to report the details of the *World Seafarer's* collision with a Japanese freighter.

"How bad is the damage to the hull, gypsy?"

"There's a dent—rather a deep one. But it'll be repaired within a fortnight."

"And the engines?"

"Minor damage. I had our team of engineers from Glasgow flown in. The parts we ordered will get there by tomorrow evening, it won't take them long to make the repairs."

"Any trouble with those fucking idiots who own the freighter?"

"It was an old boat, probably they were relieved it went down. They had it well insured."

"Any claims on us?"

"Lloyds will fight it out with them. Their man came over and we went over the whole business."

"I hope you didn't forget to smash Captain Yiannopoulos' face in while you were about it."

"We have to back him up until the whole affair is settled. We were in the right, we admit nothing."

"I'll smash his face in myself when I meet him."

Mark heard a crash at the other end of the long-distance line; he could visualize Leonides' face as he thumped the desk. The rights and wrongs of a matter never interested the Old Lion—only the results.

As if to confirm his thoughts, Mark said, "There are three dead and one missing."

"Ours?"

"Theirs."

"Four Japs less won't make any difference to anybody."

Mark noticed Eva stop as she was applying lipstick and look at him in the mirror.

"I'll fly over in two weeks to check things out myself," he said.

"You will, will you? Check on Odette, too, I bet. How is she? She's got lovely tits, a great asset to the Buenos Aires office, isn't she?"

"I'm afraid I was too busy to notice," Mark said.

This seemed to amuse the Old Lion.

"Don't say you're overworked as much as that, gypsy, because if you're thinking of asking for a raise, the answer's no. I'm sure you're making up for lost time in Athens, anyway, aren't you? Why did it take so long for the operator to locate you? You're not in your apartment, are you? You're with a cunt?"

"Of course not."

"Fuck her for me, you young dog, fuck her good-bye, because I want you on the first plane to London in the morning."

Mark put down the telephone, bent down, and kissed Eva's bare shoulder.

"You needn't come back," she said, busy with her jars. "I'm going to the club and I think I shall be late tonight."

"The ancients must have been made of sterner stuff, especially bottom-wise," said Hilary as he pulled out of the car-park at the foot of the Acropolis. It had been a long performance. The Herod of Atticus Theater had been packed to capacity for *Antigone*, and although small cushions had been provided, the marble benches beneath them were extraordinarily uncomfortable.

"Aristophanes has the Persians in *The Acharnians* speak of the soft-bummed Athenians—well, the Persians obviously hadn't sat for an evening at a Greek play."

Isabel could still see the chorus of Theban Elders swooping and stamping, raising their hands to pray to the sun, "The brightest of all that ever dawned on the City of Seven Gates, City of Thebes," or lying prostrate on the *orchestra*, beating the ground, calling on Iacchus, the "healer of all ills," to "come swiftly over the high Parnassian hills," to come to Thebes "where thou lovest most to be." She felt shaken by the strange magic of the play; its poetry still possessed her. They had bought the Penguin translation beforehand and she almost knew the verses by heart, but nothing could have prepared her for the actual performance.

"I doubt that the colonels would take their guests of honor to *Antigone*," continued Hilary as they drove down Syngrou Avenue. "Did you notice the applause every time Sophocles got a dig in at the tyrant?"

Isabel had put on the turquoise necklace for the evening, hoping that Mark might suddenly turn up at the theater. No, he was busy, he hadn't even given them a definite promise that he would come to the hotel to say good-bye. As the little car turned into the Sounion road, she unclasped the turquoise necklace and put it in her bag; she was angry with herself and with Mark, she would go straight up to her room.

"I wonder if it wasn't too much for you, Isabel, besides the discomfort . . . all that wailing and howling in a language you don't understand."

He thought he caught a glimpse in his rear-view mirror of a Jaguar coming up behind them, but he lost it in the traffic.

"Remember, Mark is coming around to see us if he can."

"Couldn't you see him alone, Hilary? I'm tired and I don't want to have to talk. You know I'm no good at this hour, I'd rather go to bed."

"You can't do that, Isa love. Just think—he's our friend, he's lost his wife, he's had his share of bad luck. Couldn't you stay and say hello?"

He noticed how frail she looked, how withdrawn, and patted her knee gently.

"Tender paw, Isa love, tender paw. It's as you like. I'll explain to Mark, go and get some rest tonight. Tomorrow we'll be on the sea, the air will do us good."

There was no response from Isabel and Hilary withdrew his hand, embarrassed, as though he'd been caught committing an act of indecency.

"Please forgive Isabel, Mark. She's been packing all day, she's tired and the play took a lot out of her."

68

"It's all right."

Hilary, noticing immediately how quiet and subdued Mark was, felt sorry that Isabel had opted out.

"It's good to see you before we go," he said. "When you come to the island you'll look us up, won't you?"

"I expect so. . . . You know, it's late, you must be tired, too."

"Tired? Mark, I only start waking up about this time. I know the right place for us now—only a short walk from here. Just one drink, a farewell drink. You can't say no to that, now can you?"

They walked along the corniche. It was almost midnight but the tavernas were still busy, the tables still crowded under the colored lights.

"I'm sorry about your wife, Mark. Isabel and I were—shocked, very sorry, how shall I put it?"

"I understand, Hilary."

"It was a dreadful thing to happen."

Hilary thought that Mark's eyes clouded and he grasped him by the arm, feeling great affection for him, determined not to ask him about the circumstances surrounding Jennie's death.

"I called several times, but I couldn't get you. I heard from Eva that you were in South America."

At the curb Hilary noticed a green military jeep, a soldier at the wheel, speaking into a microphone. Remembering what Lazaros had told him about Mark, he guided him away from the lights down onto the pebbles by the sea.

"I think somebody is spying on me, Mark."

"That's routine these days. Don't worry. We've learned to live with it."

"The FBI has a file on me. They questioned me once, I'm sure they check on all my movements."

"Why did they question you?"

"I went to Russia one summer. For a fortnight."

"I shouldn't have thought that was incriminating."

"Perhaps not now. But the Red scare was gripping the country then, it was a little different."

"Why did you go?"

"At Columbia I got mixed up with a group of liberal students. We discussed the affairs of the world, we wrote poetry. A poem of mine, unknown to me, was translated and published in a Russian literary magazine. Vanity, that's what made me go. The Russians invited a small number of young poets from America to see their country, all expenses paid, of course."

"I shouldn't let that worry you."

"No, no, but I couldn't get a job in the States after that. It really put a hex on me."

It was dark; Hilary thought he heard somebody following them, looked

69

back, missed his footing, and clasped Mark in order not to fall. In an inside pocket of Mark's jacket he felt the unmistakable shape of a small gun.

"Perhaps I should start wearing a jacket, too," he said.

"I think you were right not to," said Mark. "It's too hot." He took off his white jacket and held it with one hand over his shoulder.

Hilary picked up a pebble and threw it into the sea.

"Now if only there were some sea in Baghdad instead of just bloody desert and camels."

"What made you go there?"

"Sometimes I wonder myself. I suppose there wasn't anywhere else to go. Actually, it was very simple. I saw the ad in the *Times Educational Supplement* and applied."

"How do you like it?"

"It's all right. But I wonder if I shall be able to go back, they don't like us anymore."

They left the beach and walked through the arched doorway at the back of the Zephyros Bar, an old converted house. In the summer only the courtyard with the plane trees was used, and they took a table by the low wall which was covered with jasmine. Hilary sniffed its sweetness appreciatively. It was these simple things that had made him love Greece when he first came to the country fourteen years ago.

"I was twenty-nine at the time," he told Mark. "It was only three years after I collected my academic laurels, my book was published, I thought I was somebody then!"

Mark put his jacket on the back of the chair between them. When the whiskey came, he poured a generous amount into their glasses.

"You should have been with us tonight at the Herod of Atticus," said Hilary. "You should have heard that crowd burst into applause when Haemon says to Creon—'A one-man state? What sort of state is that? You'd be an excellent king—on a desert island.' It was a protest, Mark, as clear a protest as an intimidated people would dare to express. A footnote should be written on this for the historians of Greece to record some day."

Hilary stopped talking, took a big swallow of the whiskey, and looked at Mark. Had he subconsciously expected to see some change in him since learning about his past? It was difficult to imagine him with handcuffs on his wrists, his hair cropped, disgraced, wretched. Mark was the antithesis of this pathetic picture. From what little Hilary had heard of Greek jails he assumed they were pretty grim institutions. He felt a kind of morbid curiosity and would have liked to ask Mark a question or two, but of course he couldn't.

"It's the mystical quality in Sophocles that impresses one so much," Hilary said. "It was like being present at the celebration of a religious ritual. Antigone, poor girl . . ." He sighed. "Every time I go to a classical tragedy, I wonder if

70

there isn't, after all, some sense somewhere, the drama all around us, a cosmic drama, our parts assigned, our destinies already decided."

He stopped and watched Mark. What was troubling him? Why was he carrying a gun? Perhaps he hadn't been so innocent when he was sentenced to three years in jail. How much did the death of his wife mean to him? Hilary wished Isabel had come along. In the distance he could hear the muffled noises of the traffic on the road to Sounion. He finished his whiskey and held out his glass for more. He could feel it glowing warmly in his chest; the familiar, pleasant sensation of well-being was beginning to take over.

"Our destinies . . ." he continued. "The Olympians feast on ambrosia and nectar and plan, unconcerned, the destinies of mankind. Life is a drama and our roles have been assigned to us."

"What happens if we dry up in the middle of the drama, Hilary? If we make a mess of our cues?"

Mark was there, Mark was listening to him, and Hilary stabbed a pontifical finger at his friend.

"Ah, that can never happen. Character is destiny, you see? We are what we are, we can't change or choose."

"We must all play our parts, then," Mark said thoughtfully.

"We must, we must!" Hilary felt a wave of euphoria surging. "Let's put up a good show," he said. "Let's drink to the Olympians and pray that we may never feel the heavy hand of their displeasure."

He poured a little whiskey upon the ground. "This for Mother Earth. A libation for our souls."

The crickets chirped, the birds rustled among the leaves of the plane trees, the sea lapped smoothly on the nearby shore.

Hilary swallowed the rest of his whiskey and hurled the glass, Greek fashion, against the wall on the other side of the courtyard.

"Whoops, I'm breaking the colonels' law now, aren't I?"

The waiter was on his way over to protest when a round of shots shattered the night air. A young man with unruly black hair vaulted over the low wall from outside the courtyard and landed in front of them.

"What's this?" said Hilary.

The young man took the chair with Mark's jacket on the back and sat between them, breathing heavily.

Mark pushed his full glass of whiskey in front of him and asked the waiter to bring two more glasses.

"We've got a start on you," Mark said to the newcomer. "Drink it up."

He had hardly finished his drink when a police whistle sounded from the yard next door and two soldiers jumped over the parapet. The fugitive sprang up and dashed toward the arched back door; another soldier materialized there, tripped him up, and clubbed him on the head with the butt of his gun as he hit the ground. The other soldiers closed in, handcuffed his hands behind his back, searched him. As far as Hilary could see, they found nothing.

The soldier who had wielded the club turned back and leveled his gun at the customers.

"Nobody leaves!" he shouted. "On your feet! Hands up!"

Hilary was amazed at the docility with which they all obeyed, including Mark. He himself filled up his glass and remained seated.

An officer who had just arrived in the wake of his men walked between the standing customers and came over to him.

"Get up!" he ordered.

"Thank you, no," said Hilary. "I'm not playing your game. Did you learn these cops-and-robbers tactics from American television?"

The officer, realizing that Hilary was a foreigner, left him where he was and supervised his men as they searched the male customers and looked into the women's purses.

After Mark had been searched, the officer reached for the white jacket on the chair.

"Kindly keep your hands off my jacket!" Hilary said irritably. He picked the jacket up and put it on.

The soldiers left with their captive.

"I've some papers to look through," said Mark. "I'm flying to London in a few hours. I should go home and try to get some sleep."

"What's the hurry? You can sleep on the plane, can't you?"

But he followed Mark out to the street. "Look, I'm putting on weight. My clothes are getting too tight for me." He patted the jacket.

"That was dangerous, Hilary," said Mark.

"Nonsense!"

"You saved me a lot of trouble tonight, you know." He touched Hilary's arm.

"What will they do to that poor devil?"

"It's not for us to ask."

They walked along the corniche silently, each thinking his own thoughts.

"Shouldn't you give me back my jacket now?" Mark said at last.

"Somebody may be following us. Anyway, I should keep it as ransom. I'll return it when you come to see us on the island."

"I'll come and see you if you promise to show me your manuscript on the Greek ballads."

"That will take some time."

"The island's a peaceful place. You'll be able to work there."

"I've done a lot of field work. And Isabel's promised to help with the typing. The only thing I need is some enthusiasm and inspiration to get me off the ground."

72

"Isabel can be your inspiration," said Mark.

But Hilary was talking half to himself.

"Poor little devil, I hope they don't lock him up in an underground chamber like they did Antigone. Yet Antigone stepped on the tail of the serpent, she defied the dictator, remember?"

"Do you teach Greek drama at the university?" asked Mark.

"Christ, no! But last year they did, they truly did, *Macbeth*. How I remember."

He brooded on this for a moment and then said: "The three witches invented special curses in Arabic for the occasion, it was most effective."

Mark laughed.

"You will show me your new book, won't you, Hilary?"

"Do you think I can do it? Do you think I have it in me? Frankly, now."

"I'm sure you do."

"Do you know how old I am, Mark? Forty-three. Next month, forty-four. Sometimes I feel I've been living for centuries."

"Don't be foolish. That's not old."

"Ah, well, I suppose you envy me, Mark. After all, I'm married to Isabel. She's mine, isn't she? Other men may look at her, that's their privilege, but she's mine."

Mark wished the whiskey had affected him as it had Hilary—he would have suffered less. As it was, Isabel's deep blue eyes tormented him, the sculptured mouth, the fragrant skin, those long fragile fingers, the slender wrists: like a piece of music known and yet not known, like something once known well and long forgotten.

"Mark, are you listening?"

"I'm listening, Hilary."

"Now, Shelley's idea of Utopia was to go to a quiet spot with a select group of friends and share out their women among them. It never came to much, though, the women wouldn't cooperate and look what happened to Percy Bysshe. Washed up on the beach and a horrible great marble statue of him in the nude at University College to this day—divine retribution, wouldn't you say?"

Mark closed his eyes.

"I wish you could have come to the play tonight, Mark. Poor girl, she knew she couldn't fight destiny, nobody can . . . 'Antigone, what agony to watch you die. Hilary, what tyranny the perfect eye. . . .' Now how do you like that? Those are *my* verses. I used to write poetry once."

Mark felt Hilary's weight heavy upon him. He was a good man; no one had the right to threaten his happiness.

"Come on, Hilary. We're only the dice in a mad game, we know that. Why worry about it?"

"The dice of God, the irrational . . ."

"The dice of God fall as they will," Mark quoted.

Hilary stumbled and stopped for a moment.

"Mark. You will come to see us on the island, won't you?"

Mark simply put his arm around Hilary's shoulders and helped him along.

"You're a good friend, Mark. I don't care what other people say about you, you're my friend, and a good one."

As Hilary rambled on, Mark managed to steer him toward the hotel and up the steps to the deserted terrace. He helped him out of the jacket.

Hilary looked up, scanning the row of balconies above. All the windows on the second floor were in darkness; he flung an arm upward, pointing theatrically:

"That's our room there, that's our balcony. What a pity Juliet is asleep!"

Mark stood watching Hilary as he entered the foyer, swaying a little. He could almost sense Isabel's cool fragrant presence somewhere above him; he imagined her lying in bed, the magnificent eyes closed, the lovely features in repose, her mind asleep, her spirit free.

He was trembling. It was the cold of the early morning, he thought, already the silent lawns were drenched with dew. He saw the light go on in the room above and the lump in his throat tightened until he thought it would choke him. He turned and walked quickly to the Jaguar, slammed the door and raced toward Athens.

Part Two

□

7

"Your eyes are amazing—a few minutes ago they were violet and now they're the most wonderful sea blue."

Isabel smiled, but ignored Sir Clive's change of subject. "And you haven't been home since then?"

"I'm an islander. I shall live all that's left of my life in Alea."

"You've made a good choice. I can't imagine any place more lovely."

She watched Clive as he painted.

"I'll never be able to do justice to you," he said. "Botticelli, perhaps . . ."

His admiration soothed and comforted her. He was kind, near him she was safe, she was sorry about his bad leg. The terror of the morning seemed far away.

"There's something elusive in you I want to capture," he said. "Something fresh, something magical . . ."

He stood back, looked at the painting from various angles.

"I think it's enough for today."

He put down his brush.

"Come to the window, Isabel. Come to see the Venetian castle."

She hesitated.

"The castle is in its glory in the late afternoon sun. Do have a look."

"I went there this morning," she said, walking to the window.

As the bright light fell on her, she closed her eyes.

"Now I've got it. I'll paint a burning disk of sun in the distance. I want to match its light with yours, with your face. I want to connect the mystery somehow."

"Mysteries frighten me, Clive."

Isabel turned away from the window.

"Give me a few minutes longer," he said.

She watched him spreading the red paint on the palette, mixing it, working up a blotch of blood. She was trembling.

"I'd like you to come with me to the castle one day. I'd like to see you framed against the Queen's Window."

Isabel wavered on the ledge, seeing her people being slaughtered by the Saracens on the rocks far below.

"I'm afraid," she whispered, her eyes trapped in the pool of red paint as she plunged down the walls in a haze of blood. *They're killing my mother, they're taking her from me.* She was only a little girl, she heard the crying through the closed bedroom door; when she turned the knob her mother was spread across the bed, her head lolling like a rag doll's, whispering in pain, her skirts pulled up, a streak of blood on one thin white thigh, the red-faced man naked as he strained over her. He shouted at the child . . .

"My mother died very young," she said to Clive.

"Is your father alive?"

"I don't think so." The child hid in a cupboard, numb with terror; she never saw the man again—except for the day of the funeral.

"The war?" asked Clive.

"I don't know. He was a foreign correspondent, he was always abroad."

When her mother was being lowered into a pit in an ugly black box and everyone was crying, he reappeared and walked toward her, his arms out- stretched, his face so red; she ran away, down the long graveled aisle between the tombstones. . . .

"Isabel, are you all right?"

Clive put his paints away and came to her.

"I'm through for today. Come out into the garden and I'll ask Irene to give us some tea."

They walked outside together, Clive holding her arm, Isabel trying to focus her attention, following his pointing finger down to the harbor, the Black Mountain, the White Hills, the grove of cypress trees in the distant cemetery, the ramparts and towers. No, she didn't know about the earthquake, but she remembered the custodian, Demetris, explaining how the drawbridge had fallen into the moat. The island was volcanic and had suffered three major tremors in the nineteenth century and the worst of all in 1912.

"Why?" she asked, but her mind was preoccupied as Clive told her about the volcanic belt that stretched from southern Italy to Turkey and Iran.

"We're standing on unstable ground—geologically speaking."

"Yes," she said. "Geologically speaking."

Her hands shook as she took the cup of tea Clive handed her.

"Isabel. What's wrong? Did something happen to you today?"

"No, I'm . . ." she stopped and took a sip of tea.

Isabel was back in the castle; the infidel was after her and she fled through the underground chambers, through the open arched doorways, down the stone-wall corridors. The labyrinth closed in upon her, she checked herself in mid-flight, not knowing which way to run, how to escape hands stretching out to seize her, the heavy breathing of her pursuer that echoed in the vaulted chamber. She turned to see his face in the distance, the face of a butcher, the flesh red-stained as it caught a beam of sun from a skylight somewhere high above. Her hands groped along the wall until they reached emptiness, and she plunged into the darkness beyond.

The tunnel was endless; running, she stumbled against some steps, tripped, got up hurriedly, and started upward, the palms of her hands tracing the stone walls. At the top of the steep staircase the corridor turned left and she ran toward a rectangle of light at the far end of a narrow passage, certain that she could not make it, that his hands would reach out and grab her by the ankles and bring her down. The daylight startled her and she stood outside the tunnel, closing her eyes against the light. . . .

"Let me put a drop of brandy into your tea," said Clive.

She was back, she was safe.

"I think I must have got overtired this morning'" she said. "That's all."

Isabel began blaming herself for having been so emotional, so unreasonably hysterical. It was she who had insisted on seeing the dungeons. She had listened attentively as the custodian told her of Byzantines and Saracens, Franks and Greeks and Turks; the Venetians had defended the castle for six months, watching the Ottomans waiting in their camp below, scanning the horizon in vain for sails from Italy to bring forces to raise the siege. No rain came that year, and at last the great cistern stood empty, mocking their thirst; when the fortress was stormed the few survivors were too weak to fight back. The conquerors flayed the commander of the garrison alive, stuffed the skin with straw and sent it as a present to the sultan in Istanbul. . . .

Isabel shivered as she remembered Demetris putting his hand on her shoulder when she stepped forward to look into the pitch dark of the cistern, trying to control her nausea. As if in slow motion she saw his face approaching hers and, with a gasp, stepped back and began to run. . . .

Her hands were shaking. She tried to put her cup on the saucer, but the tea spilled on her dress.

Clive took the cup from her.

"Would you like to lie down for a few minutes?"

She shook her head.

"Shall I take you home?"

"Hilary is expecting me at the *plateia* for dinner."

"Do you think you can make it?"

"Yes. Please come along."

Irene mopped at her dress and she stood up, but her feet were rooted, she couldn't move.

"Of course I'll come, Isabel. I wish I could always be near you to help you, to take care of you."

"How kind you are, Clive."

"You need looking after, Lady Isabel—isn't that what Hilary calls you? Were I your knight, I could step between you and all the pain of the world."

"Clive . . ."

"You belong to another age, it must be difficult for you. A medieval princess besieged in her tower. Isabel, please let me take care of you. Please." He pressed her hand.

A military jeep caught up with the two men outside the town. Inspector Notaras sat next to the driver; Demetris was in back.

"Who was that lame man with the Englishwoman?" asked Notaras without turning around.

"A foreign resident here," Demetris called back. "Settlers, we call them."

"I thought I saw her husband at the taverna as I was coming to meet you. Do you think this foreign resident is hanging around the wife?"

"He's English, too. They had dinner at Kavouras' but the husband stayed behind."

"That's what I call consideration." Notaras spat out the window. "Cuckolds, these foreigners. All of them."

"She came to see the castle this morning—alone."

"She's a nice piece, all right. I had to ask the husband some questions in Athens—he's a bit addled, but the wife is a beautiful piece."

"There's something queer about her, don't you think?"

"I'd say that husband of hers isn't much use to her. Women go off the rails when they're not getting it socked to them regular."

Demetris leaned forward so that the inspector could hear every word. "I was showing her around when she started running away as if the devil was at her heels. I still don't know why."

"You should have gone after her and given it to her there and then—that's what she needs."

The jeep followed the unpaved coast road past the cemetery, but as it approached the chapel the driver switched off the lights, drove off the road, and parked under a tree in the churchyard.

"You wait for us here," Notaras ordered him. Then he noticed Demetris holding his pistol.

"Put that away," he said. "You won't need it tonight."

The commandant had told him to keep the gun out of sight when he issued it to him earlier that evening, but this was Demetris' first revolver and he was anxious to try it out, to recapture that sensation of holding a weapon, of firing at somebody, as they had trained him to do in the army. The path down to the shore was steep, and although a new moon offered a little illumination, it was dark enough to excite Demetris' sense of danger. He had seen a stack of these shining new pistols waiting to be issued at the camp; it was the first consignment he had known to arrive on the island since the U.S. government resumed arms shipments to Greece.

"Whatever they say," he said, "the Americans know who their friends are."

Inspector Notaras had no romantic notions about weapons.

"Put it away, Demetris. Don't get trigger-happy. That thing could be fatal—for you. If the Armenian sees you flourishing it, he won't wait for you to get in close."

"Not if I shoot first."

"You won't. We want Nubar alive."

"Why don't you arrest him, then? I can tell you his whereabouts most of the time."

Notaras cleared his throat and spat on the ground. Papademas had spoken of Nubar Ohanessian. The Armenian had contacts; he knew others in Turkey, in Syria, in Lebanon. Of course, Papademas couldn't have acted; he had taken his cut, and his official protection kept the trade flourishing and motherfuckers like Nubar crawled about like lice. Yes, it would be easy enough to round up Nubar, hang him up by his one good arm, pull out his toenails with pincers, one by one. But Lazaros had said they must watch him first, they must let him lead them to his accomplices. Inspector Notaras knew he could find these with far less effort, but he had a bad record for violence—he'd had a prisoner die while undergoing questioning; he'd been transferred to the Bureau of Narcotics and warned not to lift a finger without his chief's instructions.

"His whereabouts!" he said. "What we want to find out is who else is in it, what his contacts are, where the lab is."

"It can't be here, Inspector. The police have combed the island."

"I know it isn't here, but the Armenian is, and that's something to follow up."

"Could they collect the stuff here and take it to Piraeus or Marseilles or somewhere else to process it?"

"They could. They could do many things." And the best way to find out was to talk to them. The only thing Notaras asked for was to have one of them in his hands. The method was such a simple one and it never failed.

"What about Stephanou? Any sign of him on the island yet?"

"Not yet, sir. But he's bound to come. The Italian engineer who's installing the lifts was saying yesterday that Stephanou is expected. Soon."

"Where does he stay when he's here?"

"By himself in an old house. Belonged to a sea captain, an ancestor of the Lions."

"Does the Armenian visit him?"

"Not as far as I know. But he takes women there, I'm sure of that."

"What sort of women?"

81

"Any woman he can lay his hands on."

"Does he really? Wait till *I* lay my hands on him."

"We've seen Katia Kommenou going there, Leonides' niece. She's Jason's sister."

"I know Jason."

"He's a troublemaker, that one. He has his friends, he speaks against the government. I pointed this out in my reports, but he's still around, alive and well, pouring scorn on the Revolution."

"I could explain the reasons why he's still around, but don't ask me."

"Don't you think, Inspector, that his sister's visits to Stephanou may have some significance?"

"Yes, if they don't use contraceptives."

"I mean, Jason and his subversive activities."

"What the hell are you talking about? Because the bastard is banging the sister, have you come to the conclusion that he's planning to overthrow the regime with her brother?"

"Markos Stephanou might well be a secret Communist, a traitor. He's only half Greek, you know, which I should think would be enough to explain his lack of patriotism."

"I know all that, but you're barking up the wrong tree. Stephanou doesn't care for politics. It's easy money he's after."

"If he catches Katia, *that's* easy money."

"Drugs. He's been in jail for it once, he's an old hand. Now show me this place where the Armenian keeps his boat."

Demetris led Notaras to the two boats, one tied on the small jetty, the other drawn up on the shingle. Then he took him inside the hut. Notaras switched on his flashlight and looked around at the nets, the wooden table, the bare wooden bench. They were just coming out of the hut when they were stopped by the sound of a distant explosion.

Demetris pulled out his gun and looked around wildly.

"Let's go," said Notaras. "For Christ's sake, put that away and let's go."

This time the thud of two explosions, one after the other, reached them through the night.

Isabel grasped Clive's hand.

"What was *that?*"

For a moment they were silent, half expecting something else to follow.

Her hand was nestled, trusting, in his.

"As far as I can make out, the explosions came from the direction of the barracks—on the other side of town."

"Do you think any harm will come to him?" She took back her hand. "I mean to Hilary."

"No, why should it?"

"He was deported from Greece before, you know."

"I'm sure nobody will bother Hilary."

"I worry sometimes, seeing him friendly with so many people. He's so outspoken."

"The colonels know what they're after. Hilary will be as right as rain."

"I hope he doesn't get soaked tonight, anyway—he's been drinking a lot recently."

They had very little in common, these two people, thought Clive. Hilary would never appreciate a woman like Isabel. Nor was she the sort of wife he needed.

"Do you think this is the beginning?" she asked.

"Of what?"

"The revolution that will overthrow the junta."

"It will take more than a few bombs to do that. Now, if something happened within the army . . ."

"The colonels control the army and the police, don't they?"

"And the courts and the media and the unions and the universities. Does it sound familiar?"

"Is it really very bad?"

"Not if you're one of them. Or at least know your place, see what you should see and don't see what you shouldn't."

"How dangerous could it be for a nonconformist, for a . . . revolutionary?"

"The revolutionaries usually know how to take care of themselves."

"But if things go wrong, if . . ."

"That's a risk they're prepared to take, Isabel, just as we did in the war."

Clive saw her glance at his leg.

"It hurts sometimes, Isabel. I just ignore it."

"How did it happen?"

"I was dropped in Epirus to work as a liaison officer between us and the guerrillas during the occupation. There was an attack on a German convoy one night in the mountains and I caught a stray bullet right here, on the knee. Of course, there was no doctor. An *antartes*, a genuine brigand type, took it out with a knife."

"How dreadful for you!"

"Oh, that was quite a while ago. I should do my exercises more regularly. The best thing for it is swimming."

"Let's go to the beach together, then. Hilary is busy with his writing and I have to go all alone."

His bad leg was wasted, he was shy.

"I'd rather not, Isabel dear."

Clive hadn't minded Margaret, he had got used to her. Thinking of his wife

83

was an old sorrow. She had been married when they fell in love, she was a Catholic and they had thought it hopeless until her husband was killed in a plane accident; but fate seemed to mock their unexpected happiness and soon after they were married Margaret died of leukemia. Clive left Britain for good and chose to live in a place free from memories. Isabel, he suspected, had her own private grief, but she was young, she could be comforted.

I may be an ordinary sort of chap, but I could make Isabel happy, he thought, and, forgetting, pressed down on his bad leg to swing the hammock. The pain shot up, excruciating.

Looking at his face, she touched his shoulder gently.

"Clive . . ."

"It's nothing, it won't last a moment."

He waited a little for the pain to subside, then got up.

"I think I should go to bed," said Isabel. "I'm not any good this late."

Isabel led the way to the front porch and Clive followed. She offered her cheek like a child, and he kissed her awkwardly.

"Will you come and see me tomorrow?"

She nodded and his heart beat so fast that he turned immediately to leave. As he quickened his step, his lame leg began hurting—to remind him, to warn him.

They dropped Demetris in a dark spot not far from the small museum by the castle and drove directly to the camp. Dust still hung in the air, thick in the glare of the floodlights. A helmeted sentry with fixed bayonet was guarding the gate.

Inspector Notaras put his head out of the window.

"What's going on?"

"Three time bombs, sir. Some damage, but nobody hurt."

The inspector climbed down and walked across the parade ground, past the whitewashed chapel to the new wing of the barracks where the cloud of dust looked thickest. A number of police and military were standing around; apparently the bombs had been planted in some of the newly built apartments for high-ranking police and army officers, three of which were reduced to smoking ruins. A fire had spread to a nearby store, and the island fire engine was spraying water on the blaze.

"Is this only local?" Notaras asked a police officer. "Or did they throw any bombs in other places?"

"Local, as far as we know."

"Any special reason they picked on us tonight?"

"Tomorrow a bunch of hard-core political prisoners are being transferred here from Yaros. But instead of the new cell block they blew up the apartments. Fortunately, they were unoccupied."

84

"They timed it right," said Notaras, "but it's schoolboys' work. Not a chance, not as long as the old-timers aren't involved."

Notaras saw an army colonel in pajamas standing with hands locked behind his back, surveying the scene, accompanied by the apologetic commandant. The colonel was visiting the island, he had been in bed at the time of the explosions—in one of the two apartments in the row which remained miraculously unscathed. The colonel looked as smooth as Notaras' own boss; probably he was as much of a filthy queer as Lazaros. Notaras spat on the ground. He had wanted the opportunity to bring himself to the colonel's notice when he arrived · the day before but hadn't quite known how to do it. Now he went over and smartly saluted the two officers.

"Are you all right, sir?"

The colonel nodded. "You know the proverb," he said. "God loves the burglar, but He loves the landlord more."

Notaras didn't have much use for God, but he crossed himself anyway, his fat hand moving mechanically across his thickset chest.

"God is with us, praise be to His name!"

"God is with us, Greece will prevail!" said the colonel. He turned abruptly and strode away to his undamaged quarters.

As the commandant walked toward his office, Notaras overtook him.

"How did all this happen, sir?"

"We shall soon find out."

Even as he spoke, two military trucks turned in at the gateway, bringing suspects picked up in the middle of the night for questioning.

"Of course, of course," murmured Notaras. "Can I be of help, sir?"

"When we need your help, Inspector, we'll ask for it."

Notaras had never liked the military. Since they had tried to get him out of Athens, he had detested them. He thought privately that it was a good idea to plant a bomb under their asses from time to time, shake them up a bit. In the old days the police had had a clear field and Notaras had been a happier man; now he had to watch his step, he had to butter them up and defer to them.

They arrived at the main office block as the straggling file of suspects was being led in. One of them was Jason Kommenos.

"I know that young man, sir. He's one of the Leonides family, the son of the Leonides' sister."

The commandant did not respond.

"I think I would like to ask him a question or two myself, if it's all right with you, sir."

The commandant looked him straight in the eyes, and Notaras remembered, yet again, that his job was in their hands.

"Not about the explosions, sir. And not until you've finished your investigations, of course."

The commandant simply turned away. Notaras, afraid that he might have said the wrong thing, hurried after him.

"May I use the wireless, sir, to send a report to my chief later this morning? I was on reconnaissance tonight and I have something most confidential to tell him."

8

Hilary unfurled his handkerchief and flourished it like a flag, gave it a final shake and tucked it loosely into the breast pocket of his white linen suit. Then he went to his untidy desk, picked up Mark's handwritten note and read it again.

"Good old Mark. I thought he'd catch up with us."

He waited for Isabel to say something, touched his pockets anxiously to make sure he had his keys and money, found his comb, and, stooping a little to see his reflection in the pane of an open window, ran it quickly through his hair which somehow always became rumpled when he was excited.

"Aren't you going to change?"

"I'm not coming, Hilary."

"What do you mean? Mark's our friend."

"Everybody is your friend. We hardly know him."

"I thought you liked him."

"I'm tired and I've got one of my headaches coming on. I think I'll go to bed early. You can make my excuses to him, can't you?"

He shrugged. "As you like." He started to go and then turned back. "It would have been nice to have gone together. Sure you won't come?"

He spoke the words softly, not insisting; in the course of his life with Isabel he had never won an argument.

"Please yourself, then. But if you feel like it later, Zafiro can get you a taxi."

Hilary made straight for Kavouras', waved a general greeting to everybody, called for a carafe of retsina, and, from a vantage point on the pavement, kept an eager watch for Mark. Soon some of his cronies moved closer to share his wine and swap tales. The ritual evening promenade past the taverna was in full swing. The tables were filling up, and Kavouras had some difficulty in crossing the strip of paving stones to reach the other half of his clientele, who were sitting under the pine trees overlooking the harbor.

When Hilary caught sight of Mark, he hailed him across the *plateia*, got up and put an arm around him, drawing him down.

"Isabel isn't feeling too well this evening, but she may turn up later. We can keep an eye open for her here."

A few men drifted over to welcome Mark back to the island. Some of them worked for the Kalamos Village, or one of their relatives did, and Mark was popular in the community. More glasses were brought, and Hilary poured drinks all around.

It was Mark who spotted Isabel's carriage and went forward to help her down. He took one small hand; felt its bones—fragile, like a bird's bones—as it rested for a moment in his.

"How nice to see you, Mark."

She smiled at him gravely. For a moment he did not know what to say.

"Why, Isabel, I can see you're feeling better!" Hilary said happily. He clapped his hands. "Retsina all around!"

"*Amesos*, Mister Ilarion," Kavouras called back. "And for the madame?"

"Retsina for the madame, too," he announced.

Isabel found Hilary's perpetual democratic bonhomie irritating, but she was too shy to refuse and she tried once more the resinated wine. Once more she shuddered. It tasted like varnish, it was impossible to allow any more of it to pass down her throat.

"Why don't you try something else?" Mark asked. Their eyes met; she blushed and didn't answer him.

Hilary clapped his hands again and ordered Mavrodaphne.

"Have a glass of this, old girl, you like this sweet stuff, don't you?"

"Yes," Isabel said. She was embarrassed at being treated like a child, particularly in front of Mark.

"I imagine you've been away," she said. "Haven't you, Mark?"

He only nodded. Was he still grieving for his dead wife, she wondered? He wouldn't confide in her, he didn't want her sympathy. The thought made her angry. Perhaps he was not grieving at all, perhaps he was glad the poor woman was out of the way. Mark turned and looked into her eyes and she was afraid that he could read her thoughts. Some day I'll say something to hurt him, she promised herself; I'll smash that composure some day. . . . She stopped her thoughts, surprised at her own vindictiveness, drank a little more wine and smiled at him. Mark did not smile back.

A surly-looking villager walked slowly past their table, a little white goat following him like a dog. The man moved from group to group, greeting people, writing their names in a notebook. He reached Hilary's table and the little goat stood next to Isabel, waiting. It had golden eyes and Isabel gently stroked its rough white head; the creature responded by pressing against her hand, butting gently.

"How friendly it is," said Isabel.

"It's to be raffled at the island fair, madame," Kavouras explained.

"Will it have to find a new master? When is the raffle?"

87

"August the fifteenth—no, the day before that."

"But *why?*"

"It's a local custom, Isabel," said Hilary. "Come on, drink your wine."

"Why?" repeated Kavouras. "Because the lucky winner will need time to prepare it for the feast."

Isabel shrank back in her chair. She had thought it was a pet. She watched as the kid quickly but daintily ate the lettuce offered by Joanna, Kavouras' slow-witted sister-in-law; then, realizing that its master had already moved on, it abandoned the rest of its treat and trotted away to catch up with him. The men continued their rapid, noisy conversation, but Isabel's eyes watched the little goat as it went down to the harbor at its master's heels.

"It's the ram caught in the thicket," said Hilary, following her gaze.

Kavouras leaned over and gave her a complimentary ticket for the raffle.

"Good luck, madame," he said.

Isabel, too distressed to say anything, didn't pick up the creased green piece of paper; in the end Kavouras slipped it back into his apron pocket.

Mark noticed her expression.

"I thought we might move to the Golden Dolphin," he said, turning to Isabel. "Would you like that?"

Isabel nodded.

"Let's finish our drinks and go," said Hilary.

Joanna returned and bent over their table, unloading a tray of *meze*. Hilary, enjoying the abundance of flesh thus revealed, poured liberally from the new carafe and drank off his tumblerful.

"I'll tell you what, Mark. The Dolphin's a good place, I'm sure, so why don't you and Isabel run along ahead of me and get things organized?" He leaned back, smiling at them amiably. "It'll be more interesting for you there, Isabel."

"You always know what is best for me, don't you?" Isabel felt she was being handed over like a parcel.

Hilary, unconscious of anything wrong, stood up, moved the chairs, and made room for them to go.

"Are you sure you won't come with us?" she asked.

"Don't worry about me. I'll join you later. You young people go along and order my drink. I'll be there in no time."

As he held the door of the Jaguar open for her she saw him looking at her legs; she pulled the door shut herself, a little too abruptly, and tried to smooth down her dress, to look poised and unconcerned by the time he came around to the driver's seat. In silence he switched on the ignition, shifted into first gear, released the clutch, accelerated.

"It was good of you to come tonight," he said at last.

"Thank you for asking us."

They were reserved and guarded.

"I'm sorry about Hilary's lagging behind," she said, watching Mark's face. "He has so many friends."

"He'll be along," Mark said tonelessly.

She tried again.

"Hilary"—she had started to say "my husband," but it sounded odd and unfamiliar—"Hilary gets so involved with people."

"It's all right," he said.

"When did you get back?" she asked. Then, "How long will you be staying?"

"Two days ago, and I don't know yet. It depends."

She wondered upon what it depended. "How is the building getting on at the Kalamos Village?"

"Well enough, I suppose. Buildings going up right and left, there's no end to it. But we have at last completed the cinema and the shopping center."

"I should like to see the village one day," she said.

Mark slowed the car. The colored lights from the Golden Dolphin were streaming along the coast road.

"I'll look forward to showing you."

In the space in front of the nightclub there were cars and taxis and five or six horse carriages, the drivers talking in small groups. While Mark parked the car, Isabel walked a few steps toward the horses and stood watching them, waiting, suddenly apprehensive.

He surprised her.

"You look just beautiful," he said, taking her hand. "Just beautiful. Let's go." He led her up the steps toward the lights and the music.

A floor show was in full swing as they walked in, but Mark guided her to a table at the far end where they could talk to each other. The table was reserved for three, but he called the waiter and ordered dinner for the two of them.

"What a lovely place," she said. "I'm sorry Hilary didn't come with us."

"I suppose I should say I'm sorry, too. Don't you think we are managing quite well?"

"I . . . don't know what you mean."

She had hardly got the words out when a young girl came suddenly from behind, put her palms over Mark's eyes, and talked to him in Greek. Isabel had seen Katia Kommenou before, on the yacht at Vouliagmeni. Mark seemed uninterested, even when Katia embraced him, her hand producing a letter from his coat pocket.

"This is what will happen to you," she said in English, waving the letter. "He'll seduce you and he'll abandon you and you'll write to him and he'll never answer."

"How is Jason?" He took the letter back; it was from Eva. He still hadn't had the time to read it.

"I bought the curtain material," Katia said. "Tomorrow I'll come to take the measurements."

"Not tomorrow. I'm busy."

"When?"

"Some other time. How is Jason? I can see his hair is growing."

"I'll come tomorrow, anyway," said Katia. "I've got a second key." She walked away.

"She's Jason's sister, isn't she?" said Isabel. "She seems to be very fond of you."

Mark smoothed back his hair with both hands; Isabel noticed his platinum wristwatch, matching his cigarette case and lighter. On the back of his right hand she saw the livid scar and took his hand, touching it with the tips of her fingers.

"It doesn't hurt any more," he said.

She drew back, embarrassed.

"You know, Mark, I worry about Hilary. He's not exactly a model of discretion—I should have insisted on his coming with us. . . . Perhaps we should have stayed with him, he might need us."

"He won't."

"You know, he drinks a little more than he should sometimes, more than he means to."

Looking at her, he felt certain that he had done the right thing not to get involved with Nubar again. He hadn't—not for Isabel, but he was glad, and the only thing he wanted now was to take hold of her fragile hands and empty his heart to her. He wouldn't be able to buy his ship soon, as he had planned; the rich would still keep him out, but with hard work and patience the future could be arranged. He had never been lucky, yet as Isabel gave him a trusting smile he thought perhaps his luck was beginning to change. He wondered how much she needed Hilary, how much she really worried about him.

"Hilary will be all right," said Mark. "Don't let our politics spoil your holiday."

"It must be worse for you. I mean, for the Greeks."

"We're used to this state of affairs here. As long as I can remember we've had political prisoners in Greece. We all have our file with the security police. People learn, they teach themselves to be careful from the time they're young."

"Have you learned to be careful, too?"

"I'm no reformer, Isabel. I keep clear of politics."

"How can you at a time when so much is in the balance?"

90

"I suppose I'm not made of the stuff that makes martyrs and heroes."

"It's true, isn't it? People are being arrested and interrogated and tortured and sent to concentration camps without trial?"

Yes, it was true, but how to explain all this to a naive foreigner like Isabel?

"I just don't see how anyone can sleep when others are rotting in jail for their ideals," she said.

"History is always tragic—when the time comes it will claim its victims. How can we be the conscience of the whole world, Isabel? How can we bear such a cross?"

"We lack imagination," she said. "The cleverest man of our century was Bernard Shaw, but even he only gave up eating meat after seeing what went on in a slaughterhouse."

"I didn't know you were against eating meat."

"I'm against cruelty, all kinds of cruelty. I always wanted to be a vegetarian but I'm weak."

"Is it weakness or is it because you know whatever you do won't make much difference?"

"It's lack of imagination. Mark, if I were strong, if I were free—I mean, free from my own bondage, free in my own self . . ."

"What would you do?"

"I'd try to help. I'd join some sort of organization, devote my energy to helping the sick and the poor."

"They'll always be with us, you know."

"Do the tyrants have to be with us always?"

"We can't change the world, Isabel."

"We can try. Some people, even here in this country, are trying."

"They're simply stepping on the tail of the boa constrictor. The only way to kill a snake is to smash its head in."

"Why don't you do it?"

"I don't know. . . . Perhaps for the same reason you haven't yet renounced the world. Because I'm not free, because I'm weak . . ."

"You're strong and you're free, I'm certain of it. Unless . . . unless you're a supporter of this regime. You said as much once!"

"Do you believe everything I tell you?"

"Should I? You're an evasive person, Mark. I feel I can never be sure of your motives. And, anyway, some of the nicest people tell all kinds of lies."

"It isn't so terrible to tell a lie when it's in a good cause, is it?"

"What *is* your cause?"

Mark felt lost in her eyes. She was so beautiful, so intense.

"I don't know myself," he said.

"Is that a lie, too?"

"I don't know that, either."

"You don't know very much tonight, do you?"

She was watching him closely, leaning toward him.

"Isabel, when you look at me like that I don't know *anything*."

She laid her hand on his arm. "But you *do* care, Mark, don't you? If there's justice, if there's freedom?"

"My own. Very much."

"You're an utterly selfish person!"

Mark, suddenly hurt, fell silent. However selfish, he had been strong enough to break away from the Armenian.

He raised his glass to her. "You have marvelous eyes, do you know that?"

"Yours are nice, too."

Her hand was on the table and he took it in his and pressed it. "Tell me more."

"You're vain, aren't you?" She drew her hand away.

"I'm selfish, according to you."

She watched him drawing deeply on his cigarette.

"Mark, I have no right to criticize you. I was rude, I'm sorry."

"You weren't rude. It's all right."

He took her glass from her hand and put it on the table.

"Let's dance, Isabel."

He didn't wait for her to say yes or no, but took her by the hand and led her through the tables onto the floor. As they joined the crowd of dancers under the dim lights, the small band was playing something sweet and slow and plaintive. When he drew her to him, her head rested on his chest; she could feel his hand pressing gently against her back, guiding her with practiced skill. He did this as he did everything else, she thought, with a kind of understated grace. People were watching them, she felt proud and exhilarated. She looked up at him and he pushed back the lock of dark hair falling over his forehead. Near them she suddenly saw Jason, dancing with his sister.

"Hi, Markos!" he called.

Mark answered in Greek. He was a rebel, all right, naturally he had to be careful. . . . His cynicism was a mask he used to outwit his enemies. For the first time in her life Isabel felt close to a crusade, and the idea of Mark fighting a secret war almost intoxicated her. She lifted her head a little and felt the sweetness of his breath, the brush of his lips against her hair, his hard chest and legs. . . . She had never felt so physically attracted to a man in her life.

"You're a bad character, Mark," she murmured.

"I know it. But I'd like to reform."

"Really? How disappointing."

"I can change slowly if you like, so it won't be too startling."

92

"You mean you'll sort of taper off into goodness?"

"I'd do anything for you, Isabel."

He put his arms round her waist and drew her even closer.

When they got back to the *plateia*, Hilary was there, well pleased with himself, still the center of attention. Seeing the two of them, he stood up.

"Now look who's here. Come and join us."

"I'm tired, Hilary. Can't we go?"

"Look, Isabel, I can't abandon everybody just now. Won't you let Mark drive you home?"

"It's late, Hilary. Please come along."

Hilary went over to Mark's side and patted him on the shoulder.

"Take her home, will you, Mark? I'll be much obliged."

Mark drove slowly around the harbor, through the old gate and under the ramparts of the castle, down the narrow streets of what had been the Turkish quarter. Neither of them said anything, but when they left the town and took the coast road to the east, Mark found her hand and drew her near. Isabel did not resist but leaned against him and put her head on his shoulder.

He raised her hand to his lips, his eyes on the road ahead, his left hand on the wheel. Isabel drew her hand away but her head still rested on his shoulder, and he put his arm around her waist and hugged her close to him. A sensual tide surged around her breasts and when she breathed in this new happiness —deeply, her mouth half open—she felt her nipples, taut and eager against the tight bodice of her dress. His fingers stroked her soft hair and her body shook with pleasure.

They left the main road and took the turning that led to the *kalivi*. At the gate he stopped, switched off the headlights.

"Shall I walk up with you to the house?"

It was dark and Isabel would not go with him through the hedges and the trees, among the flower beds.

"No, thank you. It's all right." But still she sat in the car, waiting. "Well, good night, Mark. I'll remember this evening."

He took both her hands and stroked them gently, feeling her excitement mounting, giving her time to get used to his touch.

"Mark," she said, more to herself than to him "I never had a chance to tell you how sorry I was about your wife. But you understand, don't you?"

"Yes."

Again they were silent for a moment.

"Was she very beautiful?"

He stroked Isabel's hands, but it was Jennie who stared at him. As long as she was alive, his heart had stayed obstinately bound to her, whatever else he

93

did, whatever other women he had. Now she was dead and he was free. He must teach himself to forget her rippling laughter, the small mole under her lower lip, her lovemaking. But the vacant eyes stared at him from the mortuary bed, and he felt such uncontrollable misery that he shivered, pulled his hands away from Isabel's, laid them on the wheel and leaned his head against them.

She looked at him and felt his pain.

"I'm sorry," she whispered. "I'm so sorry."

She drew closer and stroked his hair.

"I must go now. Good night." She leaned forward and kissed him lightly on the cheek.

"Good night," she said again.

She was ready to leave him when he turned and drew her into his arms, and she felt his mouth, hard and demanding against hers. When he released her, she was breathless, and her cheeks were wet from his tears. Somehow she opened the car door and ran all the way through the dark garden to the shelter of the small house.

9

"It's a question of stamina, Isabel. I know the book's here, all stored inside me. I know I can do the job, but can I stay the course? That's the question."

"The race is not always to the swift," she teased him.

"If it weren't for my neck, Isabel . . ."

"What about it?"

"It hurts. I'm afraid it might turn into permanent arthritis and affect the spinal cord and my brain. Multiple sclerosis, *that* would be the end of me."

"But the Persian doctor said you were as strong as a lion, as strong as a horse."

"A sick lion, a horse ready to collapse between the shafts."

He glanced at her, lowered his head, and, like a sulky sheep going back to his grass, returned to his papers.

Isabel raised her eyes from her book. He was boyish in his white shorts and loose white shirt with the red and yellow toy bears on it, his hair hanging over his forehead and his naturally fair skin burned by the sun. He looked younger than his years though the line of his jaw was growing slacker and his waistline was thickening.

"You must have got up very early this morning," she offered. "I didn't hear you."

Hilary had noticed her watching him, thought she was being critical and resented it.

"You wouldn't hear me, you know."

"You could surely always have called me if there was anything I could do."

"There isn't much you *can* do, is there?"

He looked at her, his eyes quizzical behind his glasses, and switched to a new theme; he was dreaming aloud to Isabel now of academic laurels, of a niche at a European or American university where one could walk on clean green grass, or, at any rate, on clean concrete, and drink water without having to boil it.

It was not a new dream; it had not materialized and Hilary, now desperate, was ready to accept anything to better their lot, to give Isabel the small luxuries of life, to prove to her that he was not, after all, a laborer unworthy of hire. Success could be his even now, with a little encouragement. He didn't want it as a favor, but if he had someone by his side to help him, someone who really cared . . .

"What a man needs is a little affection, Isabel, but you wouldn't know about that."

The telephone rang, and Hilary hurried to the hall to answer it.

"It was Mark," he announced, coming back. "He's invited us to go swimming with him this afternoon at Akroyiali. Five o'clock."

"I heard you. You always sound hearty when you talk to him. You might have consulted me first."

She said this calculating the effect. She did not want Hilary to think she was pleased, and, obstinately, she refrained from asking if there was any other news from Mark. Till five . . . She sucked in her lower lip and still felt the taste of his mouth.

Hilary rubbed his chin.

"I must shave today," he said. "Akroyiali is *the* beach for the smart set here, and I must give all those golden girls a treat."

He was suddenly in good spirits, and Isabel smiled at him.

"Did I say anything funny? What are you laughing at?"

"You *are* funny, Hilary. You just are."

"Other people think so, too," Hilary said and clapped for Zafiro.

The servant girl was wearing a cocktail dress obviously passed on to her by some previous employer, and she had never thought of readjusting the low neckline to a more decorous level for everyday wear. Hilary watched her surveying him impudently, twisting a strand of hair round her finger. She could do with a spanking, that one.

95

Funny, he thought, burrowing among his papers. *That's me.*

"One Nescafé with milk and one *metrios varis,*" he ordered without lifting his head.

The beach at Akroyiali was beautifully clean and organized, with changing rooms, a snack bar and restaurant, and rows of colorful umbrellas along the shore. *Flesh,* thought Hilary, looking around appreciatively at the strong, tanned bodies: *healthy flesh.* Water-skiers were skimming along in the wake of speedboats; he narrowed his eyes against the sun and watched them admiringly.

"I bet that one could teach me the ropes," he said, his eyes lingering on a girl in a black mesh swimming suit. He was still wearing his loose shirt with the toy bears and the white Bermuda shorts Zafiro had rinsed out and ironed for him. He breathed in deeply and thumped his chest.

"This is the life, Isabel, this is the life!"

As she was towed at high speed, the skier lifted first one leg and then the other, balancing skillfully. She swept in between the marker buoys, her black hair streaming behind her; then, after several runs around the bay, the boat made for shallow water, the engine was cut, and she dropped the rope. Hilary watched the man at the wheel go back and pull the girl up on board.

"It's Mark," said Hilary and waved.

Isabel was obscurely disappointed that Mark was already in the water, not on the beach to greet them.

"You go and change, Hilary," she said. "I don't think I'll swim today, I'll stay as I am. I'll wait for you here."

She sat in a deck chair, placed her beach bag on the sand by her side, and shut her eyes. She was not going to take off her clothes and set herself up in competition with that girl or any other girl. It was an unsuitable spot for a meeting—a public beach where everybody was wearing hardly anything, where she was expected to do the same. To suggest such a place showed a lack of finer feelings, an impertinent familiarity. Or, most probably, a desire to see her undressed.

She suddenly heard his voice speak her name; he was close, very close, waiting for her. Isabel turned and looked at him. Water dripped from his lean, tanned body. She said hello but glanced away quickly.

Mark was toweling himself vigorously.

"Is the water nice today?" she asked him.

"Yes, it is. Why don't you come in?"

When she didn't answer, he sat down beside her chair.

Hilary returned, wearing his baggy khaki swimming trunks and straw hat, singing discordantly under his breath, full of goodwill.

"I think I've put on a little weight this summer," he announced as he flopped down beside Mark. "Isabel'll probably tell you it's the retsina, but it

96

isn't—look at Tryfon, he drinks the stuff like a fish and he's lean as a rake. It must be Zafiro's cooking, that girl's a menace."

He patted his waist gently and sighed. He liked the sound of cheerful, healthy people all around him, the murmur of the sea, the hot benevolent sun penetrating every tense muscle and bone. He tilted his straw hat over his face, grunted contentedly, and stretched out on the sand.

"Are you sure you won't come and have a dip with us?" Mark asked Isabel. She shook her head.

"Would you like to go in the boat?"

"No," she said. "I like it here, on the beach."

"I think Lady Isabel is not in her playful mood today," said Hilary. "Let's give her a drink and then abandon her. . . . What would you like to have?" he asked her.

"An iced lemonade, please."

Mark was surprised at her reserve, at her hostility. I shouldn't have kissed her, he thought. But the more he looked at her the more he wanted her and he told himself that he must give her time, that the prize would be worth the waiting. He looked at her again, a long look that took all of her in. She didn't want to take off her clothes, he realized. *One day I'll take them off myself.* He saw Hilary happily flexing his muscles, waiting to go with him into the sea, and he felt a twinge of guilt at his own thoughts.

Watching them go off together, Isabel was nettled that she was being left behind, apparently not missed. It was hot, she was tired, the anticipation of coming to the beach had destroyed her siesta and she dozed off. . . . She was at her mother's funeral, an earthworm was crawling over the coffin in the pit. Her aunt put her arms around her, but the worm grew big as though engorged by blood, a sinister serpent rearing up its red head, poised to strike . . .

Isabel was shuddering uncontrollably when she heard Hilary's voice through the wide wastes of her subconscious. She struggled to wake up, to be part of the present moment. She opened her eyes and heard the sounds of the beach coming back. Then, reconciled to her environment, she got up and walked to the edge of the sea.

Hilary was perched precariously on the seat of a small canoe, paddling vigorously toward the open sea, wearing his straw hat at a jaunty tilt. Isabel watched him make a wide turn and paddle toward her, almost running over two unwary swimmers in the process.

"I'm getting the hang of it now," he shouted, flourishing the paddle. "I'm sure I could shoot Niagara in this thing!"

At that moment Hilary overturned in a shower of spray, with a great flurry of arms, legs, and hat. She heard a shout of laughter and saw Mark swimming out to him. The two men came to her through the shallows, dragging the canoe behind them.

"Don't celebrate too soon, Lady Isabel," called Hilary. "I'm not drowned yet. In fact, it's practically impossible to sink me. Now—just look!"

He fell back noisily in the water and demonstrated his newly acquired skill for them: he lay on his back, completely still, eyes shut, holding his nose with one hand, his body buoyed up. Isabel could not help smiling.

"He's like a little dog," she said. "When he's happy he makes a lot of noise."

She said it lightly, almost lovingly; Mark, stung for a moment, caught hold of her hand and burst out laughing. Hilary splashed and cavorted in the water, as if rising and sinking to the rhythm of their laughter.

Later, on the terrace, the two men hardly noticed her. Hilary drank iced beer and told stories Mark seemed to find uproarious: the three nights he had spent with the Bedouins at H4 on the border between Jordan and Iraq, his adventures in the desert between Basrah and Kuwait in a sandstorm. Isabel had heard them all before and was well aware of how much the details were embellished for such occasions. Once or twice she thought that Mark was looking at her through his laughter, but she sipped her gin and tonic and pretended not to care.

There was a commotion behind them as some girls came over and laid claim to Mark.

"That's the girl, the peachy one, who was skiing with Mark when we first came," said Hilary. "We've seen her before, haven't we?"

"She's Leonides' niece," said Isabel.

"Katia—yes, of course! I hardly recognized her. She does look a dish without clothes, doesn't she? I'll bet she and Mark are having it off together, don't you think?"

"I don't think anything!"

Hilary turned and peered at her, noticing her flushed face even in the bright sun.

"You do sound strange, Isabel. You aren't in love with him, are you?"

"Don't be ridiculous."

Standing up, Hilary caught sight of Tryfon on the small quay that marked the end of the Akroyiali Beach. He waved to the fisherman and went down to talk.

Mark came back for the cigarette case and lighter he had left on the table. As he picked them up, he spoke to Isabel in a low voice.

"I'll be here tomorrow. Come and have a drink with me"—he hesitated —"I'll be here from five o'clock on."

Isabel did not reply, but as she reached out her hand toward her sunglasses, his fingers, strong and hard, closed over hers.

"I'll be waiting for you," he said quietly.

"I'll come," she said, her voice softer even than his.

98

He moved away and drifted down to the water's edge, where Hilary was talking to the fisherman.

They were lying at the edge of the sea, their bodies soaking up the brilliant, burning sun. Mark rolled over on his stomach and stuck his fingers into the sand, dug a hole, found the sea water and made a little lake. Isabel was sifting the hot white sand through her hands. As he leaned on his elbow to show her a shell, delicate pearl-pink with veins of coral, she noticed the grains of wet sand on his chest, the skin around the nipples smooth and brown.

"I want the shell. Please give it to me."

She stood up, her long fair hair streaming over her shoulders.

"Come on," she said and pulled him to his feet.

As they walked along the sand to their clothes, Mark began urging her to visit him, as he had whenever they'd met over the last two weeks. This time he described the old captain's house, the stone staircase, the well in the yard, the carved ceilings and thick wooden doors.

"Do you occupy this mansion all by yourself?"

"Well, yes. I mean, the house is empty but I had to arrange a corner for myself when I moved in. There are still plenty of historical relics for you to see—scimitars and pistols and flags from ships and a marvelous painted figurehead of a mermaid. I think there's probably a lot more stuff in the basement, but the place is locked up and I shouldn't think anybody has gone down there for years. It's rumored that there are some skeletons of the early Lions—more of them were killed in family feuds than by the Turks."

"Isn't the Leonides family interested in preserving these things?"

"The Old Man took away the portraits of his ancestors and hung them in his cabin on the yacht, but the rest of the things have stayed there in the old house—it makes a good setting for them."

He looked at her expectantly.

"No, Mark, you will *not* persuade me."

"Not even for the mermaid?"

"No."

"The skeletons?"

"They're locked up, you said so."

"I could always unlock them. Probably the place is haunted—doesn't that intrigue you?"

"I hate ghosts," she said with a shiver.

"Have it your way," he said, unperturbed. "But if you come, I'll make some good English tea. Doesn't that tempt you?"

"I thought the secret weapon for seducers was wine. I've never heard of tea."

"I can brew it with the secret water. That makes all the difference."

"All right, what *is* the secret water?"

"It's an old legend in Greece. If you promise to come I'll make a point of looking it up for you."

They collected their things and climbed up to the little *kentron*; it was deserted, but the proprietor, who had come to know them as frequent visitors to the secluded beach, welcomed them warmly. He brought them a bottle of chilled wine and two glasses, then went back and fetched the tray with the many small dishes of *meze*.

"It's a nice custom, serving hors d'oeuvres with drinks," Isabel said.

"We have a nice way of doing things here," Mark clinked his glass against hers. "*Yiá chará.*"

"*Carpe diem.*"

"To the most beautiful girl on the island!"

She flushed, suddenly confused. "That's rather conventional, isn't it?"

Mark cut a piece of brown bread, spread it with cheese, and offered it to her. "I suppose I'm rather a conventional person when I'm given the chance."

"And a little romantic?"

"Sometimes."

"What made you choose not to stay at the Kalamos Village or a hotel in town but in an old house alone with scimitars and skeletons?"

"If I stayed at the village, I'd be on the job twenty-four hours a day. If I stayed in a hotel, I travel so much I'd always be checking in and out. I like the old house, and even though I'm not one of the family I feel part of its tradition. It was built in the late eighteenth century, you know—twice it was attacked by the Turks and once by the original admiral's brother."

"You almost make me change my mind about coming there. But I shan't."

Later they went down to the beach. Mark helped her into the boat, raised the outboard engine, and unfurled the sails. He knew of a quiet place where they could have the sea to themselves. He turned back and saw Isabel's golden hair flying free in the wind, the blue Aegean in the background, and at once he imagined her naked in his arms, writhing and moaning under him among the nets, Nubar's nets—yes, he had done the right thing to say no to Nubar, he was sure of that now. He looked at Isabel's thin fingers holding on to the side of the boat, at the slender wrists . . .

"I think I love you," he called over the wind. When no answer came, he turned away. He had done the right thing, the only thing. Happiness was at hand; Isabel was with him and he was taking her to Glaros Bay, to the hut where Nubar kept the nets and the boat.

Isabel trailed her hands in the water as he busied himself with the canvas. They were friends by now, they knew each other, she knew he would not force her. She was conscious of his desire for her but she was confident of her ability to keep things manageable, to draw back in time. They would take turns at the wheel of the speedboat; later, they would wander around the narrow streets of the town, eating and drinking at the local tavernas or dancing until early morning at the Golden Dolphin. People were beginning to talk about them, but they were too absorbed in discovering each other to care.

There was a small jetty at the foot of the overhanging precipice and in a clearing, half buried in the body of the rocks, was a hut with stone walls and a flat roof. Inside the hut, dark and gloomy after the bright sunlight, Mark showed her the rows of nets on racks and the piles of rope.

"Some of these belong to Tryfon," he said.

"Isn't he afraid someone will come along and steal them, with the door unlocked like that?"

"No fisherman would steal from another," he said and suddenly he put his arms around her and tried to kiss her. Isabel, avoiding his lips, leaned against his chest, happy to feel his wide, hard shoulders, to be so close to him. But when she turned away from him, Mark bit her neck at the nape and slipped his hands down her bodice. They had been swimming and she was not wearing a brassiere and Mark stroked her gently, feeling the nipples rising. He buried his face in her soft neck and silky hair: A wonderful feeling of emotional freedom was rising in his veins, as if nothing bad had ever happened to him, as if all the past simply did not count. It was like being given another chance, and as he breathed in the fragrance of her hair, touching her behind the ears with tender lips, he felt humble and earnest and free.

"Isabel, Isabel, I'm crazy for you. For how long—how long?"

Isabel was trembling as she freed herself from his arms.

"It's too dark in here," she said and stepped outside.

Mark followed her, took her hand, and climbed with her the path that ascended the precipice. The reddish-brown rocks were steep and barren, offering treacherous footholds. In some places the path cut through the rock face, rising so steeply that he had to pull her up after him. Yet somehow this challenge was exactly what she needed after that moment in the boathouse, and she labored until they reached the top. He held her hand tightly while she looked down over the sheer cliff at their boat, now only a toy moored at the jetty on a sheet of blue glass.

They had not spoken and Isabel, flushed and dizzy from the ascent, was panting a little as Mark caught her again in his arms. Some gulls were circling in midair, calling with harsh, raucous cries. One of them dived past them so close that Isabel could see clearly its black beady eyes.

"Jemima! Jemima!" she called.

"Who's Jemima?"

"A sea gull, it's the name of a sea gull."

"Do you know them all by name?"

He sat her down on a rock, thinking that he would take her to the Kalamos Village when they went back down. I could give her a drink to relax her, he thought, watching her excitement as she told him the story of Jemima; how she had found the bird covered with tar and taken her home, how Hilary had cleaned her up and been so good about helping care for her . . .

She stopped in confusion, suddenly realizing that she had mentioned Hilary too often, but once mentioned, he was there.

Isabel, now silent, wondered if she ought to feel guilty about seeing Mark; she was only sorry for Hilary, sorry for herself, too, and grateful to him. Hilary could easily have abandoned her a long time ago—other men would have.

She took Mark's hand.

"Hilary has always been very good to me."

Returning, they passed a small chapel on the cliffs overlooking Glaros Bay. The road had originally stopped at this point, but the firm had extended it to run down to the Kalamos Village. As they came nearer, they heard the sound of chanting from inside and Isabel turned to Mark, her eyes pleading with him to accompany her.

The door was open and the sun streamed in, lighting the dark icons and their golden halos. Father Athanasios was standing on the single broad step leading to the altar, intoning passages from a large book. Some women stepped forward, knelt, and bowed their heads under his book. Mark touched Isabel's arm, but at that moment Father Athanasios finished his prayers and closed the book, offering it to the members of the small congregation to kiss. Isabel had met him with Hilary at the *plateia;* she stepped forward and waited until the women and a few shepherds and fishermen had finished before kissing the silverplated missal herself.

The priest withdrew into the sanctuary and Isabel, her eyes shining, turned back to where Mark was standing in the background. She took a candle, lit it, and placed it carefully on the stand in front of the icon of Our Lady the Compassionate. Isabel's lips moved . . . *Holy Mary, Mother of God, pray for us sinners, now and at the hour of our death* . . . The Virgin lay asleep on her bed, the golden paint around the edges of her mantle fading with the centuries. *For us, pray for us sinners, pray for us* . . .

As soon as she joined Mark outside, he started walking back toward the cliff.

"Aren't we going to the Kalamos Village?"

"Some other time."

"Why not now, Mark? Hilary isn't home—I'm not in a hurry, are you?"

"It's too late now. We'll go there one morning."

She had never seen him so edgy and abrupt. He led her down the cliff path, not giving her a moment to pause, retracing their steps to the boat. He jumped in and pulled her after him, almost roughly, then brought down the sail and started the outboard's engine.

"I'm sorry I was so long in the chapel," she said.

"It's all right."

102

"We've met Father Athanasios before. He's such a nice person, don't you think?"

"I try to keep away from priests."

"I thought you would have liked the chapel, Mark. It was so peaceful, so . . ."

"Churches and chapels don't appeal to me. I've been in many, I had to go."

Was he thinking of the time he had spent in the navy? Or of his wife's funeral service? Isabel took his hand.

"My mother used to say we should pray whether we believe or not. If we pray, he may give us a sign, he may talk to us."

She looked up at him, loving him with her eyes, but he was still hostile.

"In any dialogue like that I'll bet he would steal all the best lines."

Remembering her mother, even for a moment, made Isabel feel lost. She drew closer to Mark and put her head against his shoulder. The sun had just set, and a light breeze ruffled the waters; white paths rippled along the sea, running miles out and away to the other islands, busily traveling the length of the Aegean.

Mark looked ahead, steering the boat around the coast, thinking of Jennie. No man, no God, had gone to the help of Jennie.

10

Hilary was typing with a great show of industry: quick little stabs of the index fingers, spectacles sliding forward on his nose, a timetable pinned neatly over his desk. "Ideas," he murmured. "Ideas, I mustn't let them escape me. *Vita brevis, ars longa.*" Dr. Hilary Grey, the distinguished scholar who brought to the West the splendors of demotic poetry . . . But, as if the thought was too much for him, he stopped and stared ruefully at his timetable with its gaily colored drawing pins. " 'Drawing pin'—an abstraction. Back home they are thumb tacks. . . . An Elizabethan use of the language, concrete and vivid." He was in arrears with his work; after the first few days of high enthusiasm he had fallen off and never again quite attained his daily quota.

"Work!" he ordered himself now. "You can still do it, you can still dazzle them!" Now was the time, he knew where he stood now. "I am more philosophical nowadays."

Last night he had visited the villa for the second time since Angela's arrival last week. She had not been expected, at least not to his knowledge, and when he heard the news of her return, he was so perplexed that he was afraid to walk in the grounds lest he run across her and not know what to say.

When at last he gathered courage and went to the villa, he managed not to mind the puma circling within the confines of a golden chain. But he was afraid of the Old Lion, who materialized in front of him with no warning, his dark opaque eyes casting a chill when they fell upon Hilary.

"I suppose your business this evening is with the Baroness? I'm afraid she won't be able to see you. Is there a message I should give her?"

"No, thank you. It's not necessary."

No message . . . He only wanted to see her; they had loved each other once, and he wanted to ask her about her child, their child—Hilary's secret, his pledge for the future, a treasure hidden away that made him breathe faster on those rare occasions when he thought of it.

"Just say hello for me, will you?" he mumbled.

"Of course. After all, you were one of the old friends of the Baroness, weren't you?"

The words were polite, but there was mockery in Leonides' use of the past tense.

"Poor Kriton, although an excellent man in his way, didn't appreciate your qualities, Dr. Grey. I wonder if you realized that at the time?"

"I think I did."

"Ah, but you must not misjudge Kriton. He had no hand in your being asked to leave Greece. I believe somebody else accused you of being a Communist and that was how it was done. Even in those days, to be branded as a Communist in a bigoted little country like ours was no light thing."

"No doubt, Mr. Leonides. No doubt."

He turned and left, convinced that he had departed with dignity. But he spent the next few days in misery, unable to return to his work, unable to rest. The villa seemed to be pulling him like a magnet, and the image of the child he had hardly stopped to think about for so many years tormented him suddenly.

As he walked toward the villa the second time, he had rehearsed his lines, wondered how to greet the boy, if he was there. Could he embrace him? Or should he embrace Angela and give the child a friendly pat?

Angela had been lying on a couch, eyes fixed on some distant point, face immobile and heavily painted—almost, for a moment, unrecognizable. Inge sat by her side, her hand in Angela's, the puma lying at their feet. Leonides, seated in an armchair near the head of the sofa, was smoking a cigar and reading the newspaper.

Hilary stepped back, as if to give himself a moment to get over the shock. Then he bowed, not knowing what to say. The Old Lion looked up; Inge smiled lazily at him and caressed her mistress's hand; Angela turned slowly, like a wax image, toward Hilary, her eyes looking through his as if she did not recognize him. Nobody spoke and nobody asked him to sit down.

104

At last Hilary managed to speak.

"I thought you might care to come and have a drink with us at the *kalivi*—we'd like to thank you for everything."

The blond servant who had ushered Hilary in returned and offered him a whiskey and soda on a tray. Hilary raised his glass in Angela's direction—as if he wanted to welcome her, as if he were drinking to her health—but no words came out, and when he tried to drink he could not. He looked around him, half hoping to see a boy coming in through the open door or through the French windows. Then Angela's abstracted stare pulled his eyes back to her.

Leonides folded his paper and took the cigar from his mouth.

"The Baroness is tired, but when she feels better she will be pleased to accept your invitation."

The blond man came back, silently took the glass from Hilary, hovered to show him out.

Could it be that she was really out of her mind? It was not possible that she had forgotten. He had fantasized their meeting, he'd had great hopes. He couldn't quite bring himself to believe that it was all over, that no pieces were left to be picked up. . . .

He remembered walking with her in a sunny town (was it on Corfu?) holding her hand, loving her, Angela enjoying his admiration, preening like a cat. It was the first time he had managed to get her away from Athens and her brother, and they had made the most of it. That unfortunate devil Kriton Kontopoulos had known all about it, of course.

She's still tormenting me, Hilary thought as he turned to go. Leonides rose at once to accompany him to the door.

"I think you know my assistant, Stephanou, don't you? A friend of yours and of Mrs. Grey? I suppose you first met him in Athens."

"Yes, we did."

"Was it on the *Hesperides?*"

"Yes."

"Was Eva there—the cabaret girl? Eva is Markos' mistress, one of his mistresses. He has a way with women, I don't know where he gets it from."

Leonides glanced quickly at Hilary, smiling at some private joke.

"I understand his father was a most God-fearing doctor from Patras," he added. Then his amiability vanished.

"Now listen to me, Dr. Grey. I'm leaving for the States tomorrow. The Baroness will be in the care of Felix, her servant, and no one is to disturb her. And no one is to disturb her secretary Inge, whom I'm sure you noticed. If anyone disturbs them, the least that will happen to him is to be told to leave—immediately. I'm sure Felix will see to that. And, by the way, the wild cat really is wild, when necessary . . ."

The old scoundrel hadn't liked him, *that* much was clear. Hilary remembered almost being killed when his brakes failed a few days before he was deported from Greece—Angela had given him the gun, but she hadn't advised him to check his brakes.

At his typewriter Hilary felt the sweat running down his cheeks; his neck went stiff, his head ached. What had happened to the child Angela was carrying when he left? Hilary passed the back of his hand over his forehead; it was burning. He would find out one day, he had to find out. Work, he reminded himself, and went back to his typing.

Isabel came in, went to the end of the veranda, and stood looking out to sea.

"How's dreamboat these days?" called Hilary.

There was no answer, so he got up and went to her.

"Where's Mark? Don't tell me he's stood you up?"

"Please leave me alone."

"I've been doing that for the last five years." All the humiliation he had felt going to the Villa Artemis was stinging him; Isabel was there to receive the brunt.

"You're a human crossword puzzle," he told her. "But I suppose I'll find out all the clues if I live long enough."

She stood near the parapet, an ice princess, a fair lady in a medieval tapestry, framed within the window of a high tower, aloof, remote, impervious to the need for human communication.

"Hell," said Hilary and went back to his typewriter.

Argos started howling again—a new habit he had developed since the coming of the Baroness and her puma. Hilary went to the kitchen to ask Zafiro to banish the dog. She was more than a servant now; in the evenings, coming back late from town when Isabel was either out with Mark or shut up in her room, Zafiro would help him take off his clothes and put him to bed. In the beginning, he had tried to make love to her but she always managed to push him back and comfort him by taking hold of his penis and jerking him up and down until he came in her hands. Hilary, now accustomed to this compromise, looked forward to it as a baby to its bottle. But he had not been able to find her the night before, and the impudent girl refused to tell him where she had been. Now she prepared the coffee and pushed his hand away from her bottom.

"You go to your desk and then I follow."

He winked at her when she arrived with the tray.

"What about some of that nice honey cake you made yesterday—is there any left or did you give it all to Andreas?"

When the cake came he took the plate to Isabel, who shook her head.

"That cake is very fattening, Hilary. All honey and almonds."

"I thought you'd say that."

She watched him eating, using both hands, licking his fingers appreciatively.

106

"That's hardly the way to begin a diet." He had been talking about reducing quite a lot recently.

"I know, but how can I ever forget the Hungry Forties? It's only natural. Psychological compensation, you see."

"Don't tell me you were around then."

"No, but I've heard that some of my ancestors from County Cork died from hunger on the road."

"I don't think that will happen to you, somehow."

"I'm still bossed by the British, aren't I?"

Argos howled from the outhouse to which he had been banished and Hilary cursed.

Isabel hated to think that she didn't appreciate him, didn't understand him; but she never really tried to boss him—how could one boss Hilary?

"You've been up working early today, haven't you?" she said for the sake of peace.

"Yes, and now I remember, you promised to do my typing and wrestle with this uncooperative machine."

"You haven't mentioned it since we've been here."

"You've seen me working. You could have offered to help."

"You never asked me."

"I don't like *asking* you to do things for me, Isabel, don't you understand? I hate favors."

"Yes," she said softly. "I do. Tell me, how is the book progressing?"

"It isn't, Isabel. I think it's in its last agony."

"What on earth do you mean? The translations you read to me seemed very fine."

"I'm just too late. There's always somebody a step ahead."

He picked up the Penguin paperback of *Greek Verse* and handed it to her. "I got this yesterday at the local bookstore."

Isabel leafed through the book.

"But your project is different. Your book's a stage beyond this."

"Yes, I know. I have an intellectual problem to solve, I have to move further than the translations, reach somewhere."

"It sounds marvelous, Hilary."

"Does it? Trypanis is an Oxford don. Who's going to be interested in a book by an unknown like me?"

"You've got the ability to do it, Hilary. You don't have enough drive—that's your problem."

"Have I ever claimed to you that I had?"

"No, but I sometimes wonder what you *have* got."

"Thinning hair, thickening waistline, and absolutely no illusions—Grey, the Jesting Philosopher, that's me."

107

His complacent self-deprecation exasperated her.

"A bit melodramatic, isn't it? You'll be laughing through your tears next."

She sometimes adopted for his benefit this tone of brisk common sense, and it infuriated him. He closed his eyes wearily.

"If my head doesn't get any better, I'll pack it in for the morning and go back to bed." He leaned forward expectantly, waiting for her to touch his forehead, for his fever to be confirmed. "It's burning," he announced, "but we won't talk about it. I know other people's suffering bores you."

He called for Zafiro, who brought his plastic bag filled with medicines and placed it on the table. He lined up a wide assortment of pills and powders and syrups, and lingered over his choice, awaiting Isabel's advice, yet unwilling to be snubbed.

"Why don't you get on with it and swallow down the whole lot?"

He looked at her, calm and fresh in the strong morning light, watching him, pitying him, criticizing him.

"Shut up, you blasted Rhine maiden with your flowing hair and your cold çow's eyes."

He waited for her to react, but she only stared at him as if he were something unclean brought to her reluctant attention.

Hilary shifted ground.

"Our common friend, Mark—I hear he's common to many, by the way—he's run into difficulties with you, hasn't he? Well, for him I have a fellow feeling. He's not used to it, it must be more trying for him."

Isabel stood watching him coldly, defying him with her presence. Hilary waved her away.

"Don't keep staring at me like that, damn you. Go away, go away!"

"I only wish I could," she said quietly and left him to ramble on alone.

She walked briskly at first, smiling to herself. The path followed the curve of the hill for a while, then turned steeply upward. Isabel walked slowly now, her feet hurting from the loose gravel.

She reached the flat top of a huge boulder overhanging a ravine and stood on the natural platform to get her breath back. The *kalivi* was hidden behind the thick hedges and bushes of the gardens, but she could see the red-tiled roof of the Villa Artemis through the tops of the cypress trees. At the sea's edge the walls of the Venetian castle glowed in the last of the day's brightness. The harbor was hidden under the medieval ramparts, but she could see the whitewashed Cathedral of Ayios Nikolaos shining in the afternoon sun. Beyond the town and around the shores of the island, the blue sea was turning paler as the brightness of the sky faded into evening; on the opposite shore across the channel, the tops of the mainland's ancient mountains were still shining, their foothills floating in purple shadows.

108

Isabel started off again and was soon on the brow of Aspros Lophos. From there she could see the terraced vineyards on her left and, below, the olive groves sweeping in a descending curve to the sea. The coast road skirted the island, passed the cemetery, then wound out of sight beyond the far slopes of the hills. Behind the wild ridges of the Black Mountain lay the other side of the island; from where she was standing, it must be only a short distance through the wild forest over the ridges of the Black Mountain. Our Lady the Compassionate was under these ridges, and as Isabel scanned the mountains she saw at one point the white path climbing over and then disappearing into the darkness of the dense forest.

As soon as she started on her way again she heard footsteps following her, but when she looked back there was nobody. Her feet hurt in her thin-soled sandals as she picked her way along the stony path to the cottages above the town. She walked a little faster and then faster, until she was almost running. The road was not far away, she knew that, but the more she hurried the more uneasy she became. The cicadas chirped incessantly, orchestrating her panic. She lost the path for a short while and ran under some pine trees, unable to turn back or to stop; she could distinctly hear someone behind her, and as she ran over the slippery pine needles, she missed her footing and fell heavily on her side. For a moment she stayed there, too frightened to look up or get to her feet. She heard the sound again and raised her head. Argos, the handsome hound, was standing over her, his grave brown eyes regarding her, his mouth open, the red tongue lolling as he panted. He came nearer to nuzzle her, his long tail wagging briskly.

Isabel patted him, got up, and started off again, the animal trotting at her side. Soon she found the rough road, the road Mark lived on. Some of his secrets must be hidden in that house, she thought, wondering if she could surprise Mark, open the door and walk in. Perhaps he'll be having a shower after the day's work, she thought. Or a drink. . . I'll only have a look, I'll spy on him just a little and he'll never know.

Mark had said he didn't expect to be free before eight that evening.

"I'm painting the garden wall," he had said. "When will you come to see it? I'll fix you the most marvelous drink you've ever tasted."

"Not at your place."

"Anyone would think you didn't trust me."

"They'd think right. You could always offer me a drink at the Kalamos Village, you could take me there to see the Aquamarine Bar."

"Let's make it the Poseidon Palace. We can sit on the terrace and listen to the band."

"I can see you're determined not to be seen with me at the Kalamos Village—a girl?"

"Many girls."

"Have you promised to marry them all? Will they lynch you or something if they see you with me?"

"I owe money to the barman, I'd rather we went somewhere else."

"You're not telling me the truth. But never mind."

"Why not the Poseidon Palace? Why don't we meet there about eight?"

Isabel stopped her climbing to draw a breath; she could see the captain's house now on the opposite slopes overlooking the town, not very far from Clive's: Until eight, until eight. For now, she would only have a look at the house, just to see what he was doing.

Feeling more confident, she hurried along intent on her purpose, speaking occasionally to Argos, glad of his company. But when she saw the gray-tiled roof of the old house only a hundred yards or so from the road, she stopped and tried to make the animal understand that he must go home, that he must not betray her. She finally sent him back with a firm command, left the track-road, and took the path to the house through the pine trees and the wild gorse.

As she approached she heard a peal of laughter, a girl's laughter, music—a Greek song coming from a radio somewhere. She was ready to leave when she heard again the high-pitched laughter. If she turned back they would probably see her and she didn't want that; she would rather wait a little for the darkness and then slip quietly away. She left the path and stood back in a clump of trees. I can go to Clive's, she thought. It's not far, he's bound to be in; he'll take me home safely.

Then she heard Mark and the girl who had laughed speaking in Greek. She couldn't understand it, she felt alien and unwanted, but his voice, the knowledge that he was there, drew her closer.

Katia was sitting on a low parapet, sewing, piles of crumpled, brightly colored material by her side. She wore red shorts and a tight, sleeveless cotton sweater. Mark was standing barefoot on a ladder, stripped to his shabby blue jeans, whistling as he applied whitewash to the garden wall with a large brush. From time to time Katia would call up some remark to him and he would shout back, but it was all in their language and Isabel couldn't understand.

Katia suddenly picked up a pair of curtains and stood at the door of the house, calling to him; when he didn't come, she pulled at his feet until he came down, threw the bundle of curtains over his head, giggling, and began to tug him inside. Mark disentangled himself, turned, sloshed her bottom vigorously with his dripping brush, and went back to the wall. Katia twisted around to look at the splash of white on the seat of her shorts, gave a squeal of dismay, threw down the curtains, and snatched up the bucket of whitewash. Several times she made as if to throw it over him, feinting, laughing, drawing back. When she finally flung it at his head, Mark ducked and the flood of white splashed over the wall and the pile of curtains; she put down the bucket and started running along the path, Mark in pursuit. He caught up with her and pulled her down by her hair, seized her under the arms and knees and lifted her off the ground. Katia, shrieking with delight, kicked her heels and tried to bite his hands.

Isabel wanted to run, but they were too close. She shut her eyes and waited for them to go by; when she opened them, Katia was kissing Mark on the throat as he carried her into the house.

She's only a mischievous child, Isabel told herself. Yet she was shaken and depressed out of all proportion to the scene. Seeing Mark like that with another woman humiliated and confused her. She bit her lips as she finally walked away into the shadows.

Argos was waiting patiently for her near the road, lying down, his powerful paws outspread. Isabel bent down and touched the massive head.

"It's all right, it's all right. Argos, my good boy, my good dog, nobody can take me away from you, nobody." The big brown hound arose, stretched, and began trotting down the hill into the gathering dusk. Isabel tossed her hair back from her brow and hurried to catch up with the gentle animal.

Somewhere outside Argos was howling dolefully. Isabel lay wide awake in bed, unable to sleep. Let Mark wait for her, let him amuse himself at the Poseidon Palace, go to others for comfort.

She raised herself on one elbow and looked again at her watch on the side table. It was past midnight, but she would wait until one to take her capsules. He hadn't even bothered to telephone, perhaps he was still busy with that giggling girl. Or could it be that he was waiting? More likely, he was gambling at the hotel, Katia looking on, fetching him a drink, brushing herself against him. He hadn't telephoned; for all he knew, something could have happened to her. . . . She would take her sleeping capsules later, after Hilary came back and she could find out if there was any message from Mark. But Hilary was late tonight.

Isabel buried her head in the pillow, trying to cry, courting the release of tears.

When she heard Hilary talking to Zafiro, she got out of bed and put on a housecoat. He was sitting on the wide stone step, his head in his hands. She went to him and tried to help him up, but he would not move and she sat near him, watching him. Would she be able to ask him about Mark? Hilary was talking about a child, some boy he had never seen.

"They don't want me now, the Lion is afraid I'll claim the child, the old scoundrel never liked me."

Isabel drew closer and put her arm around his shoulders, not knowing how to comfort him.

"Which child, Hilary?"

"I didn't tell you, did I? It's my secret. I haven't told you all my secrets."

Zafiro appeared and handed him a cup of black coffee.

111

"I've put lemon peel in it and no sugar," she whispered.

"Come on, now, drink it, it will do you good."

"You haven't seen Mark, have you?" asked Isabel. "Were you at the Poseidon?"

No, he was with some friends at the taverna, he hadn't seen Mark, there was no message.

As Isabel sat close to Hilary, she smoothed his hair with her palm, their separate miseries bringing them closer together.

"You wouldn't give me a child," he said. "You wouldn't have me near you, but I have my little secret."

She was close, her leg was touching his, even through his misery something stirred in him, but when he tried to embrace her she drew back.

"Come on, now," said Zafiro. "To bed."

She tugged at his arm.

"Leave me alone, I want to stay here and . . . think."

But the two women managed to get him to his feet, Zafiro holding him under the arms and coaxing him along.

He tried to shake her off—"Leave me alone, can't you?"—and stretched out his arms to Isabel. He needed her just now, his desire for her was like the old days.

"It's me," he said, swaying a little. "Hilary."

"Let's go to bed," said Isabel, backing away.

"Hear my ever-loving wife? To bed, she says, to bed. She just can't wait for it. She's jealous about the child, she's jealous, and I haven't told her all my secrets yet. . . . I'm coming, Lady Isabel, I'm coming."

Isabel stood at the entrance to her room, staring at him, barring the way. Hilary was angry, then the old memory came back and his courage ebbed, leaving the familiar taste of drink and guilt and frustration. He blinked at the light, staring at her through narrowed eyes, leaning on the maid.

"Lady Isabel, when I look at you closely, I can see an owl behind each of your big blue eyes."

He had started for his room when the dog howled again; he stopped and turned back.

"I'm no good, I'm just a drunk. I'm an animal. You love animals—why don't you love *this* one?" He waited for her response, waited until he heard the hound again. "Just you wait, Argos, my honest, dirty dog. Tonight, I promise you, I'll come and we'll howl together."

Isabel could not bear it any longer, and she walked out to wander in the garden. She thought she heard Hilary calling for her and came and stood outside his window. The shutters were not completely closed, and she could see into the room. Zafiro was sitting on his bed and Hilary's head rested on her breast; with her left hand she was stroking his head and her right hand was under the bedclothes. Isabel could see the sheet moving. Suddenly he gave a little gasp and fell back and, almost immediately, he was asleep.

Watching them made Isabel feel lonelier and colder. She walked away quickly and took the downhill path to the steps in the cliff and the landing-stage and the sea below. The small waves around the rocks were edged with silver, but further from the shore the sea was black and quiet. Isabel stood there, staring.

A breaker dashed in, and the boat tossed on the swell and tugged at her moorings. Isabel was frightened of the night, but she shook her head as if shaking the fear out of her head and pulled on the rope. The boat, after a moment's resistance, came to her—then, secured by the anchor on the other side, it swung back again before she could hold it. Isabel waited for the swell, pulled again. She measured the distance. The boat would come within three feet of the landing stage, then swing back as far as five feet away. She pulled on the rope again with both hands, and, when the boat came near, she jumped; she lost her balance but landed safely among the coiled ropes and tarpaulins. The boat reared up and she was afraid it would capsize, but back it came again.

A slice of moon hung over the Black Mountain, and the air was still. Suddenly she wished that her mother could be there. It was strange to think that she had been not much older than Isabel when she died. Isabel saw her mother's peaceful face, the coffin being lowered, her father trying to pick her up. . . . She had run away among the tombstones, terrified, struggling to escape. Now she realized that her father had only wanted to comfort her. After her mother's death she had lived with her aunt; her father had gone abroad and she never saw him again. He only wanted to comfort me, Isabel said to herself, but the memory made her shake uncontrollably.

There was a sudden gust of wind, the secret phosphorescent sea creatures glowed in the moonlight with the swell, the moored boat dived down in the abyss with the suck of the sea and rode high again with the return. Isabel was thrown among the coiled ropes, still shivering, still with the dead.

11

"Balls!" said Nubar behind his dark glasses. "And, by the way, do you know what the balls are always complaining about?"

"What?" asked Luigi, the Italian engineer from the Kalamos Village.

"Of being left out."

"*Santo cielo!*"

Mark was not listening. He hadn't seen Isabel for days; she hadn't come to meet him at the Poseidon, he hadn't called to ask why. Hilary was his friend, perhaps it was better this way.

The Armenian jerked his head toward Ted and Terry behind the bar.

"*They* don't have any trouble. If worse comes to worst, they've got each other."

Terry dispensed three whiskeys, mindful of his green silk shirt. His hair fell to his shoulders in shining chestnut ringlets; Ted affected a flowing bow tie and a wig—he had many and was fond of describing being mistaken for a tart in his auburn one. Tonight, in his Charles the Second, he looked like a saturnine cherub. Taped music played in the background, and as a lively popular tune started up Ted emerged from behind the bar, smiled, and plunged joyfully into the chaotic tempo with half-closed eyes, clicking his fingers, swaying his hips and shoulders, his small moccasined feet weaving intricate patterns.

The two rooms were connected by an open archway; both were furnished in plum-colored damask—alcoves, sofas, carpets, draperies. The two brothers shared a passion for Victoriana which had inspired a great swath of black horsehair funereal plumes, an old street barrel-organ and stuffed monkey bought from a junk shop in the Plaka, and various other period pieces. The resplendent mahogany and brass bar, itself an antique, stretched along the far wall of the larger room.

The Old Lion was celebrating tonight, but he hadn't invited Mark to stay for dinner after the cocktail party. The Baroness was with him, Leonides was with the family—well, after all, it was the Old Man's show, it was he who had fixed the deal with the colonels. Mark wondered at what price. With the firm expanding at its present rate, the government's appreciation was predictable. Nobody commented about the virtual monopoly the Old Man had pulled off. Instead, well briefed in advance, the newspapers played up the story that the *World Seafarer* had today hoisted the Greek flag. No journalist found it necessary to mention that Leonides still kept the Liberian colors on the *Hesperides*, traveled on a Brazilian passport, had much of his money in Swiss banks.

Leonides had called Mark to his office to brag about the deal.

"You need experience for this kind of thing," he said. "You need a lot of patience, a lot of understanding of human nature—especially when that nature belongs to a soldier who came from his village with the hope of a field marshal's baton in his knapsack."

"When you were in South America, you must have known quite a number of soldiers with that sort of ambition."

"What's that? Are you trying to be clever?"

"I don't mean ordinary soldiers. What about the oil-greased sheiks, the cunning Jews, all those wily orientals you've told me about?"

114

"Now listen to me, you young bastard. If you think you can make it while gambling at the Casino du Liban, or shaking your ass in the discotheques in Paris, you can think again. *I* sat down cross-legged in the desert and ate sheeps' eyes with the Bedouins and drank camels' milk from the same filthy bowl. *I* got hepatitis in Egypt, typhoid in Hong Kong, dysentery in Venezuela, I know what I'm talking about."

And probably the clap just about everywhere, thought Mark, while keeping a diplomatic silence.

Now the Lions would be drinking their champagne on the veranda of the Villa Artemis and he was not of enough consequence to be invited. Katia was probably there, she would no doubt tell him all about it tomorrow.

"Women are creatures of instinct," said Luigi, apropos of nothing. He had a way of pronouncing platitudes as though he had just stumbled upon some important, undiscovered truth. "Their instincts sometimes get the better of them."

"And I could tell you what their instincts are," said Nubar.

"I feel sorry for them," said Luigi. "Even sorry for Francesca, but what could I do? What *can* one do when they lose their reason? I loved her—mind you, I love them all—but one is powerless. I spent a fortune on that girl and what did she do?" He paused rhetorically.

"Screwed your brother?" suggested Nubar. "Made you a present of a little bundle the image of your best friend?"

"*Oh, Dio buono!* I can't bear to dwell on it."

He waited for someone to press him for details, but no one did.

"Just tie them up and screw them," said Nubar. "It's the only language they understand."

Luigi leaned over and nudged Mark.

"I've told you about Francesca, haven't I?"

"Yes, you have, Luigi."

Nubar slapped Mark on the back.

"I've got some good news for you—I'll tell you later. Cheer up!"

Earlier that evening Mark had seen Hilary sitting alone at Kavouras' taverna, but he had walked quickly past. Their time together at the Zephyros seemed very long ago; the summer would soon be over, the Greys would be leaving. Hilary had his books, his ideas, his wife. Hilary was free and he would take Isabel with him, while Mark stayed behind, flying here and there, buying and selling, approving tenders, making the way easy for the Old Lion.

The music changed to something quick and African which Ted apparently found irresistible. Brushing past Nubar, he winked at him and moved to the center of the room. He pulled off his red handkerchief, brandished it in the air, and started the tribal dance, his pelvis thrusting back and forth rhythmically.

"I wonder how much he'd pay me to screw him?" said Nubar.

115

"More likely he'd charge you for the privilege," said Luigi.

Mark noticed Demetris come in and pause on the threshold, glancing about the room before sitting down in a shadowed alcove.

"I'd better go and ask him what he'll have," said Terry. "He's my favorite agent." Looking at Demetris, he shuddered theatrically. "Look how he glares—it sends shivers down my back."

The music changed again, and Ted tangoed prettily around the room, humming and flirting an imaginary cloak from side to side.

"Women can't eat *his* guts, lucky devil," said Luigi as Ted finished his dance and bowed in their direction. He came over to them, shaking the black curls out of his eyes, asked his brother for a drink, closed his eyes and took a deep breath. "Delicious!" he said. "Mr. Nubar, what do you think of our bar? Give me your hand—how *thrilling*, your only having one!—now put your finger in this bullet hole in the counter."

"Sure you wouldn't like me to put it anywhere else?"

Ted went right on.

"Two *gorgeous* hairy bush rangers shot it out in a *notorious* saloon in Sydney about a hundred years ago. *Now*, what do you feel?" He guided Nubar's finger into the hole in the gleaming wood. "Tell me, dear, what do you feel now? Terry declares that it's really alive and speaks to him sometimes. And the things this bar has *seen*—it traveled with us all the way from Australia, you know. There was a dreadful storm coming over, and we had a horrid moment when the captain started looking round with his steely blue eyes and talking about jettisoning *unnecessary* cargo!"

Mark was remembering Isabel's jasmine perfume. They were together and she was in his arms, dancing at the Golden Dolphin. . . .

"Do you think Signor Kommenos is very jealous?" Luigi asked him.

The jasmine filled the room and they moved against each other, their bodies pressing close.

"Oh, I don't want any trouble, Mark, I don't. If necessary, I shall leave the Poseidon Palace."

The voices and the heat and the cigarette smoke floated in Mark's nostrils, in his lungs, burning out the jasmine memory.

"Why don't you move to the village?" he asked Luigi.

"Don't get me wrong, Mark, I like it—I should, I helped to make it—but the Poseidon suits me. It's just that there's enough trouble in the world without looking for it, don't you think so?"

The room was too hot, the air was stale and heavy.

"Let's be going," said Mark. "I'll walk with you as far as the hotel."

"Thank you, but for me the matter is more complicated. For me it's too early to go home."

The Armenian laughed and turned to leave with Mark.

"That's the price you pay for home comforts, signore—that is, if it's somebody else's home."

The Old Lion came in with Inge on one arm and Katia on the other. Inge's slacks were low cut at the hips to show the beginning of the cleft of her buttocks; around her breasts she wore a twisted silk scarf. Katia, cuddly in hot pants, put out her tongue at Mark and twined herself around her uncle. Leonides, proud and possessive, held the girls tight, one under each arm.

Mark gave the whole party a slight, formal bow and turned to leave.

"Going off, gypsy? Who is she this time?"

"I was about to go to bed, sir."

"Alone?"

"Naturally."

"You must be saving yourself. Right, gypsy? Come and have a drink with us—I insist. Just one, and then I'll let you go."

Van Sullivan came in with Thalia suntanned and smiling. They had just returned from their cruise on the *Hesperides*. Thalia glanced at Mark. They had an innocent friendship, but in the presence of the Old Lion they were self-conscious. Van shook hands with everybody, and Thalia invited them all to the wedding.

Leonides squeezed Katia's arm.

"She asked me to bring her here to meet you," he told Mark.

"I didn't! I never want to see him again," Katia announced.

"Can't you see the girl's madly in love with you? Give her a chance. When I was your age I didn't rush off when a pretty girl entered the room, I can tell you."

Katia, as she rubbed against her uncle, looked at Mark and flicked her tongue across her lips. The little bitch, he thought, I should have fucked her there and then to show her. She had gone to see him last night, had managed to drag him to bed and pull off his clothes. "We'll get married. Why waste time?" She was a virgin, she claimed, she wanted him to be the first. "What are you afraid of? My mother knows about it and she fully agrees." "Not your father?" "If you make love to me, if I told him I was pregnant, he wouldn't have much choice, would he?" Even now her giggles grated on him.

Nubar was trying to tell the Old Lion about a telegram confirming the arrival of eight hundred German tourists, but Leonides would not talk business.

"Gypsy, where are you going?" he called, without turning to look at Mark.

Mark had finished his drink and was saying good night.

Leonides' hand slipped down from Katia's waist to her buttocks.

"You can't stay put, you young dog, can you? Gypsy, gypsy, who put pepper in your arse? Come here and tell me how you rate the local talent."

117

Mark stood perfectly still.

"Signore," began Luigi, "if I am allowed to intervene, if I dare to offer an opinion . . ."

"You shut up," said Leonides.

He turned to Mark.

"You call me an old man, it's good the girls don't believe you."

He released Katia and tried to put an arm around him, but Mark recoiled.

"Relax, gypsy, relax. What's this face you're putting on? Has your caique gone to the bottom?"

How long, Mark wondered, would he have to put up with the Old Lion showing off at his expense in front of women? It was a kind of serfdom, it was what happened when you weren't your own man.

"Who's this one, gypsy? What are you hiding from me?"

This time Leonides put an arm around Mark and hugged him.

"Weren't they something, those girls at Innsbruck?" he said in his ear. "You say I'm an old man, bastard, but you saw how I screwed them both, didn't you? I could have done the whole cathouse if we'd had the time."

They had been in Munich, Leonides had just settled some business with Angela's former husband, the Baron; they were walking along Bayernstrasse when, without warning, the Old Man walked into a car showroom, bought a black Mercedes, and commanded Mark to drive him over the Brenner Pass to Italy.

At Innsbruck, where they spent the first night, Mark remembered Leonides' high spirits, his sudden confidences, his changes of mood, one moment affectionate, the next vicious. As always, Mark both envied his success and resented putting up with him. Nothing would have gratified him more than to have thrown everything in his face and walked out; yet he also admired his guts, his business ability, the sheer audacity of his dealings with the world.

Leonides, without consulting Mark, had booked them into a twin room. "I want to stay awake and talk to you tonight—watch it you don't get drunk and fall asleep." After dinner the Old Man announced that he wanted to explore the red-light district. Ignoring Mark's protests, he waved down a taxi and told the driver to take them to the best brothel in town.

He's always wanted to drag me down, thought Mark, he wants me to be like him.

He shifted under the Lion's embrace and turned away from Katia and Inge.

At the brothel the Old Man had moved into the parlor, completely at ease with the group of half-naked prostitutes, ordering champagne for everybody. Without wasting any time, he stripped off his clothes and proceeded to make love to a girl in front of all of them, encouraging Mark to do the same. Mark left the parlor and went to a private room with one of the girls. When he returned

118

Leonides was still busy, a different girl under him, the other whores cheering him on. . . .

Mark remembered wandering the streets of Innsbruck for most of the night after the Old Man was safely in his bed, snoring.

"Markos and I are returning to Innsbruck one of these days," Leonides announced to the whole company. "We've got some unfinished business to do there."

He turned to Mark with a leer: "I wonder if our business associates still remember us."

Mark put his glass on the counter, ready to go.

Inge took both his hands playfully in hers.

"Are you certain you want to leave us?"

As she spoke, she pressed a slip of paper into his left hand.

"Gypsy," said Leonides, "I've decided to take Leandros with me—you'll be all by yourself, but remember who's the boss."

As Mark went through the outer room, he saw Demetris sitting alone in the shadows, watching everything, missing nothing.

Nubar caught up with Mark outside.

"You shouldn't misjudge the Old Lion," he said.

"Leave the old bully alone. I've had enough of him tonight."

The two men started to walk along the corniche toward the town.

"Markos, you're too touchy, you're bitter. He's very fond of you, I'm sure."

"He's a pain in the neck. But he has the money, he pays the piper and everyone has to dance."

"Be that as it may, I've never heard him say anything but good about you when you're not there."

"He beefs enough when I *am* there, anyway, but one has to suffer him, working for him."

"It could be tough for you to get a job as good as the one you have now."

"You're trying to say I've got a record. All right, go on and say it."

"I wasn't thinking . . ."

"It's true enough. And there would be questions. . . ."

"Leonides wants you near him, I'm certain of it. You remember when you gambled your salary for six months and lost it to him? Five thousand bucks. Did he really tell the accountant not to pay you?"

"What do you think?"

"Me? Nothing. But I remember how you got it all back from me soon after, when you wiped out all the money I made from that Dutch business."

"I offered you your revenge. You wouldn't take it."

"I would have, but somebody else wanted to make sure you kept the money."

119

"You mean . . .?"

"Yes. The five thousand came from him."

Mark was perplexed at the Old Man's devious generosity. To this day Leonides enjoyed twitting him about that game. He didn't understand; he should be grateful but he wasn't, he felt treated like a child.

"I only want your good," Nubar was saying. "I know how much Leonides thinks of you. If you play your cards right, you needn't always work for him."

"What do you mean?"

"You could become a Lion."

"How?"

"Marry a Lioness—join the pride."

Mark stopped, flicked his lighter, and read the slip of paper. The Baroness was inviting him for a drink at the villa, at midnight. Mark remembered that Leonides' private plane was leaving at eleven-thirty.

He crumpled the piece of paper and dropped it. He could screw the Baroness, that was one way of joining the pride. He had seen her staring at him at the cocktail party, a flamboyant, sensual woman, the Old Lion by her side, keeping a close rein on her. Mark, who was not invited to the dinner party afterward, had stayed obstinately at the far end of the lawn with Luigi and Nubar and other hirelings of the firm. Not that Mark cared. Let the Baroness screw herself.

"I saw you lose thousands of drachmas last night to Kommenos," said Nubar. "I think you're on the way up, Markos, whatever you say, but you're not rich enough yet to afford to throw away as much as that." His voice dropped. "There are hundreds of thousands to be made, my friend, and this isn't a joke. I've just had a tip for a job—a big one. I know you've given it up . . ."

"I'm not interested, Nubar."

"Sixty kilos of morphine base, nicely packed and waiting in Istanbul. I paid my man in Afyon three thousand dollars for the six hundred kilos of opium. Plus a thousand for the conversion."

"You paid fifty doltars a kilo for opium? The Turkish government only pays ten to fifteen."

"It's a crime, I know, but what could I do? The Turks first took our land, now they overcharge us for its produce. The least we can do is to make something out of it."

"I admire your patriotism, Nubar, but I'm out of the game. You'll have to find somebody else."

"How can I? You're my good friend. You know the right people. Every day that goes by increases the risk. Papademas is still in their hands, who knows how much he's talked? But he never knew you, you're clean, I can trust you."

"I'm still not interested."

Nubar went right on.

120

"When I saw you losing all that lovely dough to that cuckold Kommenos and his bitch of a wife, the cunt Luigi's screwing these days, I said to myself: Look here, Markos is a good sort, you've been in some tough spots together and he's never let you down. You've got a plum in your hands and you don't want the undeserving to get a bite of it. And then I remembered Napoli and how you saved my life there when the Mafia boys turned nasty. . . ."

Mark instinctively glanced down at the empty sleeve. The Armenian, depending on the company he was in, might claim that he had lost his arm fighting with the partisans or the royalist army.

"You don't owe me anything, Nubar."

"You were good to poor Sarkis, I'll always owe you for that."

"I know you mean well, but I'm still not interested."

"And Markos—"

"Yes?"

"Forget Jennie, can't you? We're only businessmen, after all. There's a demand, we supply."

Mark heard the name and saw again the dead body, the red hair and the beautiful breasts, the glazed eyes staring at him for eternity.

"Leave me alone, Nubar, won't you? I've explained this before, I've squared it with you, now leave me alone."

"Never mind all that. If you're joining the Lions, and I think you've a good chance, you won't want to be the poor boy of the family, will you? I know you, Markos, I've worked with you—you're proud. You won't like to go running to your father-in-law to borrow money every time Katia flies to Paris or New York to do a little shopping. The Lionesses are used to such jaunts—for them, it's like a trip to the supermarket."

Mark looked at the platinum watch: his talisman. It was the first thing he'd bought after he walked out of a Geneva Bank, collecting his share from the first job. The watch was the most expensive in the shop; he had bought it in three minutes, joyfully extravagant, even throwing his old watch into the lake. Well, everything came to an end, sooner or later.

"I know you mean well, but no. Good night, Nubar."

The Armenian gripped Mark's arm with his only hand.

"If you change your mind, you'll have to change it fast. I've got to send word soon to Polis. The patient's in a critical state and there may have to be an emergency operation. If you're not coming in it'll have to be another—but I shan't feel so sure about it then. So think quickly, will you?"

Mark heard the timid tap on the door and waited, listening. The tap came again, louder.

He opened the door.

Isabel stood in front of him, pale in the light, her golden hair shining on her shoulders. She was wearing a simple dress of white linen that buttoned down the front and made her look very innocent, very girlish.

"I came to see the mermaid," she said, an actress speaking her lines a little too carefully. "You remember inviting me, don't you? You owe me a drink, you promised me one."

For a moment he was lost.

"Come," he said finally. He took her hand and lifted it. As his lips touched the slender fingers, a wave of tenderness overcame him.

"I'll get some ice," he said, releasing her.

For days he had labored to convince himself that he was better off without her, that she was better off with Hilary, that she would be all right. Every morning he would resolve to call Eva; he would even arrange his files, determined to move to Athens, to find an excuse to travel abroad, as far away from Isabel as the firm would send him. He never called the girl in Athens, he stayed put on Alea as if serving a life sentence.

He mixed the drinks carefully and waited. He could see Isabel examining herself in the mirror.

When he handed her the gin and tonic, she looked at him with candid eyes. He watched her long slim fingers clasping the glass; his eyes moved down to the slender waist, then back up to her face . . . . .

Isabel finished the drink and gave him the glass, trying to appear poised and self-possessed.

"I'd like another," she said and turned again toward the mirror, arranging her hair over her shoulders.

"You look very beautiful," he said as he handed her the drink. He had made it very strong.

"Do I, Mark?"

"The most beautiful woman in the world, *agapoula mou.*"

"Greek is a loving language. Tell me more in your language."

"Isabel, *agapoula mou, moroudaki mou, kouklitsa mou.*"

"You like me, Mark, don't you?"

"I'm crazy about you."

She finished her drink quickly and set down the glass.

Then she began unbuttoning her white dress, very slowly, starting from the top, going all the way down. She was wearing nothing underneath. She held out her arms.

He picked her up and carried her to the bed, knelt by her side and kissed her mouth, neck, shoulders, nuzzled his head between her breasts.

"Dear Mark."

He took off his clothes, lay by her side and drew her into his arms.

"*Agapoula mou.*"

122

He kissed her deep and sweet in the mouth, crushing her head against the pillows, his hands traveling down her perfect body, over her hips, between her thighs.

"I want you, Mark. I need you," she whispered. "Please love me."

He kissed her on the throat, his hand still stroking gently, giving her time, feeling her body tense with excitement.

As Isabel ran her fingers through his hair and down his back, she was intensely aware of his hand brushing gently between her legs. Her skin tingled; her hips moved.

"Take me, love me, Mark."

She half opened her mouth and breathed in expectantly. *I must be brave, it's for Mark, just this first time. It's so easy, really, it must be, and it's Mark I love, Mark who loves me.*

She opened her eyes and saw his face, flushed with passion; felt his hardness besieging her—and down she fell into the abyss, blinded by circles of snow stained with crimson. . . .

"No!" she shouted, beating desperately with her fists on the chest of her tormentor.

Mark saw the terror in her eyes, felt her body turn cold and dead even as he released it.

"I can't," she sobbed.

He left her crying and pulled the sheet over her and walked out of the room. He could still hear her bitter weeping; he went into the bathroom and turned on the shower hard, so that her sound was lost in the sound of the water splashing on his back.

When he came out there was no Isabel anywhere and he felt numb and dull, shattered into a thousand pieces. He poured himself a drink and wandered from room to room, unable to understand, his mind unfocused.

He went to the telephone and dialed Nubar at the Kalamos Village.

"You can count me in," he said. "I've changed my mind." He put down the receiver before the Armenian could reply.

At the Villa Artemis he was received by Felix.

"The Baroness is watching a film, Mr. Stephanou. She will be pleased to have you join her."

"My pleasure."

"Come with me, sir."

Felix led the way upstairs, opened a wardrobe and handed Mark a kimono.

"You'll be sitting on cushions in the screening room, sir. You'll be more comfortable in this."

Mark took off his jacket and Felix at once started unbuttoning his shirt.

123

Mark suffered him, but when he moved to take off the trousers, Mark brushed Felix aside and removed them himself. The eunuch went down to the floor and unlaced his shoes.

Mark put on the kimono. It was of soft, brightly colored silk.

"How many will be watching the film?" he asked.

"The Baroness and her secretary, sir."

Was she really deranged? he wondered. Was that why the Old Man protected her so carefully? He thought of the portrait he had seen, the lustrous eyes, the full breasts . . . Suddenly he saw Isabel's small, perfect breasts and he felt numb.

"It's a film about vampires," Felix was saying. "You'll like it, sir."

"Tonight I could jump from the ramparts into the sea and like it."

The screening room was lit only by the film; he couldn't see his way. A woman was screaming on the soundtrack.

Felix guided him forward onto the floor, pushed several cushions toward him, brought him a drink and left.

As his eyes grew accustomed to the dark, Mark looked around for the Baroness and Inge. The first thing he saw was an animal stretched out a few feet away from him, it could have been a dog—no, a cat, but much larger. At its side was the Baroness, lying behind Mark on cushions, her eyes fixed on the screen. He lifted a hand in salutation, but she made no response.

Inge, who was sitting near her, came over to him and sat down on one of his cushions.

"How's your drink?" she asked.

"It's fine."

"The film will be over soon."

"I'm in no hurry."

"The best part is yet to come."

"The best part always is," he said.

She got up and left the room.

On the screen a black creature was sucking at the throat of the girl, blood dripping from its jaws on to her white breasts.

Mark watched, but he was not there, he was in Istanbul, where Nubar's merchandise was waiting. The *World Seafarer*, unloading at Odessa, would soon be sailing down the Straits, past Alea, heading for Libya to reload. Never before had Mark felt so alone, so much on his own.

The film came to an end and a red spotlight fell on the platform beneath the screen. A tall woman—heavily made up, with blonde curls, wearing exaggerated high heels and a flowing blue dress—came on the stage and began a striptease to taped music.

It was Felix, of course. His impersonation was clumsy, but Mark was surprised at how seriously he went about his business. He executed a particularly high kick, and Mark laughed.

124

No response came from behind him.

Felix lifted the hem of his dress, exposing black lace panties. But as he pulled the garment over his head his blonde wig came off, and, for the first time, Mark heard the husky laughter of the Baroness.

"He's the best impersonator I've ever seen," he said.

She didn't reply.

Felix, who had a dog collar around his neck, went down on his knees, lifted his head, and brayed like a donkey.

Inge came onstage dressed as a circus ringmaster, whip in hand.

"You can do better than that, beast!"

She cracked the whip in the air. Felix looked up and pulled down his panties with both hands.

Mark, watching the spectacle, felt the Baroness gliding next to him.

"Now eat your hay," said Inge.

She kicked a bucket in front of Felix, who tried to munch at it.

"Eat, beast!"

As the whip came down on the exposed rump, a hand gripped Mark beneath the silky kimono. He was stiff and it hurt terribly.

12

Hilary put his hand on her knee and patted it gently.

"Tender paw," he whispered, but Isabel did not react.

"You've still got good old Dr. Grey-Elephant on your side. I want to help—you know that, Isa, don't you?"

Isabel made no answer. She had lost weight, she was too thin. Hilary didn't like the way she looked.

"I think I should get the quack to have a look at you."

"It's not necessary. I'll be all right."

"We must both try to be sensible, you know."

Being sensible was not quite Hilary's line, but Isabel was his responsibility. He was husband and father and brother and the only friend she had. At first he had thought she might have picked up some virus which would account for the shadows under her eyes, but then he recognized her overwhelming unhappiness and understood that it was something quite different. He had met Mark a few days ago, by chance; they had been ill at ease with each other and neither of them had mentioned Isabel.

Hilary tried a smile.

"I'm your friend, Isa, love. Whatever happens, I'm your friend. Think of all we've been through together, the places we've seen, our travels in the desert, the picture I took of you with the little white camel at Ur. . . ."

He felt guilty—for a thousand small failures, for promising her more than he could ever give, for never trying hard enough. When it had finally dawned on him that Isabel wasn't seeing Mark any more, that she was alone, he started going to the beach with her, taking her out in the evening, cutting down on his drinking at Kavouras', sometimes taking her to the Poseidon, which he knew she liked better. Thinking back over the summer, thinking of how he had encouraged her to go out with Mark, he felt that once again he had done the wrong thing.

They left Josephine in a side street and walked down to the *plateia* and the harbor. It was the fourteenth of August, the Eve of the Feast of Our Lady, and pilgrims had come to the island to take part in the celebrations, to pass under the icon, to ask the Mother of God to heal their sick, comfort them in their bereavements, bless them in the coming year. They came in caiques and steamers and with them came the holiday makers from Athens and the neighboring islands.

Strings of bright pennants were suspended across the streets from wall to wall; from the upper windows of the dazzling white houses hung the *Yalanoleuki*, the blue and white flag, the traditional cross prominent at the top of each flagpole. Slogans of the regime were painted blue against the white walls: *Long Live the 21st of April, Hellas Hellinon Christianon, Long Live the National Army, Long Live the Greek Fatherland.* Hilary explained the slogans and chattered about the festival, then helped Isabel onto a low wall so she could see over the heads of the people in front.

The military band played patriotic songs and martial music; the tourist police, in white gloves and white helmets, pushed back the crowds as a contingent of officers and men of the Royal Navy marched to the quay-side and formed up in four ranks. The caiques and other craft sounded their sirens as the motor launch carrying the icon of Our Lady the Compassionate rounded the promontory of the lighthouse. The bells in the cathedral tower began to peal; the guns from a frigate in the harbor and the cannons from the ramparts fired a welcoming salvo. The band crashed into the national anthem, the crowds stood at attention as the launch touched the quay-side where the mitered archbishop, wearing golden vestments and carrying a golden scepter, was waiting, flanked by his clergy, to receive the Holy Virgin.

Now over the amplifiers came the chanting of the priests, intoning the Byzantine hymns. The archbishop lifted up his hands, crossed himself three times, and kissed the painted wood. Four sailors raised the holy relic high above their heads, its golden bejeweled canopy shining in the afternoon sun. First marched the naval party flanking the four sailors bearing aloft their sacred burden, then came the clergy, then the army officers, then the notables of the town. The pilgrims stood in a thick, straggling line in the middle of the road along which the procession would pass on its way to the cathedral; as the icon approached.they fell to the ground and Our Lady the Compassionate passed over them. A mother wailed loudly, clasping her paralyzed child in her arms; a handsome young man dragged his withered legs after him; an old man was helped by his family to lie down and wait with the rest for the passing of the *Panayia Eleousa*.

Hilary, holding Isabel firmly by the hand, joined the people ascending the hill to the cathedral. Our Lady passed; the fair was under way. On each side of the road the shops exhibited merchandise, the stalls began selling soft drinks, cotton candy, ice cream, sweets—*lokmades, loukoumia, karamelles*—and some sideshows opened for business. Hilary paid two drachmas for a lovebird to pick out his fortune from a basketful of paper scraps. *Soon you will go on a long journey with a woman in green.*

"That's Josephine, of course," he said. "You don't wear green, Isabel, do you?"

He expected her to be amused by the bright-eyed little creature busily dispensing destinies with its sharp, curved beak, but she shook her head and he had to lead her away. One stall was festooned with pictures of saints, film stars, athletes, the prime minister, the archbishop, and other celebrities, and you could have your photograph taken inside. An old man sold small crosses carved in olive wood; a little girl sold white wax candles and bunches of jasmine.

"Buy me a candle, Hilary," said Isabel. He paid six drachmas for a large candle and a small bunch of flowers.

Some food stalls were already serving customers, and the smell of frying olive oil and onions wafted down the hill. From the loudspeakers came the chanting and praying; now and then the people outside the cathedral would cross themselves and mutter rapidly under their breath. They had been brought up in the Church, they were very businesslike about it all.

"You don't want to go up to the cathedral now, Isabel, do you?"

"May I? To light my candle?"

The crowds were densest in the courtyard before St. Nicholas and on the other side of the hill. Some of the pilgrims were camping under the trees with their mules, donkeys, cows, goats, and sheep.

As the icon was placed on a table before the doors of the cathedral, the faithful pressed forward to say their prayers and kiss it. Some people opened a way for Hilary and Isabel, but they soon found themselves in the middle of a throng that bore them this way and that, making retreat impossible, jostling and shoving so that their hands were pulled apart. Hilary found himself separated from Isabel by a solid barrier of bodies.

127

"Isabel!"

There was no way she could hear him; she was being carried further and further away from him by the living current. Isabel, at first exhilarated by the noise and confusion, found herself panicking as she was pushed backward and forward like flotsam tossed upon a restless tide, until, suddenly, she found herself nearing the icon's gorgeous canopy. The crowd hemmed her in and she had to go forward, yet the icon itself seemed to be drawing her near, claiming her. Black-kerchiefed women in front of her murmured prayers, bowed down and touched the dark ancient wood with their lips. Isabel knew the icon's spare, angular features from the chapel on the east coast. Two angels supported the holy head as the *Panayia* lay on her bed asleep; Isabel placed her bunch of jasmine in front of her along with the honeysuckle, the roses, the wild lilies, the cyclamen, the carnations . . . Her limnéd soul struggled to be free! *Holy Mary, Mother of God, pray for us sinners, now and at the hour of our death . . .*

The lower half of the icon was blurred with a film of red grease from the imprint of many lips. Isabel leaned forward, but her faith failed her and she could not kiss it. Others surged to take her place, elbowing her away, and she moved on, still holding her candle.

Inside the cathedral the archbishop was intoning the *hesperinos* at the high altar, and Father Athanasios moved among the worshipers, his lips moving silently, swinging the censer over the bowed heads until the air was heavy with incense. Isabel lit her candle and placed it carefully in one of the sconces; as she turned to go, she saw Zafiro absorbed in prayer, hands clasped, eyes closed.

Isabel slipped out the side door and wandered aimlessly among the pilgrims. The *bouzouki* bands were playing now, she could hear the waterfront songs so beloved by the Greeks. Men and women, joining hands in a circle, danced the *kalamatianos* while their children played on the swings and merry-go-rounds or rode hired donkeys up the hill and back. The fourteenth of August was a fast day, but the butchers, their white aprons stained red, were busily slaughtering kids, lambs, and calves. Worshipers coming out of the church stopped to buy chunks of the fresh, raw meat to take home and prepare for tomorrow's festive meal. For fifteen days the more devout among them had not touched meat or cheese or milk or eggs; tomorrow, after partaking of the Holy Sacrament, they would make up for their abstinence.

Isabel was moving away, trying to escape, when she saw the tall, dour peasant who had won the raffle earlier that day: the little white goat with liquid amber eyes, the kid she had petted at Kavouras'. Isabel saw it all. The butcher, the knife between his teeth, seized the front legs and brought the animal to its knees with a thud, pressing its shoulders hard against the ground while the peasant held its hind legs tight. The butcher took the muzzle, forced the head back, and slit the throat; the thick blood pooled on the ground and the flies buzzed greedily around it. The butcher wiped his knife on the rough white coat of the carcass, then straightened up and lit a cigarette. The animal was still twitching, its gentle eyes glazed in death.

Dusk was falling and Isabel drifted down to the harbor and along the thronged corniche, passed under the ramparts, walked into the old quarter, lingered beside the Venetian fountain, leaning against the marble and trailing her fingers in the cool water. *Here's the smell of the blood still.* . . . She looked around wildly, then started off again, almost running. She was out of the town, on the road to the *kalivi*, but still she heard the tumult behind her; when she reached the fork in the road, she chose the hill.

She was tired now and walked more slowly, bracing her knees for the climb. The lights were on in some of the cottages, but Clive's house was dark. A hare in front of her bounded into the night; an owl looked down at her from a branch above her head. . . . Isabel thought she saw a flash of light from the captain's mansion. Mark never came to the Akroyiali Beach, she hadn't seen him for days. She left the road and took the narrow path leading down to the old house, defying the darkness, pushing ahead eagerly now.

She left the path and walked beneath the trees; the ground was soft with pine needles and she stretched out on it, suddenly exhausted. The mountain air was cool after the heat of the day, the sounds of the night were hushed and secret, blurred shapes flickered, undefined, as though in a dream. . . .

When Isabel opened her eyes she was conscious of someone moving along the path quite near her. At once she was certain it was not Mark. The man was carrying something heavy, stooping slightly under the burden as he advanced slowly toward the dark house. But he did not approach the front door; instead, he laboriously hefted his load down the steps to the basement. Isabel waited, still hidden among the trees, now fully awake. She heard the wooden door of the basement creak, saw a gleam of light playing upon the trees nearby. Then the light went out and she heard the door being shut, the rattle of the padlock.

The man climbed the steps and started walking up the path. The moon had risen and Isabel saw him clearly. It was Jason, Katia's brother, the brave student who had been arrested in Athens and was now confined to the island. Mark must know about the basement, Mark was in this, he couldn't pretend any more to her. Dear Mark . . .

Isabel got up, went to the front door, knocked with her fists. There were no lights, there was no answer. *I must find him tonight, I must tell him now, now I am ready for him, now I know I can.*

She took the path Clive had told her led through the forest to the other side of the island, to the chapel and the Kalamos Village. It was a stony, meandering path beset with thorn bushes, the loose stones were sharp and treacherous under her feet. Several times she lost her balance and fell on hands and knees, bruising herself. The moon made the path white, but the trees and bushes merged to form grotesque shapes. The twisted ribbon of moonlight in front of her beckoned her and she pressed doggedly forward, conscious of nothing but her desire to find Mark. Running, she stumbled against a boulder and sank down, feeling the blood oozing from a cut on her knee. She stayed huddled there, gathering her strength.

Isabel started walking again. She was weak but determined; when she reached the brow of the hill, the salt breeze from the other coast brushed against her face. The moon was hidden behind the Black Mountain, but down by the dark mass of the sea the lights of the Kalamos Village shone out—from the gardens, from the hotel entrance, from a window here and there. Isabel held her breath; listening, she heard no human sound, only the rustling of the breeze among the branches. She picked her way carefully along the dark path, descended to level ground, and walked through the gates into the village.

Seeing a light at the entrance of the hotel, she headed for the reception hall. A night porter at the desk raised his eyes, looked at her sleepily and waited. But only her mind asked, no words came from her mouth: *You haven't seen Mr. Stephanou, have you? No, I thought not. . . .*

She stepped back from the desk. The reception hall was vast, all black marble and mirrors. Isabel saw herself in them, her dress torn, her hair tangled, her arms and legs scratched and bleeding, her face dirty and distraught. The night porter went back to his newspaper, not interested in her, and she wandered outside.

It was still very dark, but there was light in some of the bungalows down by the sea; perhaps he was there, perhaps she would find him now. A man lay snoring on the grass in front of one of the small houses; Isabel walked through the open door of a bungalow, carefully threading her way among the sleeping bodies on the floor.

She walked down to the beach and drifted into the open-air bar. Two girls in bikinis were asleep on a bench, but they wouldn't know. . . . She saw a man lying in a deck chair on the beach—he might have word for her, he might know Mark. She went to the chair and put her hand on his shoulder. But the head drooped forward; the eyes in the night face were closed tight. . . .

She took the coast road, away from the Kalamos Village. On the cliffs the Chapel of Our Lady seemed desolate, robbed of its treasure, and Isabel hurried past it. . . . She would climb the cliffs of Glaros Bay and wait for the bird colony to wake up with the first sun and, perhaps, one of the gulls might be Jemima.

The dawn was breaking; a feathery streak of crimson slashed against the eastern horizon had reached the mountain peaks of other islands beyond. Below the cliffs the sea was gray and smooth and suddenly Isabel saw, far from the shore, a small black speck, a moving object—a boat, surely. It slid slowly across the water, growing larger as it approached the land. A man was sitting in the bow, another man was rowing. Could it be Mark? Out on a secret errand, working quietly under cover of the night, risking his life? If he were carrying arms or ammunition, if he were found out, if he were captured . . . She tried to dismiss her fears, to be reasonable. The men in the boat were probably fishermen, bringing in their catch. The world was waking up, Mark was far away, she could not reach him. Surely these men were fishermen—Andreas, perhaps, and Tryfon, who kept his boat down there.

The dove-gray sky began to change a little and soon the peach-blossom pink turned a magnificent gold. A large bush marked the end of the forest, half of it overhanging the cliff; Isabel took hold of the branches, parted them and looked down. The drop to the sea below was easily two hundred feet. The water was gray and green in patches and rippled in the morning breeze, but further out it was smooth and silver. At the foot of the cliff she could see the fishermen's hut and the path winding upward, the one she and Mark had climbed; she could see one of the fishing boats up on the shingle and the racks for nets outside the hut. If she got down there . . . She could wait for the fishermen to go, climb down, push the boat off by herself, get in it, and float out to the open sea.

Her grasp tightened on the parted branches as she watched the boat gliding into the shallows. The man at the oars stood up. She recognized Mark. *I was right! I'll call down to him. . . .*

At that moment she heard a man's voice shouting from an overhanging platform of rock halfway down the cliff. As he called, he fired a round of gunfire in front of the boat. The bullets spattered in the shallow water, Mark slowly raised his hands, Isabel took an instinctive step forward. Her foot dislodged a stone which rolled down the cliff; a flurry of gulls rose with harsh cries.

What happened next seemed a matter of seconds. The man with the gun stiffened and swiveled around, but an overhanging branch obscured his face and she could not see who it was. Immediately there came a shot from below. Isabel saw the man's body twist in a desperate effort to stay balanced on the rocky platform; she saw it hurtle through the air, the right hand still clutching the gun as it spun down into emptiness. She closed her eyes tight and kept them closed until she heard the splash as the body hit the sea far beneath.

Without looking down again she hurried back to the coast road and stumbled along its dusty length, following one of the parellel ruts worn deep by the wheels of cars and carriages. Every time the road sloped downhill she began to run feebly; when she came to a difficult stretch, she would turn back to see if she were being followed and then push her feet forward again.

Nobody followed her, and she met no one on the way.

Part Three

□

13

Felix worked with expert hands on her breasts, her stomach muscles, around the hips and down the thighs, all the length of her legs. From time to time he would stop to apply more oil, then he would resume his ministrations, kneading and rubbing the tawny flesh. He moved the supple arms and legs, pushed her over onto her stomach, and began working on the shoulders, the back, the hips, and buttocks. Kriton had been crazy about her buttocks. As she crouched on all fours on the bed, he would grab at her rump the whole time. The Baron had been more conventional; if he wasn't sucking her, he was masturbating.

Suddenly the Baroness sat up. The puma, couched on the floor at the far end of the large bathroom, stared at her with its secret jungle eyes.

"Did you feed her today, Felix?"

"No, madame."

"Be careful, Felix. One day I shall tie you up and offer you for meat."

"You told me not to feed her, madame, if you recall."

"Did I, Felix? Well, you give her that plump lamb tonight, the one with the black ears."

The Baroness pushed aside her blond attendant, got off the couch, and examined herself in the mirrors. The guests had all left. She was alone with Inge and Felix, and Ted and Terry would be coming soon. If Brother Leon should suddenly break in upon them, he might be provoked to violence. She smiled. Perhaps one night she would arrange for Brother Leon to break in upon them.

She caressed her breasts, rubbing her palms against the nipples. Why hadn't they let her nurse him? The boy had gone and was not coming back; they kept on about it and she had pretended to believe them and Brother Leon, to reward her, took her out to a nightclub and let her invite the *artiste* back to the hotel for the night. They all tried to deceive her, but Angela knew that Philip was in Egali, waiting for her. She hadn't nursed him for such a long time, he must be getting hungry. And very lonely.

She moved closer to the mirror, put both hands under her breasts, hugging them, feeling the texture, the elasticity. Both men and women had loved them

135

and sometimes had handled them too roughly, biting and scratching and spoiling them. The nipples were firm and the areolas large and dark, but as she stroked the breasts, she thought that the suppleness had lessened, surely they would begin to sag in a year or two. She lifted her arms and looked at her body from all angles in the mirrors lining the walls: the curve of the hips was full but not exaggerated, the thigh-line flowed smoothly from the hips, the legs were strong and feminine.

Felix came toward her, but she waved him away. She didn't want her neck massaged, she never liked the blond man to massage her neck; she could do it herself another time, when only she could see the telltale lines. She went to the deep pink marble bath and Felix helped her to climb in. He knelt by her side, soaped a large sponge and smoothed it over her back, under her armpits, between her breasts and buttocks and thighs. Then he rinsed the soap away, helped her out of the bath, wrapped her in a robe and led her to a couch he had covered with soft towels.

"Isabel Grey is beautiful, don't you think so, Felix?"

"Yes, madame."

"Did you notice how she tasted her drink?"

"As if she were sipping a Borgia brew, madame."

"You could have fixed her up if I'd thought of it in time, couldn't you, Felix?"

"I suppose so, madame."

He went to the dressing table and chose a scarlet varnish; then he trimmed her toenails a little and began painting them.

"Tell me, Felix, was I in good face this evening?"

"Very good, madame."

"Did I behave correctly?"

"Perfectly, madame."

"You don't think any of that crowd suspects, do you?"

"No, madame."

"I was natural, wasn't I? I shocked them a little, I like to shock them, but I was natural, wasn't I?"

"Very natural, madame."

"I think Zurich was good for me, Felix. You will tell me when I should go there again, won't you?"

"I will tell you, madame."

"I think, Felix, you're the best inheritance the Baron left to me."

"I am your servant, madame."

"You mean my slave, Felix. You are loyal to me, aren't you? Brother Leon didn't ask you to spy on me, did he?"

"I am in your hands, madame."

"If you deceive me you will die in my hands, Felix. My puma will look after you for me if I ask her. Or I could tell Brother Leon what you've been up to."

"Please don't do that, madame. Please."

She gave him her other foot and the blond man concentrated on painting the nails.

"Was it in Berlin the Baron picked you up, Felix?"

"Hamburg, madame."

"Ah, yes. I always forget, don't I? In the Two Foxes Bar, I think?"

"No. In the Three Crocodiles, madame."

"Did you make much money in Berlin, Felix?"

"Hamburg, madame. Not very much. It was very difficult just after the war."

"And you never saw the SS man again?"

"He was tried and executed by the Allies, madame."

"For what he did to you and the girl?"

"For other things, madame. I never told anybody."

"This castration, Felix—did he cut off your balls by himself?"

"He had me tied up first, madame."

"And was the girl watching?"

"They forced her to watch. Then he shot her through the stomach."

"A lingering death, Felix?"

"She was screaming for a long time, madame."

Angela's fingers beat a nervous rhythm on the couch.

"Mark is not coming tonight, Felix. He's all right, but he's not one of us, is he, Felix?"

"I thought he wouldn't be, madame."

"He's a good fuck, Felix. Did you notice him at the party? A killer, he looked a killer. It would be a pity if Brother Leon got him in the end, wouldn't it?"

"Yes, madame."

"And probably he is a killer—did I tell you what he asked me this afternoon? To say that he was here with us the whole of last night and all this morning. What time did I ring for you this morning, Felix? He had gone by then."

"It was almost five, madame. I saw him slipping away just after midnight, after you'd fallen asleep."

"I wonder whether I should help him."

"If you feel the need for his company, madame, perhaps you should."

"You didn't see him talking to Isabel at the party, did you, Felix?"

"No, madame. I had the impression he was avoiding her."

"I thought so, too. And the reports—what do our spies report?"

"They haven't seen each other for over a month."

"I think we'd better give him the alibi, Felix."

"I should think so, madame."

"Hilary Grey—did you notice Hil? Isabel's too beautiful for him, don't you think so?"

137

"Yes, madame."

"What do you think happens when he gets her in bed, Felix? Do you think she cries? She looks the type who would. . . . That white dress suited her. She's tall and fair and she looked beautiful in it, but she's probably cold, probably she never allows herself to be fucked properly. . . . I kissed her cheek, Felix, and it was like cool satin. And the way she stood—so erect, staring into the distance while Hil chattered on. He seemed different, not the same as I remember him."

"Then you knew him before, madame?"

"Years ago he was a lover of mine, a good one. Now he's changed—he's older, he's drinking too much. Brother Leon was furious with me for offering the *kalivi*."

"When will he be coming to us, madame?"

"Soon, Felix, soon."

"I hope he doesn't find out about Mark, madame."

"Mark's a good fucker, he's coming tomorrow evening. I'll ask Inge to join us—do you think he'll disapprove?"

"I shouldn't think so, madame."

"He likes only women, doesn't he, Felix?"

"All our reports indicate that, madame."

"Explain this to Inge. Let her be ready."

"I understand, madame."

"And, Felix, you've been good. Tomorrow you may watch."

"Thank you, madame."

He put a silk cape round her shoulders and began brushing her hair.

"Inge, my girl Inge, do you think she's very beautiful?"

"Not very, madame." This was the correct answer.

"But she's young, isn't she? Twenty, twenty-one?"

"At least twenty-four, I should think, madame."

"What is she wearing tonight, Felix?"

"She's not wearing anything, madame, except a ribbon. She's lying on the velvet couch, posing as Olympia."

"I shall be a nun tonight, Felix."

"Black is very becoming to you, madame."

The Baroness unwrapped herself and stood on the scales. She had been dieting for the past two weeks, but found that she had lost very little weight.

"You're not working hard enough, Felix. Or is it the highballs?"

"It could be the highballs, madame."

She put on a black lace brassiere, then changed her mind and threw it on the chair where the lace panties were.

"A good nun doesn't need these things, Felix, does she? Nothing shows under the habit."

138

She sent Felix to bring her the nun's habit and he helped her to put it on. At first she thought she wouldn't use markeup, but her face looked too stark against the black garment. She looked at the face, striking and well preserved with massage and creams and oils, but the eyes were too bright and she could see the net of fine lines spreading underneath and at the outer corners.

Quickly she began opening her jars and tubes, working to camouflage the lines; she could see the beginnings of crepiness in her neck, and her chin was loosening a fraction.

"You're certain I was in good face at the party, Felix?"

"You were perfect, madame."

"I looked old. And you noticed it, Felix. You're waiting for me to become old, Felix."

"You were perfect, madame."

"Don't provoke me, Felix."

"I said you were perfect, madame."

"Because I shall tie you up and make you cry again, Felix."

"I know, madame."

She sent him to fetch her the ivory crucifix, then she allowed him to slip the beads and crucifix over the headdress, arranging them on her breast.

"Did the brothers come tonight, Felix?"

"I haven't seen them, madame."

"They will, they will. Which of the two do you like better, Ted or Terry?"

"There is little to choose, madame."

"There's a chance for you there. I'm sure they're both nice boys, they'd go crazy over your new equipment."

"I haven't tried, madame."

"Try, Felix, try. Balls or no balls, nothing happens unless one tries."

She walked over to the puma and took the soft-furred feline head between her hands.

"My puma is hungry, Felix. Take her and introduce her to her supper. I'm a nun tonight, it's too much for a nun to watch. You watch her make the kill. After that, bring her back to me to smell my guests, to see which ones she doesn't like."

Hilary emptied his glass and left the bar. He was a little unsteady on his feet, but his mind was clear. He had sent Isabel home with Clive after the cocktail party at the Villa Artemis. A drink by himself, that's what he wanted, his unhappiness shared by no one. When people tried to talk to him he walked off, drinking his way from Kavouras' to the Two Brothers. But the brothers began to shut the bar and pushed him out. It was late and the boys had a date, Ted reeking with perfume, Terry had put on his cowboy leathers.

Hilary started walking toward the town, then stopped in the middle of the deserted street, waiting for a taxi or a carriage, talking to himself. Why, she must be waiting for me. All this being cool to me and attentive to Isabel was a bluff, a smoke screen—why did she lend me the bungalow if she didn't want me to come back to her? It was the old game again, he knew his girl and what she liked. . . .

Hilary suddenly felt keyed up, impatient, remembering the immense black eyes, the luxuriant breasts. *"Bite me, Hil. . ."*

A carriage stopped for him. What better thing could she hope to happen tonight than for her old teddy bear to go back and screw her? He was good at screwing her, she couldn't have forgotten that. Hilary smiled to himself. He *should* have kept a journal, a sentimental journal, an erotic journal.

The carriage took the track road to the Villa Artemis. When Hilary saw the lighted arches, he called to the driver, paid him, and got out to walk the rest of the way. He was surely mistaken, but he felt that he could, even now, breathe in the heady perfume emanating from Angela's body. How idiotic he had been to lose contact with her, to give up his claims on her.

He remembered reading the news in the paper: Angela had married Baron Ludwig von Gotthard—"for the sake of her son," the newspaper quoted Mr. Leonides as saying. When he heard about her divorce, he sat down and wrote a long letter.

The wheel had been spun, the cycle was almost completed. . . . He was afraid of the puma and avoided the front door, went to the terrace and pushed open the French windows.

Angela was standing in the center of the room, hands folded over her breast, dressed in a nun's habit. She stared blankly at him and he stopped, perplexed. For a moment he wavered; then he opened his arms, hurried to her, embraced her.

"Angela!"

The Baroness allowed him to kiss her on the cheek, on the neck, then guided him to a sofa.

"Let me get you a drink," she said. "I'll get one for myself, too."

"Thank you. Whiskey, if you please."

She summoned Felix, who reappeared in moments with the drinks.

"It's only you and me tonight," she said, and for the moment she believed it.

Hilary raised his glass, but he could find no words to toast her with. Why was she dressed like this? What was wrong with her?

Angela's eyes softened and she smiled.

"Hil, honey, I'm so happy to see you again. I was certain you'd turn up one day."

She put her hand on his knee.

140

"They made me leave the country and you didn't care," he said. "I wrote once, but you didn't answer."

"I waited for you to come." She took his hand and brought it to her lips. But when Hilary turned to embrace her, she moved away.

Hilary moved closer, then eased himself down onto the floor, and folded his arms on her lap.

Angela caressed his forehead, smoothed his hair back—once this man had been a favorite lover—not this man, but another Hilary, younger, confident, flamboyant. He belonged to the better days, before the headaches started, before her troubles really began.

"You said in your letter that you still loved me, Hil, and yet you got married—you were lying, weren't you?"

She tugged at his hair gently.

"Why didn't you write before? Where were you when I was sick, when I was alone?"

"I'm sorry about Kriton. . . ."

"Kriton is in paradise, fucking little angels, I'm a nun and I should know."

Hilary leaned back against the couch. The past was gone, he felt old, there were no threads for him to pick up.

Hilary raised his head and looked her in the eyes; perhaps she was mad after all, as they said, but he had to ask, he had to find out.

"When I left you were expecting, you were pregnant, can you hear me? It was our love-child and you said you'd bring it up like a prince."

Angela stiffened and the blank look came into her eyes.

"Philip is all right, Philip is a prince."

"I'm glad. Where is he now?"

"They tell me he's gone, but how could they know? They don't know, I'm the only one who knows."

"You will take me to see him, won't you, Angela?"

"If you're good enough, if you deserve to see my Prince Charming."

Hilary's eyes filled with tears. "My child, *our* boy, Angela."

"You weren't the father. The father was of no consequence, I didn't care for him as I did for you. Philip is my child, now, and no one else's. A marvelous child, a prince, I'm only waiting for him to grow up to take over his empire. He'll be so handsome, he'll have the world at his feet."

Hilary felt numb. He stood up, avoiding her eyes. He wanted to leave, but he lost his way and walked through the archway into another large room. At once the scent of marijuana hit him, sweet and strong; there was a row of narghiles and several people, Ted and Terry among them, were sitting on the floor, smoking contentedly. Hilary backed out into the first room to find Angela kissing Inge on the mouth, one hand between her thighs.

"Let the others wait," she was saying. "We'll borrow Felix's equipment."

As he walked through the French windows, Hilary saw Felix standing beside the lintel, made up and dressed like a follies girl, holding the puma on a golden chain. The animal stretched lazily and flexed its paws; Hilary noticed that the sharp claws were lacquered scarlet.

He walked around the grounds, still dazed, still unable to get things into perspective. The child was not his, it never had been his. She was sick, she was changed, she rejected him now, not even the boy had anything to do with him. He would not go back to the *kalivi* to collect the car, he didn't want to see a single soul. But as he shambled along toward the town his natural resilience kept him going, his mind compensated him for his loss with memories of happier days.

Hilary remembered being with her on the Philopappos, sitting on the wooden bench in the darkness. She had opened his trousers and sat astride him, galloping. She liked to do that, she had done it in the taxi driving her home to her husband and brother Leon, and in the deserted grotto of St. Anthony on Mount Helicon while the rest of their party was out in the sunshine taking snapshots. He remembered that day in her royal golden bed in Egali, when a cable had arrived from the Old Lion announcing that the papers for a new ship to be named after her had been signed in Japan—"Hil honey, I'm a ship now, come and launch me!" Yes, he was her Hil then and her teddy bear. *I should have kept a record. I should have put it all in a personal diary,* la vie amoureuse *and all that.*

14

The Baroness looked at the card again and poured herself a stiff shot of whiskey. Philip? Could it be Philip? Could they have found out and have come to ask questions? She had had to answer a lot of questions in the past—about Nick, the Piraeus boy, and about Kriton's accident. But always Brother Leon had been around to help, truly a lion of formidable strength. She could always refuse to answer the questions, she could insist upon calling her lawyer first. . . .

"Send Felix to me," she ordered the maid. (But Felix had gone to the sea. Inge was with him.) "Tell the superintendent to wait."

As she turned his card over and over in her hands, Angela felt alone, exposed, vulnerable. They had abandoned her, all of them; when the critical moment arrived no one was there to help. She drank off the whiskey, found her blue capsules, and took two to give her courage. Whatever he wanted, this man must not learn her secrets, he must not. Despite all resolutions, she felt herself growing tense and she leaned back in her chair, vague apprehensions crowding her mind. She allowed the capsules five minutes to start working, then told the maid to show him in.

Still seated, she held out her hand.

Superintendent Mikhail Lazaros took it, kissed it, and made a little bow.

"Baroness, I must ask you to forgive this intrusion. I trust that I've not called at an inconvenient time."

His eyes were gray and intelligent, the skin pale and clear, the hair touched with silver at the temples. Angela silently indicated the sofa and he sat down, sighing gently as if exhausted.

"What a lovely room! How fortunate for you, if I may say so—the mistress of this beautiful house. And how doubly fortunate the Baron!"

"I'm divorced."

Lazaros studied her for a moment before responding; having heard about the mad Baroness, he was intrigued by this forbidding woman in the flowing sari of cerise silk.

"Divorced? I didn't know. Forgive me if I distressed you. Doubtless there were sound reasons for your decision."

He contrived to turn this statement into a half-question, but Angela ignored it. He had probably known all along.

"A cigarette, Superintendent?"

"Yes. Thank you."

He took one from the silver box on the table by his side and leaned back as if very tired. Certainly the flight that morning from Athens, the strain of establishing his authority at the barracks had told on him a little. The apartment seemed comfortable, and after a light lunch he had tried to have his siesta, but Inspector Notaras came in with Mark's statement. *He chose the thing that would hurt me* . . . Mark had always taunted him with his women and now he had chosen this blatant woman to torment him—perhaps he had actually spent the night with this aging apparition, it didn't bear thinking about.

"Alea is a delightful spot. And your villa—so lovely, such a haven of peace!"

The capsules were taking over, and Angela breathed deeply, savoring the relaxation. What did he want, what did he want?

"*Such* a paradise! And yet, Baroness, tragic things do happen here. You will have heard, perhaps, of the death of the castle's young custodian? Some fisherman spotted his body early this morning, washed up in the shallows of Glaros Bay. He had a bullet through his chest and the opinion in some quarters is that he committed suicide."

No. It wasn't Philip he was interested in, and she didn't care about

Demetris. She had had the young man up at the villa; he had been amusing for a night or two, but he wasn't important.

"You sound skeptical, Superintendent. Don't you believe he killed himself?"

"No, Baroness, I don't. There are certain technical indications that simply do not support this convenient theory."

"Really. But how do I come into all this? What brings you here, what do you want from me?"

"Nothing very much, just a little background information which we can use to fit into the larger picture. I shall be most grateful for your cooperation."

He looked at her, his gray eyes all gentle confidence.

"The unfortunate victim was planning to go to the States, Baroness—to do graduate work at Harvard, such a shame. Apparently he was a fine young man, upright, law-abiding, and most patriotic."

"I knew Demetris," said Angela, ringing the bell. "He had other qualities, but I didn't realize he was such a paragon in the community. . . . Tea, coffee, or a drink?"

"Really, I don't think I should impose my presence on you for too long, Baroness. I wouldn't want to ups t your plans for the evening."

She didn't want him to think hat she was in a hurry to get him out, that she had anything to hide.

"Why not have a drink with me first? What would you like?"

"Are you sure, Baroness, I'm not inconveniencing you? I came here uninvited and I should not exploit your kindness."

His elaborate politeness exasperated her.

"Quite sure, Superintendent."

"May I have a whiskey, then?"

"Of course. How do you like it?"

"With a little water and lots of ice, if I may."

He rolled the whiskey on his tongue, savoring it. Angela was looking out across the smooth lawns and terraces toward the sea; he studied her unobtrusively, wondering how mad she really was and how mad she pretended to be. The hand holding her drink was steady, and he noticed the long fingers, the nails lacquered crimson. She was a handsome woman in a lavish, theatrical way, but there was a kind of stiffness behind the facade. She was like an animated puppet whose strings were pulled by some enormous effort of will. There were permanent lines of stress around the sensual mouth, and when she turned to him he noticed how taut were the cords of her throat.

"I've heard, Baroness, that the fair was extraordinarily successful and crowded this year. Did you see much of the festivities? Did you go to the cathedral on the fifteenth? No? Then perhaps you saw the procession of the icon on the eve of the great day?"

"I stayed home, Superintendent. I'm not interested in religious festivals."

"They are *rather* exhausting, I admit. Did you venture into the town at all? The worthy citizens of Alea had a fine old time of it, I gather—unclouded of course, by the knowledge of the tragedy that had taken place in their midst."

"I stayed home," she repeated. "I had a friend for dinner that night, and when the subject came up he didn't want to go into town."

"Didn't he? May I ask who your friend was?"

She settled back on the couch, enjoying her performance.

"Look, Superintendent, I don't usually like giving an account of my actions, but if you're quite certain that this will help you . . ."

"Dear Baroness, how kind of you. Please don't feel that you are obliged to tell me anything, that I am such a tactless barbarian as to intrude into your personal life."

"It's not an intrusion, Superintendent. But can it be treated in confidence, just between the two of us?"

"Absolutely, my dear Baroness, I assure you."

"My friend that night was Markos Stephanou, if the name conveys anything to you."

"Yes, it does. What time did he come here on the night of the fourteenth?"

"About seven o'clock, I think. I don't remember exactly, but certainly no later."

"Seven? Do you dine as early as seven, Baroness?"

"You're very inquisitive. Mr. Stephanou happens to be a particular friend of mine, he comes and goes any time he likes."

"And he left some time after dinner, I suppose?"

Angela smiled confidentially.

"I can see you're determined after all to make me confess all the details of my private life," she said. "No, Markos did not leave after dinner. He spent the night and the following day here, with me."

"Really? The *whole* night *and* the following day?"

"He left in the evening actually. Why do you ask?"

"What time in the evening?"

"I'd say seven, perhaps seven-thirty. Just after my cocktail party."

Lazaros nodded. "What a fortunate man. And how good of you, if I may say so, Baroness. *Such* hospitality!"

Angela, highly pleased with herself, let the innuendo pass.

"Is that it, Superintendent? Or is there anything else you want to ask me?"

"May I? You are very patient with me."

He offered the silver cigarette box to her and when she shook her head, he again fitted one into his amber holder.

"I will be very frank with you, Baroness," he began. "But before I can be frank with you, you must promise to be frank with me. How long have you known Markos?"

"I really couldn't say. Quite some time, anyway."

145

"Could we, perhaps, try to narrow it down a bit? Would you say a year, or six months?"

"No, not so long as that."

"Perhaps a month or so?"

"Yes," Angela said calmly. "I think the time is nearer a month. I consider that to be quite a long time for a friend of mine, Superintendent. I've come to know him well."

"I'm sure you have, Baroness," said Lazaros. "And impressions from you, from a woman of your intelligence and sensibility, might be very interesting."

"Impressions of what?"

"Of Markos. What sort of a man would you say he is?"

"An upstart. And ambitious, quite ambitious."

"You don't think, do you, that Markos would be planning to marry Miss Katia Kommenou? To promote his ambitions? We have it on record that Katia and he are friends. But Katia's father, Mr. Kommenou, who is a serious sort of person and who could recognize the young custodian's solid qualities, had already given his consent to Demetris. Still, the girl refused to accept Demetris and she had her mother on her side and her uncle, your brother, Mr. Leonides. You don't think, do you, that Demetris picked a quarrel with your friend and that this quarrel resulted in his death?"

"It's possible. I wouldn't put it past Markos to shoot it out."

"The police surgeon tells us that Demetris was in the water some twenty-four hours—they found the body early this morning, so he must have been dead at least as early as yesterday morning. We also know that he was seen at approximately nine o'clock on the fourteenth, the eve of the festival, which means that he must have met his fate between then and six o'clock on the morning of the fifteenth. Now, if Markos was with you from seven o'clock until the following evening, the fifteenth, he could hardly be involved, could he?"

Angela smiled and stretched.

"You seem to have reasoned him out of it, anyway."

"True, true . . ." He turned and faced her. "But Demetris was working for us here, you know. On that fatal evening he was instructed to keep a close watch on Markos, to follow him. Now it is possible, Baroness, that Demetris came to his death while following certain police instructions. In any case, we are endeavoring to find out—how shall I put it?—to find out where certain people were and what they were doing on the night of the fourteenth when this unfortunate young man lost his life. I must thank you, Baroness, for your cooperation. No one will be able to question the account you have supplied of your friend's movements. If all the men who might possibly be involved have such comprehensive alibis, we shall, indeed, be faced with an insoluble mystery."

Angela ignored this.

146

"So Markos was being followed," she said. "You must have had some suspicions about him already to have done that. You don't really need my impressions, do you?"

"My department, Baroness, is anxious to collect all the data it can on a person like Markos."

"May I ask exactly what your department is, Superintendent?"

"Certainly you may ask. Narcotics."

"You surprise me. I'm sure I would have noticed from his skin if he had the habit. No, I don't think Markos is an addict, I really don't."

Lazaros winced at the thought of Mark's skin: smooth, olive, suntanned.

"My dear Baroness, drug addicts themselves are not of great interest to my department. Does that sound heartless? It's not meant to. We don't hunt victims, Baroness. But the victims now run into thousands in western Europe and the situation in the States is even worse. Every moment more lives are ruined because some unscrupulous persons, for personal gain, transport and distribute these hellish substances. . . ."

As he talked on, Angela found herself becoming restive under his old-fashioned rhetoric. She stirred impatiently and lit a cigarette.

"Have you ever met a heroin addict, Baroness? I have met many—their misery is indescribable."

He had dropped his affected manner; he sounded oddly sincere.

"It's appalling, really. Drug addicts are pitiful creatures."

He was silent for a moment, remembering a certain young merchant seaman, a nice boy despite his addiction. Lazaros had gone beyond the requirements of his job, paying for medical treatment, even putting him up at his apartment for a few weeks. He remembered the boy down on his knees, begging him to let him go out and get a fix, the very last one. It had been an uphill battle, but people were ungrateful—when he was better, when he had quit it with Lazaros' help, he had gone back to sea and the superintendent had never heard from him again.

"I knew a young man," he said aloud. "A boy, really, who was on heroin. His friends tried to help him, they did help him, but it wasn't a very nice thing to see."

Lazaros stood up, quite upset. What was it about Markos that made him unreasonable?

"The men who destroy human lives for gain—nothing is too bad for them."

Angela accompanied him out onto the terrace. He looked over the parapet, surveyed the path, the cliffs, the landing stage, as though registering everything for future reference.

"You've been most kind, Baroness. And now, if you will excuse me . . ."

"I'm happy to be helpful, Superintendent. But now your business with me is over, isn't it?"

147

She linked her arm through his, tightly enough to make sure he felt the fullness of her breast.

"So it's drugs, is it, that you think he's mixed up with? Very interesting, Superintendent. Well, Markos is coming here tonight—perhaps you'd like to stay a bit and meet him?"

She squeezed his arm.

"I've always admired men who get out into the world, who take risks. I think you must be one of those. Your life must be very exciting, isn't it?"

Lazaros looked at her quizzically.

"There are moments, Baroness, that might certainly be described as exciting."

"Is that meant as a compliment to me?"

She took his hand and found it pale, dry, cool.

"I'm certain, Baroness, that you receive far too many compliments to feel the need of any from a poor policeman."

She smiled, her original diagnosis of him confirmed, and withdrew her arm.

"By the way," he said, "from which point on the cliffs did the late lamented Kriton Kontopoulos *precipitate* himself? Oh, but I shouldn't ask such questions—I withdraw it, particularly as you have been so kind and so patient. And, to be sure, what lovely grounds you have, what a delightful place!"

She smiled graciously and accompanied him to the drawing-room door. In a moment, he would be gone.

"Goodbye, Baroness," he said as he turned to leave. "I can't thank you enough for supplying Markos with such a total clearance—before I had so much as mentioned him."

"It's a good story, Stephanou," said Notaras. "This Baroness must be some lay to keep you busy for so many hours."

He continued searching the rooms Mark used in the captain's mansion. In one drawer he found Mark's passport. He leafed through it, put it in his briefcase.

"I'll take this, jailbird, you won't be needing it now."

But as he stepped onto the veranda he turned back.

"What's down there in the basement, Stephanou?"

"I've no idea. The place is locked up."

"Have you got the key?"

"No, and I haven't seen anybody going in there."

The inspector went down the steps and examined the rusty padlock.

"The skylight is broken," he announced.

"That explains the noises I hear sometimes. Birds must fly in, perhaps swallows nest on the ceiling—see, up there?"

"Bats," said Notaras and left.

Mark was worried. As the occupant of two rooms in the old house, he could easily be made responsible for whatever might be found in the rest of the place. He went upstairs and telephoned the Poseidon.

"What is it?" asked Katia's father.

"I wonder if you happen to have the keys to the basement."

"What do you want them for? The place hasn't been opened for years, I have no idea where the keys are."

Kommenos hung up.

Mark waited for the dark, then went downstairs with a flashlight and some tools he had brought from the car. He tried to force the basement door, but the padlock was well secured.

As he was going up, he worked out the probable dimensions of the basement; he went from room to room looking out for any opening through which he might enter. There was none. He went into the bathroom that had been installed for him when he decided to stay in the house. It was small, he realized—too small to take up the whole space of the original room. Some part of it must have been left closed up. He knocked on the back of the cupboard he used for a linen closet. It was hollow. Using his tools, he removed the shelves and forced the back out. He stepped into the other side and switched on his flashlight, then pushed aside a few pieces of old furniture covered with dust sheets. He soon discovered the trapdoor, which opened easily. Below him in the dark was the basement; he lowered himself down and flashed his light around. As above, there were a few pieces of sheeted furniture.

As he explored the room he wondered how trustworthy Angela would turn out to be. The alibi had been an act of desperation. If she made a mistake, if they found out, they were bound to come back with more questions. Perhaps he had been unwise, but now he had told his story to Notaras and it was too late to think of something else.

He lifted one of the dust sheets. Beneath it was a Roneo duplicating machine, shining in the beam of his flashlight; on the table by its side were piles of blue duplicating paper. Some of them were smudged, and when he touched the smudges with his finger, the ink was fresh. He explored further. In a box he found sections of metal pipe, empty tins, and bottles; in a corner, wrapped up in waterproof material, he found a machine gun. He picked it up and was examining it with his light when suddenly he heard his name being called from the trapdoor above.

It was Katia.

"Wait," he called back to her. "I'll come up."

He put back the gun, covered up the box and the Roneo machine, and climbed up through the trapdoor.

He found Katia stretched out on his divan bed, smirking.

149

"Demetris made such a beautiful corpse at the funeral this afternoon," she said. "I wanted to kiss him, but they wouldn't let me. You weren't there, Markos. Why?"

"Shut up," said Mark and went to wash his hands.

"Perhaps he committed suicide for unrequited love of me. Or perhaps he was shot with that machine gun you were holding."

Mark walked back into the bedroom.

"Is it really true, Markos, that you only like old women?"

She kicked off her shoes, drew her knees under her chin and put her tongue out at him. Mark threw down the towel with which he was drying his hands and began taking off his clothes. He had resisted making love to Katia up to then; her father disapproved of him, she was only a child, his life was complicated enough. But if that was the only way to keep her mouth sealed . . .

"Take off your clothes," he said.

"I'm a virgin. What do you think you're going to do?"

He sheathed his penis in a condom, but when he came to the bed, when he was ready to go inside her, she tore it off.

"I've been on the pill since I met you," she said and lifted up her legs.

He hadn't expected it, but little Katia turned out to be a real virgin. Mark tried to pull back, but she held him with her legs and arms, panting and working at him for some time.

"Not bad for a first-timer."

Katia released him at last and wiped the blood off her thighs with the edge of the coverlet.

"Demetris always came without going inside, he wanted to wait for us to get married first."

She followed Mark to the bathroom.

"My duty is to help the law to catch the guilty, to help justice, to punish the murderer. But as your friend, as your future wife, my duty to you is greater. I shan't tell anybody."

He soaked a hand towel with water, turned his back to her and cleaned his penis thoroughly, not wanting her to see his face.

15

"You just can't wait, can you?"

For an answer, Angela pulled out his shirt, unbuttoned it, and helped him take off his trousers. Mark's skin was cold, and as she touched his unawakened sex, he shuddered; but she took him in her mouth until he was ready, pulled him toward her and guided him in.

"I love you," he said, his mind far away.

"Liar."

He grabbed her by the hair and pulled her head back and kissed her. At first he fought and struggled as if trying to force his body through hers, then he stopped and looked directly into her eyes and she could feel the immobility of the moment, perfect and final.

"Angela," he whispered, his eyes bleak.

"Come!"

He worked on her brutally, sweat streamed down his forehead, but his face was drawn and his skin stayed cold. Suddenly, as if he had lost the thread of an argument, he stopped and stared down at her sadly and felt himself going limp inside her. He rolled off and reached for another cigarette and lay smoking, staring at the ceiling.

"Never mind now," she said. "I'll call Felix to get us a drink."

He disliked Felix snooping around, but before he could stop Angela, she had rung the bell and the blond valet appeared in the doorway. His face was flushed with excitement, and Mark wondered if he had some means of watching them. He wouldn't be surprised.

"Whiskey," she ordered.

Mark was staring at the ceiling, naked, desolate; like the solitary survivor of a great calamity, or someone on the verge of a great disaster. But when the whiskey came, he drank it down and smiled at Angela, an odd, disquieting smile, as though he were seeing her for the first time. His eyes softened and he took her hand and looked at her with a kind of weary affection.

"Why do you smile?" she asked him.

"You said once that we were two of a kind."

"Did I? What a stupid thing to say."

He stroked her hair. "Just tell me what you said to Lazaros, and what he said to you. And ask Felix to bring us more whiskey."

"I will, when you tell me what you were up to that night."

"I was with you here. Don't you remember?"

"And you slipped away after midnight, after I had fallen asleep. Where did you go?"

"To my place."

She smiled. "It would have been a long way from your place to carry a dead man and throw him into the sea."

"Didn't you know? I stayed here with you all that night and all the next day."

"The superintendent told me Demetris was keeping you under surveillance. He caught up with you somewhere at Glaros Bay, didn't he?"

He pulled on a robe and went to the balcony. Damn it all, Glaros Bay had

151

been an emergency, a special case. He drained his drink and went inside and called the eunuch for another.

"Once in Chicago, when I was very young, Markos, I knew a gunman, a real gangster. He'd worked with John Dillinger and he had several bullet holes in his body from the old days—I know it was true, because he showed me."

"Sorry I can't oblige. I'm *not* a gangster." He was only a businessman; there was a demand and there was a supply, just like any other trading anywhere else in the world. He put the glass on the side table, crossed his arms behind his head, stretched his legs.

Angela got up and went to her mirror. Mark was good for her. Her eyes were bright, and her complexion had never looked better. Automatically her left hand went up to her throat; she smoothed the flesh, then picked up a bottle and sprayed herself lavishly with scent. Lazaros was insufferable; she could not forgive his sly smiles, his malicious talk—already she felt forlorn, betrayed, forsaken. Isabel . . . that cold, arrogant woman—perhaps Isabel had spent that fatal evening with Mark, her icy breath blowing on his warm body, chilling his blood, freezing his heart . . . She cursed aloud and went back to the couch.

"You're not carrying on with Isabel Grey, are you? She's mad about you, even that little bitch Katia is mad about you."

"There's always some woman mad about me."

"It must be quite exhausting for you."

"One gets used to it."

Angela wondered to what extent he was being flippant and to what extent he was genuinely proud to be a potent, sought-after male animal.

"The more you treat them rough, the more they fawn on you; the more you neglect them, the more they fall down and worship you—that's how it is, isn't it?"

"That's the way it is."

He seemed preoccupied, and his coldness stimulated her desire. He's here, naked, in my room, she thought. He belongs to me.

She sat on the edge of the couch and leaned over and kissed him lightly on the mouth, stroking his forehead and his cheeks with her fingertips. She pinched his lips and opened his mouth and pushed her fingers inside, but he was unresponsive and kept staring at the ceiling while the gilt clock on the mantlepiece ticked on.

"I thought Isabel looked sick at the party yesterday evening." And aloof. Exquisite and aloof. An authentic modern version of "La Belle Dame sans Merci," wild eyes and all. "Why didn't you tell me you knew each other in Athens?"

Her hand moved over his broad, hard chest, found the nipples and kneaded them, gently, absent-mindedly.

"Whiskey, Felix," she called.

152

The blond man entered again, refilled their glasses, and left the room. They drank in silence. They were both on edge, Mark staring at the ceiling, Angela pretending not to watch him. . . .

Her mind reeled and she floated into a world of fantasy. She sat on the floor, Philip by her side, and they played with his trains, his soldiers and tanks. The cannon? Philip held his cannon upright, shooting up the soldiers, killing the general and the brigadier, the other officers, and then the men. The cannon grew larger and larger, too large for little Philip to support, too heavy: Angela held it up, teasing, pretending she would shoot Philip. The precious boy, thinking she was in earnest, started screaming. *Poor Philip, he must be so lonely, all by himself and nobody to play with . . .*

She left the room, found Felix, and asked him for her medicine.

"Am I sick, Felix, do I look sick to you? Am I in good face?"

She swallowed the two blue capsules, then asked for a red silk scarf. Felix arranged it loosely around her throat.

"Do I look better like this?"

"You look lovely, madame."

She offered her cheek. "Kiss me, Felix," she said, but she was trembling. Then she went back to the bedroom.

Were Mark able to love her now, perhaps she could pull herself out of the abyss, back into the world of light and sense. As she knelt by the couch, almost religiously, lucidity ebbed and flowed.

"I believe you love me," she whispered. "I love you, too."

He was small and soft and she caressed him gently, taking his testicles into her cupped hands. She bent and kissed the tip of his penis, then took him in her mouth, licked him around and around, squeezing his testicles, fondling him deep between the buttocks. His taste excited her and she tongued him greedily, feeling him quicken and swell; she began sucking rhythmically, long and slow. When the crisis approached he tried to pull back, but she held him there, her hands squeezing his testicles as she worked on him. Sweat poured down her face and she grunted occasionally like an animal. When his orgasm came, she swallowed the warm liquid greedily, drinking him up.

Mark took her by the hair and pulled her off; she sank to the floor, flushed and disheveled, her eyes staring, the pupils dilated. Just then she looked old, an old lecherous woman whose coarseness repelled him. He wanted to wash, but she came back to him and licked him clean, lingering over him.

"You know, you don't have the biggest cock I've ever sucked and you aren't the best fuck I've ever had, but you sure taste good."

Later, when he finally began to stiffen again, she wanted to climb over him, but he pushed her aside and got up and found his cigarettes.

"What's the matter? What's bothering you?"

He wouldn't tell her.

"It's that stupid, selfish, priggish bitch you're thinking about, isn't it? Why didn't you tell me you were thick with her? Does she make love to you better than I do? Does she give you bigger kicks—does she know how?"

"Shut up," he said. "You don't know what you're talking about."

"Don't I?" She pressed the burning cigarette tip against his chest and held it there.

He struck her hard across the face, a blow that sent her staggering against a chair. Dazed, she raised her hand to her cheek—the blow had stung badly.

"You dirty bastard," she whispered. "You filthy shit, I'll make you pay for that!"

She snatched a Meissen vase from the side table and aimed it at his head; it missed him and crashed against the wall. There was a small baroque marble Cupid she had found one day in an old shop in Florence; she had had it long enough, it had existed long enough. As she picked it up, she saw her face framed in gilt in the mirror on the opposite wall, and she hurled the statue at her shadowed self, smashed her reflection into fragments. . . .

Mark moved toward her and she grabbed up the decanter and hurled it at him, striking him on the shoulder.

"Filthy, fucking bastard! Motherfucker!"

She knocked the tray to the floor, then swept everything off the mantlepiece with both hands.

She tugged at the draperies and a wooden pelmet came down, one end going through a pane of glass, jagged pieces falling on her hands and wrists.

"I'll cut your guts out, murderer!"

She snatched a piece of glass and flew for his face, but Mark moved in time and she fell heavily against an oval table. She held onto the edge, panting and glaring.

Mark turned away and finished his drink.

"I'll show you, you shitty murdering swine!"

She rushed to a cupboard, took out a whip, and cracked it in the air. But when she took a step forward, Mark jumped on her and wrested it from her hand.

"Stop it, Angela. Do you hear? Stop it!"

She attacked his face with her scarlet nails.

"I'll kill you!"

Mark grabbed her by the hair and pulled her down.

She went for his genitals, but he caught hold of her arms, twisted them behind her, and shoved her face downward on the bed.

"Bitch!" he said and beat her across the buttocks and thighs, turned her over and hit her once more across the face.

She fought back and he took her by the wrists, pinned her down on the bed, and threw himself full-length upon her.

154

"You rotten bastard!"

He handled her violently, as though her body were a barrier against which he threw himself, a battlefield on which he was waging a desperate war. Angela spread her legs wider and arched her back.

"Deeper, deeper!"

Seeing the blood on his shoulder, she raised her head and licked up the drops with her tongue.

"You're just a tramp."

"A whore, Mark, I'm a whore, tell me I'm a whore."

"A fucking, bloody whore."

"I'm a whore, tell me you want my cunt, tell me it's the hottest cunt you ever fucked."

"A fucking, whoring cunt."

"Yes, yes, *yes!*"

The climax approached; she clung to him while his body racked convulsively, her contractions crushing the sperm out of him.

Mark lay spent, panting.

"Felix!" she called. "Felix! Tell Inge to come and keep us company."

He threw the stub of his cigarette over the balcony and went back inside. On the wide bed Angela and Inge were asleep, Inge's flaxen hair spilling over Angela's thigh, one long suntanned leg over Angela's head. All the lights were on. The room was still a shambles, but Felix had cleaned up the broken glass.

Mark tightened the sash of his robe around his waist, went downstairs to the hall, and left through the French windows leading onto the terrace. It was almost four o'clock; the moon had vanished and a fresh breeze was blowing from the sea. He could see lights from villages on the distant mountains on the mainland across the channel.

He knew the way down the steps carved out of rock to the beach. The pebbles were cold, but the water was warm and he took off his robe and plunged into the sea. He swam steadily with long, even strokes until he was tired, then turned on his back and floated in mid-ocean, his face to the dark sky. He had always liked being alone in the sea, his limbs and spirit freed from bondage. In the navy they'd told him he could have been a champion swimmer, but he swam always for his own pleasure and couldn't be bothered to be competitive. Now, drifting on the water, he felt whole again.

In Athens he would sometimes leave his friends and drive along the Sounion road, park in a quiet spot and spend the night in the sea by himself, letting the waves wash away his tensions. In a flash he recalled swimming with Isabel, teaching her water-skiing, showing off to her—he banished the memory and began swimming vigorously back to the shore. His clothes were up at the villa and he wanted to get away before the coming of the new day.

But when he lay down on the sand, he felt suddenly exhausted, unwilling to move; for a few minutes he dropped off, then woke again and resigned himself to staying awake. Sleeplessness was an old enemy which had grown worse this past year. He tried to keep his mind blank, but he couldn't help worrying. Notaras, Lazaros, Angela, the alibi . . . it was damned bad luck, Demetris' death was the last thing he'd have wanted to happen. He could get out of the country secretly, arrange for a false passport—yet he had a curious feeling of fatality, as if everything had passed out of his hands and there was very little he could do. He had to stay, and so he found reasons for his decision: to keep his eye on Nubar and wait for his cut from the deal.

He would retrieve his passport from Notaras. Then, once the money was properly stashed away, he could get out of the country in the normal way. He had broken his pledge never to deal with the stuff, but this was the largest consignment he'd ever been involved in—it would mean over a hundred thousand dollars for him when accounts were settled. . . . He had made a secret bid for a Norwegian cargo boat, but hadn't had the cash for the down payment; now, very soon, he would have it. He had gone over the ship of his choice, under the pretext that Leonides might be interested in it. Mark smiled, remembering the private verdict of the firm's chief engineer: *It's pure music to listen to those engines down there. It'll need a refit, but minor things—the engines are pure music.*

With any luck she would be his first ship, the first of the many that would enable him to meet the Old Lion as a competitor. Mark's mind traveled the oceans, to Japan, to Brazil, Beirut, Sydney, New York, Rotterdam—he was there, he saw the building, the refitting of many ships, moving between many shores, all registered under his own name. For the launching of his first freighter, he'd invite everybody and serve champagne and then—let the orchestra play, let the party begin; Mark would circle the floor, Isabel in his arms.

When he opened his eyes, the day was breaking and the sea had turned a steely white. He went back into the water and washed the sand off, then ran back up the steps and into the house. Inge had left, but Angela was still asleep on the bed, curled up like a child. He showered and shaved, rubbed himself with Angela's cologne, and began putting on his clothes.

When the hammering on the front door broke the silence in the room it was not, somehow, unexpected. Angela opened her eyes, muttered something incoherent, raised herself on one elbow, and flung out an arm in his direction. He pressed her back gently, telling her to be quiet. During the moments of silence that followed, he took out his letter of resignation to the firm, unfolded it, and applied his lighter to the edge of the paper. As if on cue, the knocking resumed when the letter had crumbled completely in the ashtray.

"It's the police," he told Angela. "No need for you to get up."

"But it's *my* door they're knocking on!"

"No matter. They've come for me."

Now the bell pealed imperiously.

"They're suspicious of everyone these days," he said, remembering what he'd discovered in the captain's basement. "I expect it's only to ask me some routine questions."

"At this hour?"

"Precisely at this hour. It's part of the technique."

"The alibi . . ."

She smiled, and Mark bent down and kissed her on the cheek.

"I'm sorry about last night, Angela."

Mark went downstairs, and Angela could hear him calling to the men outside in Greek. Felix was standing in the hall, holding the puma by its leash.

Angela put on a negligee and went to the balcony, just in time to see Mark being taken away between two uniformed men. Even when they had disappeared into the trees, she stayed there, the cool air chilling her flesh through the thin material. *Killer*, she said to herself, *murderer*, and she was pleased.

She wandered back into the room; on the floor among the torn curtains lay the small gilt clock, still busily ticking away the minutes. She bent and picked it up—it was ten minutes to five.

"You sweet bastard," she whispered and went back to bed.

16

The jeep was waiting. Inspector Notaras heaved himself into the front seat by the driver while the two policemen climbed in the back with their prisoner. Nothing was said to Mark on the way, and he saw no point in asking questions.

The castle was a dark mass in the gray mist that hung over the Aegean. Kavouras' taverna was desolate, the chairs and tables piled up against the wall, the pebbled *plateia* bare and empty, like a stage set from which the actors have departed. Some fishermen were sorting out the night's catch on the quay, but when they saw the jeep approaching they turned away and bent over their baskets.

Security Headquarters was half a kilometer or so from the sea, on the outskirts of town. Inspector Notaras was known by now to all the camp, and the helmeted sentry with fixed bayonet saluted and waved them in.

Notaras had Mark hand over his papers to the sergeant in charge, who entered the details in a ledger and told him to empty his pockets. Mark placed on the counter his cigarette case, his lighter, his wallet, his keys, and his comb; then he took out his handkerchief.

"You can keep that," said the sergeant. "But leave your watch here."

He wrote down each item, counting the money in the wallet, and Mark signed that the list was correct.

One of the policemen led the way and Mark followed, Notaras plodding heavily after them. The policeman unlocked a door and stepped back for Mark to go in first.

"Strip," ordered Notaras. He looked inside his mouth, felt under his tongue, examined his fingernails, toes, armpits; then he nodded to the policeman, who lifted Mark's penis and testicles and examined them carefully.

"Bend over," said the Inspector.

The policeman pulled apart the cheeks of the prisoner's buttocks and probed inside the anus with his fingers.

"You can put on your clothes," said Notaras.

They left Mark in the cell, sitting on the plank bed. His hand went mechanically to his pocket, but then he remembered that his cigarettes were in the platinum case. He lay back, wondering whether this latest investigation could be the work of Katia. Early light filtered in through the iron bars over the skylight; Mark noticed a bucket in the corner of the cell and at once remembered Sarkis, Nubar's brother, spitting blood. . . . The prison doctor had pronounced him healthy and there was nothing Mark could do except give him his own blanket, give him water, sponge his burning forehead.

He heard the bugle call and instinctively ran his hand through his hair. Angela's cologne lingered on his fingers—it would be nice if the scent lasted until he was free again. He could handle Lazaros, it might prove useful if Lazaros were in charge. He tried to doze, but it was no use: the political prisoners in the neighboring cells were singing hoarsely and someone was monotonously chanting his morning prayers.

Hours later two policemen came and took him back down the green corridor to a large office and told him to wait on a chair that faced a desk by the window. The men stationed themselves outside the open door; Mark sat perfectly still and waited.

"Please don't get up. Please stay where you are," came the familiar silky voice from behind.

Mark had made no move to do so. Lazaros shut the door after him, went directly to the desk, seated himself behind it, and took a file of papers from his briefcase.

He glanced across the desk. He mustn't weaken. He hadn't seen Mark for some time, his mouth still went dry at the sight of him. He had shampooed his hair that morning, using a blue rinse for the silver streaks around his temples; he

158

had patted on more lavender shaving lotion than usual and carefully manicured and varnished his nails, rubbing his hands and wrists with hand cream. He hoped that he hadn't overdone the lavender.

A man came in carrying a tin tray suspended on three chains, poured Turkish coffee into two small cups, put one in front of Lazaros, and gave the other to Mark.

Lazaros took a sip.

"I think perhaps they don't know how to roast the coffee beans properly —they burn them, the way they burn them in Egypt."

He sipped again, opened a desk drawer, took out Mark's cigarette case and lighter, murmuring something about tiresome formalities. He handed over the cigarettes, keeping back the lighter.

"Could I ask you for one?" he said softly. He turned the lighter over and over in his hand. "I like English cigarettes," he confided. "Perhaps you remember? Won't you have one?"

He came around the desk and flipped open the lighter. There was a breeze coming from the open window and the flame went out; Lazaros tried the lighter again and Mark shielded his cigarette with cupped palms; as he did so, he touched Lazaros' hand and held it for a second. Lazaros took a step back and lit his own cigarette.

"You won't forget to take your lighter," he said, placing it on the desk.

He went back to his chair and fitted the cigarette into the amber holder that protected his smooth, slender fingers from nicotine stains.

"I'm sorry to have got you up so early," he said, leaning back in the leather chair. "I hope the Baroness wasn't too much disturbed. I'm certain she'll think the worst of me now—it's so dreadful to be a policeman, every one hates you in the end. I don't know why we go in for it." He picked up a leaflet printed on cheap blue paper and began reading it to himself. "We get all the blame in the end—us and the army. Of course, now it's the army everybody hates. Ingratitude, sheer ingratitude, one of the less endearing characteristics of our race."

He pushed the leaflet in front of Mark.

"Look at this rubbish. Of course we know the facts, but abroad we are the tyrants and every *soi-disant* liberal considers it his duty to cry out to heaven for justice, one of the latest, who else, but the former director of the BBC. God give me patience!"

The leaflet looked very much like the blank sheets of duplicating paper that Mark had seen in the basement. He sipped his coffee and watched Lazaros, wondering what he was leading up to.

"They all expect the army to do the dirty work, to kill, to be killed, to leave their homes and families, so the rest can stay in their comfortable beds, cheat in their shops, make money and get fat—and play at politics. . . ."

159

He went on in this vein; Mark had heard it all before, but he listened patiently, preparing himself for what was to come.

"Why did you kill Demetris Christoforou?" Lazaros asked suddenly, without changing his tone.

"There was no reason. I didn't."

"It might be of interest to you, Markos, to know that we are certain here that you killed him. You shot him somewhere, we don't know where yet, and you threw him into the sea and the body was washed up yesterday morning at Glaros Bay. Was it there or nearby that you shot him?"

"I didn't kill Demetris."

Lazaros took a cigarette from his own pack and fitted it into his holder.

"I would advise you to be frank with us, Markos. I want to help you, but you must help me as well. Perhaps it was really an accident, not a premeditated killing. Perhaps you had a fight and the gun went off."

"There was no fight."

"Perhaps he provoked you, insulted you. Or was it that he wanted to marry Katia, Kommenos' daughter?"

"I wouldn't know. It wasn't my business."

"But it was your business all right to have her in your house, to do whatever you did with her in there?"

Lazaros pictured Mark making love to the girl, Demetris watching them, suffering, jealous, unwanted. The custodian had reported her visits to Mark. He opened a drawer and placed Mark's dossier on the desk in front of him.

"I'm sure any court in Greece would be sympathetic if this is a *crime passionel*," he said.

"I still didn't kill this man."

"Perhaps one of your friends did?"

"I don't have that kind of friends."

"No? I have here a list of your known friends and acquaintances. I don't think an affair like this would worry some of them at all. Perhaps you believe that Demetris committed suicide?"

"It's a possibility, of course."

Lazaros sipped a little water, dabbed his forehead and throat with his blue silk handkerchief. He was getting soft and sentimental, he must be on guard against that. A man shadowing Mark on Lazaros' instructions had been killed and it was Lazaros' job to see that the crime was solved and justice administered.

The game of questions and answers went on for another half-hour. The telephone rang; Lazaros listened without comment for a few minutes.

"I see, I see," he said finally. "You'd better come in, then."

He turned to Mark.

"Nubar Ohanessian was arrested half an hour ago at Piraeus, just as he was boarding a caique bound for Algiers. The interesting thing was that in the course of searching the boat the police found two kilos of heroin. Well, I

160

wanted to help you, Markos, and I still may, but as you can see things are getting rather complicated. Ohanessian, now, I suppose you met him through his brother Sarkis, the brother who died in jail when you were in. Ohanessian is a friend of yours."

"The firm did business with his agency. I haven't seen him for over a week."

"You went out fishing together in the evening, didn't you?"

"Once or twice."

"I'm sorry, but I don't think you will go fishing together again. I only wish you would tell me how the Armenian proposed to deliver the merchandise. Had he arranged a rendezvous with some boat on the open sea?"

He's bluffing, thought Mark. The big haul was on a private yacht bound for Marseilles—what was this talk about two kilos? Unless . . . unless Nubar had kept back two kilos, trying his hand at a shady job on the side.

"Now Markos, be sensible and let me help you. If you will tell us the whole story, how it all happened, how Nubar shot Demetris or how Demetris was killed accidentally in your presence, I promise you I'll do my best to get you out of this, do you understand? Because I want to get you out of it, I want you to stay free."

He smiled, a slight, coaxing smile.

"I want to be your friend, I want *you* to be *my* friend, do you understand?"

"Yes, of course I understand. You know, I feel I am your friend already, I've felt so for some time. But you see, I can't help in this case. I've told you all I know about Nubar, and I know nothing about the killing of Demetris. Surely you don't want our friendship to start off with lies, do you?"

Lazaros got up and went to the window, looking out, his back to Mark.

"It's such a pity," he said. "You're much too good to be wasted like this. You're not really a criminal, it's just that your loyalties are misplaced."

He turned and looked wistfully at Mark until there was a knock at the office door and Inspector Notaras entered with a sergeant. Lazaros glanced at them, then looked away and touched his chest.

"Go on, ask him," he said as he searched a drawer for the little box with his tablets.

Notaras and the sergeant questioned Mark in turns, Lazaros leaning his head against the back of the winged chair, looking almost asleep, only opening his eyes to make an occasional note on the pad in front of him.

An hour later, Notaras asked the superintendent if he and his sergeant might have some food. Lazaros nodded stiffly, amazed at the self-confidence of these younger men. It had not been so in his earlier days.

He declined the glass of beer and sandwiches Notaras offered him. Mark was given nothing; as time passed and the day wore on, the afternoon hours hot and heavy, he found it difficult to concentrate, to keep his mind always a jump or two ahead of his interrogators.

Notaras sent for water and a policeman brought it in a jug, frosted with ice.

Mark's throat was dry and he saw all three of them waiting for him to ask. He would not.

At four-thirty Lazaros got up. He had had enough. Inspector Notaras always made him feel vaguely uncomfortable; he had the feeling that too much emotion lay behind the man's cool exterior and he found his personality oppressive.

He walked to the door, and came back.

"Since you've been brought in, Markos, one of our people has had another word with the Baroness. She admits that she made a mistake before, that you left the villa during the night, although, of course, your car was there. What do you have to say to that?"

"Nothing. I was with her the whole night and stayed on all next day."

"Were you in bed with her until the morning?" asked Notaras.

"Yes."

"Do you mean you were having intercourse with this woman intermittently throughout the night?"

"Intermittently."

Lazaros set the corners of his mouth to stop their trembling.

"That's not true," he said. "We know for certain that you left the villa during the night. You were followed by Demetris, whose body was found at Glaros, almost five kilometers from the villa."

Lazaros walked over to Mark's chair. There were small beads of sweat on the prisoner's forehead, and Lazaros fought the impulse to take out his blue silk handkerchief and wipe them away. He spoke slowly, keeping his voice steady.

"I don't want you to say that I didn't give you every chance, Markos. Think over what I've said to you. I'd hate to see you in difficulties."

He left the office, and Notaras turned back from the window to resume the interrogation.

Mark was awakened at dawn by a long, drawn-out scream which seemed to come from somewhere above him. A door clashed noisily; then there was silence.

He had no idea what would happen next, but he had given nothing away so far. Had Angela? Had Nubar? Or were they bluffing? He despised Lazaros, but he would rather have him than Notaras. The old queer, in his plodding conscientious way, would want to act on concrete facts, not on suspicion and inference alone.

The door to his cell was unlocked and a guard led Mark away to a large washroom. Mark stripped to the waist, cupped his hands and drank the water, washed his face and hands. The towel on the rail nearby looked well used, and he dried himself as best he could with his handkerchief.

Two guards came in with three prisoners, and Mark moved away from the basin to make room for them.

"These are the revolutionaries," his own guard said to him and laughed.

One prisoner was very old, with long white hair and beard. The two others opened a door for him and held him by the arms, one on each side, as he crouched on the latrine to defecate. Then they brought him out and helped him to wash. His hands shook as he dried himself; he dropped the towel, stumbled, and stepped on it with his dirty feet.

Mark offered the old man his damp handkerchief, but his guard saw him and started to push him back. The old prisoner gripped Mark's arm, his eyes burning.

"Have my blessing, my boy. Be brave! I've been in their hands for twenty-six years, I've seen all my companions die, one after the other, in the concentration camps. Let's die as brave men, true Greeks, true patriots."

Mark felt ashamed. The old man was mistaken, Mark was not one of them. And yet, watching that skeleton of an old man being led away, only his enormous black eyes alive—yes, he felt he could kill a few bastards who destroyed people's lives because they would not go along with their way of thinking.

"He's an arch-Communist," Mark's guard explained as he took Mark to the Security Building. "He and his men burned two villages where the royalist troops were given shelter. In one village he tied up the priest while the guerrillas raped his daughter in front of him, one after the other. In the second village they couldn't find the girls, so they hanged the priest from the belfry tower and burned the church."

They entered the room where Mark had been questioned the day before; Lazaros put aside his morning newspaper and gave a nod to the guard to leave them alone. Then he smiled amiably at Mark and told him to be seated.

"We have a message for you, Markos, from your friend Nubar. He sends his best regards, he says you were good friends and he's been worrying a bit about you. He says now that the game is up, he doesn't want you to be foolish and get yourself hurt. Ohanessian chose the wise course and I'm sure the police won't forget. If you decide to do the same . . ."

"I can't. I didn't kill Demetris and I've got nothing to do with drugs. I don't take them and I don't handle them."

"I can see you don't take drugs. The point is that you're an old hand in handling them."

"I told you in Athens—I was framed."

"Probably your wife's lover, so conveniently run down by a car shortly after you were released."

Lazaros withdrew a brown envelope from Mark's file and took out some photographs.

"Your Jennie was an attractive girl, wasn't she? I've got a picture of you both here—somebody must have taken it when you didn't know. One can see she had a roving eye, even then."

He looked across at Mark, studying him. Talking about Jennie gave Lazaros the illusion of getting closer to Mark, of standing between him and Jennie.

He leaned forward and held out the photograph.

"Why did you marry her in the first place?"

"Isn't there any part of my life I can call my own?"

"You forget how the unfortunate woman died, you pretend to forget, you don't want to be reminded."

A sudden intensity lit his pale face as he looked at the other photographs in front of him.

"She was a pretty girl. I wish now I had enjoyed her favors, you and I would have had something in common. She gave me the lead, but I didn't pursue it."

As he talked about Jennie, the superintendent imagined Mark's body over her, over other women, over the Baroness and Dr. Grey's wife.

"I've got several pictures of her," he said. "Come, now, and look at them."

"No, thank you."

Lazaros got up and went over to him, holding out one photograph.

"This one you *shall* see."

He held it in front of Mark's eyes: Jennie was lying naked on her back on a tumbled bed, her fists clenched, the scars and punctures clearly visible on her arms and legs, her hair dull and matted, her breasts still beautiful in death. The dead eyes stared into space, the mouth was half-open.

"This has nothing to do with me, Superintendent. She'd left me long before she was an addict."

"Some criminal started this wretched woman on her downward course. It could have been your good friend, Nubar. Or one of his people—don't you think so? The Armenian has already given us the names of a number of men involved with him."

"If you've got a genuine list, I'm not on it. I've got nothing to do with drugs, I don't want to know anything about them."

"I wonder why, as you're so innocent. Most people are mildly interested, we find."

He propped the photograph on the desk against an inkstand near Mark. Mark looked, and felt the same head-spinning nausea he had felt at the mortuary. Under the gaping mouth, he could make out the small beauty spot that he had kissed so often . . . *Oh Jennie, Jennie, my love Jennie, how could it have come to this? I would have taken care of you . . .*

There was a knock at the door, and Inspector Notaras came in and handed Lazaros a slip of paper.

"This just arrived, Superintendent."

Lazaros read it; he was even paler than usual, his lips contracted.

"Take him away," he said. "Then come back here. I want to talk to you."

Mark spent the next twenty-four hours in his hot cell, pacing the floor or tossing on the plank bed, hungry and burning with thirst. That night, when he was trying to doze, a guard came in and took him across the gravel yard to the newly built barracks apartments, one of the two that was still standing among the rubble. The guard rang the bell and saluted smartly when the door opened. Lazaros stood on the threshold.

The superintendent dismissed the guard, then put an arm around Mark and drew him inside. He was wearing a shirt of tangerine silk open in front, cream-colored slacks, and soft white leather moccasins. The scent of lavender was strong.

"My dear boy, I'm so sorry. I've hated what's been happening to you the last few days. You remember, Markos, you said once that I was just a policeman. Well, I've been a policeman, but I've hated it. Now I'm off duty, so come in and relax. What can I give you to drink?"

"Water."

Lazaros looked embarrassed.

"The brutes! Haven't they been looking after you?"

He turned to get the water, but Mark, seeing the door of the adjoining bathroom open, went in, cupped his hands under the tap in the basin, and drank.

When he finally lifted his head, Lazaros was standing at the door.

"I suppose you'd like to wash. But come and have a proper drink first. I've got some Metaxa here. You see, I haven't forgotten you like brandy." He poured two large shots into tumblers. "I like mine with lots of ice. Surprise! Look."

He produced a bucket of ice, but Mark had already drunk the brandy neat. He took the bottle and refilled his glass.

"*Lots* of ice," said Lazaros, putting several cubes into his own glass.

Mark looked at him, defiant.

"I'm sorry, Markos. I didn't mean to hurt you. I don't want anything to hurt you, ever. Now let me give you some ice."

He held a cube in midair, suspended by tongs.

For a moment Mark looked at him, hating him; then he relented and held out his glass. Lazaros smiled, gratified, and at once got up and brought a tray of sandwiches.

"I thought we might have a snack together," he said and began to eat one with quick bites. "Come on, Markos, help yourself." He moved about the room, watching Mark eat, returning to fill his glass with brandy and ice cubes. "I've told one of our people to collect some clean clothes from your place. You'd like to change, wouldn't you?"

A jeep pulled up outside.

"This must be he, I'll go find out. Perhaps you'd like a shower when you've finished eating—use my razor, if you like. You'll feel better after a wash."

He went out and stood for a moment on the porch. The police officer got down from the jeep, saluted, and handed the superintendent a parcel wrapped in newspaper. After he had gone, Lazaros waited outside the bungalow, as if afraid to return, listening to the hum of the electric razor in the bathroom. It would be possible, if he wished; it would be possible to get him put inside, even before the mystery had been resolved. Lazaros was certain, or almost certain, that the death of Demetris, the drugs picked up on the caique in Piraeus, Nubar and Markos, all were connected somehow. The facts, he must get the facts. And then? He didn't want to think about that. It would be like caging a beautiful, predatory creature; such a lovely boy, a Greek god, an Apollo . . . He must speak to Markos, he must try to get it through to him how much misery and suffering he had been instrumental in causing through his pursuit of easy money.

When he reentered the bungalow, the water was running in the bathroom. He made a pot of coffee and then walked about the room, his breathing shallow, envisioning streams of water glistening on the smooth skin. He's guilty, he thought, and he's strong, and he's in my hands. The discarded clothes were strewn about on the floor; Lazaros bent down and collected them, piling them neatly in a corner. When he came to the briefs, he held them in his hand, glanced at the bathroom door, then swiftly brought them to his face, laid them against his cheek and inhaled the smell of masculine sweat, his eyes half closed, his lips apart. He heard a movement from the bathroom and quickly put the garment down, picked up a cup of black coffee and went in.

"I've brought you some coffee," he said, avoiding Mark's eyes. "Please drink it."

Mark stood naked, challenging, and drank the coffee.

"Thank you, Superintendent."

"There's some more. And, Markos, please call me Mikhail."

Lazaros brought a second cup, holding the coffee like an offering as he contemplated the naked man. The shoulders were broad and strong, the hips narrow, the buttocks small and firm. Mark noticed him watching and went on with his shower, soaping up once again. What the hell; let the blasted cocksucker have a treat. His penis hung down full and heavy and he soaped himself slowly, pulling back the foreskin, then rinsing himself thoroughly, rubbing the loose skin in his hands.

"If you tell us that Nubar shot Demetris," said Lazaros, "I'll get you out of this before you know it, you could walk out of here tonight."

Watching the naked body before him, Lazaros found it difficult to continue. *I'm a policeman, I have a duty to perform.*

166

"I know you think the Armenian is a friend of yours and that you should stand by him. He doesn't deserve it, let me tell you. And you can't make things much worse for him, can you? The drugs were found in his possession, not in yours." He waited but there was no answer. Then he added, "Unless you killed Demetris yourself."

"I'd like to cooperate with you and get out of this. Particularly now, because you're in charge of this and I know you want to help me. But I'm telling you the truth."

"Are you?" asked Lazaros.

"Mikhail Lazaros, do you really believe that I killed Demetris? Do you think I could be a murderer?"

"Yes." Lazaros smiled as if at some shared secret. "Let me give you a towel."

Trembling, he watched Mark dry himself. Mark did not hurry. His penis stood out, partially erect, but he didn't turn away. When he had finished he handed the towel to Lazaros.

"Your clothes are in the next room, I'll give us some more brandy."

Mark walked barefoot into the living room, a little water still dripping from his legs and genitals. As Lazaros handed him his brandy, his free hand moved down and he took hold of Mark's penis and began stroking him gently.

"Do you want to make love to me?" he asked softly. "I don't care what you've done, I don't want you hurt. The only thing I really care about is you. Markos dear, I *do* care, I really do."

As he spoke he sank to his knees, took Mark's penis in both hands, caressed him, brushed him against his face, kissed him on the tip; then, with a glance of pain, he opened his mouth to suck him in. Mark took a step backward.

Embarrassed, Lazaros stood up. He watched Mark arranging his hair in front of the mirror, then he put his arm around his bare shoulders.

"You're so strong, so beautiful, Markos."

He leaned forward and kissed Mark on the mouth.

Mark stepped back, touched his mouth with the back of his hand. He began dressing. His decision to go along with Lazaros, if that was the only way to gain his freedom, had left him. He just couldn't.

Lazaros looked up at him, his eyes intense, accusing, suffering. Mark recognized the look—he had seen it on the face of more than one woman.

Mark took the bottle and poured more brandy into their glasses.

"You could do with a drink, yourself, Mikhail. Cheers. Remember, we're friends."

Lazaros slumped into a chair, his body huddled together, his head buried in his hands. Mark went over to him and touched his shoulder.

"Mikhail, please, you mustn't take it so hard. I'm sorry, but it wouldn't be fair. For either of us."

He picked up the glass of brandy and held it out to Lazaros; the superintendent pushed his hand away violently and the brandy spilled on the table

Mark put on the blue slacks and the white shirt. It felt good to be clean, shaved, fed.

"Thank you for the clothes," he said. "You know I don't think you really *are* a cop—why do you have to work for them?"

Lazaros lifted his head and looked at him coldly. Then he pressed the button on the table and Mark understood that his time was up.

He threw back his drink and went to the bathroom to have another look at himself, to comb his hair again, to be ready for them.

Mark was taken back to the office in the Security Building, but the desk was now occupied by Inspector Notaras. The sergeant sat at a table to the side and took Mark's statement, the same story, stressing his alibi, denying all accusations.

At a signal from Notaras, he took Mark back to his cell. As soon as they were inside, he tore the statement into pieces and threw them on the floor.

"All right, Stephanou. Superintendent Lazaros has already left tonight for Athens—he's washed his hands of you. Inspector Notaras is now in charge of your case and he isn't as patient as the chief. If you don't tell us what we ask you when we ask you . . ."

Mark said nothing, and the sergeant went away. Five minutes later he was back with two guards. Behind them was Inspector Notaras, gripping the end of a heavy leather belt with its sharp buckle, his eyes unfocused, his mouth working loosely.

"Take off your clothes," he ordered.

By the time they had finished with him, Mark was more dead than alive, but he had given away nothing.

17

"Now, friends, I put it to you; what would you do if you went in and found a bedraggled seagull, black with oil, lying on the bathroom floor and squinting up at you one fine morning? I ask you, what would you do?"

"Come on, Hilary," said Katia. "Tell us . . . what *did* you do?"

"And how did it get there, anyway?" said Thalia.

"At first I thought it was all part of my hangover; then, when I prodded it with my bare foot and it took a vicious peck at my big toe, I began to understand the damned thing was real."

168

Hilary had abandoned Isabel soon after they had arrived, she was not there to dampen his spirits, the wedding party aboard the *Hesperides* was a grand affair, and he was enjoying himself.

"It was all Isabel's doing—Lady Isabel, our dumb friends' friend. She found this horrible fowl lying amidst the seaweed in a pool of tar on the shore, and brought it home."

"What did you do then?" asked Thalia.

"Gave it to the fat ginger tom who lives in the garden, of course," Hilary said, draining his glass.

"You didn't!"

"Of course I didn't, it'd have been such a waste. I made some delicious gull kebab on the grill and ate it for breakfast. Isabel cried all through the meal, she could only manage a little toast that morning."

"Now I know you're teasing," said Katia. "Isabel would never have allowed it."

"How right you are! She had me giving that blasted bird a foam bath—used a whole bottle of Royal Drene, in fact. Then Isabel wouldn't hear of our throwing it out of the window. She said it had suffered a shock and needed to recover its strength. I can tell you, while that gull was recovering its strength I was losing mine. Isabel filled the bath tub with cold water, permanently. The theory was that the invalid would just float peacefully, convalescing, but in reality it spent most of the time flying round and round the room like a caged eagle and making practice dives at my face. With Isabel, of course, it was tame as a dove. And then, I couldn't use the bathroom, I was just too embarassed. She used to sit there and take me all in with her beady, lascivious eyes. She wouldn't turn her beak away."

Katia giggled. "Is she still there?"

"She would be, if Isabel had had her way. But, after she had eaten my shaving cream and dashed my only bottle of good cologne to the ground, I decided it was time Jemima said good-bye."

"Jemima?"

"That's what Isabel christened her. Ghastly name, but it suited that ghastly bird. It took a pretty smooth diplomatic line about the cruelty of keeping wild things in captivity to persuade Isabel that Jemima was fit to fly. Even then, she insisted that Jemima be taken back to the same spot where she was found, so she wouldn't lose her bearings. Fair enough, I said, and I edged my way around the bathroom door to find our guest sleeping with her head tucked into her feathers, floating on the bath water as good as gold. 'So there you are,' I said. 'Wake up, the party's over.' I closed the door behind me and made a grab at her—she flew up and started circling, keeping close to the ceiling. Once she dropped her card on my head *and* I had Isabel outside calling to me, 'Do be gentle with her! Don't frighten her, will you?' I climbed on the stool, but I couldn't reach her.

Then I flapped a big towel at her, hoping to bring her down. But Jemima, not wanting any unpleasantness, flew up to the top of the cupboard and sat there, waiting for me to make the next move.

"Well, I wasn't going to give up so easily. I climbed on the edge of the tub, and that damnable bird waited till I stretched my hand out and then dived into my face. Of course, I fell backward into the tub. The water spilt over like a tidal wave, but I kept my nerve, and wouldn't you know, there's Isabel knocking on the door, crying desperately, 'You're not hurting her, are you?' 'Not yet, but you never know.' I dipped the big towel in water to make it heavier and resumed the chase. When I caught her in the end she fell, beak first, into the lavatory. The crisis had come—I had a savage impulse to pull the lever and flush her out of my life forever."

"You didn't, did you?"

"Well, no. I remembered Saint Isabel of the Birds keeping vigil outside, and I fished Jemima out and washed her with warm water in the basin. Mercifully she was dazed and submitted without a struggle, otherwise I would not have been responsible for my actions. Then, grasping her by the wings, I opened the door. Not only Isabel, but the maid and her fiancé were for some extraordinary reason standing in a row, staring at me.

"Isabel gave me a dirty look and asked me what I'd been up to in there for so long. 'My goodness, I hope you haven't upset poor Jemima.' I just said, 'I hope not, dear,' and handed her the cause of all the trouble. 'I also hope I haven't got hydrophobia from that poisonous beak of hers.' To end this horrible tale, we took Jemima to the place where Isabel had found her and she released her and I closed my eyes—I just didn't want to know which way she went. To this day, every time I see a gull I close my eyes and hope it'll go away."

Van Sullivan the Second came over and claimed his new daughter-in-law. Thalia was looking almost pretty. Her homely features had been made up by a beauty specialist flown out from Athens, her dull brown hair had been subtly streaked, and the long golden dress by Balmain did all that could be done for her figure. Around her throat was a double string of pearls, the gift of her husband. Sullivan the Third joined them and the proud father put an arm around each of them, for the benefit of the photographers.

Katia saw Luigi on the other side of the room and went to him; she had caught him in bed with her mother a few days before and enjoyed reminding him of it. "Did you see the news in the paper today?" she asked him. "A brother in Preveza split the skull of his sister's lover with an axe—while he was asleep, naturally."

Hilary, having lost his audience, went over to the long table, helped himself to pâté de foie gras, piled fresh Iranian caviar on a toast triangle, washed it down with champagne, and raised his glass and his voice above the din of the guests. "Long live the newlyweds—*Chrónia pollá!*" But as nobody paid any attention, he refilled his glass and went on with his feasting.

170

The Baroness arrived late, accompanied by Felix and Inge. Hilary spotted her immediately, but made no move toward her. *I know what is not expected of me and I quite understand.* She was a pagan goddess tonight in a silver gown and long emerald earrings. Her hair was piled up extravagantly on top of her head. As the heavily made-up eyes swept around the deck, Hilary thought that she looked more like a splendid waxwork than a human being. She handed her pale mink stole to Felix.

"He's not here, Felix."

"Mr. Leonides is talking to him in his cabin."

"We shall wait."

A faint doubt touched her full red mouth.

"What do I do now, Felix?"

"You congratulate the bride and groom, madame. And may I suggest a glass of champagne?"

"You're right, Felix, as usual. Go and get me one. Inge, lead me to the happy couple."

She embraced Thalia perfunctorily and gave her hand to Van to kiss, then took a glass of champagne and sipped at it, her movements stiff and mechanical. She stood motionless, looking straight through people, turning wherever she was led like a sleepwalker.

Hilary, watching her, was firm in his resolve not to go over to her, not to degrade himself further. *I know what is not expected of me and I quite understand.* Understanding was his major talent, his intellectual specialty, the thing he did best. Angela turned in his direction and he admired from a distance the opulent white breasts half spilling out of the silver dress. The Baroness, holding Inge by the hand, was already the center of a hushed, respectful group. I understand, said Hilary to himself, and turned to get a glass of champagne.

Leon Leonides crashed his fist down on the desk in front of him and the golden *World Seafarer* rocked on its base; Clive's portrait of Angela shook and came to rest slightly askew.

"What the devil's been going on here?" he shouted. "No sooner do I turn my back than I find my personal assistant has been pulled in by the fucking police for questioning."

Leonides saw the cut on Mark's lip and smote the desk again: It was as much as he could do to keep his hands off him himself. *I was right, after all. And he expected me to believe that story of the frame-up which landed him in prison? That he had nothing to do with the death of his wife's lover?* Often while away on his travels he would start worrying about Mark and try to reach him, pretending that he needed his help, ordering him to stop what he was doing and join him at once. *I was right, he's wild, I'd better get him chained to a wife and hope for the best.*

"Speak, gypsy, speak! Say something and make it convincing."

171

"It wasn't my idea, you know."

The Old Lion glared at him.

"Are you trying to be clever?"

"There have been some bomb explosions, somebody has been scattering leaflets against the government in the streets. One of their agents was killed. They're very edgy these days, they seize anybody who . . ."

"Women? Is that it?"

"No, sir."

"Blackmail?"

"No. I've got a previous conviction, I suppose I'm always a suspect in the eyes of the police."

"It's dope, then."

"No, sir."

"You're lucky I'm around, you bastard. You're lucky I don't count the drachmas when I entertain the fucking ministers."

But as he looked at those gypsy eyes his anger ebbed, he couldn't go on shouting at him indefinitely.

"Tsavellas asked me for a position for his godson, by the way. The goatherds have ambitions, you see, they want to turn into shipowners."

He pulled open a drawer and took out Mark's passport.

"Here, take this. And keep out of trouble. You have a responsible job and you're expected to behave like a responsible citizen, a man of business, not a hooligan. It's bad enough that because of your record the police have an excuse to pick you up every time someone is found dead. If I ever find out that you're using this organization in any way as a cover for drug running on the side or for any other dirty trick, I'll kill you myself. Do you swear that you have nothing to do with this filthy business? Do you swear?"

"Yes, sir, I do. I have nothing to do with drugs."

"And you didn't know that Armenian was mixed up in it, did you?"

"I didn't know."

"Did the police tell you that Ohanessian had escaped from custody?"

"No, they didn't. How did he get away? When?"

He seemed anxious, and one part of Leonides' mind doubted him. No, he couldn't believe it. He didn't want to believe it.

He got up, went close to Mark, and examined the bruises on his face. They looked bad and he shook his head and swore under his breath. He put an arm around Mark's shoulders; Mark winced in pain.

"For God's sake, go to the sick bay and ask the nurse to give you some codeine, or something stronger, if she's got it. Then come back, I want to talk to you."

Leonides returned to his desk, sank into the leather chair, rested his head on the back, and closed his eyes. It was a winter afternoon, four years ago, the *World Seafarer* was expected at Piraeus after being launched at Clydeside. To

172

celebrate, Leonides was giving a party aboard to which he had invited government officials, the press, Athens society, and the archbishop, who was going to bless the ship and the waters on which she sailed. The party was to start at nine o'clock; that afternoon he left the office soon after lunch, went home, put on a blue jersey and a sailor's beret, and took the bus down to the great port. He wandered among the crowds, looked into the cafés, spoke to the stevedores on the dock, walked the back streets of the Troumba with the girls of the port. Nobody recognized him.

It was getting late, the tanker would be coming in soon, he should go back to rest, to change . . . But he walked across to the wharf, bought a round loaf and a bottle of duty-free bourbon smuggled by a deckhand. He jumped on a tram, and, on impulse, pretended he didn't have the fare: The conductor put him off at the next stop at the far end of the port and he walked along the barren rocky promontory carrying his paper bag of provisions to eat and drink while he watched his own ship entering the harbor.

A young man was sitting among the rocks, down by the edge of the sea, a forlorn figure in the late light of the winter afternoon.

The Old Lion hurried down to the sea, sat on a rock opposite him, opened his paper bag, and began eating.

"Like some bread?" he called.

The young man turned but made no reply. His clothes hung on him, the face had no flesh; but the eyes had a dark, wild, familiar strangeness.

Leonides went closer and offered him a chunk of bread. There was no response, and he put the bread on the rock. Then he drew out the fifth of bourbon, drank some, and placed it between them.

"It's nice," he said. "Wish you'd join me. I'll have to finish it by myself and that's not good at my age."

"Who are you?" asked the young man.

"I'm an emperor. Who are you?"

"I'm an admiral."

"Where's your fleet?"

He pointed to the horizon. "Out there."

"I could do with an admiral for my empire. Cheers."

Leonides drank more bourbon and handed the bottle to the young man.

"Won't you toast your emperor?"

He was proud, even then. He was starving and the Old Lion had to press him to drink, to eat a little bread.

"Now if you join my empire, your salary will be one dollar a day, but you can eat and drink as much as you like and there'll always be a hot bath and a clean bed for you."

The young man held the bottle poised halfway to his lips, his eyes flashing as the giant tanker, the biggest in the world that year, dressed overall, with the Lion's insignia on the funnel, sailed into the harbor.

173

"That's one of mine," Leonides said.

The young man turned and looked straight at him for the first time.

"You're not an emperor. You're a crazy old man."

"You're not an admiral, either. You're just a wandering gypsy."

"My mother was from Hungary. How did you know?"

"You may call me Old Man, but on one condition: I shall always call you gypsy . . ."

He felt a hand touch his shoulder and opened his eyes. It was Mark.

"Mr. Sullivan is asking for you," said Mark.

Leonides got up, put on his white jacket.

"How are you feeling, gypsy. Better now?"

"I'm all right."

Again he noticed the bruises on Mark's face.

"But why all the rough handling? Why did they beat you up—or are you going to tell me you were in an accident?"

"There was a maniac there who had it in for me from the beginning. If I ever get the swine on neutral ground I'll kill him for what he did to me."

"You will, will you? What's his name—do you know it?"

"Oh yes, I know. Inspector Panos Notaras."

"Keep out of that kind of trouble. Who knows, I may fix him myself."

Mark was silent and brooding, the Old Lion didn't like it.

"Come on, gypsy, let's go up. I've got my ugly duckling off my hands today *and* I've pulled off a deal that will have Onassis and Niarchos gnashing their teeth. Come, it's a day of celebration. Cheer up and we'll have some champagne together."

As they were leaving the cabin, the Old Lion took Mark by the arm.

"The commandant brought your passport back in person and apologized. By the way, he says he knows nothing about the rough handling, so it's no good for us to quarrel with him. I asked him to come along tonight."

Mark turned to go.

"Now, wait a moment. You can't stay still, can you, gypsy? My niece is waiting for you, I'm sure—she must feel left out in the cold, seeing Thalia settling down. Come with me and we'll find her."

The Old Lion put on his black bow tie, then took Mark by the arm.

"A strong boy like you needs a hot cunt to fuck every night, that's what will keep you out of mischief. I made a mistake—no, it was more bad luck than a mistake. I was already married when the right woman came along, it was too late, it was too complicated, I was a coward."

He gripped Mark's arm tightly.

"As for that raise, I know you didn't ask me, you know you don't deserve it, but I'm giving it to you all the same. I've already told the accountant to double your salary. Is that fair, gypsy?"

174

"Fair enough, Old Man."

As they came onto the deck, Leonides went immediately to the Baroness. Mark congratulated Thalia.

"I've done the right thing, haven't I, Markos?"

"Of course you have. Van's a lucky man."

"I can't tell anybody, Markos, only you. Sometimes I don't know if I've done the right thing. If my mother were alive, I could speak to her."

Mark pressed her hand warmly.

"Don't worry, Thalia. Everything will be all right."

She smiled at him, raised her eyes, saw Van with a pretty actress, and looked down again.

"If my father has chosen Van for me, it's my duty to love him, to marry him, and give him children."

Mark pressed her hand again.

"I'll see you later," he said and went to the rail where it was darker and lit a cigarette. There was gambling in one of the cabins, but he had to stay on deck, if only to see Isabel from a distance.

Katia, who had been searching for Mark all evening, saw him walking back from the rail. With her were Ted and Terry, one on each side, sporting identical satin dinner jackets of palest gold with voluminous cravats. Linking her arms through theirs, she moved toward Mark.

"Do you think I'm terribly bad, Markos? Don't you think you should carry me off and protect me from these desperate characters?"

"At least we're not incestuous," said Ted. "The nearest we came to *that* was at Port Said with the most *gorgeous* he-man. We shared him like a lollipop!"

The Old Lion was talking to Jason: "I've had a talk with your father. You don't deserve it, but you'll go to the London School of Economics. They tell me it's a good school and you can demonstrate and protest there to your heart's content. You leave next month."

"But, sir, I don't want to . . ."

"Quiet! When you finish your studies we'll have another talk, but not before. I've no time for milksops." And with this he turned away and returned to Angela.

Mark went over to Jason.

"You'd better move all those things from the basement," he said in a low voice.

"Why? Does the typing keep you awake at night?"

Mark, who was really quite angry with Jason, was about to say so when he caught a glimpse of rich, golden hair.

"Excuse me," he said and walked away.

He was still some distance away when Isabel's eyes met his. He stopped

175

where he was, watching her; her gaze faltered and the blood rushed up, staining her face crimson. Mark felt a lump in his throat and he turned slowly away; the lump turned into a rock and scraped its way down to his heart and a spasm of pain moved through his whole body. His face was shuttered, his features hardened, his eyes misted.

Across the room Angela saw Isabel's color change from crimson to ashes and then she saw Mark, haggard and elegant, moving away among the guests. *The cheat. The bastard.* She handed her glass to Felix and pushed her way through the crowd, holding Inge firmly by the hand; she caught sight of Mark's bruised face, the discolored left eye, and was gratified. She imagined him naked, his back scarred and lacerated, his penis raw, his testicles bleeding . . .

"What's the matter with your face?" she asked as she reached him.

"Hello, Angela. Nothing serious. How are things with you?"

"You haven't come to see me. Have you been busy?"

"Very busy."

"Brother Leon is back. You've seen him?"

"Yes."

"Come tonight. Brother Leon is busy tonight."

"Do you want me that much?"

"I hate your guts, damn you—but come tonight."

He nodded noncommittally and snapped his fingers for more champagne.

Across the room, Hilary was trapped by Father Athanasios.

"And what would you say was the most important doctrine in your faith, Father?"

"The Resurrection," said Father Athanasios. " 'For since by man came death, by man came also the resurrection of the dead; for as in Adam all die, even so in Christ shall all be made alive.' "

"Really? Now, I was brought up as a holy Roman—I remember them always telling us about the Immaculate Conception."

"That also is part of our faith, as you know. The real difference between us is your belief that the Holy Spirit issues from the Father *and* the Son—the doctrine of *filioque.*"

"I do wish all you people would get together and hammer something out—strength in uniformity, Father."

Hilary spoke in Greek, but using the patronizing tone he reserved for children, fools, and clergymen of all denominations.

"Strength in unity, my child . . ."

Father Athanasios had launched into a discussion of the schism that divided the two churches when Hilary saw Angela approaching, Felix behind her. He smiled, nodded to the priest, and slipped away into the crowd.

Angela had heard that the robust priest had swum the wide, treacherous straits between the island and the Morea several times.

176

"I've seen you swimming off the headland, early in the morning," she began. "My father was a good Orthodox, I don't know what I am. You must come to the villa and have a go at bringing me back to the church of my ancestors. I do want to be saved, if the business isn't too tedious. Shall we start by going swimming together, Father? Tomorrow morning, perhaps? *I* can swim quite well, too. . . ."

Sir Clive joined Hilary at the buffet.

"Where's Isabel?"

Hilary made a vague, sweeping gesture.

"Somewhere."

"She hasn't come to see me in quite some time. Is she all right?"

"Can a statue bleed? Can a work of art suffer? Don't ask me."

"Let's go and find her."

Hilary rapped his glass on the counter. "Give us some champagne," he ordered the barman, deliberately slurring the words. "Fill 'em up, old boy, that's the style."

"You haven't got seriously drunk yet, have you?" Clive teased him.

"Not yet. But I shall, very shortly."

"Let's find Isabel first, then."

"Good idea. Then you can take her home if I decide to go on a blind." He saw Leonides coming toward them. "You wait here," he said. "I'll get her."

"And this is the artist, Sir Clive Bellingham," Leonides informed Van Sullivan the Second and his other guests. He had just taken them to his office-cabin and shown them the portrait of Angela.

"It certainly is a fine piece of work," said Sullivan. "May I congratulate you, sir."

"I'm most obliged to you, Sir Clive," said Leonides. However brash he might be with others, in the presence of the former ambassador he was always suave and courteous.

Clive, who had returned the money for the portrait, had had to accept the kiln which arrived from England with the compliments of the Old Lion.

"Thank you again, Mr. Leonides, for the kiln. It's exactly what I wanted —how did you think of it?"

"I just thought I must send you something too heavy for you to return!"

He smiled, well pleased with himself, and moved on with his guests.

Hilary found Isabel, who had been cornered by Ted and Terry. He put his arm around her and drew her toward the buffet table and Clive.

"Now, Isabel, I never thought I'd have to rescue you from these two. If you knew how many women they've raped—why, the whole female population of the island trembles at the sight of them."

Clive took Isabel's hand and pressed it.

"I'll get us some champagne," said Hilary and went away.

Clive let go of her hand.

"Those blue eyes of yours . . ." he said. "Why haven't you been to see me? You haven't been ill, have you?"

"I'm all right," she said softly.

"Isabel . . . Come with me. I have something to tell you tonight."

He put a hand on her back and led her along the deck.

"It's quiet here," he said when they were alone. "Look at the lights on the islands. . . ."

Isabel paused, drinking in the night.

"It's beautiful," she murmured.

"The world is charged with the grandeur of God, do you remember? I've got a new album of Hopkins, read by Margaret Rawlings. I had it sent especially for you."

"How kind of you, Clive."

"I want to be kind to you, Isabel, I want to take care of you."

She pressed his hand.

"I wonder if you know how very much you mean to me, Isabel."

"I'm sorry I didn't come to see you. I've been feeling sad and silly."

"I love you, Isabel. I want you to marry me. I can't promise you much, but we'll have the sea and the islands together."

"You know that's not possible, Clive."

"You don't belong with Hilary—why carry on in such unhappiness?"

"I'm useless to him, I feel so guilty."

"Then marry me. I'll never ask anything from you, only to look at you, to paint your perfect face, to be with you."

"Dear Clive," she said. "You wouldn't have asked me if you knew more about me."

She reached up and touched his hair, but as he looked into those blue eyes he could sense that they were not for him, that her thoughts were with the wedding guests where Mark moved here and there. Clive had noticed them looking at each other that evening and his "proposal" was more like a final act of despair.

"We could be happy together, we share so much. I can give you some things nobody else can give you."

Acutely embarrassed, Clive raised her hand to his lips and took her back to Hilary. She was young, it was only natural, he told himself; if he hadn't been lame they would have gone swimming together, he, too, would have taken her to the Golden Dolphin and danced all night. *I have her portrait, nobody can take that away.* It was all he would have of her. He limped slowly along to the gangway where he would take the motor launch back to the shore.

Hilary gave Isabel his own glass of champagne and disappeared toward the bar. Unescorted, she wandered among the guests, saw Mark at the other end of the deck, moving through the chattering throng—pale, handsome, different. *He's back, he must have outwitted them all and he's back. How brave he is.*

Angela, who had been watching Isabel, came up to her.

"Why, Isabel, you look lovely—angelic, as always. Spiritual seduction, that must be your line. How many conquests tonight?"

She paused, but Isabel did not respond.

"And what a lovely dress. I always think of you in white, I wonder why."

"Thank you. You look very nice, too."

"I have to, for the occasion. My dear little niece Thalia has done it at last—she's managed to bring home her very own millionaire."

Angela signaled to Felix for cigarettes and offered the case to Isabel.

"Thank you. I don't smoke."

"Ah, I'd forgotten. Felix, go get us some champagne."

Angela moved closer to her.

"Tell me, do you tint your hair? No? I thought not." She leaned forward and touched Isabel's cheek lightly with her fingertips. "That marvelous English skin . . ."

Isabel recoiled like a cat stroked by a stranger.

Angela unperturbed, slipped an arm through hers.

"Queen and huntress, chaste and fair—does your quarry ever get away?"

She must be nearly forty, thought Isabel, seeing the faint network of lines around the enormous eyes.

"Where's Hilary?" Angela asked her. "Hilary and I were friends once, very close friends, but your spiritual spell reached over the oceans, over the continents, and he abandoned me to go to you."

Hilary joined them, he felt self-conscious and restless, he didn't know what to say.

"Let's celebrate," he said, lifting his glass. "Before you can say wedding bells, I bet they'll give birth to twins."

The two women looked at him blankly; they were strangers and he hated them.

"I'm funny and I'm drunk and you both pity me and I know it."

Isabel, embarrassed, brought her glass to her lips but barely touched the wine. Hilary looked around, suddenly wanting to get away, and wandered off.

Angela and Isabel watched him go to Mark, who was standing in a small group of people nearby; then the two women turned and, as if by mutual impulse, stared at each other for a long moment.

"This quarry you will not kill," Angela said finally. "You did your best, but your bows and arrows are useless against him. He's mine, I've got him in a cage and I've thrown the key into the sea."

Hilary went to the bar, drew up a bottle of champagne from an ice bucket, and, beckoning expansively for Mark to follow him, walked over to the swimming pool area where many guests from the party had spilled out. He filled his glass to the brim and drank it down.

"You're not looking too well, Mark. And you're not drinking, either."

"I'm all right."

"I was sorry to hear you'd been in the calaboose."

"Calaboose? What's that?"

"The clink—oh well, I meant at the police barracks. Anyhow, I'm glad you're back in circulation again. I must say, some of those cops look ugly customers to me. I hope there wasn't any rough stuff, was there?"

"No, nothing like that." Then he caught Hilary's gaze and grinned. "Well," he amended, "maybe a little."

Hilary poured him a glass of champagne.

"You know, old boy, if you're feeling a bit down about things, a little drinking is the best way to put it right. It never fails with me, anyhow."

Some men came along the deck holding Petros Kommenos by both arms, talking soothingly to him as the pale, thin man kicked and struggled ineffectually and swore.

"He knew all along about his wife and Luigi and he picks this evening to get annoyed about it," said Hilary.

He sank down upon a bench.

"I thought it was a paradise here when I first saw the island. Now I wish we were all back in Athens."

His shoulders slumped. If he were in Athens he would see Daphne, he would go and listen to Eva singing her haunting songs.

"*Some* paradise! We're all dice in the hands of the Almighty—you were right, Mark. I wish somebody would explain the rules to us."

Mark saw Isabel standing alone at the railing, looking out.

"Drink up," said Hilary, watching his face. "There's plenty here."

He waited for Mark to empty his glass, then leaned over and whispered confidentially.

"You know, Mark, to be honest, I used to be sorry for you because I know what a satanic bitch Isabel can be, but then, God knows what you did to her—now, I'm not asking, I'm not even curious anymore—but she came home one night looking like a bloody ghost and she's not really been herself since. You didn't, did you, Mark?"

"You've had too much champagne, Hilary. You don't know what you're saying."

"I *knew* you didn't. Mind you, it's not my fault—God knows, I tried. It's just no use, an emotional block or trauma or something, you know how the quacks and the shrinks go on about these things. She just can't, that's all."

The two men sat silent. Hilary, suddenly deflated, bent down to put his empty glass on the deck. Misjudging the distance, he set it down too hard and the glass broke on the boards. The splintering of glass focused Mark's thoughts and understanding crystallized in his dazed mind.

"I'm sorry," said Hilary, putting his arm around him.

Mark shuddered as the pain traveled up to his bruised face.

"Poor Mark—those bloody pigs. I'm sorry."

Mark started walking away; Hilary followed, swaying a little.

"I say, I think I've been a bit indiscreet, haven't I? It's the drink, you know, it's the drink."

But Mark did not wait for him and Hilary lost him in the crowd. He then had an idea to go and get another bottle of champagne, but the Old Lion was standing by the bar, Angela on his arm. Isabel was still alone at the railing, and Hilary shambled his way toward her; it was dark and he knocked over a small table and a large box of cigars fell on the deck—Havana cigars, the real thing, each encased in its glass tube.

Hilary took one out, lit it, and breathed in contentedly; they were too good to leave and he took a handful and pushed them down into his pockets. A few cigars won't put the Lions into the bankruptcy court, he thought, the glass tubes tinkling a little as he walked gingerly to collect his wife.

18

Mark stared up at the dull sky, feeling the drops of sweat forming on his forehead. The sunset had been lurid and the air was still hot and close, hovering over the sea, pressing down on them like an enormous weight. Angela lay next to him, naked like himself.

She turned over on her side, waving one leg in the air, running the hot sand through her fingers. Brother Leon had left her to go with Van and Thalia—he and the Sullivans were accompanying the newlyweds on a cruise as far as Rhodes, where the happy couple would spend their honeymoon. Brother Leon's desertion rankled, and Angela drew nearer to Mark.

"Brother Leon still doesn't know about us."

Her fingers wandered over his face and chest; then she sat up, bent over and kissed his nipples.

"I'm envious of Thalia," she said. "I think it's about time I got married myself. Have you ever thought of getting married?"

"I was married, once."

"Are you joking?"

"It was certainly no joke."

"I suppose it would be asking too much to expect you to tell me about it?"

"Much too much."

She lay back on the sand, arms spread wide.

"The most beautiful woman at the party was Isabel—that skin, and hair, and those eyes! I'd like to love her myself, but she'd never allow it. You haven't seen her lately, have you, Mark?"

"No."

"Pity. You could have helped, you could have arranged something."

Mark said nothing.

"When is your next assignation with Isabel? It must have been a bad scene. A fight? I'm sure you'll see her again."

"No."

"You sound very certain. I'd like to think that you were certain. Tell me, what made you break it off?"

"Is there only one way to make you shut up?"

She waited expectantly, but he made no move; she turned to him, pulling herself closer, her hand traveling down his body.

"Bastard," she murmured.

She buried her head between his legs and kissed and tongued him, feeling him grow big in her mouth, until he grasped her by the hair and pulled her off.

He stood at the helm of the boat and turned it toward the anchorage at Kalamos Village. Angela lay on the deck, still naked, smiling lazily up at him, but Mark avoided her gaze. The job was done, the stuff was on its way to Marseilles, what was he waiting for? Several of his contacts had been arrested; Nubar was still at large, but for how long? *Why am I waiting? I don't love Isabel. I don't want to love her. She's sick. I can't cope with her.*

His papers had been returned to him, his passport was in order. Now he could make his bid for that Norwegian ship and establish himself in a small office in London—or Buenos Aires, or New York, or Paris. . . . Already he felt like an exile. He would miss this coast, these blue waters, this salt breeze: Now that the time had come for him to leave, he felt an unexpected attachment to his country.

"Brother Leon will get you in the end, just you see."

He ignored the interruption. He would miss Athens and the islands, he would miss Eva, waiting loyally for him to come back.

"I'd like to see what happens when he gets hold of you. He'll be back any day now. I'd like to see how he'll mess you up—castrate you, I hope, make you my slave, like Felix. You won't be much good to that beautiful white lily when Leon gets through with you."

"It's nice to know you've got my good at heart."

182

"Don't believe me if you don't want to. We'll see. Brother Leon is extremely jealous of men like you, he's a good brother who knows what's best for his baby sister. Kriton didn't understand him, poor Kriton, but Ludwig was more intelligent and got out in time. I wonder if you'll be in time."

Mark realized the risks he was taking, all right. *Let him try, let him just try.*

"When he catches up with you your only hope is to offer to marry me. But I won't accept."

She slipped on her dress, not bothering to put on briefs or brassiere; Mark helped her out of the boat and they headed for the Kalamos Village restaurant.

"Send for the waiter to tell us what's on tonight," she said. "I'm famished."

The restaurant was spacious, but many of the tables had been brought outside and arranged beneath the two large plane trees, only fifty yards from the sea. Some people were eating in their swimming costumes; others had dressed for the evening.

"Bring us some of everything," Angela told the waiter. "Give us everything you have."

"Bring us a good bottle of wine," said Mark.

The waiter returned with the wine and a tray crowded with small dishes of savories; Angela sampled them all, loading her plate. Mark sat back in his chair and sipped at the iced wine.

"A lobster, a nice juicy lobster, alive and kicking, that's what I want." The lobsters, perhaps fifty of them, were in a fenced-in rock pool fed by the sea. It didn't take Angela long to choose the one with the most life in it. "That one!" she cried, pointing. "He must be the stud of the shoal. Let's boil him alive and eat him up."

Her eyes glittered as she watched the lobster being fished out and carried, dripping and struggling, to the kitchen. When it was served, Angela pushed some of the lobster on to Mark's plate.

"Delicious," she said, sucking at a tiny leg.

Watching Angela's moist crimson lips as she devoured her prey, Mark couldn't bring himself to eat any of it.

Someone recognized the Baroness in the glow of the table lantern, and several people came over to share their food and wine. Angela kicked off her sandals, shook loose her hair, and joined the crowd of dancers gyrating to the frenetic beat of the music.

Mark emptied his glass and left for the converted beach house where there was gambling every evening.

The man collected the notes into a pile, folded them in two, and slipped them into his hip pocket.

"Well, that's all for tonight."

"Lend me a hundred more," said Mark. "Just this once."

"I'm sorry, Mr. Stephanou. You owe us enough here. Don't worry, I'll be around whenever you want your revenge."

"I'll give you a nice sum for that watch," said another man. "It's platinum, isn't it?"

"How much will you offer for the Jaguar? It cost twenty-five thousand drachmas."

"I'll give you ten."

"Come off it, you can't be serious. I can get twenty thousand any time from the first dealer in Athens."

Having never thought of selling the car, he found himself drawn into the ritual of bargaining.

"Twelve thousand," said the man. "And that's it."

"Make it fifteen . . ."

For the next thirty minutes fortune seemed to smile on him; but then his luck turned, nothing came his way. When he got up an hour or so later, minus the Jaguar, he was surprised to find that he was not really disturbed at his losses, only relieved that he had been able to cover his debts. He still had his watch, his talisman, and he could always get another car. He looked at the watch now. It was five minutes to one.

He felt lighter, he needed a drink. The bar was closing, so he bought a bottle of Scotch, poured some into a glass, and walked away with the bottle. Further along the shore, only a few yards from the sea, was the bungalow from which Nubar had directed his operations. The man who worked there was a local and went home at night; Mark had a key and he had stayed several times, mostly with Angela. When he entered, he didn't bother to turn on the lights but walked through to the veranda, sat on the low stone parapet, poured himself some more whiskey and tossed it back, feeling the glow in his stomach.

He finished his drink and poured himself another. And another. A girl had once told him that a Welsh poet had drunk himself to death in a New York bar on eighteen double whiskeys; it seemed quite a good idea and Mark got up and found another bottle of Scotch, almost full. But he needn't kill himself just that moment—he went to the sink and ran some water into his glass. His legs were already unsteady and he found himself leaning heavily against the wall; then he made his way out to the veranda and set the new bottle next to the other on the parapet. These good friends would keep him busy for quite some time. Suddenly very tired, he slipped down and sat on the floor. His back hurt as he leaned against the stone wall, but he would not—could not—get up.

He wished there were someone to talk to. He thought of Isabel and poured himself another drink. It was true now that he did not want to see her again—not Isabel, not Eva, not Katia, not anybody. Angela was part of his daily life, the life in which time was running out. Hilary—if anyone, it was Hilary whom he would like to have a drink with just then.

He heard the door open and recognized Angela's voice, offering drinks to some people. Then she came outside and sat on the parapet near Mark.

"Are you all right?" she asked.

"Yes, yes. Come and join me and send the mob away."

"They're not staying. Why did you sneak off?"

Mark laid his head against her thigh and slid his hand up her skirt.

"You've been hitting it, you mean bastard. You're drunk."

"It's your smell that makes me drunk."

"It's the whiskey," she said, but she liked his hand touching her under the skirt. "Give me the bottle."

"Why? Are you afraid I won't be good enough in bed?"

"You always think of that, don't you?"

"Don't *you?* Come on, take off that dress and let's have a swim."

"Honey, you'd sink in your present condition. It's not a good idea."

"All right, we'll go to bed. Let's drink and let's fuck and let's spit on everybody."

"Don't overdo it, honey. One day there'll be no more candle and no more ends."

"Do you know, once, I didn't have any drink or any woman for three whole years? I'm only making up for lost time."

"You never told me about those years," she said, her hand caressing his hair. "I wish you'd tell me . . . Did they mistreat you?"

He shook his head.

"They beat you up? They made you crawl, but you won't tell? Did you let the screws fuck you for cigarettes? Did you lick their arses for extra food? Why didn't you try to escape? Or did you like to be punished for your crimes?"

"Escape—where? You can't live permanently on the run."

"What is it like when you come back into the world?"

"First you wash, second you stare at the stranger you see in the mirror—you haven't exactly improved, you tell yourself. Then you have a drink, then you eat, then you have another drink. Then you walk around, looking at the people, wondering if they know about you. Then . . ."

"What?"

"Then you go and look at yourself in the mirror again."

"*If* you're as vain as Markos Stephanou!"

It was true. But in prison he had lost the habit of taking care of himself. On that first day of freedom he had moved close to the mirror in the cheap hired room and stared curiously at the face that reflected only part of the bitterness he felt. He had looked down at his hands; they were a mess, the nails black and broken, the palms calloused, the skin rough.

He put down his glass now and looked at his hands. Even in the dark he knew that the skin was clean, the nails well cared for. He turned them over and ran the fingers of his left hand over the smooth ridge of the scar on his right hand. A sharp rock in the quarries had crushed his hand wide open; when the deep wound had begun to turn septic, the prison doctor had drained and stitched it. He hadn't used an anesthetic. . . .

"Where's your wife now? What have you done with her?"

"Jennie's at rest."

"How did she die?"

There was a pause. Then he said quietly, "An overdose of heroin."

"Jennie's a nice name for a dead wife," Angela said. "I appreciate her being dead, it's very considerate of her. I know some other women who should die, too, but they don't seem to realize it."

"What do you think makes people take drugs?" he asked abruptly.

"They like taking them, I suppose."

But he was not listening. The dreaded vision had come back; he walked about the veranda, stretching out his hand as if to close her eyes, but the lids were stiff and would not yield to his touch.

"If I ever kill somebody," he said, "it'll be a dope merchant."

He reached the wall and rested his hot forehead against the cool stone and mentally laid a gun against his throbbing temples. He could see his guilt now, he could see now the thing that was not to be looked at, the thing he had always managed *not* to see.

He held up his glass and started to pour more whiskey. For a moment he held the glass and the bottle, one in each hand, undecided. Then he shouted, "Am I Christ? Am I their keeper?"—and hurled the bottle violently against the rocks below. Seeing the jagged shards of glass gleaming as they caught the light, he laughed.

"Who's for a swim?" he called to Angela. "Who's going to swim to the other shore?"

Angela thought that it was all very studied, very staged, but Mark was in dead earnest. He began taking off his shirt; then suddenly he faltered, swayed, and collapsed in a heap on the ground.

She looked down at him, prodded him gently with her foot, but when there was no response she lit a cigarette and sat there watching him for a while. Poor devil, she thought, he's had his share, he deserves something better. I'll marry him, I'll make him happy.

She went inside and ordered Felix to put Mark in the car and drive them back to the villa.

By the time they got back, drops of rain were falling on the terrace. Mark sank down into a deck chair, liking the rain, waiting for a cloudburst. But the rain stopped. There was lightning but no thunder, the storm was far away. The air was oppressive and he found it difficult to breathe. The sea below lay black and still, a monster couching dormant, biding its time.

186

Felix came out and helped him through the French doors and up the stairs to the large bedroom.

"I'll go and fetch some black coffee, madame," he said.

Soon Mark was dropping off to sleep, barely conscious of the woman by his side, but when Felix returned he took some of the coffee.

"Thank you, Felix."

Mark finished his coffee and dragged himself to the balcony, leaned over, and vomited. Now and then hot, heavy drops of rain fell; the storm was approaching but the sea was still quiet, still waiting. Then he heard music coming from the piano in the drawing room below.

When he went in, Angela called to him from the bed, but he lay down on a couch and dozed for some time. The roar of the storm finally woke him up. Angela was not there, the piano was still playing downstairs, and he went down to see what was going on.

The drawing room was lit by candles, dozens of them; Felix was sitting at the piano, wearing a monk's robe. The French windows were open, and Mark could hear Angela crying on the terrace. As he went outside, a streak of lightning broke the dark sky, and a crash of thunder made the windows shudder. Another flash of lightning illuminated Angela's face, distorted in agony.

"Markos—take me to him, take me to my boy!"

She was dressed as a nun, she was barefoot, her hair streamed out from beneath the hood.

"Who is your boy?" he asked, but he stepped back involuntarily, afraid in the presence of the insane.

"He's all I've got, all I ever had—they can't take him away, I won't let them! Philip, Philip, I'm coming."

She fell to her knees, her arms raised up, her voice rising to a crescendo. "Philip! I'm coming!"

"Angela. Who is Philip?"

"Take me to him, Markos, and I won't tell Brother Leon. Save him and I won't tell Leon and I'll marry you, Markos."

She was wailing, tugging at her hair. The rain fell in earnest now, and strong gusts of wind made the curtains flare out from the open windows. There was a peal of thunder that went on for several seconds—he heard pictures falling from the drawing-room walls, and from the sea there came a roar as if a giant monster had just been awakened.

The rain became torrential; Mark tried to take Angela inside, but she held tightly to him and wouldn't move. Her hood was blown back and the violent rain soaked the nun's habit as she clutched him, her voice rising and falling in the same monotonous octave.

"Philip, Philip, mother is coming, darling, don't fear anything, I'm coming to you, I'm coming my boy, my little prince—can't you hear him, Markos?

187

He's calling now, take me to him, Markos, and I'll do anything you ask, always!"

Mark tried to hold her close, to protect her from the rain, to pull her by force away from the storm, but she rocked and swayed, crying out to him, beyond the rational world, through the malicious roar of the elements.

"Take me to him, Markos. I'm coming, Philip . . ."

Suddenly Mark heard Andreas calling through the tempest. He tore himself away from Angela and ran to the edge of the terrace. Andreas came up, wet and panting, shaking the streaming water from him like a dog.

"It's Mrs. Grey, she's in the boat and it's adrift, she's on the sea . . .!"

Mark rushed down the steps to the landing stage, jumped into the motor launch, and started the engine. The waves were mountains, it was pitch dark, the rain was drowning the sea, the wind was roaring, and Andreas, standing helplessly on the landing stage, could see neither the launch nor the sailing boat in which Isabel had slipped out to sea.

Angela lay sprawled on the terrace, lashed mercilessly by the rain, the piano music breaking through the wind to mock her fears.

Part Four

□

19

The lightning split the black sky; the thunder roared from the center of the earth. Mark fought desperately in the treacherous channel. He traveled as far as the mainland, but the gale tossed him back—he could not keep the wheel steady, he was carried east and south. Isabel's boat had to be ahead of him, chased by the tempest. . . . As he rode full speed with the wind, he felt her presence somewhere in that vastness between the sky and the ocean; sometimes he even thought he could hear her calling to him through the roar of the thunder and the mad howling of the wind.

Suddenly the searchlights of the motor launch fell upon floating chairs and tables: This must be the Akroyiali Beach. Mark turned south, desperate. . . . A crash of thunder sent the launch up in midair, then down before the giant waves, then up again. Lightning lit the sky for a moment and Mark sighted a dark floating mass two or three hundred yards away. An upturned boat? Isabel's presence was overwhelmingly near. He struggled against the raging elements to reach her, to rescue her, to be near her.

For what seemed ages he was lost, the motor launch no longer under his control, until the wind finally began to die down. Isabel was floating close to the launch, holding onto a sail; Mark put the engine in neutral, dived into the sea, caught her by her thick hair, swam back, and lifted her up.

The storm was not yet over, the wind swept in from the west, there was no way of turning back. Mark let the launch travel with the waves until he managed to turn into Glaros Bay. When he picked Isabel up in his arms she was like a frightened child, dazed but alive, clinging to him. He carried her to the hut, took off her sodden clothes, put her on the nets, dried her, and wrapped her in an old blanket he found there. Around her neck she had the long turquoise necklace he had given her, and he arranged it carefully over her breasts. Then he took off his clothes, lay down, and took her in his arms.

Outside the hut the wind whined through the cracks of the door; from time to time their hideout would be brightly lit as lightning flashed through the skylight. Isabel nuzzled in Mark's arms, kissing him on the throat. He pulled the blanket over them both, holding her close, feeling her body, tense and vibrant, pressing against him. Already hard, he tried not to move, not to frighten her.

But Isabel's hands touched his shoulders and chest, moved down and found him and held him tight for a moment. She rolled onto her back, still holding him, and Mark got on top of her; at the first thrust inside he felt the barrier and stopped.

"There!" she cried.

Lightning flashed and Isabel closed her eyes, ready for the sacrificial act. Their bodies seemed to vibrate with the electric current of the storm, and when a crash of thunder shook the hut, Mark's thrust came naturally. Her sudden cry of terrible pain, part of the blast, was carried away by the wind sweeping the distant skies. They were united and Isabel felt warm and moist, tingling inside her body, her brain, her heart. As the climax approached, she was praying inwardly for the hour of our death, and then for a frightening moment she *was* dying, a lamb devoured by a tiger. . . .

They stayed together for a long time, Isabel's head drooping like a tired flower on Mark's heart. And when they returned to themselves Mark was a god to her, strong and gentle and all-loving; the pain of the sacrifice was vindicated.

Mark saw her eyes opening; the first faint glow of dawn seemed to make her flesh translucent. . . . He kissed her and held her close. In all his life he had known no pleasure greater than this.

The storm, attendant to their act, was pacified; the wind died down, the rain stopped, and silence returned to the cliffs and the bay.

Neither Mark nor Isabel spoke until the new day broke through the skylight. Then Mark left her body, helped her to get up, and opened the door. As they stepped outside, a snow-white gull swept by them, crying for the morning.

"Jemima?" asked Mark.

"The birds are free," said Isabel.

Holding hands, they walked naked down to the sea and bathed in the glowing waters. Then they spread their clothes on the pebbles to dry and lay nearby on the sand, their bodies and spirits awake and at rest.

Isabel rested her hands on the parapet and watched the Parthenon changing colors, a jewel set among the shining lights of the city. She felt Mark's lips brush her hair and instinctively her hand went up, her fingers playing with the turquoise necklace. His hand closed over hers, took it up, kissed it, and placed it against his cheek.

"Dear, dear Mark."

They stood on the balcony of his apartment in Kolonaki and listened to the sounds of Athens, conscious of their love and desire for each other; now, that very moment, happy to be together, to know that the night was theirs. Mark kissed her open palm, the wrist, the long slender fingers, her bare, cool arm. . . . Something had been reborn in him, something youthful and free—he now had that capacity to feel which he had thought long dead.

192

He caught the scent of the perfume he had bought her earlier that day; he turned her around and kissed her again and again.

"I'll never have enough of you," he said.

She laid her finger against his lips.

"Greedy . . ."

"Just hungry," he said and kissed her on the mouth again.

"Your eyes, Mark . . . Your mouth gives everything, but your eyes always hold something back."

They drove to a fashionable restaurant in Pendeli; they had dinner, drank iced champagne, danced till late in the night. Mark was totally absorbed in her; she was the only woman in the universe, she loved being cherished and Mark loved doing the cherishing. He courted her and flirted with her, pressing her hand, brushing his knee against hers, sketching a delicate kiss across the table.

"*Yiá chará!*"

"*Egészeségére, Isabel!*"

"No sooner do I learn one language than you come up with another."

They had made love twice that afternoon, but as they left the restaurant and she took his arm, Isabel was conscious of an intense, secret sexual thrill. Her skin was glowing, her cheeks were flushed with excitement, her eyes were shining. . . .

Neither of them wanted to go back to the apartment just then, so Mark drove the car to the foot of Lycavitos and suggested that they climb the hill.

"We'll watch the sunrise," he said.

It was not yet four o'clock so he led her away from the main path to lie under the pine trees. They were tired but not sleepy; they made long slow love and he fell asleep inside her.

Isabel lay quite still, holding him for as long as she could. She bore his weight contentedly, but as he fell into deeper sleep, she pushed him gently down by her side and looked at her lover.

He had the trusting innocence of all sleeping creatures; one arm lay across his face, the other was flung out, palm upward, strong and graceful and relaxed. She kissed the scarred hand and then his sleeping face; Mark murmured something in Greek or Magyar but didn't awaken.

Isabel sat up, put his head on her lap, and covered him with his jacket. As she was arranging it, she felt something heavy in the pocket and took it out so it wouldn't press on him. It was a gun. She put it back in the pocket. When he was away from her, she had always imagined him as struggling for a cause, fighting secretly for freedom. Now she knew she had been right all along.

When Mark woke up, she helped him on with his jacket; but as she embraced him, she pressed her hand against his pocket.

"You thought you could hide it from me, but I knew all along," she said. "Which group do you belong to? The National Resistance Movement or the Free Greeks? Or is it the Greek Democratic Movement?"

193

"Don't ask me these questions," he said. "Please."

Why was he afraid of her knowing? Could it be that he was mixed up in something else, something she didn't know about, something she didn't understand?

"Even now you don't trust me, Mark. Even now."

"I do trust you."

"But you won't tell me."

"I can't."

"You've taken an oath, isn't that it? Tell me this, only this. That night when the government agent was killed, was it arms you were carrying in the boat, arms and ammunition for the struggle?"

Mark stopped her questions with a kiss, and they set off again for the top of the hill.

But as they climbed each of them was thinking about the gun in Mark's pocket, and they put their arms around each other as if to protect themselves and their love from the unknown.

Mark was driving the winding uphill road that led past the Tatoi Palace to the top of the Parnes Mountains. By the time he got there, his watch read ten to eight; he waited in the parking lot of the Xenia Hotel, smoking a cigarette.

Nubar Ohanessian was hidden only three hundred yards away in the forest. He tried to embrace Mark with his one arm but Mark stepped back.

"I've got good news for you, Markos, you lucky bastard. Don't worry that you didn't catch Katia—the English girl's the most beautiful creature I've ever seen, next to her Katia is trash. Never mind that she's penniless, you can be as rich as any of them."

"What is it, Nubar?"

"I knew you'd get my message, I knew you'd come."

"What is it?"

"Good old Markos, I've missed you, my good friend, I miss the old times. Now, you haven't asked me how I am, so I'll tell you. I'm pretty snug now, but it's terrible not being able to show one's face and there are agents everywhere. They won't report on me, not if I have anything to do with it—remember, I don't do so badly with a left-handed draw, do I?"

"What do you want, Nubar?"

"When I remember how you saved my life in Napoli, when I think how good you were to my poor brother—you're my good friend, Markos, and when I get to Italy, the first thing I'll do is send you a card to come and have some wine with me on the Via Veneto. Bring along your girl and show her the catacombs —right, Markos?"

He laughed, not at all the desperate fugitive.

"How much do you think your cut was from the job?" He added.

194

"I don't know, it should be over a hundred thousand."

"One hundred and thirty-five thousand dollars. In your numbered account in Geneva, as safe as the treasury in the Vatican. Don't say I don't do well by you."

"You do. You have."

"Well, won't you say thanks, haven't you anything to say to your old friend?"

"What do you want from me now, Nubar?"

"I want from you? Nothing my good friend, only your love, I pray to God to give you good health, you and your *philenada*. Now, if you wanted, if you're interested, we could make some more thousands, just to wind things up before we clear out."

Mark waited.

"It's a safe job. *Very* safe. I've got it all organized, but I can't run around as I used to, the pigs are looking out for me. So I say to myself, Markos is your best friend, he's getting married, perhaps. He needs friends, and money is a man's best friend. There's plenty in this job, Markos, I'm telling you. What about making your cut double? Well, what do you say?"

Mark shook his head.

"The stuff is all waiting in Teheran. I can't get it over the Turkish border or the Iraqi border, we had some trouble there."

At once Mark knew the correct route, but he wasn't going to be tempted.

"Sorry, Nubar. I've other plans now, I'm busy."

Nubar went on as if he hadn't heard.

"I know that our ships are plying up and down the Persian Gulf."

"That coast is very far from Teheran."

"It would take my friends only four days, but let's give them a week in case the bus breaks down and they have to use mules over the mountains."

Nubar laughed and his white even teeth gleamed in the dusk.

"No, Nubar, I'm giving up my position in the firm. Sorry, I can't help."

"Now, Markos, you're turning soft. You *are* getting married, aren't you?"

"Yes, I am."

"You never learn, do you? This English woman must be some lay."

"Shut up!"

"Well, well, we're touchy now, aren't we? I wonder how that cuckold of a husband is taking it."

"None of your damned business."

"How do you do it, Markos? What do you promise them? *La dolce vita?* Well, here's the chance to make some real money for you and your girl."

"Listen to me, Nubar. I'm out of the game for good, I'm making a fresh start. Going abroad. And I don't need any more money."

"I'm sure your girl doesn't agree with you. I'll ask her myself."

"You'll do nothing of the sort."

Mark's hand fondled the gun in his pocket.

"Yes, I'll call her and explain the situation. I think she'd be interested."

"You do that and I'll kill you."

"I like you, Markos! You were always hot-tempered. I'll speak to your girl, she'll calm you down."

Mark took his hand out of his pocket, defeated.

"This business is strictly between us," he said. "You tell anyone and I'll . . ."

"Good old Markos, why do you get angry with me? Because I'm going to make you rich?"

He clasped Mark's arm.

"Now, you fix up your end and leave a message for me at the kiosk. . . ."

It was after ten, he had promised to take Isabel out that evening, but he kept on Piraeus Avenue and went directly to the firm's main offices. Somebody was always there, day and night, receiving and sending messages, transmitting to the far ends of the earth the orders that came from the Old Lion. Mark himself had done this many times, and as he went up in the elevator, he couldn't help feeling wistful. Yet it had to be done; he couldn't spend his life in the Old Man's shadow, he couldn't ask Isabel to live beneath it.

The telegraphist was busy, but he still waved a quick hand to Mark. On the world map marking the positions of the Lion's ships, Mark instantly recognized the code number pinned at Abadan. Number seven, the *World Seafarer*; he pulled out the right drawer and checked the ledger. The giant tanker had docked four days earlier; to load she needed thirteen days and, yes, she was expected to sail for the States nine days later. Mark shut the ledger and put it back. The telegraphist removed his earphones and stood up to greet Mark.

"I need to speak to the second mate of the *World Seafarer*," Mark told him. "Would you get him for me?"

Once the man was finally on the line, Mark asked about his wife and family in Athens, promised to look them up.

"If Ida comes aboard to look for me," he said, "give her a drink and make her comfortable. You know, she always wanted to give me an antique prayer mat—if she comes up with one, do take care of it."

It could be a prayer mat, a copper jar, a set of worry beads—the code word was always "antique." As Mark went to his office he felt exhilarated. He was in the game again, he was on the move.

His desk was bare, but he found a pad and sat down and started writing; . . . *It is with regret that I tender my resignation. . . . You've been good to me and I appreciate it. . . . In choosing to go it alone, I am only following your example, so I expect you will understand. . . .* He signed and folded the paper, then started looking for an envelope.

196

At that moment Leandros came in, dressed as always in immaculate white.

"I've a letter here for your father," said Mark. "I came to see him, I wanted to talk to him."

"Mr. Leonides is on the island tonight. He won't be back until the day after tomorrow, as I'm sure you very well know."

"Damn it, I can't find an envelope in this place. Could you take care of this? Hand it to the Old Man?"

"What is it, if I may ask?"

"It's my resignation."

"Really? Well, you've been relieved of your duties already. Sorry, I assumed you'd been informed."

Leandros, an odd smile on his face, crumpled the letter and threw it into a wastebasket.

"Did *you* relieve me of my duties?"

"Mr. Leonides, of course, made his own decision."

"I resign," Mark said firmly, but the stab had gone home. He felt betrayed.

"I quit," he muttered, more to himself. "I quit."

"You're fired," said Leandros and walked out of the room.

As Mark drove back to Athens, he was hardly aware of the traffic, the lights, the crowds in the streets. Isabel was in his apartment, waiting for him, loving him. He needed her now, her comfort and support and love, now more than ever.

20

It hurt, the pain was bad. Especially the way it had been done—as if he were of no consequence, the last to be thought of, his feelings of no interest to anybody. Hilary's foot pressed the accelerator and the little green car jumped as if she had been kicked.

"Poor Josephine, you boil and rattle, but you still go. We have good hearts, you and I."

He touched his jacket; obstinately he kept Isabel's letter in the inside pocket, a relic that hurt and must nonetheless be treasured. Now he had only himself to worry about—yet why should he worry? To keep body and soul together, that he could manage, that shouldn't take much effort; he could teach English in Athens, a few drachmas would suffice for a modest room and some simple fare. He still had Josephine, he could get around. . . .

He had driven to Glyfada, collected the few things he had left behind at the

Venus Beach Hotel, then set off for Piraeus. He could see the ships coming and going there, he could watch the tourists, the emigrants, the tarts and pimps, the strange flotsam of the big port. Here there were no pretenses to keep up, there was nobody to impress or deceive, to hurt or make happy.

He felt buoyant and he didn't see why Josephine should be overloaded—he drove down to the coast, opened his bags, and took out various things he would never need again: Isabel's clothes, some old shoes, a stack of paperbacks, a thermos flask, a brocade waistcoat he had bought in Damascus and never worn. He could have sold everything in a secondhand market, but he couldn't be bothered, and he dumped the lot into the sea, watching the thermos flask bob up and down. Then he took off his shirt, kicked off his shoes, and eased himself into the driving seat. There was no hurry, the port was always there, now unbearably hot in the afternoon sun. He would descend upon it with the first cool breeze of the evening.

He drove along the coast road and stopped at Neon Phaleron, changed into his swimming trunks, and joined the crowds in the dazzling surf. The sun was healing, the salt sea air invigorating, and he felt elated by the mass of humanity swarming around him. *I'm one of them, but I'm not of them. I have work to do.* And he dozed on the sand, turning from side to side.

With the sunset Hilary found the beach virtually deserted, so he drove over the Kastella and down to Piraeus; he stayed there that evening and the next and the next, sleeping in the car, taking a ring of hard bread with sesame to assuage his hunger. Otherwise he ate and drank very little, careful with his money, suddenly stingy and abstemious.

There was no reason for him to shave and he soon acquired a beard. Again and again he looked at himself in the car mirror, pleased with his appearance, his new identity. The pimps tried to interest him in the girls of the area, the homosexual boys wanted him to give them a ride in his car. But Hilary refused without offending anyone, and soon the harbor world accepted him on his own terms. People would ask him to join them for an ouzo or a small sticky black coffee or even a cognac. Hilary enjoyed the company of his new friends, the in-jokes, the girls' talk about their profession—and he would tell them stories of adventure in the East, giving free rein to his fertile imagination. He slept with several of the girls, not paying any money, secretly surprised and always gratified. *I've charmed them, and I haven't even kissed the Blarney Stone.*

One aging prostitute invited him to sleep in her room after two in the morning, when she shut up shop. Her breasts sagged. "They're not much now, are they? Half of the lousy country has been sucking at them for the last twenty years—what do you expect?" When she was young, she told Hilary, she had gone to a back-street "practical" doctor who had sewed her up because she was engaged to a merchant from Corinth, "and you have to be a virgin for the Greeks." But the worthy suitor, having "deflowered" his fiancée had promptly disappeared, taking with him the money she was saving for her dowry. . . .

They're nice girls, thought Hilary. They've seen the worst, they're good human beings, you can't deceive them. Nobody could deceive him either, not now. He was one of them, and as he sat in the taverna one morning watching a group of sailors, he called out to them.

"Hello! It's girls you want, isn't it? It took me some time, but I know where the best ones are."

The sailors joined him and he offered to take them to his friends. After all, he thought, it's not so terrible to be a pimp, pimps are human too. And Hilary wondered whether to accept any money if it was offered to him.

Day in, day out, he sat in the cafés, watching the ships coming and going, watching the people. Isabel's letter remained in the inside pocket of his linen jacket—he'd read the letter only once, but he lacked the heart to throw it away. Isabel, Angela, Zafiro . . . Zafiro would be getting married soon, she had said she would name a boy or girl after him. That would be posterity for Hilary, and he would not even know when it happened.

Every day he drove to Neon Phaleron to swim; he was surprised at the long distances he could swim now without tiring. And he had lost weight—his trousers were too large for him, there were no more holes in his belt to tighten up. His face, no longer florid, was as tanned as his body, his stomach was flat and as he walked among the crowds, he would straighten his shoulders and work out in his mind his ideas, as though flexing his mental muscles for the effort ahead. The people of his lost world—Isabel, Angela, Mark—were no longer real, perhaps they had never been real, only characters in a novel he had planned but never written.

Then one night, as he was making love to the old whore, a group of rowdy sailors came upstairs and she made him finish quickly and told him to get dressed outside, there was work, the navy was in.

Hilary collected his things and walked out. The next evening he drove up to Athens and parked his car in the courtyard of the ramshackle house where Madame Daphne lived.

Hilary paced about the small cool room in the Turkish house, stretched his arms over his head, then went back to his typewriter and had another bash at the old machine. All his ideas were back with him: he was capable of repeated bouts of intellectual activity. The important thing was to capture that joyful *anima* which had always eluded him, the important thing was to be organized. The important thing was to keep his mind fresh and unclouded, not to worry, above all not to worry. And so Hilary sent his gregarious self into exile and lived with his books and with the bandits and the revolutionaries, often reading aloud, enjoying the heroic cadences of their songs as he translated the Fauriel and Passow and Politis open in front of him.

As for Isabel, his lost muse . . . When the pain was bad, his confidence would ebb and he would waste precious time self-doubting. I'm the appreciative

199

type, he would tell himself; turning out yet another dull, technical book offends my better nature. This was the work for cloistered monks, not for Hilary Grey, who was of the world, who was torn and tormented by life's shocks and blows.

He worked in the small room all morning and late into the night, breaking off to have lunch with Daphne in a nearby restaurant, then sharing her large four-poster in the afternoon. At seven o'clock Hilary would leave to stroll about the streets of Athens, sometimes returning secretly to go straight to the back room and rewrite something he had abandoned earlier while Daphne gave her private lessons. He respected her sense of propriety, and, at night, when they would go to a taverna for some wine and *meze,* he might ask her seriously about her work, her students, the enrollment for the new term.

Daphne was happy to have him back, but never asked him why he had disappeared in the first place or what had happened to him. Hilary would now and then catch her looking at him with a kind of hopeless affection that belied her happy-go-lucky nature. "He's a Doctor of Philosophy, not a doctor for grippe and syphilis," she told the middle-aged ladies who came for toning and slimming. And as she tiptoed to his table, bringing yet another sweet Turkish coffee, she might hush them and let them peep at the philosopher in his den.

His hair grew longer, his beard wilder, and one day he borrowed Daphne's electric razor and trimmed his whiskers, leaving the silky hair longer around his chin. He looked rather like a benevolent missionary of some lost faith, his eyes sad but clear, but his looks did not protect his privacy and, one fine morning when Daphne had to take the bus to Kalamata, two of the plump ladies of the eleven o'clock class stayed behind, intruded into his study, tried to tempt him with some Cretan *raki.* He simply patted them on their plump bottoms and sent them on their way. When Daphne came back the next day, she insisted that they go out for a good meal and some wine, and that night they finished between them three bottles of *kokkineli.* Daphne held his arm as they walked back home, leaning heavily on him in her high-heeled shoes.

"You'll not suddenly leave me, will you, you'll not disappear and leave me alone?"

"There's nowhere else to go, old dear," he said.

They reached the Turkish house, the three poodles rushed to welcome their mistress, the bells around their neck tinkling madly.

"Give me a moment to cook something tasty for the little gentlemen," she said.

Hilary went to the back room and tried to type, but for some reason the memory of that stormy night haunted him and his fingers kept missing the keys. He gave up the effort and went to bed, remembering. When he heard the news about Isabel from Andreas, he had rushed to the town to ask for help. But he didn't like the faces of the fishermen who came to save their boats; he didn't like the coast guard telling him that if she could be saved, Mark would save her, that there was nothing they could do but wait for the storm to pass; and he didn't like it that Andreas had gone first to Mark for help. He remembered driving back to the *kalivi* among the wreckage of the passing storm—an anchored caique thrown up by the waves lay half broken in front of Kavouras' taverna, there were drowned birds in the streets, Argos was lying dead in a puddle of water, electrocuted by fallen wires. . . .

He opened his eyes, wondering for a moment where he was, still frightened, his sheets slippery with sweat. Daphne was sleeping by his side, her breathing strong and regular, one plump arm outside the sheet. Above his head was the small shrine with its glowing electric crucifix; by its light he could just make out the souvenir dolls Daphne had collected at fairgrounds over the years, their glass eyes watching and waiting for him to speak. But Hilary was sailing in a motor yacht and Angela was by his side, begging him to drop anchor, to take off his handsome white naval uniform and make love to her. The dazzling water hurt his eyes and his mind floated out over the blue waves as he stood at the helm . . .

Cum laude. He was standing in Convocation, clad sumptuously in a crimson robe, and all around him clashed the applause of the world of learning—an immeasurable contribution, Dr. Grey. He knew that from this moment his wisdom would be valued, his opinions sought. Dr. Grey, Dr. Hilary Grey, Dr. Samuel Johnson, Dr. John Donne, Sir Hilary Grey, Sir Thomas Browne, Sir Hilary . . .

He turned restlessly on his side and closed his eyes; now he was in the classroom, shuffling his notes, fidgeting with his ruler, looking over his glasses at the students and trying to make out who they all were and why they were mocking him. *As I said before*, he began, and there was giggling and scuffling; *taking one point at a time*, he attempted, but a flying book hit him on the head. He fell down, he was surrounded now, he was on his back and the giggling hurt his ears. *Pull off his clothes*, ordered Angela, pushing forward; Mark, holding Isabel by the hand, laughed at Hilary. *Cut off his penis*, cried Inge. *Stuff his ruler up his ass*, said Toni. *Get me the whip*, called Angela, and Leonides stepped on his chest. *Now when I was in Japan*, said Clive, who began tickling the soles of his bare feet. They were all there, tormenting him. . . . When Lazaros gave him a kick in the ribs, the lesson of Professor Hilary Grey came to an end. He woke up, Daphne's knee digging into his side.

She woke up. She felt his forehead beaded with sweat, reached out for a tissue and wiped his face and neck. His pillow was soaked and she turned it over, then dabbed some cologne on his temples.

"Don't worry," she said, stroking his silky hair. "I'm here, it's all right. I'm here."

One night while Daphne was with her students, Hilary put on his linen jacket and headed uptown toward Syntagma and the bustling streets of Athens. The open-air cafés in front of the American Express were packed with people; it was September and the tourists were back from the islands for one last fling in the city before returning to their cold countries. Hilary set off for a quiet *ouzeri* further down in an arcade by the Athens Cathedral. An urchin ran after him and persuaded him to have his shoes polished. *A clean pair of shoes to walk in—that's all one really needs.* He gave the child five drachmas.

"Mister, two drachmas is enough. You gave me five."

"That's all right."

The boy looked up and smiled shyly.

"Mister, I love you."

"I see."

"Mister, will you take me to your hotel?"

"I'm not staying in a hotel. Shouldn't you go home now?"

"Mister, I don't have a home. I don't have anywhere to sleep. Please take me with you tonight. I'm nice—you'll like me."

Hilary gave him another five drachmas and set off for the Bacchanalia; he had not been there since his return to Athens. The nightclub was exactly as he remembered it. When he heard an electric guitar he knew it must be Toni, but he did not turn around until he heard the husky voice singing a plaintive Hebrew air. Eva still looked gorgeous, her red silk dress clinging to her figure, her body moving slowly to the rhythm. Hilary ordered a beer and took it to one of the white sofas, sat quietly and listened and waited for her to finish.

She was about to walk past him when she stopped.

"Hilary? How you've changed! I almost didn't recognize you."

"I hope for the better."

"You look marvelous. And the beard—it really suits you."

"Thank you. It saves time shaving and I thought I might as well look the part, whatever it is."

"How handsome!"

"You look wonderful yourself. How are things with you?"

A waiter handed her her drink.

"I've been offered a contract at the Caravan," she began. "It's a fancy club in Tel Aviv."

"It would make a change for you."

"It would. I've never been to Israel. I'm still wandering."

"You should go, then."

"I don't know, I'm not certain I'm ready yet. What about you? Are you going back to your Arabs?"

"I think I've had enough of them."

Eva finished her drink quickly.

"If you're here when I'm through," she said to Hilary, "we'll go to my place and have something to eat."

She got up and ruffled his hair.

"I'm a good cook," she added and walked quickly away.

It must be worse for her, Hilary thought, she's young, she's not used to suffering like this. Isabel's letter lay suddenly heavy on his heart and he took it out and tried to read; but the light was dim, his eyes were filling up, he couldn't make out the words. As Eva was finishing her number, he got up to go, before she could return.

At the far end of the bar Superintendent Mikhail Lazaros sat alone, watching the guitarist. Toni finished playing and came over for a drink, ignoring Lazaros. The superintendent edged closer to him and started to tell him something—the young guitarist threw the contents of his glass into Lazaros' face and swore at him, then turned away. Hilary watched Lazaros wiping his face with his silk handkerchief, trying to look composed, as if nothing had happened. The sodomites have their problems, too, he thought, and walked out of the club.

The letter was still pressing on his heart, it weighed him down, he could hardly move. Hilary tried not to remember. *I must do what I have to do, please forgive me. You have always been good to me and I know you will get on better without me.*

"I do, I do," Hilary said aloud. "I get along without you very well, I get along fine," and he shambled his way through the maze of narrow streets, back to the Turkish house and his typing and Madame Daphne and her dogs.

21

Mark sent a gold bracelet to Eva, but he neither went to say good-bye nor sent her a letter. He hardly thought of Angela. The Baroness had the Old Lion and Felix and Inge to look after her.

His heart was heavy as he began looking through his things. In the top cupboard of a closet he found his old naval officer's cap. Eva had rescued it from Jennie's place and brought it to him. Mark put it on now and went to the mirror to look at himself.

Isabel came in.

"You've missed the navy, haven't you?"

"It was a good life while it lasted."

"You could have been a captain."

"Only a pirate, but the age of pirates is gone."

He threw the cap into the wastebasket.

"Isabel, you said you'd go anywhere, do anything I asked you."

"I shouldn't have said that. But you can always try me."

"Then I ask you to marry me, the first thing we do in London."

"London!"

"We'll stop first in Geneva, I'll buy you your wedding present there."

"Lovely! When are we leaving?"

"There's a plane leaving shortly after midnight."

"What shall we do after London?" she asked.

"You stay there and wait for me. I've some work to catch up on."

"Couldn't I be near you? Couldn't I come along?"

"I'm going to Norway. It's terribly cold up there, but I won't be long."

From Oslo he wanted to fly to Nassau and have a yacht standing by while he arranged for a trawler to meet the *World Seafarer* on the open seas as the supertanker made her way across the Atlantic carrying the "antique" prayer mat.

"I promise you it'll all be all right," he said, "and you'll have time to do your shopping in London before I return."

"Keep away from those Scandinavian girls," she said. "I'm terribly possessive, I've just discovered."

She showered and dressed, then began packing carefully for the flight that night.

"I love traveling," she announced to him as he was shaving. "Shall I pack your things, too?"

"Fine."

There was a sudden gust of cold wind and he went to close the balcony doors behind him. It had rained the previous night in Athens, the temperature had suddenly dropped, the best days of summer were over.

"Put on your coat," he advised Isabel. "We'll walk down to Syntagma and get our tickets."

It did not take more than a few minutes in the Olympic Airways Office to book their tickets for the night flight. Isabel was looking at the posters hanging on the walls. One showed the Tower of London and she remembered going there with Hilary. What did he really feel, now that all was said and done? When approached through a lawyer, Hilary had agreed to the annulment, he had insisted on taking all the blame and had even offered to send her money. It was beastly of her not to try to find him, not to say good-bye. As they walked back to the apartment, she rehearsed various ways in which she might bring this up—no, there was no way. . . .

As they stepped inside, a police officer in the apartment pushed the door

204

shut and a second officer pressed a gun into Mark's back; Isabel shrank against him, and Mark put a protective arm around her as he was prodded forward.

Inspector Notaras was lying on their bed, his heavy shoes resting comfortably on Isabel's filmy nightgown on the coverlet, hands locked behind his crew-cut head.

Leonides hadn't looked at the photographs since he had sent for Notaras. But now he pulled out the drawer to look at them once more, to convince himself all over again that there was no way of turning back.

He shuffled the photographs in his thick hands, then dealt them out on the desk like cards, face up.

"I'll kill the bastard, I'll kill him if it's the last thing I do!"

He struck his desk; the *World Seafarer* wobbled precariously. He had forgiven him everything—he forgave him for his old record of drug peddling, for running down his wife's lover, for abandoning his niece and running off with the English tart. This, he could not forgive.

"I'll kill him," he said again, collecting the pictures. Felix had not only watched, he had photographed Markos and Angela in bed, on the floor, on chairs, on sofas, with Inge and without. The Old Lion didn't mind Inge amusing Angela, he had encouraged them that way, it kept her quiet; but to see them both like this with Markos—he could shoot them all.

"I'll kill the bastard," he said, "but I'll destroy him first."

When Felix had told him about Markos and Angela, he hadn't believed it; he'd grabbed the eunuch by the throat and would have strangled him if Leandros hadn't intervened. Now Felix had sent him the photographs, the eunuch was getting his revenge. Why did that whey-faced son of his fire the gypsy, why? *I should have had him in my hands, I should have broken his bones with my own hands. The bastard. The bastard.*

The Old Lion was trembling so much he could scarcely hold the telephone to his ear, but he put the photographs away before his visitor was ushered in by his secretary. Inspector Notaras was holding a slim briefcase; he bowed, shook hands with Leonides and, without further preliminaries, unzipped his bag, took out papers, and placed them on the desk. The Old Lion read the documents carefully, swearing under his breath. Both sheets were signed, the signature of Markos Stephanou at the bottom was weak and shaky, not firm and bold as he knew it; they had tortured him, they had crushed his balls, the coward hadn't been able to take it. Leonides read the two sheets of paper again, then lifted his head. He found it difficult to get the words out.

"Did he actually sign this himself?"

"Yes, sir."

"You tortured him, of course."

"Not at all, sir. He was only too willing to sign anything we suggested—a very satisfactory confession, sir."

"It serves the bastard right. Now he knows who is the boss."

Obviously Leonides had picked on the right man—Notaras, at least, produced results. Still, the Old Man was amazed.

"And he confessed *all* of this?"

"He did, sir, every single word."

"Well, I'll be damned!" The Old Lion passed his palm over his face as if in pain; a nerve was twitching in his temple and he tried to smooth it away.

"We've got a witness, sir."

"Who is he?"

"Toni Melas, the musician."

"How did you manage that?" he asked wearily.

"Toni has been under our protection, sir. Ever since he broke up with the superintendent. He was the one who gave the overdose to the wife, the overdose of heroin. Superintendent Lazaros knew and turned him into his slave and kept it secret. Toni had actually moved in with Lazaros, sir. He was kept by him—a worm and a whore, that's what he is."

"Did the little bugger tell you that he gave the overdose to Jennie?"

"Not at first, sir, but when we put the broomstick up his arse . . ."

Notaras chuckled softly, wondering how far he could go, how much familiarity was permitted.

"And what do you intend to do with Toni now?"

"Keep him safely, sir, until the trial. He knows several interesting things about the prisoner, and he'll learn some more and he'll learn how to tell his story. If he's good—well, then, what he did to that woman was an accident, he prepared the injection but he wasn't certain of the dose. If he doesn't help us, it will be murder."

"Does the public prosecutor know all this?"

"It's not necessary for him to know everything, sir. But he saw the confession and he spoke to Toni."

"Well, what is he waiting for, then? Isn't he satisfied?"

"He's quite satisfied, sir. But he thinks we must get another witness. Somebody who saw him printing the leaflets, or planting the bombs, or handling the guns—he was sleeping just above them, you know, in the house you were kind enough to lend him."

"It's enough!" Leonides shouted.

Then he was silent, his head buried in his hands, and the inspector didn't dare to speak to him.

"I'll find another witness," he said finally. "Go now—go, and be careful he doesn't outwit you yet."

"Pardon me, sir, I didn't want to mention it, but the superintendent hasn't shown his face at the office since we arrested his boyfriend."

206

Leonides sighed. Why had Lazaros refused to cooperate? Could it be that Markos was also one of his sort? It didn't bear thinking of.

"I think I can do the job, as we said, sir, better than the superintendent."

Leonides could not get over it that Mikhail Lazaros could not be bribed, would not play along with him in fixing Markos. He had misjudged the guts of the old queer; now he would have to deal with this murderer.

"We'll give the superintendent a chance to resign."

"As you think, sir."

"If he doesn't, I'll speak to the minister."

"You know best, sir—and if you want, shall I go over to the island to see about a second witness?"

"No, I'll find the other witness myself."

"Relax, baby-girl, relax. There, there . . ."

The Old Lion waited for Katia's excitement to subside, for the quivering body to calm. She was one of the Lions, all right, yet even he was amazed—she seemed to be having an orgasm every five minutes. *Chisté ké Panayía*, would he ever be able to satisfy her, to control her? But she was cuddly and he liked the puppy fat, and he liked the way she was sitting astride him, working up and down on his strong, thick penis. Leonides hadn't had his second orgasm yet, he was getting tired, he had other things on his mind.

"Relax, baby-girl, relax."

Katia stretched out her legs, fell over him, and gave him a playful bite on his hairy chest.

"Was that nice, Leo?"

"You're a nice baby-girl. Tell me again, now how did you find him, did he leave the door to the storeroom open?"

"He did."

"How could you see what he was doing in there?"

"He had a flashlight."

"What was he doing?"

"He was holding a gun."

"What did he do with it?"

"He put it down, then he went on printing the leaflets."

"But there was no electricity down in the basement, how could he work the duplicating machine?"

"He was rolling them off by hand."

"Good, good, excellent! Now tell us again, how were you absolutely certain it was Markos and nobody else?"

"I know the prisoner very well. I saw his face in the light of his flashlight, and he called back for me to wait, and I recognized his voice."

"Why did he ask you to wait?"

"He's been after me ever since he set eyes on me, that's why!"

"What happened when he came up?"

"I was ready to go, but he chased me, grabbed me by the arm, and dragged me to the bed and raped me. I screamed and screamed, but . . ."

"Never mind, we shall not mention that, baby-girl, because I have a prince ready to marry you and we don't want to cool him off, do we?"

"No, we don't. Who is he, Leo?"

"Like it was with Thalia, only better—a better American, clean living, forward looking, filthy rich. How do you like that?"

She giggled.

"I like it."

"So remember, he didn't rape you because you said you'd tell your uncle and he'd lose his job. He tried to rape you, but you got the better of him."

"He tried, but I fought him back."

"That's the cleverest baby-girl in the world. Now I have a surprise for you, and then you can tell me the whole story again. You like surprises, don't you?"

Katia waited expectantly, but the Old Lion pressed a button on the intercom and asked a secretary to send for Inspector Notaras immediately. He began to put on his white trousers and his espadrilles, but he wore no socks and left his torso uncovered. Picking up Katia's bra, panties, and dress from his desk, he threw them across the cabin to her. He sat down, picked up a telephone and listened, absorbed, for some time. Then there was another telephone call and another and Leon Leonides, as he listened, swiveled round on his large leather chair and watched the twinkling lights that marked the position of his fleet on the world map.

Katia went and lay on the sofa, trying to attract the Old Lion's attention. Finally she walked to his desk and sat upon it, swinging her legs, looking at him provocatively.

"Come on, baby-girl, go and put something on. The inspector is here."

Katia kept on swinging her legs, challenging him.

"Later, when you've told your story."

She went away, pouting, to dress.

"We'll have a drink first," Leonides told Notaras.

"I don't think I should, sir. I'm on duty."

"But this is part of your duties, Superintendent."

"Excuse me, sir, you mean 'Inspector' . . ."

"Superintendent Notaras, I congratulate you on your promotion and offer you a drink in celebration. The minister appreciates your record and is sure you'll do equally well in your new job."

"Thank you very much, sir, I'm very grateful, to be sure I am, sir."

"We'll have some whiskey. Take your glass, here you are—well done, Superintendent. Congratulations!"

"To your health, sir."

Leonides emptied his drink and waited a few minutes for Notaras to finish his.

"I've got your second witness in there, Superintendent. Are you ready to take a statement?"

"I'm ready, sir."

Leonides opened the door of the adjoining cabin and called for Katia. The girl's dress was too tight but this did not worry the Old Lion.

"Come in, Katia. This is Superintendent Notaras—my niece, Katia Kommenou."

The superintendent rose and bowed; Katia sat down and told her story. Notaras, ball-point and pad in hand, made some more notes, read the statement aloud, waited until Leonides nodded his approval, and announced that the statement was ready to be typed. Leonides called for the typist; as they waited, the two men had another drink and a cigar. When the document was ready, Notaras insisted on reading it aloud again. He then asked Katia to sign it, folded the paper, and put it into his briefcase.

"Miss Kommenou will stay with me," said Leonides. "You may reach her here whenever you need her."

"That's all right, sir, thank you, sir."

They shook hands and Notaras left. The Old Lion paced about the large office; then he went back to his desk and busied himself with the papers and the telephones, trying not to think.

Out of the corner of his eye he saw Katia helping herself to a drink from the cabinet while puffing stupidly at an enormous cigar. Obviously, the little piece liked her new life style.

She choked and stubbed out the cigar.

"Markos told me he'd fucked Angela," she said. "He told me he could fuck all the women he wanted."

"He said that, did he? The bastard will find out now who the boss is. The Lion still has his teeth . . ."

Yet he was more sad than angry. On the opposite wall hung the portraits of his ancestors; Angela was up there, her place already among the dead, but not all the Lions could join the pantheon and there was only one throne, only one emperor.

Poor Angela—for her sake he had spared Felix, Felix would take care of her. Leon turned back to the magnetic map, his eyes stinging.

Katia sat on his knees, discussing her career as a favored assistant to the boss—and negotiating her salary and benefits. "What a sexy uncle you are!" she said, in the middle of demanding more and more. As she talked, she rubbed his bare chest and tickled his ears. "And a little yellow car, the smallest yellow car in the world, and a little maid, the tiniest and prettiest maid in the world."

"Why a tiny maid?"

"Well, I won't be ashamed to have a tiny maid washing me and dressing me. And if I have to punish her . . . I shall, then, live a deep and meaningful life."

"Very meaningful," said the Old Lion, watching a new member of the pride flexing her claws.

"Very deep," she said, feeling his finger inside her.

She reached down to unzip him.

"Did they teach you all this at the convent?"

Leonides was preoccupied, he wasn't interested just then, but Katia, aroused by now, was not used to leaving things unfinished.

"I'll show you, Leo—"

"Show me what?"

"What I learned at the convent."

The Old Lion sighed, suddenly more tired than he had ever felt in his life.

"No you won't show me," he said, lifting her off his lap. "You be a good baby-girl and go back to your cabin and play with yourself."

The *Hesperides* had sailed into the port of Samos, and there was a party scheduled that evening. The notables of the island had been invited—Leonides never missed an opportunity to show off to his guests aboard how esteemed and loved he was among his compatriots. The truth was that a few welcoming words from a local bishop or mayor meant more to the Old Lion than all the press stories his public relations man had been so conscientiously compiling for years.

He called the social secretary to dress Katia for the evening. He himself never liked a valet around—the idea of a man touching his things bothered him—so he put on his white suit by himself and went up to join his guests and wait for the local worthies.

The performance was repeated at Chios and Lesbos. But at Limnos, the Old Lion did not join his guests, he did not await the evening but drank steadily alone in his cabin, emerging at midnight to insult a Spanish actress and swear at a Texas oilman who had dared to defend her. The next morning he called Van a "creep"— they had picked the newlyweds up in Rhodes—and had his first real quarrel with Katia, after which he locked her in her cabin.

One evening, as the Old Lion was working late with Leandros, he stumbled and knocked down the gold model of the *World Seafarer*. The main funnel, made of crystal and bearing the monogram of the Lions, was shattered.

Leonides immediately crossed himself.

"*Ayios Nikolaos*, don't forsake me now. I've done nothing against you."

He went down on the carpeted floor and collected the pieces.

"Good saint, my ships are under your protection, do not forget me. I'll gild your icon as soon as I get to Alea."

For the next few hours he stayed alone in his office, anxiously watching the twinkling stars on the magnetic map, too frightened to send a message to find out the worst.

The news came finally from San Juan. There had been an explosion on the *World Seafarer*; the giant tanker, loaded to capacity with oil from Abadan and bound for Charleston, South Carolina, was in flames. Leon read the messages that came in, one after another—he had to go, he had to see what could be done, but when he tried to put on his shirt, he realized that his right arm was too stiff to go into the sleeve.

He summoned Leandros and the blond young man walked in, barefoot and sleepy. There was a helicopter on board and his father wanted him to have the pilot fly him at once to Istanbul; from there he was to get any plane available to San Juan.

"You should be there by tomorrow morning," he said, speaking with great effort. "So get going."

"What shall I do there?"

This was too much for the Old Man and he shouted with his last strength: "What will he do there, the dolt, the idiot! Oh, he's no son of mine. Gypsy, where are you, gypsy? . . . If only he were here, Markos wouldn't ask me what he should do in Puerto Rico while the ship's in flames and abandoned—gypsy had balls."

The next day, early in the morning, the *Hesperides* sailed into Constantinople and the distinguished guests came up on deck to admire the mythical city with the churches and the minarets; only Katia knew what had happened during the night, and when she didn't see Leonides on the deck, she went down to the office for more news of the *World Seafarer*. The Old Man was lying unconscious on the floor of his bathroom.

Leonides had a strong will to live, but recovery from his stroke went slowly. He was very weak; he refused food for the first few days and cried often, like a child.

When the doctors finally allowed him to have visitors, he refused to see anybody, even Katia. Instead he sent for his personal lawyer to be flown out from Athens and insisted on seeing him in the office adjoining his bedroom.

"This being the last Will and Testament of Leon Leonides," read the lawyer, "in which is revoked all previous wills and testamentary dispositions . . ."

"Cut the preamble," muttered the Old Man, his voice so low that the lawyer did not hear him.

"Subject to the payment of all my just debts . . ."

Leonides shook his trembling hand impatiently.

"I give and bequeath to my son, Leandros . . ."

The shaking hand was raised; the lawyer paused.

"Leave him half a million dollars," he whispered. "Only."

The lawyer made a note and began reading again.

"And to my niece, Katia Kommenou . . ."

He looked up. Leonides shook his head and the lawyer understood.

"And to my sister, Angela . . ."

Leonides nodded.

"Leave it the way it was," he whispered, and sank back in his leather chair.

He was silent for some time, then he beckoned the lawyer to come nearer. His voice was cracked, the lawyer could see the effort it took the Old Lion to speak the words, but they were not whispered.

"And to my son, Markos Stephanou, issue of Magda Almassy of Budapest and myself, conceived out of wedlock before her marriage to Emilios Stephanou of Patras, by profession physician, I give and bequeath my entire estate, all movable and immovable property whatsoever, bonds, stocks, shares, my ships, and all other interests of Leonides Maritime Enterprises— everything, all I have."

He stopped, exhausted. After a few moments he tried to straighten up, to show that he was still in control, but the tears had started and however much he tried he could not bring up his hand to wipe them away.

"I'm not dead yet," he murmured, but he couldn't swivel around to look at the magnetic map behind him. When the lawyer came and helped him with the chair, the Old Man gripped his hand.

"He'll be all right, won't he? We'll get him free again, but he'll have had a lesson to remember. . . ."

22

For the past five days Markos Stephanou had been taken backward and forward from his cell to the court; the verdict was a foregone conclusion and Mark only wished that the whole thing would come to an end so that he would know what came next, what he could do next.

To all the charges—conspiring and acting, alone and with others, "to overthrow by force the regime" and "to establish a government of a Communist type" by writing and printing "seditious leaflets and newspapers," and "possessing with intent to use hidden bombs, arms, and ammunition"—Mark pleaded not guilty.

Superintendent Notaras gave evidence early in the proceedings, describing in rich detail the perfidious supplies found in the basement of the house where Markos Stephanou had been living.

"Superintendent," asked the prosecuting officer, "what made you suspect and therefore investigate the accused and search the house?"

The question gave Notaras the opportunity to bring up Mark's old record, his court-martial from the navy for embezzlement, his conviction on a charge of transporting one kilo of hashish and his subsequent sentence of three years' hard labor. The accused, Notaras said, was also strongly suspected of the recent murder of a KYP agent—only lack of sufficient evidence had prevented his being brought to trial on that charge.

"Is the accused a single man?" asked the prosecuting officer.

"The superintendent particularly enjoyed going over the details of Jennie's death and Mark's illicit relationship with Isabel.

The prosecution dismissed Notaras and presented the accused's confession, which was read aloud.

"Is this your signature?" asked the presiding colonel.

"Yes," said Mark. "But nothing written in it is true."

His defending counsel now stood up and recalled Superintendent Notaras.

"Is it not a fact that a man died in your charge while under interrogation last March?"

"Certainly not as you suggest. The prisoner died of natural causes, of a heart attack, and I was cleared of all responsibility."

"Is it not a fact that because of this incident you were suspended from the force for one month and that you were transferred when readmitted to the Bureau of Narcotics as a junior officer?"

"No. I was transferred because they needed my services in that department, after returning from paid leave."

"Is it not true that you ill-treated my client on Alea, where he was under arrest two months ago in connection with another charge?"

"There has never been any complaint and it is certainly not true that there was any such treatment."

"Is it not true, Superintendent, that in connection with the present charge you systematically *tortured* my client until he was broken down and signed the statement you had prepared in order to save his life?"

"I have done nothing of the kind. The prisoner signed voluntarily after collaborating to compile it."

"Nevertheless, I maintain that my client is innocent, and respectfully ask the court that all charges against him be dropped. Now consider this, gentlemen—Markos Stephanou was first arrested on Alea two months ago; the house in which he was living was searched and nothing incriminating was found, which is why he was released. It was almost two weeks after my client left the island for good—what was there to stop somebody else from using

213

the same house for the purposes you claim? I suggest to the court that this so-called confession was taken after my client was submitted to methodical torture at the Bouboulinas Prisons. For three days he was tortured with the well-known method of *falanga*, then he was given electric shocks on his fingers and genitals. . . .

As Mark listened, his hands began to shake. He hadn't been able to hold the pen straight, his name had come out barely recognizable on the two sheets of paper. . . . *Is this your signature or is it not?* The white tiles on the walls were bloodstained; he was pushed in, a leg was stretched out and he tripped and fell to the floor. He tried to rise, but somebody hit him in the small of the back and he went down and they tied up his ankles with the rifle sling and hauled him up in the air, head downward. . . . He was strapped down on the bench, Notaras was hitting him with a plank of wood on the soles of his bare feet. . . . The typewritten sheets of paper were on the wooden table, the pen was there, waiting; he resisted, day after day, until the day Notaras came in with his wires and they held him down and turned on the current . . .

"And my client signed this so-called confession under physical and mental stress, because of violence and threats of violence, because he was made to sign it. He now disowns this statement and I therefore submit to the court that it be declared invalid."

The prosecuting officer sang the praises of Superintendent Notaras, "this fine officer, who has recently been promoted because of his sterling qualities. I ask the court not to take into consideration the false accusations against the Superintendent, these Communist tactics aimed to discredit the national government in the eyes of the world."

Mark's statement was admitted by the court as true and freely given. The prosecuion called Toni, who looked at Mark and trembled—*if he gets off he'll kill me, Notaras was right, he's a killer*—even as he testified that Markos Stephanou was a political agitator, an anarchist who habitually carried a revolver. Toni's evidence, the defense was quick to point out, was hardly factual.

Katia's, on the other hand, was very damaging indeed. She told her story unemotionally, as if she were only telling it to help the course of justice. Not once did she turn to look at Mark. *I don't need him, I can get anything I want, I can marry anyone I like, I don't give a damn about the cheap son of a bitch.*

The defending counsel tried to discredit Katia's story by pointing out that her brother, Jason Kommenou, who had been arrested before for political agitation, had enjoyed access to the basement of the house where his client lived.

Superintendent Notaras testified that the witness's brother had been thoroughly questioned and that his "childish" political agitation had been

214

found to be innocuous. At this point the prosecuting officer suggested that all this talk about the student was irrelevant.

"Defending counsel is making an obvious attempt to discredit Miss Kommenou and throw doubt on the patriotism and the good name of the Leonides family and of Mr. Leon Leonides himself, whose devotion to his country is beyond question and whose services have occasioned the gratitude and recognition of the national leadership. . . ."

As Katia left the court, she finally looked for the first time at Mark, who turned away.

"I hope they shoot you," she said softly.

When, at last, the elaborate farce was played out and sentence was pronounced—twenty-five years' imprisonment, in accordance with Special Law 509—there was a commotion at the back of the court. A young woman had fainted, the prosecuting officer himself handed down the jug of water from the judges' table and advised them to splash it on her hands and face. As they took Mark out, Eva was opening her eyes, but he had no chance to speak to her.

With the break of day Mark sat up on his wooden bed, giving up the effort to sleep, his anguish pressing down on him like the walls of his cell. He hated the dawn; some sensitive mechanism inside him recorded the first faint streak and he was wide awake, to watch the light creep through the prison like a predatory animal. Somewhere, at this hour, somebody was being taken away; somewhere, the executioner was lining his victim up against the wall.

It was still early to abandon hope, to abandon Isabel. All through his ordeal he had sent messages through counsel, forbidding her to come to court; she had obeyed, no doubt thinking that there must be a reason and that she could help him best by staying away. "Isabel, Isabel," he whispered and again the storm was raging, again he sensed her presence through the roaring wind, again he struggled against the elements to reach her.

I must get a message out, I need someone from outside to help. If Nubar could do it, he could do it too. But he was alone—he had no friend who could come to him in his need. I'm a gypsy, he thought, the Greeks don't accept me as one of them . . .

A guard came in later to tell him that he was to be transferred to Yaros with other political prisoners. They would send his things to his family if he gave them the address and he would be allowed to say good-bye to his immediate relatives.

"Did anybody ask to see me?" he asked, wondering if his lawyer had told Isabel which prison he was in.

"A woman came," said the warden. "She'll come again this afternoon at the

215

permitted hour. I don't remember her name, but they have it down in the book."

Then the warden noticed that the prisoner was still wearing his watch.

"You tried to hide this, didn't you!"

He grabbed Mark by the arm, pulled off the platinum watch, and threw it on the concrete floor.

"*Pagasa,*" he shouted, and stamped and ground with his heel on the watch until it was a wreck.

It was only a piece of machinery, yet suddenly Mark's fate seemed to be sealed; his fortunes were as good as his smashed talisman . . .

When he saw Eva waiting behind the wire screen that afternoon he was not surprised and kept his hands on the wire so that she could kiss them. She looked at him and her eyes filled with tears.

"Cheer up, Eva. How do you like my snappy uniform? A fashion magazine should explore the possibilities."

"Thank God they haven't cropped your hair."

"We're behind schedule from too many customers here."

Eva kept crying, her tears falling on his hands, but when she pressed her lips to the wire, Mark saw the scrap of rolled-up paper between her lips and understood the urgent pleading in her eyes. As their lips met he took the paper with his tongue and kept it behind his teeth. Eva kissed his hands once more and left.

Three days later Mark and five other prisoners were taken from the Averoff Prisons to Chalkis, where they were put on the ferry. On the quay Eva was waiting for the ferry, dressed in black as a village woman, a dark kerchief covering her hair, a basket of provisions on her arm.

The prisoners were handcuffed in two groups, Mark between two other men. The officer in charge, who had special instructions about Mark, would not let the soldiers who were with him put down their rifles. Two of the prisoners, one from each group, asked to be allowed to go to the lavatory, and the officer ordered all of them to go handcuffed, the armed soldiers accompanying them. Several village women were sitting in the corridor among the cars, some dozing off in the afternoon heat. Mark suffered the indignity, but refused to use the lavatory.

A few hours later one of the prisoners asked again to go to the lavatory; Mark and the others protested at going and the officer in charge, who was not particularly happy about his job, released the prisoner and sent one of the soldiers along to keep an eye on him.

As the sun set, the ferry was going through the straits between Euboia and the small island of Petali; they would not reach the island of Yaros until well after midnight. Eva, carrying a big plastic bottle, left the group of village women and asked permission to give water to the prisoners.

216

When she left, Mark nudged his companions and they understood.

"May I go to the lavatory?" he asked. "Please, sir?"

By now the officer was almost ashamed of his job, but he had strict orders not to let Markos Stephanou out of his sight.

"You will all go to the lavatory at eight o'clock," he said, trying to sound authorative.

"I'm really sorry, sir, for this trouble," Mark said. "I hate to ask you."

The officer ordered all three men in the group to the lavatory. The other two prisoners protested—nothing would make them move.

"I'm terribly sorry, sir, for all this trouble," Mark said again. "Might I go alone? It's urgent."

The officer was still wavering.

"If I may say so, sir, I think you're mistaken to treat us like common criminals. We did what we did for Greece, for our country. Perhaps we were misguided, but our motives were pure. We are Greeks, like you, sir, we aren't gangsters."

He was a credulous man, and he released Mark and told one of the soldiers to accompany him. He handcuffed together the two remaining prisoners in the group, then, remembering his instructions about Mark, took out his revolver to guard his charges and ordered the second soldier to the corridor, to keep an eye on the lavatory.

Mark was just opening the lavatory door. Eva pushed the soldier with her basket, threw a handful of ground black pepper straight into his eyes, and ran away. Mark ran in the other direction, reached the stairs to the deck, rushed to the railing, and dived into the sea.

The first soldier called for help; the second ran the length of the corridor and up the steps. He fired a round at Mark who, at that moment, was surfacing from his dive some distance behind the ship.

Nubar Ohanessian, waiting in a motorboat on the opposite shore of Euboia, heard the shots, noticed the ferry slowing down and a boat being lowered into the sea. Through his binoculars he watched the men taking the body from the water, the passengers gathering to see the prisoner being lifted onto the deck.

He recognized one of them. Eva pushed forward to embrace Mark, stretching out a hand to touch the shattered face, but the other women held her back. Somebody threw a blanket over him and Nubar put his binoculars away and started the engine of the motorboat.

217

23

It was late September, the women carried cardigan sweaters against the chill of the approaching evening, the summer was drawing to a close. Hilary walked up the street toward Kolonaki Square, still undecided, still not knowing how he could go to her, how he might say it to her. But he had trimmed his silky beard that morning, he'd washed his hair, he had prepared for her, just in case. . . .

The possibility of seeing Isabel brought back all the pain. Sometimes it had been almost unbearable, yet in his resignation Hilary had found a sort of peace, a clarity of vision that he had not known before. His life had its lyric moments, its comic moments, and plenty of grief; but there was no epic quality in it. He had never had a crusade to join, he had never leapt from a precipice or met an enemy upon the heath at midnight. He was satisfied with his new identity, his book was going well; he no longer needed to clown or drink or bluster, to please anybody or delude anybody—including himself. *I am not Prince Hamlet nor was meant to be; Am an attendant lord*, he murmured, wondering if perhaps he shouldn't start writing some poetry again.

Isabel was sitting alone at the Byzantion, holding a book but staring out at the street which led to the apartment—as if Mark might arrive at any moment, as if she were afraid that he might pass by and she might miss him.

Hilary, suddenly shy, waited for her to notice him.

"Hello, Isabel," he said finally. "It's me, it's Hilary. May I join you?"

He took a chair and clapped his hands for the waiter; Isabel said nothing and there was a moment of awkwardness.

"Let's have an ouzo, Isa, love," he said, trying to gather up as much as he could of his old bonhomie.

A gust of wind blew a yellow leaf onto their table. A few heavy drops of autumn rain fell; the kiosk keeper nearby began collecting magazines and paperbacks from the outside racks and the waiter came and fixed the umbrella over them.

"Now, Isa, love . . ."

He drew the book out of her hands and took them in his; she was haggard, she looked much older.

"I'm sorry, I'm sorry about Mark—I still can't believe it."

"Mark died for his country," she said. "He died for freedom."

"Did Eva come to see you?"

218

Isabel nodded and the tears began slipping down her face.

"I'm sorry," he said. "He was my friend, too," he added in an effort to share her unhappiness. After all, Isabel had been his wife, he couldn't bear watching her suffer like that.

"I'm not Mark, and I know you don't love me. But we've been through a lot together—if you think we could give it another try, if you think you might have me back . . . I could shave the beard," he said, trying to make her smile.

"No, Hilary," she said. "But I like the beard. It suits you."

"You must see my translations," he said. "You must see how much I've done. I've missed you all this time, I had no one to show my work to."

She dried her tears with her handkerchief.

"I was right, you know. You're much better off without me. The truth is, I've always been a burden to you."

Hilary, surprised at her composure, tried again.

"I can't sell myself to you, but I'm your friend."

He pointed a finger at his head.

"This old gray Grey-Elephant wants to help."

"Thank you," she said. "I know you mean it. But I'm going to England, to stay with my aunt in Cambridge. I've written to her about it. Then . . ."

"What then?" he asked, suddenly anxious.

"I don't know. We'll see."

"What's in your mind? Why don't you tell me?"

"It wouldn't affect you."

"How can you say that, Isa, love? Don't you know my heart, have you forgotten all about us already?"

"All right. I thought I might do some welfare work. Overseas, I mean. I could volunteer for Oxfam or one of those things, I could be useful for a change."

This somehow deflated Hilary completely. He paid the waiter.

"When are you leaving?" he asked, wondering if he could offer to buy her the ticket with his savings. If necessary, he could borrow some money from Daphne.

"This evening, the late flight. Twelve forty-five. I've got my ticket confirmed."

"Let me drive you to the airport," he said. *Let me be of use.*

"Thank you, but it won't be necessary. There's an airport bus, you know. The terminal is at the Olympic offices in Syntagma, a few minutes' walk from the apartment."

"What about your luggage?"

"I can take a taxi."

"Now don't be silly, Isa, love. At least let me say a proper good-bye."

He took her hands in his, gently, cautiously.

"Tender paw, Isa, tender paw."

She couldn't refuse him.

"If you're sure it's not out of your way."

"What kind of talk is this, Isabel? I've got Josephine parked nearby. Come on, let's go and collect your things first, we'll have dinner at the Venus—no, not the hotel, somewhere else. Come on."

He took her by the hand and helped her up.

"I'll wait for you here," he said when they reached the entrance hall to the apartment. Somehow, he knew he would not want to see the setting of her happiness with Mark.

They drove down Syngrou Avenue, and at the traffic circle at Phaleron he took the Sounion road to Glyfada.

"It's only six o'clock," he said. "If you like, we'll drive along the coastal road to the Cape and watch the sunset over Saronikos Bay from the temple."

Isabel nodded and he pressed on the accelerator, encouraging Josephine in a fatherly way.

"Come on, old girl, come on and show us what you can do."

Hilary spent the next day with his books, skipping his afternoon siesta, working until evening, when Madame Daphne brought him yet another sticky Turkish coffee. Hilary understood. It was almost seven, her private lessons started at seven.

He put on his jacket and wandered out into the street. He hadn't told Daphne about Isabel, he couldn't tell anybody. Still he wished there was somebody to talk to, just to talk . . . He headed for the Bacchanalia—he could see Eva, he could comfort her, he could see how she was taking it. And he could have a glass of beer, only one.

There was a new girl singing at the club and a new pianist—even the barmaids were different. He didn't know anybody and he paid for his beer and was making for the door when Inge came through the beaded curtain.

"Hi, Prof!" she said. "Leaving early tonight?"

"Yes."

"Haven't seen you around—I wondered where you were."

"And how are things with you?"

"I'm engaged to Leandros."

"Where is he?"

"I don't know, looking for me, I suppose. I like throwing him off the scent, I do it all the time."

"You haven't seen Eva, have you?"

"She signed a contract with a night club in Tel Aviv. I don't think she'll come back."

Chloe came up to them and took Inge's hand. Hilary turned to go.

220

"What's the hurry?" asked Inge. "Have you got somebody waiting for you?"

No, he had no one waiting for him, but he was broke, he couldn't offer anybody a drink.

"We'll give you a drink, Prof."

Chloe called the waiter.

"How is the Baroness?" he asked Inge.

"She's being taken back to Zurich."

"Are you going with her?"

"Don't be funny. I'm engaged to the Young Lion, remember?"

He took a sip of his drink.

"Where is the Baroness now?"

"She's in Ekali. You ought to go say good-bye to your old flame—she's been asking about you."

"Is she living alone there? I mean, is Mr. Leonides at the house?"

"She's alone tonight. Leo's been cruising around the islands with his niece, taking it easy after his stroke. He's coming back tomorrow."

Inge was cool and hard, the misfortunes of this world did not touch her. But she agreed to drive Hilary up to Ekali if Chloe, who was off duty, went along. The two girls sat together in the front of the red Impala and Hilary sat in back.

"Is Felix still with her?" he asked.

"She can't take a step without him these days. She's in really bad shape."

Inge drove as recklessly as he remembered. She brought the car to a sudden halt under some willow trees, and sent Hilary up to the house alone.

"I don't really want to run into Leandros tonight," she explained, and moved closer to Chloe.

Hilary brushed aside the maid and walked up the wide staircase alone, following the piano music he could hear floating down from above. When he opened the door, Angela was lying naked in bed with the puma; Felix was in the corner at the piano, playing Liszt. When the puma's yellow eyes turned toward Hilary, he decided to go, but Angela called to him and he stayed, uneasy, ready at any moment to make a run for it if necessary.

"I was waiting for you, Hil honey," she said slowly.

Her eyes were blazing, her movements peculiarly stiff, her skin a ghastly color. Perhaps she had on no makeup—he could see the lines in her face, quite clearly.

"I was thinking, Hil honey, of all my lovers you've been the best—you never got yourself killed in a car crash or drowned in the sea at Piraeus or pushed off a cliff or shot down while jumping from a ship. Of all my lovers you're the most reliable, Hil honey."

The combination of her hoarse, ragged voice and the puma was too much. Hilary was heartily sorry he had come.

"So reliable, so faithful! Pity the child was not yours. Poor Philip, he would have had a good father then. You would have been a good father to Philip, wouldn't you, Hil?"

She fondled the head of the big cat; it responded with a few licks of its red tongue on her breasts.

The idea of having a love-child growing up among the rich, so appealing in the past, now seemed distasteful to Hilary—thank God it wasn't he who had made a mother out of this madwoman.

"You would have loved Philip," the Baroness continued. "Philip is such a lovely boy. Would you like to see him?"

Hilary started backing away.

"No, I'm afraid I have to go, I only came to say good-bye."

The puma rose up on the bed and flexed its paws, showing scarlet painted claws. Hilary was petrified.

Angela got up, petted the cat, and began dressing herself in a nun's habit. When she had finished, she arranged a massive silver cross over her bosom, took Hilary by the hand, and led him out of the bedroom along the corridors of the old house, intoning a penitential psalm as she walked, heavy keys jangling from her leather girdle.

It was dark at the end of the corridor, but she fumbled patiently with her keys, let Hilary in, and locked the door after them. Then she lighted an oil lamp from a taper.

At first Hilary could hardly make out anything, but when his eyes adjusted to the dim light, he at once saw it in the center of the room, seated on a mahogany and ivory throne: the small deformed figure of an embalmed child, the head abnormally large, curly yellow locks of hair arranged carefully over the low forehead. The child must have been seven or eight years old when it died. It was obviously mongoloid.

Angela crouched near the throne and began arranging the toys that were spread about the floor, talking to Philip in a low, loving voice. Hilary felt he should go near her, try to comfort her, but suddenly the thought of touching the hand that was now caressing the putty-colored dead flesh was too horrible and he shrank back from the macabre spectacle.

When the key turned and the door swung open, Angela did not seem to notice. Felix came in, went to her, helped her up and led her away. The Baroness belonged to him, she was his responsibility.

Hilary left and closed the door behind him; he would not look again at the small figure seated forever on his mahogany and ivory throne. He walked quickly along the long corridor and down the stairs. *He's not my child, he's not, he had nothing to do with me,* he kept repeating to himself.

When he reached the willow trees, he saw that the two girls had moved to the back seat of the Impala. Not wanting to disturb them, he turned and walked down the long drive to the gates.

He hailed a passing taxi to run him down to Kifissia Station, where he could catch the electric train back to Omonoia and safety. *Thank God it wasn't my child. Thank God.*

24

Hilary patted Daphne on the shoulder, gave her a perfunctory kiss, and went out to see about his car and do his final errands before leaving Athens. The letter had arrived from his friend in Teheran, offering him a teaching position at the Language Institute for the next academic year. Hilary had accepted at once and he was now in a hurry to report to his post.

The green car was at a small garage being serviced and oiled and given two brand-new and two retreaded tires. Hilary had gone there every day, watching Josephine get a face-lift, drinking an ouzo with the mechanic, who shared his absolute trust in Josephine.

It was a bright day, it must have rained a little in the night because the sun shone on wet streets. With autumn there was a new bustle in the city; the lazy summer days were over and the Athenians were back from the islands, back to work. The thousands of tourists who flooded the city every summer had all but disappeared, and Hilary felt conspicuous wandering in the streets while people all around him hurried to their occupations. They would be shocked in Persia if, instead of a clean-shaven Yankee professor, they got a bearded guru who could well have come from one of their own villages. So Hilary sought out his old barber shop and sat patiently while the boys clipped his hair and shaved him clean, splashing his raw face with cheap cologne and puffing him with baby powder. He passed his hand over his chin. It felt strangely smooth, he looked so much younger! Pity about the beard, he should have had a photograph taken before it was demolished.

He talked about his plans with the boys and the other customers, explaining that now, with the Arabs being uncooperative, he would not be able to make the journey via Damascus and the Syrian desert. Instead he would drive to Salonika and on to Istanbul—"Sorry, I meant Constantinoupolis"—and then off over the Turkish plateau to Iran. Hilary's account impressed everybody and he shook hands all round, wishing them a good winter and good luck—and good colonels, he added.

"What's your job?" one of the barber boys asked him.

"I'm a philosopher," he said and stepped out into the street.

He spotted a forlorn figure moving slowly through the crowd, carrying a

223

cane. It was Lazaros. Hilary had heard that Lazaros had been compulsorily retired and that Toni had abandoned him after smashing his glass collection. Lazaros stopped at the edge of the pavement, took something from a tiny box, and put it in his mouth before crossing the road; Hilary looked the other way and waited until there was no risk of a confrontation.

The mechanic had Josephine ready as arranged, and Hilary ordered a final ouzo to say thank you properly. An assistant went for *souvlakia* and Hilary responded with another round of drinks from the cafe across the street. He had some money, he had sold his camera, which he hardly ever used, and his watch. The bill from the mechanic was much higher than he had reckoned—"I can make it, I can make it"—he kept saying as he counted his drachmas.

"We didn't charge you for the fender," the mechanic pointed out. "We used an old one, and we only charged half the usual price for labor."

"I know, I know. Look here, I can make it—just. But if I give you all this money, how am I going to pay for gas on the long journey? I tell you what, I'll pay you next summer? I'll be back. Let me sign this thing that I owe you."

The mechanic insisted that no signature was necessary—"What use are friends if they don't trust each other?"—whereupon a new round of ouzo was ordered. . . .

When he got home, Madame Daphne was having her eleven o'clock class with the fat ladies. Hilary tiptoed to the back room, brought down his battered suitcase, and started packing, hoping to finish and move out before the class was over. He would be back; he would write her but he hoped to avoid saying good-bye. He collected his notes, his manuscript, and his books, and put them in the Gladstone bag with his portable typewriter. Then, cautiously, he went to Daphne's bedroom to see if he had left anything.

An old tie of his was lying on the floor, but it was stained and he left it there for the poodles to play with. He took a pink lipstick from the dressing table and traced two overlapping hearts on the mirror, an arrow piercing through them. The lipstick broke; he was searching for another in order to write a message when Madame Daphne walked into the room.

"I was going to tell you," he began, "I'll be coming back," he tried, but Daphne would not be comforted. Then, as if the ladies had been informed, they all came into the big bedroom and shook hands and kissed him good-bye. Daphne thanked them on Hilary's behalf and wiped at her tears with a Kleenex.

"Did your wife write to you? Are you going back to her?" she asked him when they were left alone.

"I'm going East. I'll probably never see her again, but I'll come back here next summer."

"Benny Webster promised me the same, but he never came. You're all the same. You'll find new friends there, you'll forget me."

"I'll send you a ticket to come to see me, to stay with me, if you like."

"Will you, Hilary, will you? Send an air ticket for *me?*"

"I can take you to meet the shah. I can show you the Peacock Throne."

They sat on the bed holding hands, the outsize dolls looking down at them. Daphne's skin was oily from the morning exercises; she looked shop-soiled.

"You're going back to her," she said. "Why do you try to hide it from me?"

Hilary explained that Isabel was in England, that everything was finished between them, but Daphne remained unconvinced.

"I knew you were going back to her, I saw it in the cards. When Markos died, I knew she would come back to you."

"But she isn't," Hilary said.

"Poor Markos, thank God his mother is not alive to suffer this."

"Did you know her?"

"Nobody really knew Magda. She was a stranger here, she had no friends. And beautiful! Long black hair and black eyes that melted your heart . . . And how she danced—it drove the men mad to see her! The doctor she married had come to Athens for a few days; he was alone and he went to the cabaret every night and saw her dancing. One night she slipped and the doctor was rushed behind the stage to see her— it was on account of her pregnancy, she was trying to get rid of the child, the doctor found out everything. You'll not believe it, but the next day he took her with him to Patras, they got married, and he loved the child like a good man and a good Christian."

"Who was his father?"

"May God rest her soul, Magda was a saint, she would never tell."

Hilary checked his pocket again to see that he had his passport, the *carnet du passage*, his wallet.

"I say, I need some money. Could you lend me a little?"

Daphne had started for the kitchen, to make coffee.

"How much?"

"Not much, a few drachmas."

"I keep the money from my private lessons in the head of that china cowboy over there. Take what you need," she said and went out to cry alone and make the coffee.

Hilary drove by night when it was cool and stopped to rest during the day; sleeping close to the road, on the ground, using an old blanket that had been in the trunk of the car for years. He skirted the towns, stopping only to fill up with gas or to buy vegetables and fruit from the peasants or to wash his face and drink water from a public fountain. In three days he made it to Istanbul; from that point on, the journey seemed interminable. It took him another four days to reach the Persian border, it was seven days since he had washed, and he could feel the dust in his eyes, between his teeth. He was alone on this journey and the

225

passions and tragedies of the Aegean seemed unimportant on the desolate roads of Asia. . . . Now you've got only yourself, old Grey. Drink, if you can get a drink, but don't overdo it; smile at the world, but don't let it fool you. Take things as they come, then move on, traveling light. When they don't want you in one city, shake the dust from your feet . . .

Once Hilary forgot himself and stretched out his hand. "Tender paw," he began, but he touched only his jacket flung across the seat next to him and he drew his hand hurriedly back to the wheel. Isabel's face rose up for a moment, the eyes a sky blue; the golden hair washed in the clear waves of the sea. He shook his head and reached into the inside pocket of his jacket, withdrew the letter, and crumpled it before letting it flutter out of the window.

From the rear mirror he saw the paper blown here and there. He pressed the accelerator more firmly, and the small car sped along the endless road to the East.